Afghanistan

AFGHANISTAN
THROUGH THE FOG OF INSTABILITY

R.K. Sawhney

Published by
Rupa Publications India Pvt. Ltd 2023
7/16, Ansari Road, Daryaganj
New Delhi 110002

Sales Centres:
Allahabad Bengaluru Chennai
Hyderabad Jaipur Kathmandu
Kolkata Mumbai

Edition copyright © The Vivekananda International Foundation,
New Delhi, 2023
Foreword copyright © Kanwal Sibal, 2023
Copyright for individual pieces vests with the respective authors

The views and opinions expressed in this book are the authors'
own and the facts are as reported by them which have been
verified to the extent possible, and the publishers are not in any way
liable for the same.

All rights reserved.
No part of this publication may be reproduced, transmitted, or
stored in a retrieval system, in any form or by any means, electronic,
mechanical, photocopying, recording or otherwise, without the prior
permission of the publisher.

P-ISBN: 978-93-5702-065-7
E-ISBN: 978-93-5702-052-7

First impression 2023

The moral right of the authors has been asserted.

10 9 8 7 6 5 4 3 2 1

Printed in India

This book is sold subject to the condition that it shall not, by way of
trade or otherwise, be lent, resold, hired out, or otherwise circulated,
without the publisher's prior consent, in any form of binding or
cover other than that in which it is published.

Contents

Foreword   *vii*

Editor's Note   *xv*

Part I: Historical Background

1. The Historical and Geographical Frames of Contacts between Ancient India and Afghanistan   3
   Dr Dilip K. Chakrabarti

2. Buddhist Linkages in Afghanistan   13
   Sunita Dwivedi

3. Historical Trends in Afghanistan   30
   Arvind Gupta

Part II: Afghanistan and its Neighbourhood

4. Pakistan and its Afghanistan Tangle: Legitimate Interests and Illegitimate Instruments   53
   Amb. T.C.A. Raghavan

5. Central Asia's Connect with Afghanistan   62
   Amb. Skand R. Tayal

6. Iranian View: Strategic Aim and Compulsions   76
   Amb. Sanjay Singh

7. Russia's Enduring Obsession with Afghanistan   87
   Amb. P.S. Raghavan

8. China in Afghanistan: Motivation and Long-term Strategic Objectives   104
   Dr Srikanth Kondapalli

9. The Pashtun Movement in Pakistan and Its
   Afghanistan Strategy   127
   Dr Shalini Chawla

Part III: Afghanistan and India

10. Afghanistan and Its Effect on India's Strategic Security   143
    Lt Gen. (Retd) Syed Ata Hasnain

11. India's Role in the Last Two Decades in Afghanistan   156
    Amb. Jayant Prasad

Part IV: Afghanistan and the West

12. United States's Dilemmas in Afghanistan   169
    Amb. Arun K. Singh

Part V: Afghanistan in the Global Calculus

13. Afghanistan in the United Nations   181
    Amb. D.P. Srivastava

Part VI: Afghanistan: Internal Situation

14. Understanding the Taliban: Origin,
    Composition and Philosophy   199
    Rana Banerji

15. Afghan National Defence and Security Forces:
    From Collapse to Regrouping?   218
    Brig. Rahul Bhonsle

Part VII: Road Ahead

16. The Return of the Taliban: Options for India   237
    Amb. Gautam Mukhopadhaya

Notes   257
List of Contributors   278
Index   280

Foreword

A comprehensive Indian perspective on Afghanistan covering its historical past, relations with all its neighbours, the strategic consequences of its takeover by the Taliban, how the United States (US) dealt with the country, the manner in which the Afghan issue figured in the United Nations (UN), the internal developments in the country and the course ahead for India has been provided in this volume produced by the Vivekananda International Foundation.

What makes this book of special interest for readers in India and abroad is the authorship of its various chapters. These are written by retired Indian diplomats who have served as ambassadors to Afghanistan, Pakistan, Iran, Russia and the US, or have been at senior positions in India's national security apparatus. They bring to the subject either their direct experience of handling Afghanistan affairs or professionally assessing Afghanistan-related issues from critical vantage points in its immediate neighbourhood or as viewed from countries that have had a role in shaping developments there.

Enriching these diplomatic perspectives are those of retired generals from India's armed forces and those who have served in the Research and Analysis Wing (R&AW), India's intelligence agency, with intimate experience of Afghan affairs. Some prominent academics and think tank experts give this volume a scholarly touch with their contributions to ensure a better understanding of some key elements of the Afghan external and internal scene.

India has vital interests in Afghanistan. But for the parts of Jammu and Kashmir (J&K) occupied by Pakistan, Afghanistan would have been our direct neighbour today. That fundamental geographic postulate would have limited Pakistan's options in Afghanistan, possibly prevented the course of events that led to the Soviet invasion of Afghanistan and America's response in helping unleash jihadi forces against the Soviets in cooperation with Pakistan and Saudi Arabia. The terrorist threat to India and others, which has evolved since then, may not have taken the dimension that we see today.

The eviction of the Taliban from Afghanistan by the Americans in 2001, with the support of the Northern Alliance with which India had strong connections, opened the doors for us to play a substantive political and developmental role on the ground until the Taliban takeover of Afghanistan once again in 2021. In the intervening years, India's developmental assistance to Afghanistan of over $3 billion, covering 400 projects across 34 provinces, has earned India deep goodwill and popularity in Afghanistan, which endures even after the return of the Taliban. However, translating that into political influence in Afghanistan of today is not realistically feasible.

Despite a very substantial investment in Afghanistan, both political and economic, India's position there has been precarious for many reasons. Pakistan's provision of safe havens and physical support to the Taliban has led to the return of the Taliban to Afghanistan. Our missions there have been targeted by Pakistan-supported terrorists. A lack of direct access to Afghanistan has been a big handicap. Pakistan, of course, denied us transit rights through its territory to Afghanistan. The Chabahar route has provided an alternative, but that project has not realized its potential because of the US sanctions, negotiating difficulties with Iran and our own failure to give a priority push to the project.

Pakistan has also tried to keep us out to the extent possible from various formats of plurilateral discussions on Afghanistan set up by the US, Russia or China, arguing that it should be limited to the 'direct neighbours' of Afghanistan, though India has been included in some groups in recognition of our stakes in the country as a regional power. The US has pursued its interests in Afghanistan in ways contrary to our political and security interests. Its decisions to reduce its forces in Afghanistan, setting dates for its eventual withdrawal, the convening of the Doha talks with the Taliban and seeking Pakistan's support to that end, its precipitate and ignominious retreat from Afghanistan, and handing over the country to the Taliban without consultations with us testify to this. The US has kept us informed bilaterally of developments, but its strategy has been entirely guided by its own national interest. It has been fully aware that a return of the Taliban with assistance from Pakistan would seriously harm our security interests. While the US and India have been working to strengthen maritime security in the face of shared threats, on land, the US has moved in the opposite direction, adding to security threats from our western borders, also being aware of the Pakistan–China nexus and China's ambitions in Afghanistan that include the extension of the China–Pakistan Economic Corridor.

The US withdrawal from Afghanistan also meant India's withdrawal from there. India also had to take a decision on whether to engage with the Taliban and under what conditions. The Taliban is a radical Islamist organization that has resorted to terrorism in its eventual takeover of the country. Within its ranks, the Taliban government has elements that are closely linked to Pakistan, like the Haqqani group whose terrorist affiliations are well known. The Taliban have violated its pledges with regard to national reconciliation, forming an inclusive government, respecting women's rights and human rights in general, especially of various ethnic and religious groups. Terrorist attacks against the Shias and Hazaras continue, and the freedom of women has been severely curtailed. India had to decide whether to continue with a policy of not engaging with a political formation that represented all that India has been struggling against, namely, Islamic extremism and jihadi terrorism, or adopt a more pragmatic approach and establish some formal contact with it which, without giving the Taliban government official recognition, would enable us on humanitarian ground to reach out to the Afghan population. The Taliban regime also realizes the need to keep its channels open to other countries because without that it cannot effectively govern and meet the needs of the Afghan people. Eventually, India made moves to engage the Taliban at Doha and in Moscow, and has now positioned some diplomatic representatives in our mission in Kabul to provide consular services and oversee the humanitarian aid that we are channeling to Afghanistan to meet its urgent need for food grains, medicines, etc. We were able to pressure Pakistan into allowing the transportation of 50,000 tonnes of our wheat aid to Afghanistan through Pakistani territory, albeit in Afghan trucks. Our concerns about the security of our mission remain, in light of the suicide attack against the Russian embassy in September 2022.

Concerns about the continuing political instability in Afghanistan, the terrorist attacks that persist, the rising activity of Islamic State elements in the country, the dangers of spillover consequences of all this on neighbouring countries as well as Russia and China, the economic and political disarray in Pakistan have contributed in some measure to open up the doors for India for a more active diplomacy in affirmation of its regional role. India hosted a Delhi Regional Security Dialogue on Afghanistan in November 2021 and it brought together the national security advisors of seven countries—India, Iran, Russia, Tajikistan, Kazakhstan, Uzbekistan and Turkmenistan (Pakistan and China did not attend, and Afghanistan was not invited)—that aimed to firm up a common approach for practical cooperation in confronting the increasing threats of terrorism, radicalization and drug trafficking following the Taliban's takeover. It concluded with a statement that Afghanistan's territory should not be used for 'sheltering, training, planning or financing any terrorist act', called for unimpeded, direct and assured humanitarian assistance to Afghanistan and ensuring that the fundamental rights of women, children and minority communities are not violated, besides stressing the need to form an open and truly inclusive government in the country. India has participated in the fourth meeting of the Moscow Format Consultations on Afghanistan on 16 November 2022, which discussed the current humanitarian situation in Afghanistan, the provision of assistance by stakeholders, intra-Afghan talks, formation of an inclusive and representative government, efforts to counter terrorism and ensure regional security.

Tajikistan, sharing a long border with Afghanistan, is concerned about the extra risks and possibilities for drug trafficking and terrorism that the current situation gives rise to. Iran has maintained contacts with the Taliban, with the US accusing that it was providing support to it against the US. However, Iran has expressed open concern about the precipitate Taliban takeover, refusing recognition and advocating a share of all ethnic groups in the governance of the country. Iran, which already has a large number of Afghan refugees on its soil, has been concerned about a fresh crisis of migration. Kyrgyzstan, too, has concerns about terrorist organizations in Afghanistan; Uzbekistan favours joint efforts to find a collective solution in Afghanistan; Turkmenistan supports solutions to establish regional peace; Kazakhstan, with concerns about intensified terrorist activity, seeks an increase of humanitarian aid to Afghanistan; and Russia favours multilateral meetings to discuss issues linked to threats emanating from that country.

The UN was excluded from the US–Taliban talks and the intra-Afghan peace process but is now the primary avenue for humanitarian assistance to Afghanistan. Following the Taliban takeover of Afghanistan, UN agencies (20 of them) and their partners have remained there for providing the much needed humanitarian assistance to nearly 23 million people across 34 provinces. Allocations for two humanitarian funds have helped prevent a collapse of the health and education sectors by ensuring that essential workers are paid. There is an urgent need to create a functioning economy, as it hangs in the balance at present, restore basic services and the banking sector. According to the UN, 25 million Afghans are now living in poverty. The issue of food security has become critical. The United Nations Development Programme has announced the creation of a 'people's economy fund' that will provide cash to vulnerable Afghans and micro-businesses. While Pakistan has long been a choice for relief organizations to procure aid items, it is felt that the UN can help diversify aid channels through Uzbekistan and Iran as well. The US is still not prepared to give the Taliban access to Afghanistan's frozen assets.

Elements of the US policy in the region post its withdrawal from Afghanistan is a source of disquiet for India. Its operation to eliminate the Al-Qaida chief Ayman al-Zawahiri from his hideout in Kabul and using Pakistani airspace to do so raises some concerns. The assumption of reduced US interest in Pakistan has not proved to be well-founded, as the US has recently approved $450 million of US military aid to Pakistan to upgrade its F-16 fleet for counterterrorism purposes. Our External Affairs Minister has said that this explanation given by the US cannot and does not fool anybody. The US has been looking for a base in the region to enable itself to target any future terrorist threats that could emanate from Afghanistan, and some understanding with Pakistan may well have been reached in that regard. This is a development that India would be concerned about, and so would Russia, China and Iran, as all three would be against a revival of the US presence in Afghanistan.

All in all, for India, the situation in Afghanistan is difficult to manage. For the moment, our worst fears that the Taliban takeover would result in more terrorism-related pressures on us at a time when India has taken major political steps in J&K, much to Pakistan's discomposure, have not materialized. Despite their close nexus, relations between Pakistan and the Taliban government over the activities of the Tehrik-i-Taliban Pakistan from Afghanistan's soil has resulted in border tensions. The Taliban have been making reassuring overtures to India, but the movement is faction ridden and internal security is controlled by the pro-Pakistan Haqqani faction, which has to be factored into our assessments. Unless the Taliban government becomes more inclusive and rights of women and minorities are assured, international recognition will elude it. We retain the goodwill of the Afghanistan people, but our reluctance to accept refugees and maintain a restrictive visa policy is not seen positively. Our capacity to influence internal developments in Afghanistan is limited as is our capacity to provide humanitarian aid. An unstable Afghanistan impedes a more robust Indian engagement with Central Asia. In other ways too, a large Islamic country, led by a militant organization with a medieval ideology, that is unable to sustain itself without external support, which will not be forthcoming on a scale that is needed unless there are political and social changes in the country in line with international expectations, will be a source of continuing problems for the region and us.

Kanwal Sibal
Former Foreign Secretary of India

Editor's Note

The takeover of Afghanistan by the Taliban and collapse of the Islamic Republic on 15 August 2021 was essentially due to a combination of several factors, notably, a less than graceful announcement of withdrawal by the United States (US), prolonged and insincere discussions on the morale sapping peace plan negotiations, connivance of Pakistan, along with the indirect support from China. In the absence of any clear political directions or resolute military leadership, the Afghan National Army refused to offer resistance and surrendered. President Ashraf Ghani fled from the country with most of his cabinet, leaving the hapless people of Afghanistan to fend for themselves. Afghanistan was once again taken over by a fundamentalist and extremist entity from which it had been rescued almost 20 years ago. All the painstaking effort that had gone into nation-building by the US and international community, including India, came to an abrupt halt with the new regime not only committed to bringing this process to a standstill but also forcefully and irrevocably reversing it.

Although different facets of events in Afghanistan have been regularly written on and debated for their strategic relevance by the Vivekananda International Foundation (VIF), the return of the Taliban and its consequences triggered the idea of a comprehensive book on this country. Fortunately, we have a number of experts on Afghanistan, associated with the foundation, who have hands-on experience and deep understanding of this country as ambassadors, military commanders and intelligence officials. We also have academics who have historical, cultural, geographical and archeological knowledge of Afghanistan. The collective wisdom of all these experts has been pooled to produce this book, which is essentially meant to acquaint the general reader with the history of Afghanistan's journey through different eras, right up to the present time.

In this book, a long sweep of historical overview covers the period from the ancient times, wherein there was a flow of ideas, philosophies, trade and commerce between Central Asia and the Indian subcontinent, with Afghanistan acting as a bridge, to the comparatively recent times. From there on, the Pashtun monarchies, the stable rule of the last king Zahir Shah until the Daud Khan coup have also been covered. Destabilizing factors, including the Durand Line, Pashtun nationalism, irredentism, Cold War, the long-term impact of Soviet intervention as well as the US proxy war through Pakistan, and how this led to Islamization and weaponization of Afghanistan have been discussed. Surprisingly, it is the US encouragement of Pakistan against the Soviet Union in the '70s that led to the Jihadi warlordism and internecine conflicts creating Taliban under the Pakistan control and tutelage. Taliban 1.0 and the Al-Qaeda pushed Afghanistan into the stone age, economically and ideologically, encouraged terrorism, led to the Kandahar Air India hijack and the tragic 9/11 attack in the US. This traumatic event made the Americans jump into the fray against the Taliban.

The US, with the active support of the Northern Alliance, a force trained by Commander Ahmad Shah Massoud, helped Afghanistan get rid of the Taliban. Unfortunately, the Americans under the influence of Pakistan allowed a large portion of the defeated Taliban force to escape along with their regular Pakistani army supporters. Here, I must pay a compliment to the great Commander Massoud whom I have known personally. He, in my view, was one of the finest leaders, who despite the shortage of resources, put up a determined fight against the combined force of the Taliban and the Pakistan army regulars. He refused to leave Afghanistan in the most adverse circumstances till he was treacherously assassinated by Pakistani agents masquerading as journalists.

I happened to visit Kabul and other cities at the time and saw for myself the immense and systematic destruction caused by the Taliban and the civil wars. Kabul had been devastated. The civic infrastructure had been vandalized and looted to the extent of even the electric and telegraph poles having been uprooted and taken away to Pakistan. Bulk of the artefacts from the famous Kabul museum had been systematically pilfered and till today can be found in the drawing rooms of the retired ISI generals of that time. My most moving visit was to the Indira Gandhi Children's Hospital established with India's help in the '70s. It was in a pathetic state with no medicines, equipment or power supply. Majority of the staff had either been chased away or were left with only two doctors in the premises who were trying to do whatever they could within the limitations. Kabul had a forlorn look with hardly any commercial activity taking place. There were no women on the streets.

Although President Joe Biden now talks about the US not intending to attempt nation-building in Afghanistan, it did take place by the international community led by the Americans. India had also contributed almost $3 billion. Afghanistan was gradually transformed in the next 20 years. A constitution was put in place that helped define the government structure and building of the three pillars of the state of Afghanistan, i.e, the judiciary, legislative and executive. This was followed by the training of the bureaucrats, diplomats and the Afghan National Army. Elections were held for both the parliament and the presidential office. I am in no way saying that it was a perfect regime. Corruption was endemic and the systems were flawed as is the case with many newly formed democracies. With all its faults, the Islamic Republic of Afghanistan did make valiant attempts to ensure inclusiveness, education and empowerment of women. After a century of having experimented with monarchies, communist system and being subjected to extreme fundamental and radical religiosity, these 20 years of democracy would probably remain the most preferred system of governance in Afghanistan.

Coming back to the contents of the different chapters of this book, the first three chapters are primarily devoted to historical, geographical and civilizational aspects of the connection between Afghanistan and the Indian subcontinent. Dr Dilip K. Chakrabarti, in the first chapter, brings out that right from the phase of Indus Civilization, Afghanistan and northwestern areas of India seem to have had formed a broad power zone where the entire region was under the umbrella of one major force. According to him, the political power of Afghanistan oscillated between Indian territory and Afghanistan itself. Dr Sunita Dwivedi in the second chapter dwells upon the Buddhist linkages of Afghanistan. Dr Arvind Gupta, director of VIF, in Chapter 3, goes over some important landmark developments in Afghan history that defined the country over centuries. In Chapter 4, Ambassador T.C.A. Raghavan takes up Pakistan and its Afghanistan tangle, the complexity of this relation as well as the fallout of the latest takeover of Afghanistan by Taliban 2.0 on 15 August 2021. Relying solely or very substantially on securitized perspectives by Pakistan has inevitably led to excessive dependence on armed proxies and insurgents. This has negative consequences towards how Afghans view Pakistan. In Chapter 5, Ambassador Skand Tayal writes about Central Asia's connection with Afghanistan.

Iranian viewpoint, their strategic aims and compulsions vis-à-vis Afghanistan has been dealt with by Ambassador Sanjay Singh in Chapter 6. In the subsequent chapter, Ambassador P.S. Raghavan describes Russia's enduring obsession with Afghanistan since the Cold War era, it getting bogged down there for 10 years with little to show for the occupation except its contribution to the collapse of the Soviet Union. He also describes their tango with the US after the defeat of Taliban 1.0 and the present manoeuvres consequent to the 15 August 2021 event. China's role in Afghanistan, its motivation and long-term strategic objectives are analysed by Dr Srikanth Kondapalli. The Pashtun movement in Pakistan and its effect on the Afghan strategy is elaborated by Dr Shalini Chawla in Chapter 9. She also dilates on how the desire to contain Pashtun nationalism and resolve the disputed Durand Line issue in its favour contributed to Pakistan's Afghan strategy. The Taliban 2.0 regime has come to power in Kabul, but both the issues continue to pose a serious challenge to Pakistan due to continued mutual suspicions. The effect of the Taliban 2.0 coming to power in Afghanistan on India's strategic security is explained at length by Lt Gen. Syed Ata Hasnain. This change of regime affects India's security in multiple ways and requires due attention. He opines that Taliban 2.0's arrival has a profound effect on regional and international politics but its current dispensation must not be considered permanent. This, according to him, is an evolving situation that will continue to have different manifestations and must be countered with flexibility of policies.

India's positive role in the last two decades wherein it has been a significant donor to Afghanistan's reconstruction in different ways went beyond financial support or constructing Afghan parliament, the friendship damn on the Hari Rud River, building roads, erecting transmission lines and a power station to bring electricity to Kabul, executing small development projects for education, health, micro-irrigation, solar electrification, etc. Indian scholarship programmes were meant to provide Afghanistan with a new generation of educated and skilled workforce. In Chapter 11, Ambassador Jayant Prasad focuses on India's developmental efforts. He also emphasizes that India's message to Afghan political leadership has never been divisive. India has constantly advised leaders of different ethnicities to work in cohesion with each other for peace, stability and nation-building. Even after the collapse of the Islamic Republic, our humanitarian aid to the people of Afghanistan continues. According to him, Indian Afghan policy will evolve as the situation unfolds. The prevailing dilemma for the US in dealing with the current ruling dispensation in Afghanistan is elaborated upon by Ambassador Arun K. Singh in Chapter 12. In Chapter 13, the United Nation's role in Afghanistan is discussed by Ambassador D.P. Srivastava. Rana Banerji writes on the Taliban, their origin, composition and philosophy. The Afghan National Defence Forces, their origin, rise and collapse are analysed by Brig. Rahul Bhonsle. Lastly and most importantly, Ambassador Gautam Mukhopadhaya rounds up the different strands of this book to come to the recommended possible options for India to deal with the Taliban.

I would like to thank each one of the above contributors for their support, time and energy in producing very readable and relevant analysis of the different facets on a very short notice. With these words, I commend this book to the readers and hope that it will add to their understanding of Afghanistan and our relationship with it.

Lt Gen. (retd) R.K. Sawhney
Centre Head, National Security and Strategic
Studies & Internal Security Studies,
Vivekananda International Foundation, New Delhi

Part I

HISTORICAL BACKGROUND

1

The Historical and Geographical Frames of Contacts between Ancient India and Afghanistan[1]

Dr Dilip K. Chakrabarti

Before the Durand Line was laid down between British India and the Afghan territories in 1893, the Indo-Afghan boundary line was invariably fluid, dependent on the military strength and ambition of the concerned powers. On many occasions in history, the Afghan territories included Peshawar and the areas further east, and on equally numerous occasions, the Indians controlled the area south of the Hindu Kush.[2] The Hindu Kush has frequently been seen as the natural boundary of India in Afghanistan.

A HISTORICAL OVERVIEW

Gandhara is referred to in the Rigveda and also in the Behistun inscription of the Achaemenid King Darius I as a satrapy or province of his empire extending into India up to the Indus Valley.[3] This, in all likelihood, also denoted a section of southern Afghanistan, inclusive of the Kabul and Swat valleys. Kamboja is another key ancient Indian term in this context, denoting in all probability, northeast Afghanistan up to Badakhshan. The third is Bahlika, standing for the Mazar-e-Sharif area in the northern plains of Afghanistan. All these three terms are known in the two Indian epics, especially in the Mahabharata where the concerned powers are said to be interactive with one another. There is no doubt that in the epics, the modern Afghanistan territory is a part of the ancient Indian political universe. Gandhara was a major *janapada* or territorial division in the sixth century BC, but it fell to the Achaemenian power, based in Fars in Iran, towards the end of this century. The entire area between the Oxus and Indus, inclusive of the Sindh, was divided into a few satrapies, Gandhara possibly being the most important of them all.

Alexander's invasion of India took place in the wake of his conquest of Afghanistan and Central Asia. One of the *Alexandrias* (the Greek cities that came up in the wake of Alexander's invasion of Asia, including India) he set up in the region was at the site of Kandahar. Greek presence in Afghanistan and the Indus Valley marked a watershed moment in the history of the region, which was followed by its annexation in the Mauryan Empire with its capital far to the east in Pataliputra or Patna.

What is clear is the interacting political fortune of India up to the Indus Valley and Afghanistan. What lends a great measure of historical depth to this whole process of political, cultural, civilizational spread of India is the discovery of a full-fledged Indus civilization site in Shortugai at the junction of Kokcha River with the Oxus. This site came to be seen as a staging post when looking for the evidence of Indus Valley Civilization contacts in Central Asia, especially Turkestan. Shortugai itself was a trading site oriented towards exploiting resources like lapis lazuli, tin and horses. Evidence of contact with the Indus Valley Civilization has also been suggested from finds at sites like Mundigak in southern Afganistan and possibly in northern Afghanistan as well. One is not sure whether Afghanistan fell within the Indus distribution area itself or merely denoted an area frequented for trading purposes. The existing explanation suggests the latter.

That the Mauryan king Chandragupta took over parts of Afghanistan from Alexander's successor Seleucus is well known. The most direct evidence of the Mauryan control of Afghanistan is indicated by Ashoka's edicts found at Kandahar and Laghman, with the first being across the Bolan Pass and the Afghan boundary, and the second, in the area between Kabul and Jalalabad. Kandahar was linked, without much problem, to Herat via Farah and Girishk, with Herat giving access to the northeastern corner of Iran with its own network of links with Turkestan and northern and western Iran. Laghman was approached from the Jalalabad side and led to the Kabul area, giving access to the Bamian area across the Hindu Kush. With such accessibility, it appears that Afghanistan was a well-known territory to the Mauryas.

FROM MAURYAN TO GREEK ERA: A PREVIEW

Post-Mauryan history of Afghanistan is related to the Greeks of the period of the successors of Seleucus in the eastern part of Alexander's empire. The original Seleucid control gave way to the formation of Indo-Greek kingdoms, extending from Bactria or northern Afghanistan to well inside the Indus Valley. The depth of Greek occupation in northern Afghanistan and the southern section of Central Asia is clearly indicated by the site of Ai Khanum in the Kokcha Valley. This is virtually in the same area where the much earlier site of Shortugai was located. Local cultural elements exerted some influence on art and architecture of Ai Khanum, but it was essentially a Greek city, complete with its gymnasium, theatre, fountain and funerary monuments. The extent of Greek influence and the process of acculturation with local elements, such as various deities, are clearly seen in innumerable Indo-Greek coin assemblages and in the occurrence of both Greek and ancient Indian deities and scripts over a wide area spanning from Bactria to Punjab. This phase was followed by the emergence of two roughly similar political forces, the Indo-Scythians and Indo-Parthians. They were also operative in a broad zone from parts of Afghanistan to parts of the northwestern region of India.

What is important to note is that right from the phase of

the Indus Valley Civilization, Afghanistan and the northwestern areas of India seemingly formed a broad power zone under one major force. This trend was further accentuated under the dynastic control of the Kushans, whose power extended from the southern section of Central Asia to deep inside the Ganga plains, bringing the entire region within the same power belt. Afghanistan was very much within this zone. This was the period when the interaction between Afghanistan and India was possibly at its zenith in the historical context.

Buddhism was at the peak of development in Afghanistan during this period, the Buddhist stupas being the most visible sign of this interaction between Afghanistan and India. The distinct art style of Gandhara, which became a holy land of Buddhism, influenced both Afghanistan and the northwestern section of India. During this period, Buddhism spread from India to Central Asia through Afghanistan. The Sassanids succeeded the Kushans in both Afghanistan and the northwestern section of the subcontinent. There is as yet no evidence that the Gupta kings were successful in controlling any area to the west of the Indus River. The White Huns in the fifth-century defeated the Sassanids and were, in turn, defeated by the Guptas in India.

In the early days of the Muslim conquests, the Hindu Shahi kings of Kabul and the northwestern part of the Indian subcontinent continued to rule in the region, which served as a bulwark against the Muslim advent in that direction. The Shahis continued to rule until the end of the ninth century. Their main tussle for power was with the Ghaznavids and Ghurids, the latter defeating the former in AD 1148. The next major phase of the Afghan history was established by the Mongols and the Timurids. Under the latter, Afghanistan witnessed the fusion of Iranian and Central Asian–Turkic cultures. Herat was a major city under the Timurid rule.

In the sixteenth century, with the rise of the Mughal power in India, some parts of Afghanistan fell under the Mughal control, whereas the rest of Afghanistan came to be controlled by the

Safavid kings of Iran. In the sixteenth and seventeenth centuries, Afghanistan was ruled by the Khanate of Bukhara in the North, by the Sunni Mughals of India in the East and by the Shia Safavids in the West.

Around the middle of the eighteenth century, the Iranians under Nadir Shah were in power in Afghanistan, having defeated the short-lived reign of the Hotaki Sultans of Kandahar. The Iranian power did not survive the death of Nadir Shah for long, and, in Afghanistan, his place was taken by Ahmed Shah Durrani, who conquered the whole of Afghanistan, the present-day Pakistan and parts of Iran's Khorasan and Kohistan provinces. He defeated the Maratha power of Delhi in 1761. Durranis of Afghanistan gave way to the Sikhs of Punjab and Ranjit Singh took away a large part of the Kabul territory from the Durranis. In 1837, Afghans were defeated by the Sikhs in the Battle of Jamrud in the Khyber Pass.

The nineteenth-century history of Afghanistan is interesting in the sense that for some time, the British and the Russians took an inordinate amount of interest in Afghanistan, the British interest being aimed against the forward movement of the Russians in Central Asia. The British fought two Afghan wars in the nineteenth century, the result of the first (1839–42) being disastrous for them. However, the Second Anglo-Afghan War (1878–80) brought Abdur Rahman who was supportive of the British to the throne of Kabul. It was under his rule (1880–1901) that the boundaries of modern Afghanistan were established. It is important to remember that in 1837–38, there was an attempt by Iran to siege Herat, a city in Afghanistan.

GEOGRPAHICAL INFLUENCES OF POLITICS

Political power of Afghanistan throughout history oscillated between the Indian territory and Afghanistan itself. Under the Kushans, this trend was at its peak, and continued till the times of Hindu Shahi kings and the Sikhs who had their feet both in

Punjab and Afghanistan. There was no time when the historical fate of Afghanistan and the northwestern part of the Indian subcontinent was not mutually linked.

This interaction in the political domain was made possible by various intricacies of borderland geography. A large part of the concerned terrain was no doubt mountainous but riddled with many negotiable passes; the mountainous terrain did not prove to be a serious obstacle neither in the way of military movements nor in the journeys of traders. Such passes formed a large and intricate network, and can be understood by being divided into a few major sections.

1. **Passes that lead to Chitral and northern areas in Pakistan across the Wakhan Corridor:** Below are six high-altitude passes linked to the Wakhan Corridor and to the Pamir plateau beyond it.
    - Irshad Pass (4,977 m) is the first major pass in this sector and connects the Chapursan River valley in the upper Hunza Valley with the Wakhan Corridor.
    - Kalandar Pass (5,221 m) connects the Karambar Valley in upper Gilgit with Wakhan.
    - Broghil Pass (3,798 m) lies along the Durand Line border that crosses the Hindu Kush and goes towards Wakhan.
    - Dorah Pass (4,300 m) is located along the Durand Line border, with Lake Dufferin at the foot of the pass.
    - Khora Bhurt Pass (4,630 m) connects the Karambar River valley in upper Gilgit with the Wakhan Corridor.
    - Wakhjir Pass (4,923 m) at the eastern end of the Wakhan Corridor links it with Xinjiang in China.

2. **Passes that lead from the Kabul area to Bamiyan, and thus to the northern sector of Afghanistan, and the passes that are in central Afghanistan:** These passes across the Hindu Kush are located at high altitudes. There are at least eight such major passes.

- Kotal-e-Hindu Kush (4,053 m) is located north of Parwan and southwest of the Salang Pass.
- Kotal-e-Khushk (2,858 m) is in the Daykundi province of central Afghanistan.
- Kushan Pass or Kaoshan Pass (4,370 m) lies just west of the Salang Pass.[4]
- Unai Pass (3,000 m) crosses the Sanglakh Range, west of Kabul, connecting Hajarajat with Kabul.
- Silsilah-ye Koh-e-Hindu Kush (4,353 m) is located in the Parwan province near Baghlan.
- Shibar Pass (3,000 m) is the preferred route from Kabul to Bamiyan because the alternative route via Unai and Hajigak passes may be more direct but rises to 3,700 m and are, thus, not preferred.
- Salang Pass is located on the border between Baghlan and Parwan provinces, just to the east of the Kushan Pass. This has been replaced by the Salang Tunnel, linking Charikar and Kabul in the south with Mazar-i-Sharif and Kunduz in the north. Before the tunnel was built, the main route between Kabul and northern Afghanistan was via the much longer route through the Shibar Pass.
- Khawak Pass (3,848 m) lies on the route to northern Afghanistan via Andarab and Baghlan. This is said to be the route adopted by Alexander while leading his army from Kabul to Bactria in 329 BC. It is also possible that the Chinese scholar Xuanzang used this pass on his return journey from India. Ibn Battuta (AD 1333), in all likelihood, used this pass while journeying to India. Tamerlane, the Turco-Mongol conqueror, also possibly used it in the fourteenth century. This is the easternmost pass leading from the Kabul valley to northern Afghanistan.

3. **Passes leading South to Pakistan:** The list of major Afghanistan passes does not end here. A few equally important passes are oriented towards the subcontinent.

- Tera Pass (2,895 m) serves as one of the important passes, leading from Kabul to India. It is snowbound in winters.
- Khost–Gardez Pass (2,869 m) is one of the main routes linking Kabul with different locations in the subcontinent, ascending more than 600 m from the Gardez valley and then going down about 1,200 m to the Khost Bowl.
- Lataband Pass or Kotal-e-Lataband (2,499 m) is on the Jalalabad road. There is a less precipitous route via the Khord pass to Kabul, which was used in the sixteenth century by the Mughals.

There are more passes in Baluchistan and Northwest Frontier (modern day Khyber–Pakhtunkhwa) segments. There is more or less a maze of passes throughout the region, all entwined with the issues of local geography, history and ethnicity. The Kurram Pass lies on the direct route from Bannu to Ghazni, and is one of the most important routes across the Sulaiman Mountains. Lower down, in the Dera Ismail Khan area, there are about 32 passes. The Gomal Pass, which follows the alignment of Gomal River, is the most important of all, from commercial viewpoint. Powindah traders from Afghanistan used to migrate to British India during winters via this pass.

South of the Gomal, there is a whole chain of passes—the Sanghar, Sami–Sarwar, Darwazi and Draband, the last joining the Dahima Pass and forming one route to Kandahar. The Sanghar Pass is the most important route across the mountains between the Gomul and the Bolan, and provides the most direct road from Multan to Kandahar. The Sakhi–Sarwar Pass is the next most important one and is inclusive of 11 passes, Chachar being the most important. Across the Kirthars, the principal pass is Mula Pass, with 10 other passes present within 60 miles. The principal route in the south of the Bolan Pass is the Mula Pass. Further north in the map is the Peiwar Kotal Pass, which links north Afghanistan (and eventually Kabul) with the Kurram Agency area of Pakistan. This lies at an altitude of more than 8,000 ft. In Bannu, the Tochi Pass, which is about 10-km long, offers passage from Ghazni in Afghanistan to the Bannu plain. Kohat Pass links Kohat of the borderlands with Peshawar. Although not directly linked with the Afghanistan territory, this pass leads from the direction of Kohat to the Khyber Pass through Peshawar and is, thus, important in the movements of people and goods in the borderlands. In the vicinity of Peshawar, the Khyber Pass holds the pride of place, and forms the point of access to Kabul from Peshawar.

All these mountain passes and their associated highlands give the history of Afghanistan a special character. Very few areas outside the Northern Plains admit of rich agriculture. The Central Highlands, dominated by the Hindu Kush and the Pamir knot with which the Hindu Kush is linked, cannot boast of much agriculture outside the narrow valleys. The Helmand valley, although fertile in places, is hemmed in by the Seistan deserts that continue into the adjacent Iran. Even towards the border with the Indian subcontinent, the terrain may have some advantage of monsoonal rainfall, but is too rugged to permit agriculture on a large scale.

By the law of nature, Afghanistan is not destined to be famous because of its agriculture; on the other hand, its position on Asia's map and the chain of mountain passes linking it with territories all around ensure that its fate hang on the movements of armies and merchants of all kinds. Both these movements tie the history of Afghanistan to that of its neighbours: the Indian subcontinent to its south, the Iranian plateau to its west, central Asian mountains and deserts from Turkmenia to Xinjiang to the north, and, finally, a slice of China across the Wakhan Corridor to the east.

Considered as a whole, however, it is the pull of the subcontinent that was the strongest in the Afghan history, whether in the ancient or in the later periods. First, the subcontinent, because of its size and historical and natural diversities, exerted the largest pull on Afghanistan's history, including the shaping of its ancient religious destiny, in terms of Buddhism. Secondly, the economic richness of the subcontinent also ensured that the routes traversing the high mountain passes all over Afghanistan were never devoid of merchants. On the whole, geography made sure that Afghanistan's political, economic, cultural and religious fate was linked to the subcontinent throughout history.

2

Buddhist Linkages in Afghanistan

Sunita Dwivedi

From Herat to Hadda and Kunduz to Kandahar, the plethora of Buddhist heritage sites in Afghanistan epitomize the continuous Indo–Afghan dialogue on trade and culture spanning across over two millennia.

A look at the number of monastic remains in just one region of central Afghanistan, in and around Kabul, is an eye-opener on the flourishing state of Buddhism between the first and ninth centuries (Kushan to Hindu Shahi period). Several monastic establishments have been explored or dug out by collaborative teams of Afghan and foreign archaeologists during nineteenth and twentieth century excavations, all within a radius of 40 km of Kabul. These include the sites of Sarai Khuja, Paitava, Shotorak, Gol Darrah, Gol Hamid and Kafiriat Tepe at Mes Aynak, Tepe Maranjan and Tepe Narenj (on the slopes of Kabul hills, a few kilometres south of the city), Shewaki stupa and monastery, Tope Darra near Istalif.

History apprises us of regular Indo-Afghan contacts from roughly the ninth or eighth century BC when Kubha (Kabul) was the hub of Vedic sciences. This was the period when wandering scholars and creative thinkers from India flocked to the intellectual centre of Kubha to work and debate on theories of evolution and human life. Scholars pondered over the relevance of natural sciences and scientific investigation in the laws of the universe rather than blindly believing in some supernatural agency.

One of the proponents of the philosophical tradition that

believed in natural laws of the universe was the great scholar Uddalaka who worked out his philosophy in Kabul.[1] From Uddalaka in the ninth century BC to Vira Deva in AD ninth century, there were scholars travelling along Uttarapath, the northern highroad of India to the region of Gandhara, which included Afghanistan, to seek knowledge from reputed teachers who lived there. According to the Ghosrava inscription, the great scholar monk Viradeva from Nagarhara (in Afghanistan) was not only elected *sanghasthavira* of the monastery of Nalanda but was also 'worshipped' by the Pala king, Devapala (AD 810–850) of Bengal.[2] Then, there was the Buddhist priest Indragupta, also from Nagarhara, who was appointed head of the Nalanda monastery.[3] Monk Jivagupta, a master of Buddhist sutras, travelled as far as the court of the western Turk ruler Topo Khagan (AD 572–81)[4] and probably stayed at Suyab or Navekat to translate Buddhist sutras in Turki.

ANTIQUITY OF BUDDHISM IN AFGHANISTAN

It is generally believed that Buddhism assumed an international character without political boundaries and was propagated as an ideology of non-violence and compassion for all beings during the period of Mauryan Emperor Ashoka (third century BC) and subsequent periods of the Indo-Greeks (second century BC), Kusanas (first to fourth century) until the period of the Hephthalites (fifth century) and Western Turks (sixth century).

However, it was seen that the steps to propagate Buddha's teachings of the four noble truths and the eightfold path beyond the north Indian states/mahajanapadas had already been initiated during his lifetime itself, when the kings of the northwest regions of Gandhara and trans-Gandhara, of which Afghanistan was a part, received the tenets of the 'Triple Gem' engraved on plaques from the Magadha emperor Bimbisara of the Haryanka dynasty.

During the sixth/fifth century, Buddhism as a religion was being patronized by the rulers of the northwestern regions of

Gandhara. One of them, King Pukkusati (Puskarasarin), who was a contemporary of the Buddha, ruled over Gandhara in the sixth century BC, said Buddhologist Kanai Lal Hazra.[5] King Pukkusati took keen interest in Buddhism seeing the efforts of Bimbisara, with whom he had friendly relations. Likewise, King Rudrayana occupied the throne of Roruka in Sovira (or the lower Indus Valley) in the days of the Buddha. He joined the Sangha as a monk and helped to popularize the religion in Afghanistan, Himavatkuta, Nepal, Kashmir, Punjab, Sind and Baluchistan—the regions that he had conquered. Buddha himself taught in at least half a dozen different 'countries' (provinces) and established a movement above political boundaries, said British Indologist A.K. Warder.[6]

Moreover, some Sakyans of Kapilvastu[7] are said to have settled in Afghan provinces in as early as the sixth century BC, following the attack by the neighbouring king, Virudhaka, over dispute between the Sakyans and Koliyans involving distribution of water from the dam built on Rohini River. Four banished Sakyans went to the north, towards the Hindu Kush ranges; one became the king of Bamiyan, one of Udyayana, one of Himatala and one of Sambi.[8] Chinese monk Xuanzang said that the rulers of the country of Hi-mo-to-lo, to the east of Kism in Badakshan province, were of the Sakya race who claimed descent from one of the four Sakya princes driven out of Kapilvastu. Another Sakyan connection was found at Bamiyan and Xuanzang mentioned having seen the robes of the Sakyan Sankavassa, disciple of Anand (principal disciple of Buddha), who it is believed lived for a considerable time in Bamiyan.[9] After the Buddha's death, the responsibility of running the Sangha fell on the shoulders of the senior disciples.

POETIC ALLUSION TO UTTARKURU

That the teachings of the Buddha had spread to the region of Uttarkuru lying beyond Himalayas, possibly Bahli/Bahlika/Bactra, during Buddha's lifetime is indicated by the works of poets and storytellers who had followed him; the works are said to have been composed during the earliest phase of Buddhist poetry and to have been working in service of the 'doctrines'.

According to some scholars, Uttarkuru was to be found beyond the Himalayas. Historian K.P. Jayaswal identifies Mount Meru of the Puranas with the Hindu Kush ranges 'upto which we find an actual Hindu population', and locates the Uttarkuru in the Pamirs, which stretches up to the Wakhan area of Afghanistan.[10]

A verse by one such poet puts forth the idea of an ideal society which was expected to exist in Uttarkuru. The poem reads: 'In delightful Uttarkuru, near beautiful mount Meru, men are born unselfish, without any possessions they sow no seed, draw no ploughs; men enjoy rice growing wild, uncultivated.'[11]

The area of Balkh and the land along banks of Oxus River stretching up to the Wakhan and the Pamirs (the present-day Badakshan in Afghanistan and the Gorno–Badakshan region of Tajikistan) were known to the poets of the Sangha as inhabited by people who followed the tenets of the Dhamma by giving up cravings, living without possessions and eating simple uncultivated, wild rice. They followed the life of a *sramana*—a wanderer who lived either by gleaning what they could in the woods and fields (wild uncultivated rice) or by begging.

INDO-AFGHAN BUDDHIST CORRIDOR

Being at the crossroads of the 'great Asian circuit' of the Silk Road, Afghanistan possessed the key to a flourishing Indian trade and the channels through which it received the tenets of Buddhism and disseminated the teachings of the Buddha to Central Asia and China.

The over 2,000-km-long ancient corridor, the Uttarapath, joining India and Afghanistan from the Bay of Bengal to Balkh, was known as the Sher Shah Suri Marg in the medieval times and now, the Grand Trunk Road. It formed a bridge between the valleys of the Ganga and the Oxus. It was further supplemented by the Bamiyan trade corridor running between the Hindu Kush and the Koh-i-Baba ranges.

Along with the abovementioned routes, there was the crucial peripheral Ring Road running through the cities of Kabul, Kandahar, Herat and Balkh that connected with the routes coming from India via three main passes in the Sulaiman and Toba Kakkar ranges of the northwest regions, viz. Khyber, Gomal and Bolan. All these routes provided India crucial connection with the whole of Asia, China and southern Russia.

SYMBIOSIS OF TRADE AND RELIGION

The Kabul–Kandahar–Herat route that formed the southern section of the enormous Ring Road was already bustling with voluminous trade caravans when Emperor Ashoka decided to install his rock edicts at Kandahar in the third century BC. He expected to catch in this trading city a vast floating audience for his Dhamma edicts, which was easily propagated in the contiguous regions of Persia, Margiana and Trans-Caspian route. It was also meant for the traders and travellers on the Uttarapath, to and from the Khyber Pass, and all traffic passing through the Bolan and Gomal passes to and from the lower Indus region. As a result, we find Ashokan inscriptions in both Aramaic and Greek at four different sites in Afghanistan, all of which were inhabited by a large Greek-speaking population and attracted global trade from the shores of the Mediterranean in the west to China in the far east.

Like Kandahar, the eastern cities of Lamghan (ancient Lampaka) and Jalalabad, too, were located on one of the busiest sections of the Grand Trunk Road, which passed through a rich agricultural region that was accompanied by a wide network of natural waterways from the streams of the Kabul and the Kunar. For this reason, Ashoka found eastern Afghan region to be a strategic place for his edicts. Through his edicts, he was preaching non-violence and the value of concord on the busiest sections of the trade routes that reached the shores of the Mediterranean and were inhabited by a considerable foreign population.

The symbiosis between trade and religion becomes apparent if we look at the names of some monasteries north of Balkh just across the Oxus. The monastery of Fayaz Tepa in Old Termez on the northern borders of Afghanistan near Hairatan was established by the wealthy horse dealers and merchants' guild of Bactria, and was known as the *Haya* (horse) *Vihara*. Another monastery on the Oxus, now known as the Karatepa, was called the *Khadavaka Vihara* or the king's monastery. It was probably set up as hostel for pilgrims and traders who crossed into Central Asia from Afghanistan.

The great wealth of the trading city of Kapisa (as evident from the Treasures of Begram retrieved during excavations at the New Royal City[12] and patronage of its merchants) helped in the establishment of nearly 100 monasteries with 6,000 priests on the hills of Begram.[13] The list of monasteries included Shotorak, Paitava, Kham-i-Zargar, Sarai Khuja and Karratcha—all dated between second to fourth centuries. It was from these hill monasteries that several images of the Buddha in schist were recovered, which form one of the rare statuary collections of the National Museum of Afghanistan and at the Musée Guimet, Paris.

Some monasteries, in turn, aided trade through rise in pilgrim traffic. They became source of great wealth as a result of the offerings by pilgrims, and were a boon for the rulers. A case in point is the Buddhist temple of Naubahar (new monastery) in Balkh, which was destroyed by the Arabs during the reign of the Caliph Othman (or of Muawiya).[14] But in AD 725, the governor Asad Bin Abdullah is said to have restored the town and the monastery on the former site.[15] One of the reasons perhaps for the reconstruction was that destruction of the renowned monastery resulted in a fall in pilgrim traffic that, in turn, affected trade.

BUDDHA'S RELICS IN AFGHANISTAN

With a view to promote trade through pilgrim traffic, there arose a demand for Buddhist relics which proved to be great crowd pullers and brought wealth through offerings and pilgrim taxes. This resulted in several trading cities in Afghanistan being imbued with the holiness of Buddhist relics. Thus, we find pilgrims worshipping the Buddha's parietal bone, his robe and staff at Hadda, his tooth relic in Nagarhara, his washbasin, an inch-long shining tooth, sweeping brush of *kusha* grass with a gem-laden handle at Balkh, and Sakyan Sankavassa's robes at Bamiyan. Some sites became settings for important Jataka tales of Buddha being born as a bodhisattva in his previous birth. For example, the story of 'Dipankar Jataka' was set in Nagarhara and became the location of the story 'Dipankara Jataka'.

Commercial importance of southern Afghanistan had prompted Gandharan kings to install the holy relics of the Buddha, especially his *bhikshapatra* (begging bowl) at Kandahar. The precious bhikshapatra was seen by Chinese pilgrim Faxian at Peshawar, where it is believed to have been installed by Kusana ruler Kanishka who brought it from Vaishali. In the seventh century, however, Chinese scholar Xuanzang failed to find the patra at Peshawar and mentioned its absence in his records. The bowl had been whisked away to Kandahar (before Xuanzang's visit in AD 629), which was a crucial halting point for trade caravans on the Ghazni–Herat route. In 1925, the patra was found at the *khanaqa* (hospice) of Saint Mirwais at Kandahar from where it was brought to the National Museum of Afghanistan.[16] Today, the holy patra kept at the museum entrance is an object of great piety and curiosity.

Among other relics of great significance is a Kushan relinquary—the Bimaran casket of gold encrusted with gems, presently on display at the British Museum. It was recovered by Charles Masson, an Englishman, while scouring the Buddhist complexes in the Jalalabad Valley around the middle of nineteenth century. The relic casket of gold, inlaid with precious rubies and carved with the figures of the Buddha and bodhisattvas, was recovered from a stupa in Bimaran, west of Jalalabad and was dated first century. According to Nancy Hatch Dupree[17], at Hadda, south of Jalalabad, over 1,000 stupas were identified, more than half of which were excavated. The largest stupa at Tapa Kalan was opened by Charles Masson in 1841.

BUDDHIST SCHOLASTIC INSTITUTIONS

There was a time when pilgrims, instead of coming straight into India, halted at the monastic centres of Kunduz, Balkh, Bamiyan and Nagarhara for special studies on Buddhism. Here scholars composed, translated and copied Buddhist texts.

A look at the vast collection of Buddhist Sanskrit birch bark manuscripts unearthed from Bamiyan caves, copies of which are available at the National Museum of Afghanistan, will give us an idea of the scholarly work that was carried on and the considerable size of libraries that functioned in Afghanistan. A selection from the nearly 5,000 leaves and fragments, with around 7,000 micro-fragments from a library of originally up to 1,000 manuscripts found in caves in Bamiyan (in 1993–95) in Afghanistan, were on display at an exhibition, 'Traces of Gandharan Buddhism—An Exhibition of Ancient Buddhist Manuscripts in the Schøyen Collection', in the holy Thai city of Buddhamonton until February 2011.

Nava Vihara, also known as Naubahar, the main monastery at Balkh, is known to have been the centre of higher Buddhist study for all of Central Asia. *The Life of Huien-Tsiang* tells us that three eminent Buddhist scholars resided at the Navasangharama and all were well versed in the *Tripitakas* of the Little Vehicle or Hinayana[18], which was an orthodox and conservative school of Buddhism. One of them was Prajnakara, whose fame had spread throughout India. He remained at the monastery for a month to study the *Vibhasha Sastra*. Two other priests—Dharmapriya and

Dharmakara—were also staying at the monastery and they, too, were well versed in the texts of the Little Vehicle.

The most revered scholar, monk Dharmasinha who resided at Kunduz monastery, was well versed in *Vibhasha*. He was given the name Fa-Tsiang. He was the most feared as the 'priests of Su-leh (Kashgar) and Yu-tin (Khotan) dare not discuss (the doctrine) with him.'[19]

MOKSHA MAHAPARISHAD AT KAPISA

The main monastery of Sha-lo-kia in Kapisa, as Xuanzang wrote, had the tradition of holding a five-day religious congregation, *Moksha Mahaparishad*, during which scholarly debates on Buddhist texts and question–answer sessions were held to clarify and expound the doctrines. Mentioning the congregation, Xuanzang said[20] that three great Buddhist priests lived in the said convent, viz. Manojaghosh, the master of three Pitakas, Aryaverma of the Sarvastivadin School and another priest named Gunabhadra. Xuanzang participated in one of the mahaparishads along with monk Prajnakara.[21]

In this regard, Indologist P.C. Bagchi mentioned[22] a list of renowned Buddhist scholars from Kapisa and Nagarhara, who were masters in translation and were invited to China to translate Buddhist texts into Chinese or worked as missionaries. Buddhatrata, (a Buddhist monk of Kapisa) who went to China towards the end of the seventh century, resided in the monastery of Po ma sse (the White Horse Monastery) at Lo-Yang; Buddhapala (also a Buddhist monk of Kapisa) went to Wutai Shan in North China in AD 676 and finally settled in Lo-Yang, where he resided in the monastery of Si ming sse; Dharmagupta travelled from Kapisa and reached Ch'ang-ngan in AD 590; Prajna (Buddhist monk of Kapisa) went to China in AD 781 and settled in Ch'ang-ngan, and Sakyan Buddhabhadra from Nagarhara settled in Nanking in South China.[23]

Historian B.N. Puri listed names of Afghan scholars from Kabul from around the fourth–fifth century, all of who were master linguists and translators. They went to China to translate Buddhist canonical works into Chinese. Among these, we know about Gautam Sanghdeva, Vimalaksha, Sanghabhuti, Punyatrata and Dharmasya.[24]

BUDDHIST HEADQUARTERS AT NAGARHARA

We also learn from the 'Lion capital inscription of the time of Sodasa' (the Mathura lion capital) that the headquarters of the Sarvastivadins, one of the early Buddhist monastic groups, was located at Nagarhara. In the backdrop of the rivalry between the two Buddhist schools of the Sarvastivadins and Mahasanghikas, the inscription refers to the dialectician and the Sarvastivadin monk Budhila from Nagarhara.[25]

Mahasanghikas, too, had their establishment in Afghanistan as is evident from the Wardak inscription of Kushan king and successor of Kanishka, Huviska, referring to the deposit of the relics of Lord Buddha in the Vagramarega Vihara monastery, which was in possession of the Mahasanghika teachers.[26]

TREND OF BUDDHA COLOSSI

Enormous wealth accruing from commercial activities along the network of trade routes went into the construction of some of Central Asia's earliest and oldest 'Colossal Buddhas' in Afghanistan at Bamiyan (dated third/fourth century by the Archaeological Survey of India), in the adjacent valley of Kakrak, at Tepe Sardar in Ghazni and at Kafiriat Tepe in Mes Aynak.

A twentieth-century traveller to Afghanistan would have been in awe of the lofty rock cut and embellished images of the standing and sitting Buddha colossi gazing compassionately from towering cliffs of Bamiyan and Kakrak before they were destroyed in a blast in 2001 by the Taliban. These were the most amazing of colossal Buddha figures along with the 1,000-ft reclining Buddha (so far not discovered) in the mountains of Bamiyan and were part of a trend of 'colossal statuary art' that spread along the Uttarapath to the river valleys of the Oxus and its tributaries. Xuanzang mentioned[27] about the statue during his visit to Bamiyan. The Afghan colossi art is believed to have exercised a strong appeal and probably inspired the larger-than-life figures of the Buddha and bodhisattvas of the Oxus (Dalverzin Tepe, Fayaz Tepe and Kara Tepe), Murghab (Gyaur Kala) and Vakhsh (Ajina Tepe) valleys.

The colossal Afghan Buddhas told the story of the power and grandeur of the ruling dynasties and the wealthy merchants' guild that supported the embellishment of monasteries as an act of merit. They were the story of riches embedded in the ruby and lapis lazuli-laden rocks of Badakhshan, copper-rich hills of Logar, musk of the Wakhan, and horses of Kabul and Balkh, which are said to have travelled to the eastern shores of India up to Kaveripattinam.

The Afghan colossi is also a commentary on the rare art that arose as a result of the new trend in Buddhist thought regarding Buddha's divinity and the popular idea of a transcendental being.

CENTRE FOR RARE ART

Afghan sculptors and artists also carved an eminent place for themselves in the Buddhist world by propagating popular Buddhist themes as subjects for statuary and mural art. The cities and commercial hubs of Hadda, Kapisa, Bamiyan, Balkh and Kandahar formed the setting for the depiction of many a Buddhist story. In fact, in the hands of artists, clay and rocks of Afghanistan became a vast medium for the illustration of the life of the Buddha in Jataka tales and in the portrayal of a Buddhist heaven, the *sukhavati*. The 'Miracle of Sravasti' became the favourite theme for the stone carvers of Kapisa, and the story of Dipankar Buddha and his prophecy found its setting in Nagarhara. 'Gandhara Jataka' carried the story of the bodhisattva who was a prince of the Gandhara kingdom.

The foyer of the National Museum of Afghanistan displays several sculptures of Buddha from the monasteries of Kapisa performing the great miracle to prove his power when challenged by heretics. Images dated second to fourth century, showing streams of water flowing from the Buddha's feet and tongues of flame from his shoulders were recovered from Shotorak, Kham-i-Zargar, Sarai Khuja and Paitava. The representation of Naga deities and conversion of the Naga king Nagadanta to Buddhism in the statuary art of Ghazni and Hadda is another example of popular Buddhist stories adapted in the monastic art of Afghanistan. A rare picture of grandeur is witnessed in the statuaries of the bodhisattvas, from Kabul monasteries of Tepe Narenj and Tepe Maranjan, and from Kunduz. They flaunt elaborate hairstyles, stylized crowns, gem-laden necklace hanging on the chest and jewelled belt around the waist.

The portrayal of a Buddhist heaven of 'radiance and glory' was depicted in the soffit of the Big Buddha at Bamiyan (blown away by the Taliban in a blast in 2001). This was seen as an amalgamation of Buddhism and the essential features of Zoroastrianism, where the 'boundless and endless/infinite light' is the abode of Ahuramazda.[28]

The famous painting of the Hunter King from the Kakrak Valley adorns the gallery on the upper floor of the National Museum. It portrays a royal personage, presumably the Buddhist king of Bamiyan, who having renounced violence took refuge in the Buddha. The painting once adorned the drum of a stupa dome at Kakrak. The Foladi Valley at the western entrance of the Bamiyan caves presents a rare example of 'lantern roof' decorations and paintings of a thousand Buddhas on the walls and edges of cave ceilings.

To have an idea of the Buddhist art of Afghanistan, one will have to visit the National Museum. The rare life-sized Buddhas performing the Miracle of Sravasti from the monasteries of Kapisa, bejewelled bodhisattvas from Kunduz and Tepe Maranjan, Mandala paintings from the Kakrak Valley, stucco panels from

Nagarhara, Buddha head from the monastery of Tepe Sardar in Ghazni, a gigantic stele portraying the story of 'Dipankar Jataka', photographs of colossal images of the Buddha, and donors from Mes Aynak adorning the numerous galleries, all speak of the centuries-old dialogue between India and Afghanistan, and the enormous wealth brought in by trade along the Uttarapath. The rare manuscripts of the Schøyen Collection stored in the museum's library enlightens us about the high standards of scholarship acquired at Afghan monasteries.

INFLUENCE OF MATHURA ART

No study in Afghanistan's Buddhist art and iconography is complete without referring to Mathura school of art that flourished on the banks of the Yamuna in Mathura—the eastern Kaniska during the Kusana reign. While Gandhara school's art was considered to be Hellenized in style, that of Mathura school was seen as indigenous, for it was 'indigenous by birth'. The two schools of art evolved, interacted and flourished almost simultaneously under the patronage of the Kusana kings. While Mathura used the light red or spotted red sandstone (as can be seen at the present-day Government Museum in Mathura), Gandhara used blue schist or slate (as can be seen in the museums of Lahore, Taxila, Peshawar and Kabul).

However, in Afghanistan, besides schist, the use of ivory, gold, clay, stucco and terracotta was also prevalent. At some sites, like Bamiyan and Aibak, the statuary art was a mixture of carved rock and stucco. While the images at Aybak (Stupa of Takht-e-Rustam) are missing, remnants in the deep niches and arches of the hills also indicate use of rock and stucco. The same can be said about the ceiling and wall decorations at Bamiyan and Foladi caves. Large lotuses carved on the monastic walls at Takht-e-Rustam have remnants of gold polish. In Shotorak, we find a good use of schist in the depiction of Dipankara Buddha and Maitreya Buddha's Paradise. The Hadda monastic complex, with its monasteries of Tapa Kalan, Tepe Kafiriha and Tapa Shotor, has been considered the storehouse of stucco modelling.

According to eminent art historian-archaeologist and former Director General, Mathura Museum, R.C. Sharma, inspiration for motifs freely travelled from east to west, and vice versa.[29] Exchange was a natural phenomenon. In Mathura, new elements were seen in the use of winged lions, centaur, palmettes, all supposed to be of foreign origin. Likewise, we find influence or absorption of Indian motifs in Gandhara art. In the ivory statues of women carrying water pots on their head and standing on *makara* (Goddess Ganga's vahana), dated first century, found in room 10 at Begram site in Afghanistan, one can easily draw similarity between the river goddess Ganga and Yamuna.[30] Another ivory statue of elephant head, dated first century, part of a furniture at the same site, probably depicts Indian god Ganesha. Jataka story, viz. 'Rsyarnga Jataka', carved on ivory plaque, dated first century, was unearthed from room 13 at Begram. While the ivory plaques from Begram were not on display at the National Museum during my visit to the museum, photos of the same can be seen in National Museum publication, *Afghanistan: Crossroads of the Ancient World*.

Interestingly, both the art schools of Gandhara and Mathura have laid claims to the first Buddha images. While two 'earliest' images of the Buddha clad in heavy monastic robes and having a double nimbus resembling the image on Boddo coin were found in Gandhara on Kusana reliquaries dated first to second century at Bimaran, west of Jalalabad in Afghanistan and at Shah-ji-ki Dheri, Peshawar, the Buddhist icons found at Mathura have been dated to the pre-Kanishka period.

Sharma pointed out that two Buddha images belonging to Mathura school at Kausambi (dated AD 80) and at Sarnath (dated AD 81), and undated images in Mathura Museum, viz. the Maholi bodhisattva and Katra bodhisattva or Anyori Buddha, belonging stylistically to the same period, show a refined and developed stage of the Mathura school of Buddhist art by the beginning of Kusana period in the first century. Images like the Parkham Yaksha (dated third century) served as a model for colossal images of Buddha and bodhisattvas. Sharma also pointed to the *ayagapattas* (votive tablets) dated first century BC having *yaksha* and *jina* (nature spirits) figures. Hence, Buddhist icons which are close to ayagapattas may safely be dated to the pre-Kanishka period, said Sharma.[31]

CENTRES OF HINDUISM IN AFGHANISTAN

Discovery of Hindu idols at many places in Afghanistan points to the influence of Hinduism along the Kabul and Oxus valleys. Many works of Shaivite and Hindu art in general, dated fifth to eighth century, have been discovered in Afghanistan, informed author B.A. Litvinsky in the book, *History of Civilizations of Central Asia*. These include nearly 25 marble sculptures and other artefacts of Hindu art. In fact, the presence of Hindu gods has been noticed all over Central Asia, especially in the Zerafshan Valley at Penjikent, in the valley of the Syr Darya at Ferghana and in the Amudarya valley at Arytam.[32]

At Dilberjin Tepe in northern Afghanistan, a wall painting dated around fifth century depicts Siva and Parvati seated on Nandi bull. An inscription was also discovered in the sanctuary of the Dilberjin fortress that gives evidence of the propagation of the cult of Siva.[33] A white marble image of the *Surya* (Sun god) dated from the Hindu Shahi period was found in Khair Khana, which is in present-day northwest Kabul. Eyewitness accounts of Xuanzang document that both Hindus and Buddhists had their shrines in Ghazni and 'although they worship a hundred spirits, yet they also greatly reverence the three precious ones'. The heretics, who were numerous, worshipped Krishna.[34] At Nagarhara, there were five deva temples with 100 worshippers, while at Kapisa there were 10 Deva temples and 1,000 heretics.

The co-existence of Hinduism and Buddhism become apparent when we notice that the complex at Ghazni also hosted a Hindu Shaivite shrine where an image of Durga Mahisasurmardini was found during excavations. The size of the original image can be guessed from the colossal head of the goddess preserved in a glass case in the National Museum. The image serves as an evidence that female divinities were worshipped in Afghanistan. In chapel 23 at Tepe Sardar, excavators also found the decapitated body of Mahisasur, the 'Buffalo Demon', with his severed head lying beside it. This was once part of a composite sculpture depicting the victory of the many-armed Durga over Mahisasur, the demon and enemy of the gods, which was a popular cult theme under the Hindu Shahis (AD 879–1026), the Hindu dynasty ruling over Kabul Valley and Gandhara, said explorer and historian Dupree.[35]

The absorption of Hindu deities in the Buddhist pantheon, possibly during the period of the Hindu Shahis in Afghanistan and also the possibility that Buddhist shrines were converted into Hindu shrines have been discussed at length by Indologist and art historian P. Banerjee in *New Light on Central Asian Art and Iconography*. In his interesting study, Banerjee explains that though subordinate in position, these Hindu deities made their original significance felt even then in the Buddhist framework.[36] Banerjee presented several examples of the popularity of Saivism in Afghanistan and Central Asia during the late Gupta and early medieval periods. A collection of antiquities attributable to the seventh and eighth century (Hindu Shahi period) has come to light from Togao, Gardez, Khair Khana and Tapa Skandar. These include a head of Siva and that of Durga from Gardez, inscribed Mahavinayaka or Ganesa with Urdhvamedhra or erect phallus clad in a tiger skin from Kotal-i-Khair Khana, and the inscribed Uma-Mahesvara image from Tapa Skandar.[37]

A TRAVELLER IN AFGHANISTAN

It was with a sense of awe that I journeyed along the meandering rivers of Bamiyan, Kakrak, Foladi and Khulm to the quiet and forsaken abodes of the Buddha in the foothills of the Hindu Kush and the low hills of Samangan, which once echoed with adulation of the Buddha.

The gigantic left foot of the Big Buddha and the silhouette of the Small Buddha seemed to have stood the test of time even during the 2001 blasting by the Taliban. Propped up by heavy iron grills, they still adorn the colossal roofless niche. In the surrounding caves, fierce deities, Kirtimukhas, peer down from the cave walls and visibly empty pedestals speak of the grand images that once adorned them. The recently discovered oil paintings that are believed to have been the world's oldest have been preserved in the darkness of locked caves, while the two stupas that were dug out sometime around 2014 lie in the open courtyard outside a cave.

Even today, a visitor can savour the remnants of paintings, stucco sculptures, intricate ceiling and wall art, and the gigantic silhouette of Lokottara, and visualize the beauty and radiance that was once Bamiyan. Fortunately, the splendid decoration of the caves of the Buddha colossi and the soffit of its vault is alive in the records of the ASI, which was involved in the restoration of the Bamiyan Buddhas from 1976–82.[38]

At the site of Mes Aynak, 40 km southeast of Kabul, emergency excavations and documentation by the Afghan Institute of Archaeology in collaboration with La Délégation Archéologique Française en Afghanistan (DAFA) and the United Nations Educational, Scientific and Cultural Organization team of archaeologists and historians were in progress on a war footing. The Chinese mining company, Metallurgical Corp of China has a contract to extract the world's largest copper reserves in opencast mines, which pose a danger to the historical and religious treasures buried in the Baba Wali hills, where the site is located. Nicolos Engel, former vice-president of the DAFA, who I met at the National Museum in 2014, said that only a small area of the Buddhist city has been uncovered so far.

The question that bothers heritage lovers is how to preserve and salvage the remains of Mes Aynak and other splendid Buddhist cities of Afghanistan, and how to resuscitate and revive heritage routes that once formed the cradle of Indo-Afghan commercial and cultural dialogue.

3

Historical Trends in Afghanistan

Arvind Gupta

With the Taliban's takeover of Afghanistan on 15 August 2021, the country entered into yet another phase of uncertainty. The Taliban are committed to installing an Islamic Emirate and a harsh Sharia-based rule. In the 20 years since 9/11, there had been unprecedented progress in education, health, women's participation and democracy in Afghanistan. The new generation of educated Afghan youth is not inclined to accept the medieval outlook of the Taliban. A large number of educated Afghans have either left the country or want to leave it.

The latest turn of events is a manifestation of the incipient historical trends in Afghanistan: the struggle between the forces of modernity and Islamists; ethnic divisions in the country; constant external interference; and geopolitics involving external powers reflected in the 'great games'.

We will go over some important historical landmark developments in Afghan history, which went on to define the country over centuries. This will help us provide a historical context to the current developments.

BRIEF HISTORY

Thanks to its location at the intersection of Central Asia and South Asia, Afghanistan has been subject to strong external influences from all directions, particularly from Persia, Central Asia, South Asia, Greece and Mongolia. It is, therefore, not surprising that Afghanistan has evolved as a multiethnic society that has historically been subject to regional and global influences. Different parts of Afghanistan came under the influence of powerful civilizations. It was only in the eighteenth and nineteenth centuries that Afghanistan began to crystallize as a nation state with semi-fixed boundaries. Although the Pashtuns are the single largest ethnic group (about 42 per cent of the population),[1] there are sizeable non-Pashtun ethnic populations, including the Tajiks, Uzbeks, Hazaras, Turkmen and others, who together make up more than half of Afghanistan's population. There is also a Sunni–Shia divide in the country. However, the mutual interaction among these tribes and sub-tribes has been an important driving force in Afghan history.

Geographically, Afghanistan has three distinct parts—the lofty Hindu Kush Mountains in the central parts, the northern parts and plains up to Amu Darya, and the southern, southwestern plains of Kandahar and Helmand.

For most of its history, Afghanistan has been a conglomeration of tribes. The Hotak Dynasty, in the early eighteenth century, and later Ahmad Shah Abdali, from the Durrani tribe of Pashtuns, united the tribes to form the present-day Afghanistan. Abdali was earlier a soldier in the military of the Persian king Nader Shah. He broke away from Persia and established the Durrani rule in Afghanistan in 1747. The Durrani dynasty continued to rule up to 1973 when its last ruler Zahir Shah was deposed. Since then, the nation has been in turmoil.

There has been intense interaction and a two-way traffic of traders and pilgrims between India and Afghanistan for centuries. In ancient times, Afghanistan lay on the Uttarapath or the 'Northern Route' from India, which later became the Grant Trunk Road or the GT Road in the eighteenth century. As Buddhism spread to Afghanistan and over its boundaries, a dense Silk Route connecting to Central Asia and beyond came into existence.

A brief outline of Afghan history is given below to emphasize the point about Afghanistan being at the crossroads of empires.

Table 1*

A Brief Account of Afghanistan's History

From sixth century BC to AD second century	Achaemenids, Greeks, Seleucids, Mauryans, Greco-Bactrians and Parthians rule Afghanistan
135 BC	Kushans conquer Greco-Bactrians. The spread of Buddhism aided by Silk Route
AD fourth to fifth century	Bamiyan Buddhas
	Hephthalites
Fifth to seventh centuries	Sassanids
Seventh to ninth century	Turk Shahis
Ninth to eleventh century	Hindu Shahi dynasties
AD 644	Islam arrives in Afghanistan
Ninth to tenth century	Tahirids
AD 867	Safavids
AD 962	Samanids
AD 998	Mahmud of Ghazni
AD 1175	Mahmud of Ghori
AD 1206	Qutb-ud-din Aibak, an Afghan slave, becomes the Sultan of Delhi and Afghan dynasties in India
AD 1221	Mongol invasion; Genghis Khan takes over Herat
AD 1605	Timurids
Sixteenth century	Turkic Uzbeks take over Herat
AD 1522	Babur takes over Kandahar after Kabul
Sixteenth to eighteenth century	The Mughals ruled parts of Afghanistan, other parts earlier ruled by Safavids of Persia
1716	Hotakis, local Afghan rulers
1716	Abdali of Herat (Durranis) revolts against Persia

1729	Nadr Qoli Beg, later Nadir Shah
1732	Nadir Shah takes over Herat
1747	Nadir Shah assassinated, disintegration of his empire
1772	Timur takes control
1799	Zaman Shah appoints Ranjit Sigh as governor of Lahore
1803	Shah Shuja
1826	Shah Shuja signs a treaty with the British, not permitting the passage of foreign troops to India
1826	Dost Mohammad establishes Barakzai or Mohammadzai dynasty, fails to take control of Peshawar
1837	Ranjit Singh wins in the Battle of Jamrud
1838	Shah Shoja killed, First Anglo-Afghan War begins
1863	Sher Ali receives Russian mission in Kabul but refuses to receive the British mission
1878–80	Second Anglo-Afghan War begins
1879	Treaty of Gandamak is signed; Yaqub Khan allows permanent British embassy in Kabul
1880–93	Aburrahman Khan; drawing up of the Durand Line; border settlement with Russian empire
1901–10	Habibullah
1919–29	Amanullah Khan, the modernizer
1928	Tajik Baccha Saqaw
1929–33	Mohammad Nadir Shah promulgates Afghanistan's second constitution in 1931
1933–73	King Zahir Shah
1964	The Afghan constitution comes into existence
1973	Zahir Shah deposed, Sardar Daud establishes a republican government
1979	Soviet military intervention in support of the People's Democratic party of Afghanistan

*Compiled by the author from various sources

THE PRE-ISLAMIC PAST

Afghanistan is truly ancient with a long pre-Islamic past. Kabul finds a mention in the Vedic literature, where it is mentioned as Kubha. Gandhara has a prominent place in the grand narrative of the Mahabharata. Gandhari, the wife of the Kaurava king Dhritrashtra, came from Gandhara. Shakuni, her brother, is a key character in the Mahabharata. The holy water of the river Kabul was used in the religious ceremonies at the Ram Mandir in Ayodhya by the Uttar Pradesh Chief Minster Yogi Adityanath.[2] Thus, India's cultural connection with Afghanistan runs deep.

In ancient times, the Achaemenids of Persia ruled the territories that now are in Afghanistan. They divided Afghanistan into four satrapies: Aria (Herat); Arachosia (Kandahar, Lashkargah and Quetta); Bactriana (Balkh) and Sattagydia (Ghazni and Gandhara [Kabul, Jalalabad and Peshawar]). There was a centuries-old rivalry between the Greeks and the Persians. Alexander of Macedonia (330 BC) destroyed the Achaemenid empire and set up the 'Alexandrias' of Herat, Kandahar and Bagram. He got bogged down by the local fighting, tried an unsuccessful invasion of India and then retreated ignominiously in which a large number of his troops died. The Alexandrian campaigns, including Sogdia and Punjab (330–327 BC), described by the Greek historian Arrian in his books *Anabasis*, left an indelible mark of Greek culture in the region.

After Alexander's death, the Greek empire disintegrated. Seleucus, one of his commanders, established the Seleucid Empire, of which Afghan territories became a part. His rule was short-lived. The Greek soldiers rebelled against Seleucus and founded the Greco-Bactrian Empire, which lasted three centuries. A Greek city was discovered in Ai Khanoum (east of Balkh in northern Afghanistan) in the 1970s, which shows the rich remains of the Greek and Persian culture of the time. Neither Alexander nor Seleucus was able to subdue the local tribes completely. That has been the story of Afghanistan ever since.

Afghanistan's history is closely intertwined with the history of the Indian subcontinent. Chandragupta Maurya annexed southern Afghanistan to the Mauryan Empire. Ashoka (273–232 BC), the greatest of Mauryan emperors, extended his rule to Afghanistan. Ashokan bilingual rock inscriptions in Greek and Aramaic have been found in Kandahar and Laghman. The renowned ancient centre of learning at Taxila on the eastern bank of Indus River was home to some of the greatest scholars of ancient India, like Chanakya.[3] The Ashokan inscriptions, coins, Buddhist stupas and Viharas abound in Kandahar and right up to Balkh. The Mauryan and Greek cultures continued to flourish in the region for centuries. Afghanistan was also on the ancient Silk Route frequented by merchants, Buddhists and Hindu pilgrims. The Bactrian Kingdom (256 BC–c. 100 BC) at its height ruled parts of what is now Afghanistan, Uzbekistan, Tajikistan, Turkmenistan, and parts of Iran and India. King Menander converted to Buddhism and is fondly remembered by Buddhists as King Milinda of Yunani.

The northern regions of Afghanistan were also influenced by the Parthian Empire (AD 247–224) whose rule extended to central-eastern Turkey and Afghanistan. It was located on the ancient Silk Route that connected China, India and Turkey to the Roman Empire in a network of trade and pilgrimage routes.

The Central Asian tribes of Yuezhi from the north set up the Kushan Empire in the first century. It included territories of present-day Afghanistan, Pakistan and India. Kushans were patrons of Hinduism and Buddhism. Kanishka the Great (AD 127–50) was known for his syncretism. The founder of the Kushan Dynasty, Kujula Kadphises, is stated to have been a follower of the Hindu deity Siva. Kanishka's empire forms an integral part of the Indian subcontinent's history. The Kushans played an important role in spreading Buddhism in Central Asia. The Kushan Empire disintegrated in the third century. The next people to rule Afghanistan were the Sasanians of Persia. They established the Kushano-Sasanian kingdoms in Sogdia, Bactria and Kandahar. The customs and practices of Kushanas continued in this period, even when the Kushan rule had ended.

The Gupta Empire (fourth to sixth century) came next. They had conquered about 21 kingdoms including some in the Oxus valley. But the Guptas' hold on the region was tenuous. In the 480s, the Hunas (Alchon Huns under Toramana and Mihirakula) overran the territories controlled by the Guptas. They damaged India's trade with Europe and Central Asia. The numerous Chinese travellers attracted to Afghanistan and India in their quest for Buddhist literature in the pre-Islamic Afghanistan period became a bridgehead for the spread of Buddhism to Central Asia and China. The Taliban, by destroying the Giant Bamian Buddhas in 2001, were only following their Islamic predecessors, who had destroyed temples and statutes.

ISLAMIC PERIOD

With the advent of Islam in the Arabian Peninsula in the seventh century, it was a matter of time before Islam would arrive in the region. The new religion began the conquest of Persia in the same century. Zoroastrianism was practised in Persia in those days. In AD 652, Herat was conquered. An Arab governor was installed there. The Sassanian rulers were overcome, but not before the twelfth century, when the Islamic rule was firmly established in Afghanistan by the Ghaznavids and Ghurids. It may be recalled that it was from the 560s when the Western Turks had gradually expanded southeastward from across the Amu Darya and occupied Balkh and the Hindu Kush region. It was then that Herat emerged as a major centre of Islamic learning.

TURK SHAHIS (SEVENTH TO NINTH CENTURIES)

The Arabs tried to conquer Kabul several times. From the seventh to the ninth century, the Turk Shahis of Kabul, a branch of

Western Turks mixed with Hephthalites, resisted the expansion of the Abbasid caliphate for 200 years. They were patrons of Buddhism. During their rule, both Buddhism and Hinduism flourished in Afghanistan. In fact, a statue of Ganesha from Gardez is dated to the Turk Shahi period. The inscription at the base of the statue reads:

> On the thirteenth day of the bright half of the month of Jyestha, the [lunar] mansion being the Viśākha, at the auspicious time when the zodiacal sign Lion was bright on the horizon (lagna), in the year eight, this great [image] of the Mahāvināyaka was consecrated by the supreme lord, the great king, the king of the kings, the śri sahi Khi mgāla, the king of Odyāna.[4]

HINDU SHAHIS

The Hindu Shahi (AD 850–1026) dynasties of Kabul, Kandahar and Punjab resisted and checked the spread of Islam for 300 years. Afghanistan to this day has enough evidence of rich Hindu culture in Kabul, Zabul, Panjshir, Peshawar, Kandahar and many other areas. The remains of ancient Hindu temples have been found in the region. The evidence of Hindu influence has also been derived from the numerous coin collections of the Hindu Shahi rulers of Kabul.

Who were Hindu Shahis? They were the ones who ruled Afghanistan after the Turk Shahi king Lagaturman. *Rajatarangini* describes Hindu Shahis as Kshatriyas. But according to historian R.C. Majumdar, the Hindu Shahi Kingdom was founded by the Brahmin minister Kallar. The Hindu Shahi rulers who can be identified from inscriptions are: Vakkadeva, Kamalavarman, Bhimadeva, Jayapala (AD 964–1001), Anandapala (AD 1001–10), Trilochanapala (AD 1010–21) and Bhimpala (AD 1021–26).

Vakkadeva built a Shiva temple in northern Afghanistan, and issued coins with motifs of elephants and lions designed on them, carrying the legend of Shri Vakkadeva. This is mentioned in the Mazare Sharif inscription of the Shahi Ruler Veka, as reported by the Taxila Institute of Asian Civilizations, Islamabad.

Hindu Shahis supported a kingdom in Ghazni. But the areas controlled by the Hindu Shahis were repeatedly attacked by the Turks from the western side. Alp-Tegin took over Bamiyan, which has been described as 'the kingdom of infidel Hindu Shir Barak'. The confrontation between Hindu Shahi kings and the Turks who served the Samanids of Persia became persistent. The Shahis were able to hold off the Samanids for more than a 100 years. The Turks were keen to set up their own independent kingdoms. The frontier region included the Hindu Kush mountains. The literal interpretation of the term means the area where the Hindus were killed. Clearly, the Hindu Kush mountain area had substantial Hindu influence.

Eventually, the Hindu Shahis were conquered and a Muslim rule was established. The pattern of temple breaking and the massive killings of Hindus recurred in subsequent years when the Turko-Afghan rulers invaded Indian subcontinent for loot and territorial gains.

Bhimdeva, the Hindu king of Kabul, allied with the kings of Punjab to battle the Turkish threat from the west. Bhimdeva's daughter Dida was a queen in Kashmir. Bhimadeva was succeeded by Jayapal, who later ruled over Punjab. He lost a large part of his territory to Sabuktigin but continued to rule from Peshawar and Waihind. Eventually, Mahmud of Ghazni conquered Herat, Balkh and Khurasan. With these conquests, he attained a status equal to his former masters, the Samanids. The fall of the Hindu Shahi dynasties of Kabul opened the way for Mahmud of Ghazni's several expeditions into India, primarily for the purpose of loot.

The Hindu Shahis have earned a lot of praise from historians as they fought the advancing Muslims courageously for close to 200 years. Dr Yogendra Misra in the book *The Hindu Sahis of Afghanistan and the Punjab* said, 'The Shahis...collapsed against the repeated onslaughts of the Turks...but not before three generations of the Shahi kings had sacrificed themselves on the battlefield.' Under the Shahi rule, an advanced Hindu culture flourished in the region. The Shahis were seen as 'great patrons of scholars and religious foundations'. Anandapala supported art and culture, and publicized the work of his teacher Ugrabhuti. Bhimadeva built a temple in Kashmir as an act of charity. The construction of at least two temples at Udabhandapura by members of the royal family came to be known from inscriptions.[5]

The Muslim rulers routinely destroyed Hindu temples and idols. At the mountain of Zur, where there was a Hindu temple, Jabir ibn Samurah 'cut off the hands of the idol with one stroke and plucked the eyes out of their sockets but then returned everything to the priest, remarking that he only wanted to demonstrate how powerless was his idol to do either good or evil'. In AD 870–71, Yaqub bin Layth went on a temple destroying spree. 'He first took Bamian…then marched on Balkh where he ruined (the temple) Naushad. On his way back from Balkh he attacked Kabul…the capital city of the Hindu Shahis to rob the sacred temple—the reputed place of coronation of the Sahi rulers—of its sculptural wealth…'[6]

Zabul has been described as a 'large Hindu place of worship in that country, which was called Sakawand, and people used to come on pilgrimage from the most remote parts of Hindustan to the idols of that place. When Fardaghan arrived in Zabulistan he led his army against it, took the temple, broke the idols in pieces and overthrew the idolaters…'[7]

MONGOLS AND TIMURIDS

In the thirteenth century, Afghanistan faced the wrath of Genghis Khan. Kabul, Kandahar, Jalalabad and many other places were ruined, and thousands of people were slaughtered. It is said that all the male residents of Ghazni and Helmand were killed by Ogedei Khan in 1222. Afghanistan came under the rule of Mongol Ilkhanate and Chagatai Khanate. The Hazara people claim to be descendants of the Mongol and Turkic invaders. However, this is disputed.

Timurlane attacked Afghanistan in 1383–1385. Of Turk-Afghan origin, he claimed descent from Genghis Khan. He brought great misery and destruction upon the region and Afghanistan. After he died in 1407, the Timurid Empire disintegrated in the second half of the fifteenth century. Herat became one of the centres of the Timurid renaissance along with Samarkand. Timur's successors, the Timurids (1405–1507), enriched the capital city of Herat with notable architectural buildings. Under their rule, Afghanistan had relative peace and prosperity.

THE MUGHALS

During the era of flux, Babur, an Uzbek warlord from the Ferghana Valley and a descendent of Timur managed to take over Kabul in 1504 and Kandahar a few years later. He used Kabul as a staging post to invade India in 1526 and succeeded in setting up the Mughal rule. The influence of the Mughals in South Afghanistan lasted till the reign of Shahjahan. Even today, one can see the evidence of the Mughal rule in Kandahar and other areas. Kabul and Kandahar were constantly contested for by the Safavids of Persia and the Mughals. The Safavid-Mughal rivalry shaped the history of Afghanistan for over 200 years. Safavids held control in the north of Kabul, while the Mughals ruled in the south. Kandahar often changed hands between the two.

HOTAKIS, AHMAD SHAH ABDALI

In 1709, Mir Waiz Khan, a leader of the Hotaki Ghilzay tribe, led a successful uprising against Gorgin Khan, the Persian governor of Kandahar. In 1716, the Abdalis (Durrani) of Herat, encouraged by his example, took up arms against the Persians and liberated the province. The Afghan–Persian wars continued until Nadir Qoli Beg defeated the Afghans at Damghan in 1729, thereby ending the Afghan occupation of Persia. Eventually, Beg overtook Herat in 1732, along with Ghazni and Kabul. He invaded India and included the famous Koh-i-Noor diamond and the Peacock Throne in his loot. After his assassination in 1747, his empire disintegrated paving the way for the rise of the Durrani Empire.

Ahmad Shah Abdali, a guard in Nadir Shah's army, managed to unite the Afghan tribes and set up the Durrani Empire in Afghanistan that extended from the Amu Darya to the Arabian Sea. He also made a foray into India and reached Delhi where the Mughal Empire was already in disarray.

After Abdali died in 1772, his decedents Timur and Zaman Shah ruled Afghanistan. Zaman had eyes on India, like Abdali before him. He made several raids on Punjab, on his way to Delhi. However, by then, the British power in India was rising and that of the Mughal Empire was setting down. He faced stiff resistance from the Sikh armies under Maharaja Ranjit Singh. Later, Zaman also came under pressure from his cousin Mahmud in Herat. Zaman Shah died in 1800.

Mahmud ruled Afghanistan for a while. But the tribes were unhappy with him. They conspired against him and invited Zaman Shah's brother Shah Shuja to depose him. The latter ruled Kabul from 1803–09 and 1839–42.

EUROPEANS

This was the time when European interest in India began to show up. The French emperor Napoleon had a plan to invade India in collaboration with the Russian emperor. The plan never took off. In the meanwhile, Russians were pressing forward in Central Asia and eyeing Afghanistan. The British were alarmed. They saw Russians as a threat to their Indian empire. In this 'great game', Afghanistan became a pawn for more than a century. The British signed the Treaty of Peshawar on 7 June 1809 with Shah Shuja to prevent the passage of foreign troops from the Afghan territory. Shah Shuja's troops in Kabul were routed as he was signing a treaty with M. Elphinstone in Peshawar. The British had to provide asylum to Shah Shuja in Ludhiana in 1815.

The early nineteenth century was a period of great turmoil. Dost Mohammad Khan Barakzai established the Barakzai rule in Afghanistan. He took over Kabul, Ghazni, Jalalabad and Peshawar in 1818. Baluchistan and Sindh became independent. Maharaja Ranjit Singh consolidated the Sikh empire in Punjab. There was a constant struggle between the Afghan rulers and the Sikhs for dominance in the area. Ranjit Singh eventually drove the Afghans out of Peshawar. In the battle of Jamrud, 1837, a strategic town at the mouth of the Khyber Pass, the Sikh armies defeated Dost Mohammed's armies. The Sikh armies occupied the trans-Indus areas, pushing the Afghans beyond the Khyber Pass. The Afghans lost the regions of Punjab, Multan, Kashmir, Derajat, Hazara, Balakot, Attock, Peshawar and Jamrud.

THREE ANGLO-AFGHAN WARS

The First Anglo-Afghan War (1838–42)

Dost Mohammad, who reigned from 1826–39 and 1843–63, became the emir of Afghanistan in 1826. He wanted the British to help him recover Peshawar, which he had lost to the Sikhs. The British sent a mission to Kabul to negotiate the terms. Meanwhile, a Russian agent also arrived in Kabul, following which the British mission withdrew.[8] Indian Governor-General Lord Auckland, miffed at Dost Mohammad's vacillations between Russia and Britain, ordered a military invasion of Afghanistan. The purpose was to restore Shah Shuja, who was living in exile in India, to the Afghan throne. Initially, the British had major success. Dost Mohammad fled to Bukhara. Shah Shuja was reinstated as the emir. But the Afghans could not tolerate external interference and imposition of a ruler with the help of foreign powers. Insurgencies broke out. The war ended disastrously for the British. They lost an entire army of 14,000 people in the campaign. Dost Mohammad came back from Bukhara, only to be arrested and deported to India. The new Governor-General Lord Ellenborough ordered the withdrawal of British troops. Dost Mohammad was reinstated as the emir in 1843.[9]

Second Anglo-Afghan War (1878-80)

The Second Anglo–Afghan War happened for very similar reasons: the British were deeply concerned about the expanding Russian influence. The British Governor-General Lord Lytton had asked the Afghan Emir Sher Ali, the son of Dost Mohammad, to admit a British mission in Kabul. He refused. Instead, Russian General Stoletov was allowed to come in, while Lytton's emissary Nevill Chamberlain was stopped at the borders. This infuriated Lytton who ordered military action against Sher Ali in 1878. Sher Ali fled and died in exile. His son Yaqub Khan was installed as emir, following the Treaty of Gandamak in 1879. The treaty provided for a British mission in Kabul and bound the emir to follow British advice in foreign relations. The matter did not end there. The British envoy was murdered. Furious British forces again invaded Kabul. Sher Ali's nephew Abdul Rahman was installed as the new emir. He subsequently negotiated the 'boundary' of Afghanistan with the British, which no Afghan government had ever recognized. It came to be known as the Durand Line.

Third Anglo-Afghan War (1919) and Amanullah Khan

Although the British had considerable influence in Afghanistan after the Second Anglo–Afghan War, there was also a good deal of resentment against them. They were seen as the ones interfering in the Afghan affairs. The Afghan Emir Habibullah Khan maintained neutrality in the First World War, but there was support for the Ottoman Empire in the country. After Habibullah Khan's assassination, in 1919, his son Amanullah Khan became the emir and declared complete independence from the British. Amanullah favoured independence. He went against the wishes of the British and even refused to honour some of the agreements signed by his predecessors. He wanted the British to recognize Afghanistan's independence. The British were aghast. This led to the short-lived Third Anglo–Afghan War in May 1919. The war ended with the Treaty of Rawalpindi (8 August 1919), but not before Amanullah had signed a treaty with the newly established Soviet Republic. Afghanistan became the first country to recognize the Soviet Union. A special relationship between the two continued until December 1979 when the Soviet armies invaded Afghanistan in support of the communist government that was installed through a coup. The British, under the Rawalpindi Agreement, officially recognized and declared Afghanistan independent.

Afghanistan's modernization process began with Amanullah Khan. He opened schools for boys and girls, drafted a modern constitution guaranteeing equal rights for citizens and relaxed the dress code for women. Despite facing internal resistance, he managed to suppress a rebellion in Khost, but eventually abdicated his throne in 1929 and fled to India and later to Europe, where he died in 1960. After a brief nine-month rule of Habibullah Kalakani, a leader of the Saqqawists opposition movement, Nadir Shah became the king of Afghanistan. Some people believe that the British had planned Amanullah's downfall and brought 'weak' Nadir Shah to the throne.

KING ZAHIR SHAH (1933–73)

King Nadir Shah ruled for four years. After his assassination, his son Zahir Shah became the king of Afghanistan in 1933 and ruled until 1973 when he was deposed in a coup. During this period, Afghanistan developed its relations with major powers despite maintaining neutrality. Zahir Shah started the process of modernization in the 1950s. He faced several tribal turmoils but managed to keep the country intact. In the initial years of his rule, he ceded a lot of power to his uncles Mohammad Hashim Khan and Shah Mahmoud Khan, who served as his prime ministers (PMs). He was able to receive developmental assistance from the United States, Soviet Union, France, the UK, Germany, Italy, Japan and other countries. He also invited foreign advisers to help Afghanistan during the phase of transition. It is interesting to note that during the 1930s, King Zahir Shah provided aid and assistance to the Uighur and Kirghiz Muslim rebels who had established the short-lived First East Turkestan Republic. Afghanistan maintained neutrality in its foreign policy.

After the Second World War, Zahir Shah opened the country cautiously. He invited several countries, from both camps of the Cold War, to help in the country's modernization. The influence of the Soviet Union grew. Socialist ideas began to emerge, particularly among the students. In 1964, Afghanistan adopted a constitution that introduced free elections, the parliament, civil rights, women's rights and universal suffrage, and so on. Members of the royal family were forbidden from holding public offices. The preamble to the constitution envisaged a constitutional monarchy, Islam as the 'sacred religion of Afghanistan' and a 'progressive society'.[10]

Mohammed Daud Khan, a member of the royal family and a cousin of Zahir Shah, occupied high positions during the latter's regime. He was the minister of defence between 1946 and 1948 and the PM between 1953 and 1963. He was pro-Soviet in his inclinations. In 1964, when Zahir Shah forbade royals to hold official positions, Daud Khan lost his power. But he was active behind the scene. In 1963, he staged a coup and deposed Zahir Shah who went into exile. Daud declared Afghanistan as a republic. He also was a staunch follower of pro-Pashtun policies, which alienated Pakistan.

COMMUNISTS AND SOVIET MILITARY INTERVENTION

The leftists in the country, led by the Khalq, a pro-Soviet party, were unhappy with Daud Khan. In April 1978, Noor

Mohammed Taraqi staged a coup in which Daud was killed. A communist government under Taraqi, with Soviet support, was installed. This momentous event in the Afghan history is known as the Saur Revolution.[11] It triggered a chain of events that shook not only the country but also had huge regional and global implications. Taraqi faced immediate opposition from within the party as well as in the country. A virtual civil war situation developed. The People's Democratic Party of Afghanistan (PDPA), the communist party, had two factions—the Khalq and the Parcham factions. Taraqi requested help from the Soviet Union but the Soviet PM Alexei Kosygin refused to intervene. Taraqi was killed in an inter-factional fight. He was replaced by Hafizullah Amin.[12]

Hafizullah Amin could not stabilze the situation in the country. He requested military help from the Soviet Union. The Soviet army invaded Afghanistan in December 1979 on an invitation from Hafiz Amin. The situation worsened in the country. Amin himself was killed and replaced by Babrak Karmal, who belonged to the Parcham faction of PDPA. Karmal was replaced by Mohammad Najibullah who made some serious efforts at reconciliation to end the civil war in Afghanistan. But he was up against a resurgent Mujahideen who declared jihad and were being supported by the Central Intelligence Agency (CIA), Pakistan's Inter-Services Intelligence (ISI) and Saudi Arabia.

After the advent of Soviet leader Mikhail Gorbachev, the Soviet Union underwent internal convulsions that eventually led to its demise in 1991. The Afghan War was proving too costly for the Soviet Union. Gorbachev, with the help of the United Nations (UN), negotiated a withdrawal of the Soviet troops, which left Afghanistan in 1989.[13] Najibullah carried on until he was overthrown by the Mujahideen. He took shelter in the UN compound in Kabul but was taken out and hung from a lamp post by the Mujahideen in 1991. That marked the end of one phase in Afghanistan and the start of a new one that has proved to be highly unstable and violent. While the Soviets withdrew in 1989, they left behind a turbulent Afghanistan, where highly radical Islamist forces have gained prominence.

After the Soviet withdrawal, the Najibullah government lasted only for three years. He was overthrown on 16 April 1992. This was followed by the fratricidal, unstable Mujahedeen rule. They were overthrown by Pakistan-backed Taliban who ruled during 1996–2001. Taliban imposed an extremely strict Sharia rule in which stringent punishments were awarded for petty crimes, music was banned, and women were denied access to education and jobs. The Taliban also harboured the Al-Qaeda and its leader Osama bin Laden who had plotted the 9/11 terror attack on the World Trade Centre in New York.

US INTERVENTION

In 2001, the US started intervening in Afghanistan's internal affairs, and continued to do so for the next two decades. They sustained a democratically elected government by providing economic and military assistance. It took 20 years for democracy to take root in Afghanistan. The problem was that the Bonn Agreement of 2001[14], which brought an interim government in Afghanistan, did not bring stability, as the Taliban, though suppressed, were not fully defeated or reconciled. The West poured in trillions of dollars to stabilize Afghanistan, but made it an aid-dependent country. The end of the war was not in sight. It proved to be a heavy burden for the US. President Barack Obama started thinking seriously about pulling out the US troops from Afghanistan. President Donald Trump appointed ambassador Zalmay Khalilzad to negotiate a deal with the Taliban in 2018 to allow the withdrawal of the Soviet troops. The Doha Agreement, which was negotiated without the involvement of the Afghan government, was a deal between the US and the adversary. President Joe Biden reasoned in 2021 that the US was not in Afghanistan for nation-building, and that it could not remain entrenched in a forever, never-ending war. He also concluded that the Al-Qaeda had been degraded to the extent that it no longer posed a threat to the US. The US needed to extricate itself from the expensive war in Afghanistan and instead refocus on a rising China, which was posing a greater challenge. The Doha Agreement was signed in February 2020. The Ashraf Ghani government collapsed on 15 August 2021 when the victorious Taliban entered Kabul. President Ashraf Ghani soon fled the country. The US troops' withdrawal was completed by 30 August, bringing the 20-year-long US intervention in Afghanistan to an end.

CONCLUSION

This brief survey of Afghan history has been attempted to help understand the ongoing conflict in Afghanistan.

Afghanistan has a rich pre-Islamic past in which it was subject to influences from diverse cultures—Greek, Persian, Turkic, Mongol, Indic, etc. The tribes of Afghanistan have imbibed these influences deeply. Buddhism, Hinduism, Zoroastrianism and Hellenism flourished in Afghanistan before the advent of Islam. Afghanistan was located at the crossroads of major trade routes of the time. Pilgrims, merchants and travellers passed through Afghanistan for centuries. Afghanistan's pre-Islamic past is often understated. It was a Hindu and Buddhist country before the advent of Islam. Its past has been marked by extreme violence as well as deeply ingrained cultures. Time and again, Afghanistan was ravaged by invaders from different directions. Yet, several cities remained centres of advanced culture for a long time.

Afghanistan served as a staging post for the invasion of India for many invaders. Because of its location at the peripheries of India, Persia, Central Asia and China, Afghanistan has been important in the global and regional geopolitics. This, in turn, has made it difficult for Afghanistan to remain peaceful and stable. This has been true since the time of Alexander and stands true even today. British entered Afghanistan four times (three Anglo–Afghan Wars and then as part of North Atlantic Treaty

Organization or NATO-1), the Soviets, three times (in 1929 against the Saqqawists, in 1930 to fight the Basmachi movement and then in 1979) and the Americans, once (in 2001). History demonstrates that external powers have often come to grief when they intervened in Afghanistan. Going in was easy, coming out was always difficult. No wonder that Afghanistan has earned the reputation of being the 'graveyard of empires'.

India's connection with Afghanistan has been bittersweet but deep and enduring. Afghanistan has been a part of Indian civilizational history. Influence of the Indus Valley Civilization extended up to Afghanistan, which has played an important role in Indian history. Sher Shah Suri, who founded the Sur dynasty in Bengal and constructed the Grand Trunk road that connected Chittagong with Kabul, was an Afghan. Likewise, Indian influence in Afghanistan can be traced back to the times of the Mauryans. Some of the bloodiest chapters in India's history are linked with Afghanistan, like the invasion of India by Mahmud Ghazni and the repeated attacks on the Somnath temple.

At the level of citizens, the relationship has been friendly and cordial. While Afghans were rulers after tyrants, Afghan people have a far more positive image in India. Indians, too, are respected in Afghanistan. Personalities like Abdul Ghaffar Khan, also known as Frontier Gandhi, are revered in India and among Pashtuns alike.

For now, the Taliban are in power once again. They claim to represent Pashtun nationalism. Not all Pashtun are Taliban. But Afghanistan is not only about Pashtuns. Although the Pashtuns have ruled Afghanistan for a long time, there are more non-Pashtuns in Afghanistan. Therefore, the formation of an inclusive government in Afghanistan is very important. Further, Afghanistan has been subject to regional pulls and pressures. It is, therefore, important that Afghanistan maintains equilibrium in its policies.

Due to its rich pre-Islamic past, Afghanistan is of great interest to India. Even during the Islamic period, India and Afghanistan remain linked in myriads ways. In the new circumstances post the Taliban takeover, India will have to remain watchful of the developments there. It is, therefore, essential for India to keep a healthy relationship with the people of Afghanistan.

Part II

AFGHANISTAN AND ITS NEIGHBOURHOOD

4

Pakistan and Its Afghanistan Tangle: Legitimate Interests and Illegitimate Instruments

Amb. T.C.A. Raghavan

I recall hearing Riaz Mohammad Khan, a former foreign secretary of Pakistan, speaking about Pakistan's policy towards Afghanistan sometime in late 2013. The venue was the Islamabad Institute of Strategic Studies (IISS), a think tank closely affiliated with the Government of Pakistan, which also has the reputation of conducting and publishing rigorous research as also hosting discussions in which views and analysis could be put forward with candour. Khan was foreign secretary during the time when I was deputy high commissioner in Islamabad. He retired in 2008.

In late 2013, when he spoke at the IISS, Pakistan's external environment was grim: relations with the US were at a low ebb, there had been numerous frictions with Afghanistan, and clashes with India on the Line of Control and parts of the international border were increasing. All this paled into relative insignificance in the context of Pakistan's internal situation where a full-scale national security crisis was playing out. There were major terrorist attacks by the Tehreek-e-Taliban Pakistan (TTP) across the length and breadth of Pakistan, including the capital, and this time around it was often the military which was in the crosshairs of the terrorists. The blowback from the policies Pakistan had been following in terms of supporting extremist and terrorist groups seemed to be now upon it.

Khan is regarded as an astute commentator and analyst on the Afghan-Pak interface and is a scholar in his own right. He was the director-general in the foreign ministry concerned with Afghanistan during the proximity talks in Geneva that ended with the agreement leading to the Soviet withdrawal from Afghanistan. He wrote about it in his book, *Untying the Afghan Knot: Negotiating Soviet Withdrawal*.[1] Reading the book a decade and a half after it was first published, I was struck by how the Pakistan foreign office under Sahabzada Yaqub Khan as foreign minister was able to carve out a space for diplomacy in a terrain that was largely dominated by the Afghanistan experts in the Inter-Services Intelligence or ISI. Perhaps, I wondered, if this had something to do with the personality and stature of Yaqub Khan himself.

After his retirement, Riaz Mohammad Khan wrote a second book titled *Afghanistan and Pakistan: Conflict, Extremism and Resistance to Modernity*. Since it is a post-retirement work, it had even greater candour in its analysis. The book basically continues the Afghan–Pak story from 1989 to about 2010.[2] The lecture at the IISS essentially summarized and made explicit some questions inherent in his treatment of the topic in the book. I did not keep detailed notes of the lecture but my memory of it is that Khan was essentially not only talking about Pakistan's legitimate interests and expectations from Afghanistan but also saying that the means it adopted were usually counterproductive and did not suggest that lessons were being learnt over time from the shortcomings of earlier policies.

We find some elements and hints of the same in Khan's second book—a depiction of the drawbacks of an excessive securitization of foreign policy. The next part is a summary and bird's eye view of Pakistan's perspective on Afghanistan following August 2021. I will, thereafter, briefly delve into the excessive securitization aspect.

AFGHAN COLLAPSE: WHAT IT MEANT FOR PAKISTAN

Six months after the systemic collapse in Kabul, there was a mix of quiet satisfaction and triumph in Pakistan. Three principal reasons underwrote these sentiments: first, a sense of achievement that a long and risky strategy to install a 'friendly' government in Kabul had paid off; second, a mood of vindication that the US policy—long disliked in Pakistan and which united the State and street views like almost nothing else—has been exposed, both with regard to competence and credibility; thirdly, and finally, there was satisfaction amidst the Indian presence in Afghanistan, which for long has been the cause of as much psychological envy as strategic anxiety.

It is true that there were voices of disquiet and even prophets of doom amidst this triumphalism: concerns about the risks of Taliban blowback in Pakistan and the catalysing of Pashtun nationalism across the Durand Line; over-the-future cost that the US disapprobation, following its humiliating withdrawal, will lead to; or even that radical extremism will receive a huge dose of encouragement in Pakistan (even though such empowerment is also welcomed with regard to the Kashmiri outfits).

Any doubts were fewer and generally emerged from circles long seen as the 'usual suspects' and dissenters, and not really as representative of the mainstream view. The general mood, therefore, was that such problems can be dealt with in the future as and when they come up. The overall view veered towards the perspective that there was finally a good chance that Afghanistan may be on the cusp of a stability that has been elusive so far. In this view, a 'stable Afghanistan' is also seen as inseparable from a government 'friendly' to Pakistan.

If the above summarizes the mood prevalent in Pakistan till the end of 2021 or even early 2022, clearly the situation has changed dramatically since then and the triumphalism, which was so evident after August 2021, has retreated considerably. Firstly, international attention has shifted away from Pakistan, on account of the conflict in Ukraine. Donor fatigue is, therefore, evident for all crisis situations outside Europe. Pakistan itself has entered a phase of domestic instability and its economy reflects this. Also, an adverse environment on account of headwinds generated by the Ukrainian crisis and the effects of the global pandemic continue to make themselves felt. The blowback from the Taliban resurgence in Afghanistan is being felt in Pakistan earlier than was expected in terms of the re-emergence of the TTP. In brief, the external environment for Afghanistan is adverse as it is for Pakistan.

EFFECTS OF SOVIET DISINTEGRATION ON AFGHANISTAN

Some parallels with the past are worth pausing over. The resilience President Mohammad Najibullah had exhibited after the Soviet withdrawal in February 1989 surprised both his supporters and foes. The Soviet Union's disintegration in December 1991 was, however, profoundly weakening for his government and indeed for the whole architecture that had emerged over the past decade. Soviet support, rather than its troops, had been a material factor in sustaining it, and the Soviet Union's collapse meant that the government, which had so far battled the different Mujahideen groups effectively, now would come apart quickly.

By April 1992, the former Mujahideen factions were running a new government in Afghanistan. But these were not so much as different factions as different armies jostling for tactical advantage, with a civil war looming large. Pakistan's effort was to make them pull together, while at the same time playing favourites with different leaders. In September 1995, Pakistan realized a new reality was upon it when its ambassador was attacked and its embassy badly damaged. Pakistan learnt the hard way that the different factions of the Mujahideen, which it had nurtured and long supported, had personalities of their own and the behaviour they had shown in Quetta or Peshawar was going to change once they were in Kabul. More significantly, dealing with them was different from dealing with political or ideological factions. Bringing about intra-Afghan negotiation for a settlement was like getting different armies to reach a modus vivendi—settling on the battlefield is usually the preferred option for combatants rather than reaching a compromise. For Pakistan, different groups also meant that the door remained open for other external actors to step in to muddy its waters further.

The Taliban emerged as the favoured new force that would restore stability in Afghanistan and also be 'government friendly' to Pakistan. What this meant remains a subject of discussion. The view was that its sacrifices for the Afghan cause entitled Pakistan to a government of its preference in Kabul. The term 'strategic depth' also acquired and retained a certain optical and narrative value. But the arguments made in its favour suggested, as better-informed Pakistanis emphasized, a certain naivety on strategic matters.

The argument now being heard that being in government would gradually moderate the Taliban also has older antecedents and was heard in Pakistan in the late 1990s as well. Pakistan's expectation post-1996 was that the Taliban's success in controlling most of Afghanistan and its major cities would lead to international acquiescence and even acceptance of changed realities. This did not happen and support of terrorist groups, misogyny, regressive social policies and an inability to compromise forced the Taliban into isolation. By 2001, Pakistan was the only country maintaining diplomatic relations with Afghanistan. Saudi Arabia and the UAE, which had earlier recognized the Taliban, had broken relations over the sanctuary provided to Osama bin Laden. Pakistan was finally the only one left making the case for engagement with the Taliban.

Apart from these parallels with the 1990s, there are other significant similarities, too, with the Pakistan–Afghanistan interface of the 1990s. Afghanistan then was very much in a news shadow, and the US and western interest had shifted. The Cold War was over and the overwhelming focus was on a European war in the Balkans. Politics in Pakistan was also significantly different in the post-Zia phase. Nawaz Sharif and Benazir Bhutto were alternating in power and were both victims and protagonists in the civil-military contests that characterized the 1990s in Pakistan. It is easy to see the parallels today. But the differences should not be understated. A major difference lies in Afghanistan itself. The Taliban seized power in an isolated and war-torn economy and society in 1996, quite unlike the case today. While the country has numerous structural fragilities and a massive aid dependency, it is also much younger in its demographic profile today, is more educated, more urbanized and finally much more connected to the external world. Finally, what has changed most dramatically is China's role and position in the region.

Many in Pakistan who continue to be optimistic hope that this time its attempt to establish a stable order in Afghanistan with a government 'friendly' to it may be more successful. Whether that will happen remains a question, for the Taliban has changed and evolved in the past two decades. The indications so far do not generate much grounds for optimism. Pakistan is also the country, after Afghanistan of course, likely to be most impacted by the answer that emerges. But it is more than likely that what it may find once again is the surfacing of the fundamental contradiction between its twin aims of 'stability' and a 'friendly' government.

ORIGIN OF PAK-AFGHAN RELATIONS

Two different streams comprise the substance of Pakistan's approach to Afghanistan. The first is of being in the position of a larger neighbour with a significant ethnic overlap, and also a long history of frictions and disputes. Each of these factors has made for an interface that has been ridden with suspicion since 1947. The second stream is of Pakistan's concerns regarding India and Afghanistan. The grounds for this—both real and imagined—again stretch back in history. To a considerable extent, these are also derived from mainstream Pakistani views of Muslim nationalism and separatism in the first half of the twentieth century, and the position of the Khudai Khidmatgars and Bacha Khan in the old North-West Frontier Province (NWFP)—both opposed the accession of the NWFP to Pakistan in 1947. Both these streams appear to be almost static, placing an enormous burden of demography and history on Pakistan–Afghanistan relations. Yet, it is not entirely so.

The relationship has evolved and changed, and often in surprising ways. In 1965 and 1971, during India–Pakistan conflicts, Afghanistan consciously strove not to add to Pakistan's strategic anxieties. While the illegitimacy of the Durand Line as a legal border has existed as a political slogan and a rhetorical point, no government in Afghanistan has seriously pursued a policy that would give substance to occasional polemic and rhetoric. Two external great power interventions (1979–1989, 2001–2021), in which Afghanistan was totally transformed for better and for worse, did not seriously question the Pakistan–Afghanistan border, and on the contrary went to some length, at considerable damage to themselves, to respect and reinforce it. About a decade ago, Riaz Mohammad Khan noted: 'In retrospect, however, neither the Afghan's reservations to the Durand Line nor the Pashtunistan issue ever posed a real threat to Pakistan.'[3] This point is worth reiterating. In India, the contrary position is taken as a given and seen as adding extra ballast to Pakistan's notions of 'strategic depth' in Afghanistan.

The larger point is that Pakistani perspectives and concerns regarding Afghanistan have to be seen in the context of how Pakistan itself was changing in the 1980s, and how in every decade, thereafter, its pace of change intensified in a particular direction. Riaz Mohammad Khan brought out the dangers and downsides of an excessive securitization of external policies:

> The long periods of military rule and influence induced a security orientation in state thinking....security became the central strategic concern....The influence of the military elite on the polarized and often unstable politics did not allow civilian political leaders to shift the government paradigm from its emphasis on security to one that addressed the complex issues of welfare, development and political cohesion...[4]

In this context, Pakistan's real advantages vis-à-vis Afghanistan get somewhat minimized. These are its economic, social and cultural links—which in the normal course are what diplomacy seeks to leverage—that have the most potential in all interfaces between neighbouring countries. In its own way, Pakistan has been a neighbour on which many Afghans have depended upon greatly. It has housed huge refugee influxes from Afghanistan for very long periods of time. Yet, the takeaways of this in terms of accumulated social capital or 'soft power' have been minimal. The reasons for this are well known. Relying solely or very substantially on securitized perspectives to decide on policy has inevitably led to excessive dependence on armed proxies and insurgents. This has consequences, notwithstanding the current success, on how Afghans view Pakistan, and therefore any gain remains fragile. There is then the impact within Pakistan itself. Pakistan's history over the past decade and a half bears witness to the growing sense of empowerment at the opposite ends of the extremist spectrum in Pakistan: at one end, the Barelvis with the Tehrik-e-Labbaik Pakistan, and at the other, the Deobandis and the Tehrik-e-Taliban Pakistan.

In brief, in Pakistan, internal and external securitization has reinforced each other as has often happened elsewhere, too. In the backdrop of great power intrusions, adversarial India–Pakistan relations and the internal dynamics of Afghanistan itself, the consequences were even more pronounced as far as Pakistan's approach to Afghanistan was concerned. The problem is more complex than that of the military 'running' Pakistan for long periods of time. Rather it is of 'securitized' thinking acquiring a structural character. Thus, Riaz Mohammad Khan noted: 'Hawkish views on security and foreign relations often associated with the ISI and the military are, in fact, quite common within the foreign office and civilian establishment, partly owing to the long periods of military rule in Pakistan.'[5] A religious fervour in mainstream politics and an excessive securitization of public narratives lie at the core of many of Pakistan's problems.

These are pitfalls that we too have to avoid.

5

Central Asia's Connect with Afghanistan

Amb. Skand R. Tayal

Present-day Afghanistan and Central Asia have been cultural, civilizational and religious space for millennia. Greco-Bactrians (second century BC), Kushan Empire (first century), Samanids (ninth century) and Ghaznavids (tenth to eleventh century) ruled over much of this geographic space. In the sixteenth century, Babur from Fergana Valley captured Kabul from Arghun Dynasty while fleeing from Samarkand. Between the sixteenth and eighteenth centuries, the Uzbek Khanate of Bukhara, Iranian Safavids and Mughals ruled over parts of Afghanistan. In AD 1219, Genghis Khan overran the region. The present-day Hazara minority is believed to be the descendant of the invading Mongols and Turco-Mongols from Central Asia who settled down in conquered Afghan regions and married local women. Till now, this Shia minority has not been accepted as equals by the Sunni Afghans.

Afghanistan offered important routes of the Silk Road from Bukhara, Samarkand and Khiva towards Persia as well as the Indian subcontinent. In the late nineteenth century, Afghanistan emerged as a buffer state in the 'great game' between British India and the Czarist Russian Empire, which was expanding in Central Asia.

The Khanate of Bukhara, which reigned between 1500 and 1920, dominated over the northern part of Afghanistan after Muhammad Shaybani Khan acquired Balkh in 1505 and Herat in 1507. Since 1526, Balkh was one of the four main administrative regions of the Khanate of Bukhara, together with Bukhara, Samarkand and Tashkent. However, the dominance of the Khanate of Bukhara over Balkh has been fluctuating over centuries. This strategic presence led to the settlement of large numbers of ethnic Uzbeks and ethnic Tajiks in the territories around Balkh, Badakhshan, Panjshir, etc. in the North and northeastern parts of Afghanistan.

In 1839, the Afghan king Dost Mohammad, pursued by the British army, sought shelter under the Khan of Bukhara. Later, he moved to Bukhara as guest of Khan of Bukhara, Nasrullah Khan. But after a few weeks, the two had a fall-out. Nasrullah Khan even tried to get Dost Mohammad assassinated. With great difficulty, Dost Mohammad escaped from Bukhara in May 1840. Emir returned to northern Afghanistan and raised the flag of holy war against the 'pork eating infidel British'. In 1920, the Red Army attacked Bukhara and the Uzbek Emir Said Mir Mohammad Alim Khan first fled to Dushanbe and then to Kabul, where he died in 1944.

After the Bolshevik conquest of Central Asian Khanates of Bukhara, Khiva and Kokand, the cultural and civilizational links between Central Asia and Afghanistan were severed with the river Oxus/Amu Darya as the boundary. Movement of people across the borders of the then USSR also gradually came to a halt.

POST-SOVIET DEVELOPMENTS

The ill-fated intervention of the Soviet Red Army in Afghanistan in December 1979 triggered a chain of unintended consequences. The armed opposition financed by the US and Saudi Arabia spawned Islamic fundamentalism and mobilized many people across the world for jihad against Soviet occupation, with Pakistan at the epicentre for mobilization, indoctrination and training. In Pakistani madrasas, among the Afghan refugees, emerged the political force Taliban, led by Mullah Omar. The reverses in Afghanistan and growing economic deterioration weakened the grip of the Communist Party on the Soviet Union and General Secretary Mikhail Gorbachev's policies of perestroika and glasnost led to the collapse of the USSR in December 1991.

After the breakup of the Soviet Union, five independent republics emerged in Central Asia: Kazakhstan, Kyrgyzstan, Turkmenistan, Tajikistan and Uzbekistan. These Central Asian Republics (CARs), particularly Uzbekistan and Tajikistan, were apprehensive about the resurgence in the growth of religious extremism and terrorism directed towards their countries. The five CARs backed the anti-Taliban opposition, the so-called Northern Alliance, in the 1990s and later the US-led North Atlantic Treaty Organization (NATO) military campaign in Afghanistan after 2001. The Lion of Panjshir, Ahmad Shah Massoud, operated from different bases in Tajikistan.[1] The injured fighters were treated in Tajikistan, which also included the field hospital established and operated by the Indian Army at Farkhor near the Tajik-Afghan border.

CENTRAL ASIAN TERROR GROUPS IN AFGHANISTAN

The Islamic Movement of Uzbekistan (IMU) founders Tohir Yuldashev and Juma Namangani operated from Afghanistan after being driven out from an independent Uzbekistan. Its original objective was to overthrow President Islam Karimov of Uzbekistan and create an Islamic State. Later, it operated under the umbrella of the Al-Qaeda. In 1992, Yuldashev and Namangani fled to Tajikistan where a civil war was raging between Emomali Rahmon's government and a lose coalition of democrats and Islamists known as the United Tajik Opposition. From 1995 to 1998, Yuldashev was reportedly based in Peshawar where he established contacts with Osama bin Laden.

After the end of Tajik civil war, Yuldashev and Namangani

became close to Afghan Taliban. Uzbek and Tajik Islamists sought refuge in Afghan-Pak region after the Taliban government's ouster in December 2001, but started to regroup since 2007. After Yuldashev was killed in 2009 in a US drone missile strike, the IMU's new leadership relocated the group to the Haqqani strongholds of Mir Ali and Miranshah in North Waziristan. Since 2010, the IMU has expanded its presence in Northern Afghanistan, particularly in ethnic Uzbek areas. After 2015, there were reports of two factions in the IMU: one fighting with Islamic State of Iraq and the Levant's (ISIL) Afghanistan Branch, and the other denouncing ISIL and expressing loyalty to the Taliban and Al-Qaeda. The IMU is reportedly involved in smuggling of drugs through Uzbekistan and Tajikistan to raise funds.

The Islamic State Khorasan Province (ISKP) has a pan-Islamic Salafist ideology with the declared objective to replace all secular Central Asian regimes with an Islamic Caliphate.[2] While Taliban's objective is limited to rule over the geographic territory of Afghanistan, ISKP's ideology encompasses Central Asia, Afghanistan and parts of Pakistan and China. Thus, there are seeds of an ideological conflict between that of Taliban, which are limited to the territory of Afghanistan, and entities like ISKP and Al-Quaeda, which have a broader agenda.

CARs AND TALIBAN REGIME IN 1990s

In 1996, Russian engineers helped build a new bridge across the Amu Darya to provide Ahmad Shah Massoud with a land supply route from Tajikistan into the northeast Afghan province of Badakhshan. Tajikistan had also upgraded its airport at Taloquan, south of the Afghan-Tajik border, providing Northern Alliance with an air supply route. Reportedly, Tajikistan also allowed Massoud's fighters the use of airbase at Kulob in southern Tajikistan for supply of logistics. Northern alliance leaders used Dushanbe as the venue for their meetings with Russian and Indian interlocutors.

Tajikistan, supported by Russia, India and Iran actively supported the armed opposition to the Taliban regime in the second half of 1990s. On 9 September 2001, two days before the terror attacks on United States, Tajik-Afghan resistance leader Ahmad Shah Massoud was assassinated at his residence by two hitmen posing as Arab journalists. The explosive device was concealed in a video camera.

The Indian field hospital at Farkor in Tajikistan near the Afghan border is operated by 25 Indian Army doctors and male nurses, and has beds for 20 patients. A US government-funded $36-million bridge over the Panj River connects Sher Khan Bandar in Afghanistan with Nizhny Pyanj in Tajikistan.[3]

For the US and NATO invasion of Afghanistan in October 2001, Uzbekistan and Kyrgyzstan offered basing facilities for the US and allied forces, while Turkmenistan offered logistical support. The two main air bases were Karshi-Khanabad Air Base near Termez, bordering Afghanistan and Manas, north of Bishkek in Kyrgyzstan. The bases were used primarily to station soldiers and refuelling planes. Each airfield could have up to 1,000 US troops and civilian contractors at a given time.

Meanwhile, Uzbekistan had leased the air base to Americans without any charge; Uzbek government received $150 million in annual aid packages. However, US relations with Uzbekistan soured after the May 2005 Islamic uprising in Andijan and the brutal Uzbek crackdown resulting in hundreds of deaths.[4] In the midst of such strained relations, the base was vacated by the US in November 2005. However, the German military continued to use part of the air base at Termez. Since 2008, it was used by other NATO states and also by contingents in Afghanistan. Germany ceased the use of the base at Termez only in December 2015.

The Manas Air Base contributed approximately $50 million to the tiny Kyrgyz economy each year.[5] But pressured by the Shanghai Cooperation Organization (SCO) and Russia, Kyrgyzstan wanted the US to restrict operations. In 2009, the lease with US was renewed at the annual rent of $200 million, which was three times the previous rent, and the US facilities were called 'transit centre' instead of 'air base'. At the expiry of the lease in July 2014, all US forces vacated the base.

RUSSIA, CSTO AND CARs

The Russia-led Collective Security Treaty Organization (CSTO) is now active to beef up the security of Tajikistan. Kazakhstan and Kyrgyzstan are other Central Asian members of CSTO. Uzbekistan, though no longer a member of the CSTO[6], has increasingly been coordinating its defense of Afghan border with the CSTO, and has been having joint exercises with Russian and Tajik defense forces. Russia's President Vladimir Putin, in an emergency online summit of the CSTO 'expressed his deep concern over the developments in Afghanistan and the potential threats coming there'.[7] The CSTO has launched a review of how the new situation will affect its members' security.

About 7,000 Russian soldiers have been deployed at the Russian 201st Military Base in Tajikistan under an inter-governmental agreement valid until 2042. The Russian base is equipped with tanks and artillery as well as planes and helicopters. In the wake of the announced US troops withdrawal from Afghanistan, in April 2021, Russia and Tajikistan established a joint air defense system, expanding the Russian patrols of Tajikistan air space from the Ayni Air Base, west of Dushanbe. Reportedly, the CSTO has also agreed to strengthen patrolling of the 1,300-km Afghan–Tajikistan border.

Uzbekistan left the CSTO in 2012, as it did not want any Russian control over its armed forces. But in the wake of the deteriorating security scenario in Afghanistan, Russia and Uzbekistan resumed large-scale bilateral military exercises and defense industrial cooperation. In August 2021, about 1,500 Russian and Uzbek troops exercised together in Termez near the Afghanistan–Uzbekistan Friendship Bridge, the main rail and road link between the two countries. In a telephonic conversation on 15 August 2021, Uzbek and Russian presidents agreed to 'ensure close ties and cooperation in ensuring regional security and stability'.[8]

The CSTO member Kazakhstan does not have a strong home-grown Islamist movement and has been relatively immune from fundamentalist threat emanating from an unstable Afghanistan. But Kyrgyzstan, though not sharing border with Afghanistan, has seen political instability and several changes of presidents. Its porous borders were subject to infiltration by Afghanistan-based militants during the Taliban regime in the 1990s. To bolster its security, under the CSTO and bilateral arrangements, the Russian military uses the air base at Kant under a 25-year renewable lease.

The last bastion of resistance against the Taliban juggernaut in August–September 2021 was in the Panjshir Valley where Tajik fighters, led heroically by Ahmad Shah Massoud, resisted the Taliban. More than 1,000 Tajik-Afghan members of the Afghan National Army reportedly fled to Tajikistan. Tajikistan reportedly mobilized its armed forces and called up reserve officers on 22 July 2021 and redeployed 20,000 additional troops on the Tajik-Afghan border.[9]

After the Taliban takeover in Afghanistan, Russia strengthened its military base in Tajikistan with 17 infantry armoured carriers. Russia's Foreign Minister Sergei Lavrov in early September of 2021 said, 'We will do everything, including using the capabilities of the Russian military base on the border of Tajikistan with Afghanistan to prevent any aggressive encroachments against our allies.'[10] In early August 2021, Russia, Tajikistan and Uzbekistan had conducted exercises involving 2,500 troops and 500 military vehicles simulating a joint response to potential security threats emanating from Afghanistan. Russia's former Deputy Prime Minister (PM) Yuri Borisov reportedly said in mid-September 2021 that CSTO was developing military-technical ties with Uzbekistan and Turkmenistan in light of the situation in Afghanistan.

DEVELOPMENTS AFTER COLLAPSE OF GHANI GOVERNMENT

The Afghan press had reported that former Afghan President Ashraf Ghani, accompanied by 54 persons, had flown to Uzbekistan on 14 August and spent 31 hours in Termez before leaving for the United Arab Emirates (UAE). In mid-August, over 45 Afghan Air Force aircrafts flew out and landed mostly at Termez airport with more than 450 Afghan airmen and their families.[11] Afghan nationals later relocated to the UAE and the aircraft were impounded by the Uzbek government for unauthorized entry into Uzbek air space.

On 6 August 2021, the leaders of the five CARs met in Turkmenistan to boost regional cooperation and discuss about the emerging situation in Afghanistan. They reportedly shared concern over ramifications of an unstable Afghanistan and presence of anti-CAR terror groups operating from within the Afghan territory.

At the Shanghai Cooperation Organisation (SCO) Summit in Dushanbe on 17 September 2021, Uzbek President Shavkat Mirziyoyev proposed to unfreeze Afghan funds in foreign banks, which were frozen after the fall of the Ghani government. He also proposed holding regular high-level meetings in the SCO-Afghanistan format to 'consolidate efforts and broadly discuss issues of settlement in Afghanistan'.[12] In Dushanbe, the chairmanship of the SCO passed to Uzbekistan from Tajikistan.

Reportedly, former Afghan first Vice President Amrullah Saleh and Ahmad Shah Massoud were quietly offered sanctuary in Tajikistan after the resistance in Panjshir Valley was crushed by the Taliban fighters by the end of September in 2021.

Russian foreign ministry's special ambassador for Afghanistan Bakhtiyor Khakimov said in late September 2021 that the SCO was prepared to provide assistance for Afghanistan's economic reaction, but the recognition of the Taliban government in Kabul was still not being discussed.[13]

TAJIKISTAN AND THE TALIBAN REGIME

Of the 39 million Afghans, 39 per cent are Pashtuns, 21 per cent Tajiks, 24.5 per cent Hazaras and Sayyids, 6 per cent Uzbeks, 1.2 per cent Turkmen and 5 per cent Baloch. Tajikistan does have a major stake in securing a proper place for the Tajik-Afghans in a Pashtun Taliban-dominated Afghan polity as well as society.

Notably, at a time (2018–20) when Uzbeks, Russia, Iran, among others, had commenced interacting with the Taliban office in Doha, Tajikistan did not open any known channel of communications with the Taliban. After the Taliban takeover of Kabul, President Emomali Rahmon emphatically demanded the inclusion of ethnic Tajiks in the Pashtun-dominated provisional Taliban government. In late August 2021, President Rahmon reportedly told the Pakistan Foreign Minister S.M. Qureshi that Tajikistan would not recognize the Taliban rule over Afghanistan unless the ethnic Tajik minority was accorded a 'worthy role' in the running of the country.[14]

President Rahmon addressed the seventy-sixth session of the UN General Assembly in September 2021 and said, 'Various terrorist groups are actively using the unstable military-political situation in Afghanistan in order to strengthen themselves.' Casting doubt on the willingness of the Taliban regime to control terrorist outfits, he added, 'We have witnessed the release of thousands of members of ISIS, al-Qaeda and other terrorist groups.' He expressed concern that 'Afghanistan has become a geopolitical platform [for international terrorism].'[15]

When the then Pakistan PM Imran Khan was in Dushanbe on 17 September 2021 for the SCO summit, President Rahmon said in the discussion, 'The speedy elimination of the conflict and tensions in the Panjshir province by declaring a ceasefire and opening roads for providing humanitarian assistance is one of the most important tasks today.'[16] However, with active involvement of Pakistani military advisors, Panjshir fell to the Taliban on 19 September.

Tajikistan's role would be crucial in case of any eventuality wherein the international community has no option but to oppose the Taliban. President Rahmon sent an unambiguous signal of support to Tajik-Afghan resistance to Taliban ideology by awarding former Afghan President Burhanuddin Rabbani and former Defense Minister, the late Lion of Panjshir, Ahmad Shah Massoud, with the country's highest honour, 'The Order of Ismoili Somoni', in September 2021. It is notable that both the leaders had been assassinated by Taliban–Al-Qaida combined.

Tajikistan faces the threat from elements of Jamaat Ansarullah, an extremist group active in the northern border areas of Afghanistan and could threaten the autonomous province of Gorno-Badakhshan in Tajikistan. Reportedly, thousands of Afghan Taliban fighters were deployed in the Takhar province of northeastern Afghanistan, adjacent to Tajikistan. Questioning their Islamic claims, the grand mufti of Tajikistan issued an edict calling the Taliban as 'terrorist group' and Taliban's action as 'far from Islam'. Specifically, the grand mufti criticized the Taliban's treatment of women. He said that the world would recognize Taliban only if they practised the 'basics of Islam'.

UZBEKISTAN AND THE TALIBAN

Sensing the growing strength of Taliban, Uzbekistan had opened contacts with the Taliban in early 2018. President Shavkat Mirziyoyev took the initiative to organize an important international conference on Afghanistan in Tashkent in March 2018. After August 2021, Uzbekistan has repeatedly said that it is 'firmly committed to maintaining traditional friendly and good-neighborly relations with Afghanistan observing neutrality and non-interference in the internal affairs of the neighboring country'.[17]

Uzbek companies are keen to get contracts to build infrastructure in Afghanistan, along with extension of the existing Hairatan-Mazar-i-Sharif railway line to additional Afghan cities, including Kabul. Uzbekistan is vigorously pursuing rail and road connectivity towards the Indian Ocean through Afghanistan and Pakistan. At the conference on 'Central and South Asian Regional Connectivity: Challenges and Opportunities' held in Tashkent on 15–16 July 2021, President Shavkat Mirziyoyev proposed the development of modern, effective and secure transport and logistics infrastructure, connecting Central and South Asia. Uzbekistan is very enthusiastic about the proposed Termez-Mazar-i-Sharif-Kabul-Peshawar railroad, which requires an investment of about $6 billion and could become part of the Chinese Belt and Road Initiative.[18] Full cooperation of the Taliban-led Afghanistan and peace and stability there would be the essential requirements for this project to see the light of the day.

Uzbekistan has been keen on continuing its 10-year deal for electricity supply to Afghanistan. Uzbekistan reportedly supplies electricity costing $150 million annually to Afghanistan. The Kabul regime reportedly owes $170 million already to the Uzbeks for the supply of electricity. Uzbekistan is wary of incurring financial losses if electricity supply to Afghanistan is suspended. Much of this electricity flows through the 202-km double circuit Pul-e-Khumri to Kabul transmission line constructed by India.

Then Uzbek Foreign Minister Abdulaziz Kamilov led a delegation to Kabul on 7 October 2021, when infrastructure development by way of transmission lines and Mazar-e-Sharif-Kabul-Peshawar railway line was also discussed. Kamilov met Islamic Emirate of Afghanistan's (IEA) acting Foreign Minister Mawlawi Emir Khan Muttaqi and conveyed the hope that IEA would soon find a place in the international community and reportedly assured that Uzbekistan remained committed to its pledges in transit, energy and trade. In 2018, Uzbekistan already built a huge cargo centre at Termez, close to the Afghan border.

According to the Asian Development Bank, 73 per cent of Afghanistan's electricity is imported. Of that, Uzbekistan supplies 57 per cent, Iran 22 per cent, Turkmenistan 17 per cent and Tajikistan 4 per cent. It is estimated that Afghanistan spends

$300 million annually on electricity imports. This translates to Turkmenistan receiving $31 million and Uzbekistan getting $170 million annually for electricity exports to Afghanistan. Uzbekistan is constructing a 260-km section of 500-KW power line from Surkhon in Uzbekistan to Pul-e-Khumri, in north of Kabul, that would boost Uzbek electricity exports to Afghanistan by up to 70 per cent.[19]

TURKMENISTAN AND THE TALIBAN REGIME

Turkmenistan follows a foreign policy of neutrality and shares a 744-km border with Afghanistan. The Taliban have been present in the border region but have refrained from entering Turkmenistan. Following the Taliban takeover, the Turkmen government permitted border trade. In the coming months, Turkmenistan may reiterate its interest in resuming the implementation of the Turkmenistan-Afghanistan-Pakistan-India (TAPI) pipeline, at least up to Pakistan. Turkmenistan and Uzbekistan share a policy focussed on the economic potential of energy and trade routes passing through Afghanistan. Turkmen and Uzbek presidents met on 5 October 2021 and declared that the two countries would continue to provide help to the people of Afghanistan.[20] Turkmenistan is keen to implement the 1,814-km TAPI natural gas pipeline, which aims to export some 33 billion cubic centimetre of Turkmen gas annually. The Taliban had shown positive interest in this ambitious project when they ruled over Afghanistan in the late 1990s. Under the current agreement, Afghanistan would get 5 billion cubic metre annually, Pakistan 14 and India 4. Turkmenistan claims that it has completed construction of the pipeline leading from Turkmen gas fields to the Afghan border.

KAZAKHSTAN AND THE TALIBAN REGIME

Kazakh Embassy has continued to function in Kabul after the Taliban takeover. By the end of September in 2021, Kazakh ambassador expressed satisfaction with the security situation in Kabul and urged the international community to provide humanitarian aid to Afghanistan. Kazakhstan is one of the main suppliers of grains to Afghanistan, exporting 3–3.5 million tonnes annually.

Kazakhstan has allowed the United Nations Assistance Mission to Afghanistan (UNAMA) to temporarily relocate from Kabul to Kazakhstan. After the sudden collapse of the Ghani government, Kazakhstan provided help for emergency relocation, received the UNAMA personnel and offered facilities for continuation of their work.[21]

KYRGYZSTAN AND THE TALIBAN REGIME

On 23 September 2021, an official delegation from Kyrgyzstan headed by a senior security official, Taalatbek Masadykov, the deputy head of National Security Council, visited Kabul and held extensive discussions. Bishkek also sent a plane load of humanitarian aid, which was ceremonially handed over to Afghan first Deputy PM, Mullah Baradar. At the CSTO summit in early September, Kyrgyz President Sadyr Japarov dove straight to the heart of the new challenges and reportedly noted that the formation of a theocratic state in the region will undoubtedly leave a negative effect on the internal situation in the members states of CSTO.

CONCLUSION

It appears that CARs, except Tajikistan, have accepted the reality of an enduring Taliban regime in Afghanistan and are seeking ways for economic contacts, trade and sale of power, as there is no tangible threat of an internal revolt or external intervention to bring down the Taliban regime again. CARs also see Afghanistan as a bridge between Central and South Asia.

The CARs are, however, wary of the re-emergence of the

Taliban regime in Afghanistan. These strongly secular regimes are apprehensive of the virus of religious fundamentalism infecting their hitherto peaceful Muslim majority populations. Their assessment is that the terrorist organizations with roots in Central Asia, like the Islamic Movement of Uzbekistan and Hizb ut-Tahrir, are now greatly weakened—both in numbers and in support among the local populations. But still, Uzbekistan and Kyrgyzstan have sought guarantees from the Taliban representatives that the Afghan territory will not be allowed to be used as sanctuary for groups inimical to the neighbouring countries.

Uzbekistan took the lead in setting the agenda for contacts and collaborating with the Islamic Emirate of Afghanistan, with the Uzbek foreign minister, leading a delegation to Kabul on 7 October 2021. This was followed by extensive discussions between the Taliban and Uzbek officials in Termez on 17 October, when all issues, including security, were discussed.

CARs, except Tajikistan, have adopted a policy of cooperation with the IEA in contrast to the policy of confrontation in the 1990s. Their assessment is that Afghan economy should not be allowed to collapse and humanitarian assistance to Afghans should be provided by the international community. Uzbekistan has offered facilities at Termez for the transit of humanitarian assistance to Afghanistan. The CARs' approach is to prevent any flow of refugees from Afghanistan. They are determined not to open their borders for Afghan economic refugees.

The CARs' widening contacts with the representatives of the Provisional Government of the IEA amount to its de facto recognition. Formal de jure recognition of the Emirate would depend on the actions of the Taliban regime on ground. CARs have considerable economic leverage over Afghanistan and it depends on the Taliban leadership whether to choose an isolationist path of harsh medieval practices or to work for the overall welfare of the long-suffering people of Afghanistan.

6

Iranian View: Strategic Aim and Compulsions

Amb. Sanjay Singh

Histories of Iran and Afghanistan, as neighbours, have remained deeply interconnected through the ages. Afghanistan was a part of the Iranian Achaemenid (550–350 BC) and Sasanian (250 BC–AD 600) Empires. Both countries were part of the Umayyad (AD 650–750) and Abbasid (AD 750–950) Caliphates. Khorasan, consisting of eastern Iran, northern Afghanistan and southern Central Asia, was an important constituent of the Caliphates. The Mongol Ilkhanate (AD 1250–1350) and the Timurid Empire (AD 1350–1450) also encompassed the two countries. The Iranian rule of Afghanistan under the Safavids (AD 1500–1700) was marked by forced conversions to Shiism and is still a cause for resentment. The Iranian yoke was removed by the Durranis under Ahmed Shah Abdali (AD 1747–72), leading to the gradual establishment of an Afghan state. Since then, relations between Iran and Afghanistan have been marked by periods of calm as well as contention.

As a consequence of their shared history, Iran, the northern parts of Afghanistan and parts of Central Asia form a common cultural space, with similarity between their languages (Farsi, Dari and Tajik) and festivals, such as Nowruz, the Persian New Year. Firdausi, in the Iranian epic *Shahnameh*, describes Afghanistan as a province of Iran, with Rustam being a hero common to both cultures. Afghanistan's Shia Hazaras, who reside on the western fringe of the Hindu Kush range in central Afghanistan, have traditionally had close ties with Shia Iran.

THE IRAN–AFGHANISTAN BORDER

Iran and Afghanistan share a porous border, which extends 921 km from the trijunction, with Turkmenistan in the north, to the trijunction with Pakistan in the south. Its border with Pakistan extends another 1,000 km along the Pakistani province of Baluchistan to the sea. The Iran–Afghanistan border was gradually formalized over the years in the late nineteenth and early twentieth centuries. It is a border across which people, armies, goods and ideas have flowed in both directions over millennia. The routes that crisscross it were part of the arteries of the Silk Road. The Helmand River flows across this border, and the two countries have periodically had differences over the sharing of its waters.

The year 1979 was a significant turning point in the history of the region. It was the year that witnessed the Islamic Revolution in Iran, the Soviet invasion of Afghanistan and the launch of jihad against it. The Mujahideen were supported by the US and Pakistan as well as Saudi Arabia, an archrival of Iran.[1] This period also witnessed the nearly decade-long Iran–Iraq War (1980–88) in which Iraq was supported by the Sunni Gulf monarchies.

The first Gulf War in 1991 effectively neutralized the threat to Iran from Saddam Hussein's Iraq on its west. However, another threat was looming to its east with the rise of the extremist Sunni elements.

Alarmed by prospect of the takeover of Afghanistan by Sunni zealots, Shia-dominated Iran began extending assistance to the Soviet-supported People's Democratic Party of Afghanistan (PDPA) government, which was in power in Kabul (1979–92). The Taliban, after taking over Kabul in 1996, started curtailing Iranian influence and persecuting Shias, who began crossing over to Iran for refuge. The instability that has marred Afghanistan over the last half a century has bred extremist forces, some of which pose a constant threat for Iran. Since the beginning of the 1980s when Afghanistan became one of the largest cultivators of opium in the world, narcotics were smuggled across the border to Iran and from there to the rest of the world. Iran has consequently been transformed into a major transit country for illicit drugs and narcotics. This poses huge health, security and law enforcement problems for it. In 1998, the Taliban seized the Iranian consulate in Mazar-i-Sharif and 11 Iranian diplomats were killed[2], following which Iran strengthened its assistance to the Northern Alliance in partnership with Russia, Tajikistan and India.

The 9/11 attacks, followed by the subsequent US attack on the Taliban regime in Afghanistan, marked another turning point in the strategic environment of the region. Iran initially extended assistance to the US in its efforts to stabilize Afghanistan. However, after the US inexplicably included it in its 'Axis of Evil'[3] grouping and went in to occupy Iraq in 2003 following the second Gulf War, Iran perceived an existential threat from both its eastern and western flanks. The US, at that time had considerable influence in Central Asia, where it maintained military bases. Along with its bases in the Arabian Peninsula, it effectively encircled Iran. Soon thereafter, Iranian nuclear activities came to light, following which new US sanctions, in addition to a number of earlier existing ones, were imposed on Iran in December 2006 pursuant to United Nations Security Council Resolution 1696 and 1737, which demanded that Iran halt its uranium enrichment programme. The continuous tightening of these sanctions, barring the period 2016–18, when the Joint Comprehensive Plan of Action was in effect, imposed considerable economic difficulties on Iran.[4] Its GDP contracted by around 6 per cent both in 2018 and 2019, decreasing to around $400 billion in 2020 from $450 billion in 2017.

PLOTTING US DEPARTURE FROM AFGHANISTAN

It is hence not surprising that the principal aim of Iran was, and continues to be, to pursue a policy of ensuring the departure of the US from the region.

Towards this end, Iran has interacted with the Taliban's political leaders, as well as with other Afghan political leaders, some of whom it has hosted, and to some of whom it has also extended assistance. It has developed lines of communications with a wide array of diverse groups in Afghanistan, some of which did not exist earlier. Iran's former special representative for Afghanistan, Mohammad Ebrahim Taherian Fard, was active in this pursuit, and so was the present head of Islamic Revolutionary Guard Corps' Quds Force, Esmail Qaani, who was in charge of operations in Afghanistan as deputy of Qasem Soleimani, former head of the Quds force.[5] Iran, thus, has developed significant assets to pursue policies to protect its interests and expand its influence in Afghanistan. For the present, however, it seems to be restricting itself to a policy of engaging with the Taliban regime in order to promote a stable Afghanistan that is not inimical to it or to the Shia minority, and keeps a firm check on refugees, drugs and terrorist violence from entering Iran.

The two decades following 9/11 have witnessed further significant transformation of the strategic environment in the region, brought about by the rise of China and its economic dominance of Eurasia and Pakistan through its Belt and Road Initiative and China–Pakistan Economic Corridor programmes. China's strengthened partnership with Russia has also allowed it to further spread its influence through the region. This transformation has been given significant impetus by the abrupt and chaotic withdrawal of the US from Afghanistan and the drawdown of the US presence in the region. The US sanctions on Iran and Russia have created the space for China to be their main economic partner, and for Iran, an indispensable one.

China today wields great influence over all of Afghanistan's neighbours, and especially Pakistan.

In concentrating its attention on the competition with China in Indo-Pacific region and Russia in the European theatre, the US has been de-emphasizing the Eurasian region, leading to China becoming pre-eminent in Eurasia. The reduced US interest in West Asia, too, has created its own dynamics, with increased Israeli activism in West Asia, leading to normalization of Israel's relations with the UAE and Bahrain. All these are realities that Iran recognizes, and that will guide its future actions. Iran is unlikely to work against China's efforts to expand its presence in Afghanistan and do business with the Taliban regime. On 18 August 2021, in a telephonic conversation with President Xi Jinping, President Ayatollah Raisi expressed Iran's readiness 'to cooperate with China in establishing security, stability and peace in Afghanistan and contributing to development, progress and prosperity for the people of the country'.[6]

IRAN'S ATTEMPT AT ESTABLISHING RAPPORT

While Iran felt a sense of relief that the US, its main strategic threat, left Afghanistan, it recognized that this ignited new competition in the region. Its Sunni rivals from Saudi Arabia and UAE, who had largely absented themselves from Afghanistan over the past 20 years, are again trying to establish their presence in the country. Pakistan, now being the principal interlocutor for the Taliban, may not be averse to assisting them, just as it assists China vis-à-vis the Taliban. This increases the importance for Iran and its relations with its neighbour Pakistan, and with its protégés in Kabul, in order to ensure that a situation inimical to its interests does not develop there. On 26 August 2021, in a meeting with the then Pakistani Foreign Minister Shah Mahmood Qureshi, President Raisi stressed, 'The role of other countries, including neighbours, should only be a facilitator to the establishment of an inclusive and participatory government with the presence of all Afghan groups.' He further noted,

> The presence of the United States and foreigners in the region does not contribute to security, but it is [sic] also makes problems, and countries in the region, especially Iran and Pakistan, can work together to provide the ground for ethnic and active groups in Afghanistan to create security and peace in the country so that they can decide for their own destiny.[7]

Iran is working towards these objectives with other important players in Afghanistan too, such as Russia. On 18 August 2021, in a phone call to President Putin, President Raisi stated: 'The establishment of security and peace in Afghanistan has always been emphasized by the Islamic Republic and we believe that all active Afghan groups should work together to establish stability in the country as soon as possible, and turn the US withdrawal a turning point for lasting peace and stability in Afghanistan.'[8] Significantly, he also noted, 'The successful experience of Iran-Russia cooperation in the fight against takfiri terrorism in Syria has opened new windows for the two sides to increase Tehran-Moscow interaction.'[9]

Iran's approach is perhaps similar to that of Afghanistan's central Asian neighbours. While Turkmenistan and Uzbekistan have established their own lines of communications as well as working relations with the Taliban, Tajikistan continues to be Afghanistan's most suspicious central Asian neighbour. However, it seems to be under Russian as well as Chinese pressure not to take any hostile actions against the Taliban, even though it hosts the remnants of the Panjshiri resistance. As long as the Taliban keep terrorist and extremist forces inimical to its neighbours, and to Russia and China, under check, and control the illicit flow of narcotics, the latter are not likely to interfere in Afghanistan for the time being. Nevertheless, both Iran and Tajikistan seem to be keeping their future options open in dealing with the

Taliban. In April 2021, Tajikistan and Iran agreed to create a joint military defense committee that would enhance their cooperation in security and counterterrorism. In late May 2021, Tajikistan, perhaps in anticipation of a Taliban victory, strongly supported the case for Iran becoming a member of the Shanghai Cooperation Organisation (SCO).[10]

The evolving Iranian attitude can be seen from the statements made by its leaders in the recent past. The initial statements from Tehran after the takeover of Kabul by the Taliban expressed both relief as well as schadenfreude.

On 16 August 2021, the day after Kabul fell to the Taliban, President Raisi stated, 'The military defeat and the withdrawal of the United States from Afghanistan should become an opportunity to restore life, security and lasting peace in the country.'[11]

Secretary of the Supreme National Security Council Shamkani noted that 'Iran will work for establishing stability, which is the first need of Afghanistan today, and as a neighbour and brother country, calls on all groups to reach a national agreement.'[12]

In early September, Iran's president called for elections in Afghanistan to determine the future of the country, stating, 'A government should be established there which is elected by the votes and the will of the people…The Islamic Republic has always sought peace and calm in Afghanistan, and an end to bloodshed and fratricide, and the sovereignty of the people's will. We support a government elected by the Afghan people.'[13]

Iran was critical of the Taliban for appointing their caretaker government that was not inclusive, as well as of Pakistani support for the Taliban in the battle for Panjshir. On 6 September 2021, Iran's foreign ministry's spokesperson, Saeed Khatibzadeh, criticized the aerial attacks on the Panjshir Valley allegedly carried out by Pakistan in support of the Taliban, and said, 'Last night's attacks are condemned in the strongest terms…and the foreign interference […] must be investigated.'[14] On 8 September 2021, Secretary of Iran's Supreme National Security Council, Ali Shamkhani, admonished the Taliban, and said, 'Ignoring the necessity of establishing an inclusive government, foreign intervention and the use of military means instead of dialog to meet the demands of ethnicities and social groups are the main concerns of the friends of the Afghan people.'[15]

With the collapse of the opposition's challenge in Panjshir, and their leaders and cadres taking flight across the border into Tajikistan, Iran, perhaps like the rest of the region, has come to accept the reality that the Taliban have a firm hold, at least for the time being, on the reins of the government in Afghanistan. It had earlier come to terms with its allies laying down their arms and losing their positions in and around Herat. Former governor of Herat, Mohammad Ismail Khan, who is close to Iran, was subsequently permitted to flee across the border. Iran also opened new camps on its borders to accommodate the stream of refugees coming in. The UN estimated the number of Afghan citizens registered in Iran at around 1 million after the takeover by Taliban 1.0. However, the Iranian government believes that the total is much higher—at around 4 million Afghan migrants, both legal and illegal. A large number of Hazaras have crossed over to Iran since the start of the jihad in Afghanistan. Hazaras have also been recruited by Iran as part of the Fatemiyoun Division and deployed to fight on behalf of the Assad government in Syria.[16]

Iran may be of the view that ethnic cleansing and oppression of the minorities since the recent takeover by the Taliban has not been as extensive as it may have earlier feared. Further, the attacks on the Shia minority, such as the bombing of mosques in Kunduz and Kandahar, have been orchestrated by Islamic State Khorasan Province or ISKP, a common enemy of Iran and the Taliban. The Taliban 2.0 also appear to be more inclusive, with Tajik, Uzbek and Shia Hazara commanders within their ranks, such as Taliban's northern district Governor Mawlawi Mahdi Mujahid, an ethnic Hazara Shia cleric, Tajik commander Qudratullah Abu Hamza, who led the capture of Mazar-i-Sharif, and Uzbek commander Salahuddin Ayubi who co-led the takeover of Kabul.

Iran has put in place a normal day-to-day working relationship with the Taliban even as it continues to maintain lines of communications with dissident groups, to the extent of accepting a visit by Ahmad Massoud.[17] Iran also resumed fuel exports to Afghanistan in August 2021, at the Taliban's request. It also reportedly mounted a trade delegation in early October 2021, to Afghanistan; during the visit, agreements were arrived at to restart 24-hour operations at the Islam Qala-Dogharoun border crossing, and develop the land route and export via Chabahar. This land route and access to the sea via Chabahar will continue to have importance for Afghanistan, providing an alternate route towards the sea. Other areas of cooperation are inclusive of health and tourism.[18]

At the SCO summit in mid-September in Dushanbe, Iranian President Ebrahim Raisi reiterated Iran's call for an inclusive government in Afghanistan in order to promote peace and stability in the country. In his meeting with the then Pakistani Prime Minister Imran Khan, Raisi said, 'We should try to help Afghanistan form a government that includes all groups based on the will of the people of the country [...] The 20-year history of the presence of American and Western forces in Afghanistan had no result other than the destruction, displacement and killing of more than 35,000 children and thousands of Afghan men and women.'[19]

On 6 August 2021, in his talks with External Affairs Minister S. Jaishankar, President Raisi said, 'Iran and India can play a constructive and useful role in ensuring security in the region, especially Afghanistan, and Tehran welcomes the New Delhi's role in establishment of security in Afghanistan.'[20] It remains to be seen how this evolves in practice.

CALL FOR AN INCLUSIVE GOVERNMENT

At the 2nd Meeting of Foreign Ministers of Afghanistan's Neighboring Countries in Tehran on 27 October 2021, the

Iranian Minister of Foreign Affairs blamed the US for the problems Afghanistan faces and underlined the need for cooperation among countries neighbouring Afghanistan. He made the following important points:

1. He reiterated the need for an inclusive government 'with the presence as well as effective and lasting participation of all ethnic and religious groups in Afghanistan via supported intra-Afghan talks without the interference of foreign players'.
2. He stressed that the Taliban has the responsibility for 'ensuring security, fighting terrorism, respecting the rights of different groups, including women, providing basic necessities of life for Afghan citizens, stopping the violation of ethnic and religious minorities' rights'.
3. He urged the Taliban to 'adopt a cordial approach towards Afghanistan's neighboring countries and take the necessary measures to make sure that neighboring countries will face no threats from the Afghan territory'.
4. He called for humanitarian assistance for the Afghan people.
5. He proposed that in order to fight organized crime and acts of terror originating from Afghanistan, 'regional countries devise a security and intelligence mechanism where they would, more seriously and at shorter intervals, exchange information and make coordination among themselves, including Afghanistan's neighbours'.[21]

Far from the region, the US and Iran are now cautiously re-engaging in Vienna. This has its own strategic implications for the region, as well as for Iran's role in Afghanistan. The Gulf countries, recent tentative re-engagement with Iran, important by itself, could also have beneficial outcomes for war-ravaged Yemen and Syria, and also lead to some sort of rapprochement between Saudi Arabia and Iran. There are other fast-moving events that affect the region, such as Turkey's alliance with Azerbaijan against Armenia, a traditional Iranian ally. Iran will continue to keep a close eye on Turkey's activities in Central Asia, Afghanistan and Qatar, and its relationship with Pakistan. Pakistan's own behaviour and the role that it plays in Afghanistan, as well as those of China and Russia will be critical, along with the other factors mentioned above, in determining Iran's future course of action vis-à-vis Afghanistan.

Iran recognizes that what happens in Afghanistan will have deep resonance in the larger Islamic world with implications for its own aspirations of leadership in it. For the present, Iran has laid down the red lines that should not be crossed by the Taliban and is maintaining a day-to-day working relationship with them. It remains to be seen whether the Taliban will stay within those lines and how Iran will react, should they not.

7

Russia's Enduring Obsession with Afghanistan

Amb. P.S. Raghavan

In August 2021, the US troops made a chaotic exit from Afghanistan after over two decades of trying to restore peace and instil democracy in the troubled country. The Taliban, after being militarily ousted with the help of the US in 2001, swept triumphantly back into power. The elected president of Afghanistan abandoned his post and unceremoniously fled the country. America's North Atlantic Treaty Organization (NATO) allies were upset that the exit was not properly coordinated with them. Thousands of Afghans, who had assisted the western efforts to combat terrorism and restore governance, were left behind at the mercy of a vengeful Taliban.

Over the past three years or so, Russia had cooperated with the US, China and Pakistan in initiatives designed to mainstream the Taliban in Afghan politics. But the suddenness of the Taliban takeover took the Russians as much by surprise as it did other countries. The Russian schadenfreude, at the discomfiture of its adversary was, therefore, tinged with the apprehension that Afghan developments have always aroused in Russian minds.

STRATEGIES DEVISED BY RUSSIA

Russia emerged from Slavic tribes, who had been driven out of their original settlement around the Dnieper River to Moscow in the thirteenth century. Over the centuries, and particularly since the eighteenth century, Russia's strategic planning has been driven by the search for secure borders, buffer zones and warm water ports. The interests and actions in Afghanistan—of the Russian Empire, Soviet Russia and Putin's Russia—have been shaped by these perspectives.

From the early nineteenth century onwards, Russian emperors have been suspected of coveting the fabled riches of India, and every move in the southern expansion of the empire was interpreted as progress towards this goal. This suspicion was reinforced by a story that, in his will, Peter the Great (who founded the Russian Empire in the eighteenth century) had exhorted his descendants to 'approach as near as possible to Constantinople [Istanbul] and India...whoever governs there will be the true sovereign of the world...penetrate as far as the Persian Gulf, advance as far as India'. Peter's will has never been found and many historians are sceptical about its existence, but the rulers of British India were convinced that this thought dominated Russian strategic thinking.

Russia had already conquered Crimea in the eighteenth century, acquiring a warm water port, across the Black Sea from Constantinople. Its southward expansion towards Persia through the Caucasus and towards Afghanistan through Central Asia was in line with Peter's presumed exhortation. The result was an intricate web of political and diplomatic machinations between Russia and British India in the nineteenth and early twentieth century, which came to be known as the 'great game'. It was essentially a tussle for influence over Afghanistan and its adjoining territories in Persia and Central Asia as a buffer between the two empires. Three Anglo-Afghan wars were fought during this period, but the hardy Afghans used the terrain and guerrilla tactics skilfully to eventually prevail each time.

Finally, the British and the Afghans agreed on the international border between British India and Afghanistan. This border, known as the Durand Line (after the British diplomat who negotiated it), effectively established Afghanistan as a buffer state between the British and Russian empires, delineating the spheres of their respective influence in the region. It is now the internationally recognized border between Afghanistan and Pakistan. The 'great game' ended shortly after, and Afghanistan signed a peace treaty with the British; they also signed a treaty of friendship with the new Soviet government in 1921.

It may be noted in passing that while the Durand Line achieved the immediate purpose of settling the Anglo–Russian struggle for influence, it has cast a long geopolitical shadow, which continues to bedevil Afghanistan's relations with Pakistan and can cause friction with Iran. The Durand Line cuts through Afghan–Pashtun tribal areas and also through the Baloch region, which is split three ways between Afghanistan, Pakistan and Iran. No Afghan government has recognized the Durand Line as the international border, not even the Taliban government of the 1990s or the current one.

During the Cold War, the Soviet Union strove to keep Afghanistan within its sphere of influence, again as a buffer between it and the US-led West, with which Pakistan was a treaty ally. When, in 1979, the Soviets suspected that the political leadership of Afghanistan may realign itself with the West, they launched an invasion of Afghanistan to install a loyal leadership.[1] This action triggered a major standoff between Russia and the US, during which Pakistan, a US ally, became a frontline state to push back against the Soviet occupation. It received substantial US military and financial assistance, to indoctrinate, train, arm and finance Mujahideen soldiers for a 'holy jihad' to expel the Soviet invaders. This campaign bogged down the Soviet Union in Afghanistan for nearly 10 years, before its troops withdrew, leaving in its trail high casualties and a financial drain that eventually contributed to the collapse of the Soviet Union.

POST COLD WAR RELATIONS

The Soviets did leave behind an Afghan president, who supported them. But, four years later, the successor Russian government was unable or unwilling to protect him from the advancing Taliban forces, which stormed into Kabul, dragged him on to the streets and hanged him from a lamppost, after brutally beating him to death.

The direct and indirect consequences of Soviet Union's adventurism in Afghanistan in the 1980s have been visited on India in various ways. India was put in a bind since it had to balance its political and military dependence on the Soviet Union against the compulsion to condemn what was clearly a violation of Afghanistan's sovereignty and territorial integrity. The invasion hastened the collapse of the Soviet Union, which jolted India's strategic compass in the short term, but was hugely beneficial in the longer run. Of more lasting impact was Pakistan's raising of violent militias with extremist jihadi ideologies, which its army could cynically divert to Jammu and Kashmir, after their release from the jihad against the Soviet Union. The new brand of cross-border terrorism thus created remains a thorn in India's flesh. From among these militias, bred by the Pakistani intelligence services, was also born the Taliban movement. The US–Pakistan nexus during this period facilitated Pakistan's development and acquisitions of nuclear and missile technologies, since the US was willing to turn a blind eye to these activities, until Pakistan's importance as a frontline state declined.

Despite its ignominious exit, Russia could not afford to disengage entirely from Afghanistan (as the US did, for example, from Vietnam). Afghanistan remained a soft underbelly, with concerns about infiltration of drugs, Islamic extremism and terrorism from Taliban-ruled Afghanistan engaging Russia and the post-Soviet Central Asian regimes. The Taliban's links with Chechen separatists elevated Russia's concerns. India and Iran shared many of these concerns; the three countries, therefore, joined together to support the Northern Alliance (a coalition of Tajik, Uzbek, Hazara and some Pashtun elements) in the struggle to oust the Taliban from Afghanistan. After the terrorist attacks in New York on 9 September 2001, the US extended direct support to these efforts through addition of its formidable airpower, and also leaned on Pakistan to stop support for the Taliban. A unique multinational initiative (the Bonn Process) succeeded in quickly replacing the ousted Taliban regime by a democratically-elected successor government with multi-ethnic representation. Russia was fully on board in this process. It was a period when US–Russia relations were reasonably cordial. Russia supported the continued US presence in Afghanistan. It opened a transit route and an airport for the movement of coalition soldiers and supplies to and from Afghanistan. Russia and the US launched joint programmes for training Afghan narcotics control officers. The US bought 30 military transport helicopters from Russia in 2013 for use by Afghanistan's Special Forces in counterterrorism missions.[2] It is an interesting fact to note that when the US and its allies imposed sanctions on Russia in 2014 after its annexation of Crimea, the defence contractor supplying these helicopters remained outside the purview of the sanctions, until just after the supplies were completed.

The near-total breakdown of Russia's relations with the US and its allies in 2014, after the Russian annexation of Crimea (in the guise of its accession), changed Russia's attitude towards the US-led coalition troops in Afghanistan. As Russia and the West were increasingly drawn into confrontation and the hostility across geographies in Europe and Asia, Russia's suspicions of the coalition's motives in Afghanistan also grew. The Russian security establishment started accusing the coalition of slackening commitment to narcotics control. Even more seriously, the Russians hinted darkly that western special forces were transporting hardened Islamic State of Iraq and Syria (ISIS) fighters from 'liberated' areas in Iraq and Syria to Afghanistan, locating them close to Central Asia, arming them and training them to infiltrate across the border, with the intention of fomenting unrest in Central Asia and encouraging separatism in the north Caucasian republics of Russia. These suspicions drove Russia's efforts to develop and sustain an independent influence on the political currents in Afghanistan, which could be a bargaining chip with the US, which was seeking a face-saving exit from the country. The desire was also to ensure that, regardless of the complexion of the eventual political settlement, Russia had sufficient influence in Afghanistan to protect its security interests and to buttress its claim as a global power.

Sometime in 2015, reports surfaced of Russia's rapprochement with the Taliban. After initially denying them, Russia admitted that it was a tactical decision to protect its security interests. The argument was that the western coalition in Afghanistan was unwilling to curb (or was even buttressing) the growing strength of the ISIS in the country, which constituted a potent terrorist threat to the region and beyond. In Russia's assessment, the Taliban's ambitions were confined to Afghanistan and it was bitterly opposed to ISIS. Particularly in the climate of suspicion that the US and its allies were instigating ISIS to act against Russian interests, it made sense for Russia to cooperate with the Taliban through information and intelligence sharing on ISIS's activities.

RUSSIAN DIPLOMATIC PRESENCE IN AFGHANISTAN

During 2016–17, Russia spent considerable energy in improving relations with Pakistan, as the latter's relations with the US were cooling. Among the many incentives for this outreach was the fact that Pakistan had close connections with the Taliban, which, as observed by Russia, could be leveraged to encourage a political process.

Russian intelligence agencies had retained assets in Afghanistan from the '70s, '80s and beyond. They had maintained contact with all the major ethnic leaders in the country, and added President Hamid Karzai to this list, after he had a fallout with the Americans in 2014–15. Russia's Uzbek-born presidential envoy for Afghanistan, Zamir Kabulov, had been engaged with Afghanistan in various capacities, including in the Bonn Process and during diplomatic assignments in Kabul and Islamabad. In addition to these assets was the Afghan diaspora in Russia, which has the third-largest expatriate Afghan community after Pakistan and Iran: of 150,000, (as a matter of interest to Indians) about 2,000 are Afghan Sikhs. This diaspora played a useful role in furthering Russia's interests in Afghanistan, as will be described subsequently.[3]

Russia commenced a dialogue with China and Pakistan to prepare for a political process that could facilitate an early exit of the US-led forces from Afghanistan. It was the assessment of all three countries that the Taliban did have a significant following among the people of Afghanistan and, therefore, any sustainable political process needed to include the Taliban and that too without preconditions. This was clearly stated in a joint statement after a trilateral dialogue in December 2016, which called for a 'flexible approach to remove certain figures (the reference was for the Taliban leaders who had been identified by the UN as terrorists) from sanctions lists as part of efforts to foster a peaceful dialogue between Kabul and the Taliban movement'. This, of course, ran counter to the strong views of India and much of the international community that the Taliban could only be included in the political process after they relinquished violence and accepted the Afghan constitution. The dialogue was also criticized by the Afghan government for having excluded it from a discussion that concerned its own domestic affairs.

In response, Russia organized regional consultations on Afghanistan in Moscow, in which the Afghan government participated, along with representatives from India, China, Iran and Pakistan. The statement from 'Moscow format' consultations recorded their agreement to promote intra-

Afghan reconciliation, 'preserving the leading role of Kabul' and requiring the 'armed opposition' to abjure violence.

Such a duality became a regular practice. On one hand, there were regional consultations on Afghanistan, with the presence of its neighbours, including Central Asian countries, with representatives of the Taliban also participating on the sidelines of later editions of these consultations. On the other hand, there was a closed grouping, in which the US was later included, where real discussions were conducted on the Afghan political process.

A new, though short-lived, phase in the US approach to Afghanistan was launched when President Donald Trump unveiled the South Asia policy in mid-2017. Yielding to advice from the Pentagon and the US military, he committed more US troops to Afghanistan. He declared that a political settlement has to follow 'an effective military effort' in support of the Afghan government; that Pakistan should give up its double game of pretense regarding extension of support for the US's counterterrorism efforts, while sheltering terrorists, who attacked American soldiers; and that India should be more engaged in Afghanistan for economic assistance and development.[4]

Russia criticized this US policy for its 'inconsistent approach' to the Taliban, implying that the more dangerous ISIS was being given a free pass. The US was also criticized for ignoring the drug menace, which could flow into Central Asia and Russia. The US decision to inject more troops into Afghanistan upended the initiatives that Russia was promoting (together with China and Pakistan) to launch a political process in Afghanistan that would mainstream the Taliban. A Russian deputy foreign minister admonished the US ambassador in Moscow that Pakistan should not be 'selectively' targeted, and that the US policies should accommodate the interests of all countries in the region.

This US policy thrust was short-lived, and President Trump soon reverted to his original objective of an early withdrawal from Afghanistan. In his memoir, *The Room Where It Happened: A White House Memoir*, American diplomat John Bolton, in his short tenure as President Trump's national security advisor (NSA), provides an entertaining account of how Trump fulminated against his advisors for persuading him, against his better judgment, to announce his new Afghanistan policy, and asked a new set of advisors to plot an early American exit from Afghanistan. It was in this background that the mission of the Special Representative for Afghanistan Reconciliation, Zalmay Khalilzad, was framed by the US State Department to negotiate an understanding with the Taliban that would facilitate an early US withdrawal from Afghanistan. Bolton in the book described how Khalilzad was pushed into making unwise concessions to accelerate the process.[5]

With Khalilzad's appointment, US objectives in Afghanistan converged with those of Russia, China and Pakistan. Both tracks of Russia's diplomacy—the 'Moscow format' of regional consultations and more restricted consultations—acquired fresh momentum. The Moscow format expanded to include more Afghan political figures and representatives of the Qatar-based Taliban leadership to give the veneer of inclusive Afghan participation.

THE INTRA-AFGHAN DIALOGUE

A variant of this format was an intra-Afghan dialogue, initially hosted ostensibly by the Afghan diaspora in Russia, bringing together senior Afghan politicians and Taliban representatives. The US was deeply involved in helping Russia organize this dialogue. The close coordination was revealed when the second edition of this dialogue was being planned in Doha (July 2019). Afghan government representatives were invited 'in their personal capacities'. When a disagreement arose between the Taliban and the Afghan government about the size and composition of the latter's nominees (including the large number of women delegates), US Secretary of State Mike Pompeo personally telephoned the Afghan president in an effort to resolve the issue.

US–Russia consultations on Afghanistan became regular, soon including China and, eventually, Pakistan as well. This grouping, called the extended troika, met regularly and strategized about bringing the Taliban into mainstream Afghan politics in a harmonious manner. The extended troika consultations were unaffected by the otherwise tense US–Russia relationship or by the change of guard at the White House. In fact, soon after President Biden had famously agreed with a US TV anchor's description of President Vladimir Putin as a 'killer',[6] Khalilzad was in Moscow for an extended troika meeting. When asked about the incongruity of American participation in the light of Biden's remarks, the State Department spokesman simply said that Russia has 'an important stake in a secure and stable Afghanistan'.[7] It is an illustration of how big powers can sustain harmonious collaboration on shared objectives, even when they exhibit unremitting hostility across all other spheres and geographies.

The extended troika was a closed format. The four countries selectively invited Afghan political figures and, more regularly, Taliban representatives. The rhetoric always revolved around them working towards an 'Afghan-owned' and 'Afghan-led' political process. Troika statements and pronouncements of its leaders were littered with terms like 'inclusive', 'Afghan-led', 'Afghan-owned' and 'Afghan-controlled'. Many also included expressions of support for the Afghan government in combating terrorism. But the Afghan government was rarely kept in the loop of the discussions and there always seemed to be a stronger emphasis on the Taliban's preferences. For example, the Taliban's flat refusal to accept the legitimacy of the Afghan government was not challenged. In April 2019, US–Russia–China joint statement approvingly noted that the Taliban's 'commitment to: fight ISIS and cut ties with the Al-Qaeda, East Turkestan Islamic Movement and other international terrorist groups and to ensure that areas under their control will not be used to threaten any other country'—a ringing certificate of good behaviour for the Taliban.[8]

When the intra-Afghan dialogue of April 2019 fell through, the Russian government put the blame squarely on the Afghan government for trying to dictate the terms of the dialogue by not selecting a delegation acceptable to the main opponents, the Taliban. Secretary Mike Pompeo, too, put pressure on President Ashraf Ghani—and not the Taliban—to make concessions. This kid glove treatment of the Taliban was obviously a path of least resistance towards an early American exit from Afghanistan. It was actively supported by Pakistan, whose role in ensuring Taliban's 'good' behaviour was always considered pivotal by the other three extended troika members. In effect, the process eventually was US-led, Pakistan-controlled and Afghanistan-exclusive—perhaps an inevitable consequence of trying to pass off a withdrawal plan as a political settlement.

Russia's dalliance with the Taliban was viewed in India with great concern since it deviated sharply from the shared views which had driven the cooperation of the two in Northern Alliance and in the Bonn Process. The fact that India was not invited to join the trilateral Russia–China–Pakistan dialogue on Afghanistan was (correctly) attributed to Pakistan's opposition; but Indian media and the strategic community saw this as a strategic shift in Russia's orientation in South Asia. However, two facts are relevant here. First, Russia's change of attitude towards the Taliban stemmed (as noted in the foregoing) from its standoff with the West and not from a re-evaluation of relations with India. The assessment that India could not bring value to an exercise that aimed to mainstream the Taliban in Afghan polity was obviously accurate (regardless of Pakistan's view on this matter), given the state of India's relations (or lack thereof) with the Taliban. Second, India's other strategic partner, the US, was also unconcerned about excluding India from this dialogue, for the same obvious reason. Perhaps the only difference was that, while the US special envoy did go through the motions of briefing the Indian government, from time to time, about the status of the political process, his Russian counterpart did not seem to feel the need to do so; the media quoted him as bluntly saying that India could have no role in the dialogue, since it did not have any influence over any of the parties involved in the Afghan conflict.

It has been noted that Russia's motive in its engagement in the Afghan political process was to prevent its interests from being trampled upon by the western coalition, and to retain influence on a post-settlement set-up in Afghanistan. At the same time, despite the fractured relations with the West, Russia did not want a precipitate international troop withdrawal from that country because it was apprehensive about the post-withdrawal course of a Taliban-led Afghan government and its impact on the Eurasian region. Therefore, interspersed with statements that a genuine Afghan reconciliation can only happen after the exit of the US troops from that country, were also a reluctant acknowledgement that the US presence in Afghanistan contributed to stability in that country. As one example of this, President Putin was quoted as saying that a US exit would increase the costs for Russia to maintain stability.[9]

Russia's conflicting emotions were in display in the days following the abrupt and chaotic exit of the US troops from Afghanistan in August 2021. The manner in which the last of the American troops were withdrawn, the way in which the Taliban rolled into Kabul and the abandonment of his post by President Ghani provoked much glee in the Russian media and social media, seeing this as a loss of face for the US. Russia announced that its embassy in Kabul would remain open, and that special arrangements had been made with the Taliban to ensure its security. The Russian embassy was reported to have interceded with the Taliban forces on the ground to facilitate movement of evacuees. President Putin lectured German chancellor Angela Merkel a few days later (on her farewell visit to Moscow) on the futility of trying to impose external political systems and social behavioural norms on countries like Iraq, Libya and Afghanistan. The Chancellor gracefully admitted that this particular project had not worked.

But for all the gloating, the Russian leadership recognized the challenges that the Taliban victory posed. Russia did not rush to recognize their government and instead went along with the United Nation Security Council resolution, spelling out expectations from the Taliban to abjure support to terrorism and form an inclusive government. Its statements and actions demonstrated concerns about the immediate impact on its security, its influence in Central Asia and Russia–China equations.

One concern was about the inspirational impact in the North Caucasus region, in which there were simmering tensions due to jihadi and separatist movements. A tenuous peace had been restored in recent years, after suppressing new uprisings inspired by the return of Chechens and other Caucasians, who had joined ISIS in Syria and Iraq, but returned after ISIS was driven out of those regions. The victory of Islamic fundamentalists in Afghanistan and the potential migration of jihadis from there to these regions could lead to unrest. Given the Russian paranoia about the West looking for opportunities to create internal discord in Russia, there is a perennial fear that western secret services may help accelerate this process. There was also a sober recognition that a Taliban government may not have much incentive to keep these elements from moving across its borders.

President Putin immediately launched initiatives to guard against these threats. He called for an emergency meeting of the Collective Security Treaty Organization (CSTO), comprising Russia, Belarus, Armenia, Kazakhstan, Kyrgyzstan and Tajikistan, to address the critical security issues. Uzbekistan, which suspended its membership of CSTO in 2012, was also persuaded to join. The Russian President reportedly warned his Central Asian counterparts that this precipitate US withdrawal was a ruse of the West to get Russia and China bogged down in Afghanistan and to destabilize the whole region. He raised the spectre of hundreds of thousands, maybe even millions of unvetted refugees, who could be terrorists (or Islamic extremists), moving freely around Central Asia and onwards to Russia, given the visa-free regime. US overtures to Tajikistan and Uzbekistan to temporarily accept Afghan evacuees were the thin end of the wedge. President Putin warned them that their own regimes could come under threat. He is also said to have strongly warned the frontline states of Tajikistan and Uzbekistan against providing infrastructural support for the US over-the-horizon attacks on terrorist targets in Afghanistan, since it would also make them targets of terrorist attacks.

CONCERNS FROM RUSSIA

A broader Russian concern, exacerbated by continuing US–Russia acrimony, was that the US would use the Afghanistan situation to get the five Central Asian countries (C5) more engaged with it. In the recent years, the US has been devoting more attention to the C5+1 dialogue in the region. The Central Asian countries have responded positively to these overtures. They have welcomed the potential economic benefits from the partnership and the incremental political space that it could give them vis-à-vis Russia and China. Though the Kremlin's warning of the contagion of religion and democracy would resonate with them, Central Asian countries would find it very difficult to resist a US charm offensive. Uzbekistan did eventually accept Afghan refugees, their verification pending with the US authorities. Central Asian leaders have been invited to the White House and the State Department in recent years, and their achievements lauded.

Another unstated Russian concern is increased Chinese activism in Central Asia, and responding to the challenges and opportunities in post-NATO Afghanistan. Russia and China have an unwritten understanding that Russia would have the principal politico-security role in the region, while China has a dominant economic presence. This understanding started coming under strain. China's Belt and Road Initiative has not only given it a great economic clout but also increased its political clout through close engagement with the leadership of these countries. It has shown an increasing desire to take the security of its investments into its own hands. Afghan developments may further feed this desire. There are reports of Chinese presence in Tajik military units, across the border from Afghanistan. There has been a quadrilateral dialogue of the national security councils of China, Pakistan, Tajikistan and Afghanistan. There have been intensified security dialogues with Turkmenistan, undermining its permanent neutrality. Chinese private security contractors are believed to be deployed in various parts of the region.

Turkey is another player that has expanded its footprint in the region, exploiting the churn in Central Asia and Afghanistan. Its contribution to Azerbaijan's military victory over Armenia in the Nagorno-Karabakh War (November 2020) enhanced its prestige. It is now moving to consolidate its influence in the Caspian region and among the Turkic people of Central Asia. Its military partnerships with Qatar and Pakistan have facilitated its engagement with the Taliban; it has already been a part of the NATO operations in Afghanistan. Turkey's larger Eurasian presence would further complicate the already complex relationship that Russia has with Turkey across various issues and geographies.

Russia's embrace of the Taliban was motivated mainly by the desire to befriend the US and ISIS. This consideration overrode qualms over supporting an extremist organization, wedded to bigotry and violence. It found common cause with China and Pakistan, which had their own motives for their alignment with the Taliban. Such is the nature of international politics that, after harshly criticizing Russia for aiding and arming the Taliban, the US eventually associated itself with this grouping, to extricate itself from its confrontation with the Taliban.

Russia may have been hoping that the extended troika and other initiatives would bring the Taliban into power in Kabul, but with some commitment to an inclusive government. Eventually, the manner of the US withdrawal created a political vacuum, which the Taliban occupied without contest. This fact, and the consequent geopolitical dynamics in the Eurasian space adjacent to India, Russia and China, brought Indian and Russian interests more in line with each other. The churn in and around Afghanistan, the Chinese ascendancy, and the activities of Turkey, Iran, Pakistan and others in the region pose strategic and security challenges for both India as well as Russia. This was confirmed by a telephone call that President Putin made to Prime Minister Narendra Modi, just a few days after the Taliban takeover of Kabul. The two leaders agreed to establish a mechanism for regular dialogue with Afghanistan. The NSAs commenced this dialogue, and soon, thereafter, India's NSA hosted his counterparts from Russia, Iran and the five Central Asian countries in New Delhi. The fact that all eight countries were represented at the highest levels of their security establishment demonstrated that, though there are specificities of core concerns, depending on geographical, ethnic, political and economic factors, there are significant shared perspectives on what is required to ensure peace and harmony in Afghanistan, so that it does not threaten the security of countries in its neighbourhood. Their joint declaration spelt out a wider canvas of expectations of the Afghan government—that it should move towards an inclusive government that represents all the political and ethnic groups in the country, that it should uphold the human rights of all sections of the population, including women and children, and that it should ensure that the territory of Afghanistan is not used to export terrorism or radicalization to any country in the region or beyond. The last expectation is crucial to the interests of all countries in the region. The broader objective of an inclusive Afghan government, which preserves the gains from Afghanistan's democratic experience of the past two decades, can be achieved only by coordinated actions of a much wider international coalition. Whether and how this objective can be achieved is the subject of a separate discussion.

Russia continues to maintain a modus vivendi with the new Afghan government, even trying to win international acceptance for it, on the basis of the argument that this may help to moderate the Taliban's approach on governance issues of international concern. A warmer Russian relationship with Pakistan has facilitated closer Russian contacts with the Taliban leadership. This bilateral relationship now also includes a wider political and economic canvas as part of Russia's broader Asian outreach. Given that in the post-Cold War world, there is no exclusivity of bilateral relations, India can only require of its strategic partner that its engagement with Pakistan (or, for that matter, with China) does not cross red lines of India's security or strategic concerns. A strong mutuality of interests in the Eurasian space sandwiched by India and Russia, and adjacent to China, should ensure this.

It should be emphasized, however, that the triangle of relations between the US, Russia and China will have a major impact on political, economic and security developments in Eurasia. The Russian invasion of Ukraine, in search of a new equilibrium in the European security order, could profoundly alter the configuration of this triangle. India would need to carefully monitor this, and may have to make tactical and strategic adjustments to its policy in the region, depending on the outcome of the ongoing war in Europe.

8

China in Afghanistan: Motivation and Long-term Strategic Objectives

Dr Srikanth Kondapalli

Although in China's overall foreign policy perceptions, relations with Afghanistan played a marginal role historically, the latter is becoming an important, if not central, consideration recently. China's motivations towards Afghanistan include ushering stability in western areas, such as Xinjiang, and enforcing counterterrorism campaigns, controlling drug and arms exports, participation in reconstruction efforts, infrastructure projects, and so on. Its long-term strategic objectives are shaped by a desire to usher in regional balance in South Asia, search for alliances or preferably close partnerships that could cushion its rise in the regional and global orders. Afghanistan is also the testing ground for China's recently formed 'community of common destiny'.

It is argued that China's goal posts have changed over a period of time from a relatively fewer, even though positive, contacts in the formative stages of bilateral relations to an active role in Afghanistan recently; from aiming to replace Soviet/Russian influence in Central Asia and Afghanistan to replacing the US influence recently; and to exercising regional balance between Pakistan and India. In the long term, China's strategic objective is to convert Central Asia and Afghanistan into what it mentioned as partnership with Afghanistan and others. While China's concerns essentially remain tilted towards its eastern sea-board, the launch of Western Development Campaign in the 1990s and the Belt and Road Initiative (BRI) in 2013, including massive infrastructure projects, pushes the Chinese state influence into these regions. Although predominantly concerned about stability in these regions, China has also been recently exploring strategic opportunities in Afghanistan, as with other regions, specifically after the US-led International Security Assistance Forces (ISAF) exiting the region. Increase in the recent Chinese bilateral political, diplomatic, economic and military contacts with Afghanistan points towards this direction.

INTRODUCTION

Although Afghanistan is a relatively small country with sparse population and resources, some of the main Chinese perspectives on this country relate to its strategic position, straddling as it were, between three regions of Asia, viz., West, South and Central Asia as with other issues such as being the centre of global campaign against terrorism and drug exports.[1] Afghanistan also borders China for about 76 km in the Pamirs. The border dispute was settled in 1963, but the issues related to cross-border movements have become one of the main concerns for China.

China's relations can be conveniently studied by understanding the following five phases. The first phase was the historical interaction till about the establishment of diplomatic relations between the two countries in 1955. The second phase of interactions was till the time of Soviet invasion of Afghanistan in late 1970s, when China denounced the Soviet act and relations with Afghanistan nosedived. The third phase commenced from the 1970s with China's relations with splinter groups and subsequently with the ruling Taliban, till the 11 September 2001 incidents. This phase coincided with Chinese mediation with Afghans through Pakistan, its all-weather partner. In the fourth phase, China expanded contacts with the Afghan government installed following 2004 elections. This phase was relatively broad-based, with Chinese perspectives mainly emphasising on stability in relations and counterterrorism efforts, reversing its policy towards the Taliban and gradually mending fences with several Afghan groups and also the Northern Alliance. This phase also coincided with China's new initiatives, such as making Afghanistan an observer in the Chinese-led Shanghai Cooperation Organisation (SCO), extending support to the Istanbul Process, Qatar talks, parleys with the Taliban leaders and others. The fifth and current phase came in the backdrop of preparations for the US withdrawal from Afghanistan with President Xi Jinping's enunciation of three points in September 2021, which was preceded by the meeting of Foreign Minister Wang Yi with the Baradar delegation at Tianjin. These five phases are elaborated in the chapter, with emphasis on the last two.

BRIEF HISTORICAL CONTACTS

Chinese interpretations of their relations with several countries generally trace back to the historical past to underline, at a rhetorical level, civilizational links. At one level, this point is to remind of the hoary interactions that several Chinese dynasties had with these countries in the periphery, and at another, it points towards the current political and diplomatic perspectives. As most of these peripheral areas straddle strategic passes, inhabited by ethnic peoples and, as China found recently, are of economic importance (in terms of minerals, etc.), a premium is generally placed on diplomatic relations with the states located in these areas.

At a broader level, the above can also be said in relation to Chinese perspectives on Afghanistan. These accounts generally trace bilateral interactions to several thousand years. Thus, a white paper issued in May 2003 on Xinjiang region, an area bordering Afghanistan, suggested that contacts with several countries in the current Central Asian region and beyond were evolved since the time of the Western Han dynasty in second century BC. A western frontier military command was established in this period to subjugate people living in these regions, for which Han rulers enlisted Afghan military in 140 BC. Although a period of disunity had set in and left a dent in the Chinese effective control over these regions, successive Chinese dynasties in the latter period were said to have contacts with this region, including Afghanistan. The Tang dynasty rekindled links to the region from the seventh century with its Silk Road and Buddhist pilgrimages, the latter passing through Bamian, Balkh and other places in Afghanistan. Of the four main arteries built during this period linking the interior of China, the southern route passed through Afghanistan, Iran and India. A period of lull set in once again in China's interactions with Central Asia till the Qing dynasty started to expand its borders and influence in the eighteenth and nineteenth centuries.[2] This period also coincided with the 'great game' between Qing, Czarist and British empires in their quest for expanding influence and power.[3]

DIPLOMATIC RELATIONS

The broad-brush description of the historical interactions painted above indicate limited Chinese interaction with the region, including Afghanistan. Even when looking at the 1940s, one comes across the Sino-Afghan relations in similar historical contours. However, as modern states, several new factors have come to be considered by both. While Afghanistan intended to commence diplomatic interactions with China in 1950, the latter was lukewarm towards such gestures till the new People's Republic of China consolidated its position in the country's far-flung areas and formulated a 'good neighbourliness' policy in 1954. Meanwhile, the Xinjiang factor came to the fore between the two countries as they had to decide about the fate of 436 Afghans in Xinjiang.[4] Both established diplomatic relations on 20 January 1955.[5] The first high-level visit between the two countries was made by Premier Zhou Enlai in January 1957, while Afghan Prime Minister Mohammed Doud reciprocated this visit in October the same year. A trade agreement was signed in July. By August 1960, both countries signed a treaty of 'friendship and non-aggression' and by November 1963, a border treaty was signed delimiting and demarcating the boundary in the Pamirs.[6] Subsequently, King Mohammad Zahir Shah visited Beijing in 1963, while President Liu Shaoqi visited Kabul in April 1966. In this period, agreements on economic and technological cooperation were signed in March 1965, July 1966 and April 1974.

SECOND PHASE

Overall, the second phase can be broadly termed as positive in nature in its impact on bilateral relations without much of the acrimony that the subsequent third phase would witness, with China siding with one or the other Afghan group. Thus, after the Soviet invasion of Afghanistan, bilateral relations nosedived. Soon after the US Defense Secretary Harold Brown's visit, China reportedly opened intelligence posts to monitor Soviet movements, cargo planes' usage of Chinese airspace, movements across Karakoram Highway, etc., to further the anti-Soviet operations.[7] As Afghanistan went through a transformation in the last two decades, China as well adjusted its policies. These were reflected in China's covert support to Mujahideen, its overt support to the Taliban till the 9/11 events and in its measured interactions with the Taliban till 2006.[8]

THIRD PHASE

In the third phase of Chinese interactions with Afghanistan, most of such contacts were through Pakistan (which supported the Mujahideen government in Kabul), either through its embassy in Islamabad or through interlocutors. At this time, the Chinese embassy in Kabul was closed down and staff was recalled during the Babrak Karmal regime in 1979–81. The embassy was completely shut down in 1993. When Pakistan's relations with Afghanistan soured as a result of bombings of Pakistan embassy in Kabul and Peshawar school bus hijacking, China reportedly informed the then visiting Afghan Deputy Foreign Minister Abdul Rahim Ghafoorzai in February 1996 that it would use its offices to persuade Islamabad to engage in the Afghan peace efforts. A first-ever direct air-link between the two countries was negotiated during this visit, but was implemented only after Ariana Afghan Airlines started flights to China in August 2003.[9]

Subsequently, after the Taliban took over Kabul in September 1996 from Rabbani-Hekmatyar forces, despite fears of the spread of Taliban 'virus' to Xinjiang, China followed a pragmatic policy.[10] The highlight of this phase was the meeting of China's Ambassador to Pakistan, Lu Shulin, with the Taliban leader Mullah Omar in Kandahar in late 2000s—a non-Muslim leader paying a visit to the latter for the first time. A new stage came up with the tacit understanding of China with the Taliban, with the former providing protection to the Taliban in the United Nations Security Council (UNSC) and other fora.

FOURTH PHASE

The fourth phase coincided with the US strikes on Afghanistan following the cataclysmic developments of the 9/11 attacks. This upset China's carefully crafted policy on Afghanistan and the equations with the Taliban and Pakistan with the active positioning of the US and allied forces under the International Security Assistance Force in the western borders of China. Beijing then articulated the position that the US strikes should respect the sovereignty of Afghanistan, not violate UNSC resolutions and intervene in Afghanistan, and not inflict any collateral damages on the civilian population or attempt ethnic reconciliation. Though China announced reconstruction efforts, its contribution was paltry in the light of the US presence in the region. This can be compared to the assistance provided by Japan, EU countries, India and others. China, of course, participated in many multilateral efforts to bring peace and stability to Afghanistan with the articulation of 'Afghan-led, Afghan-owned' set-up in Kabul. This phase was high in political rhetoric, multilateral initiatives and less in substance from the point of view of actual assistance from Beijing to Kabul. Nevertheless, many institutional arrangements were made by the elected representatives of Kabul, including arrangements for BRI and investments in mineral exploitation and others.

Enhanced Contacts

China's inroads in Afghanistan in the fourth phase were its stepping stones in becoming a crucial player in Kabul. China became a member of the 'Six plus Two Group' in finding a solution for the war-torn Afghanistan. During the visit of Pakistan Defence Minister Aftab Shaban Mirani in October 1996 to Beijing, the Chinese Foreign Minister Qian Qichen and Vice Foreign Minister Tang Jiaxuan, China appreciated Pakistan's efforts in Afghanistan.[11] Subsequently, Pakistan's special negotiator on Afghan issues, Additional Foreign Secretary Iftikhar Murshid approached several countries, including Chinese officials to broker contacts with the Taliban.[12]

In late 1996, China and the Taliban agreed to enter into a defence understanding. Reported by *Frontier Post* from Peshawar, a 12-member Chinese ballistic missile scientists' delegation visited two sites at Helmand desert to examine two unexploded US Tomahawk missiles. Another Chinese delegation reportedly visited the Taliban headquarters at Kandahar.[13] In 1998, contacts between China and the Taliban were reportedly established at Peshawar.[14] On 10 December 1998, a defence cooperation agreement between China and the Taliban was reported, which included training Taliban pilots, maintaining and repair of equipment, etc.[15] An official delegation of five members from China to Kabul arrived on 31 January 1999. This was said to be the highest-level delegation from China to visit Afghanistan after 15 years.[16] Although the discussion between the Chinese and the Taliban were reported to be cordial, the Taliban appeared to have denied any role in their support to the Uighurs in Xinjiang.[17]

Window of Opportunity

Late 2000s appeared to be a turning point in the Chinese policy towards the Taliban, with both making adjustments towards each other. While at one level, several Chinese were critical about the Taliban support to the Uighurs, at another (official) level, a gradual makeover came to be visible in the Chinese policy. Even though till late 1999, China was critical of the Taliban and the greater dangers of this phenomenon to the stability of the region, a quiet rethinking was visible in 2000.

A Chinese scholar, Gao Rongzhu, at a seminar in Peshawar in November 2000 said that Afghanistan has become the global centre for terrorism and that the Uighur militants were being supported by several from this region, including Pakistan and Central Asia.[18] In the same month, on the advice of the Pakistan ambassador to Beijing, a four-member team from the Chinese Communist Party visited Kabul and Kandahar for a week. Around this time, the Chinese ambassador to Pakistan, Lu Shulin, was given an audience by Mullah Omar at Kandahar.[19] Subsequently, in the run-up to the approval of US–Russian proposal to the UNSC Resolution 1333 to impose sanctions on the Taliban, China and Malaysia abstained from voting, earning praise from the Taliban. The Taliban Foreign Minister Wakil Ahmed Mutawakkil, on this occasion, thanked China for this gesture.[20] This was in contrast to the Chinese support to the UN resolution to impose sanctions on the Taliban in discussions in November 1999.

In the wake of the 9/11 attacks, China's policy needed to be further adjusted, this time with the explicit criticism of the Taliban phenomenon, although official Chinese rhetoric continued to put pressure, especially on the UN, for no collateral damages, safeguarding of Afghan sovereignty, arriving at an independent solution to the Afghan internal issue, and so on.

In November 2001, China, while supporting the UN peace efforts, called for a 'broad-based' government in Afghanistan with the participation of 'all the ethnic groups' in the country.[21] On 12 November 2001, the Chinese Foreign Minister Tang Jiaxuan, attending the 56th Session of the UN General Assembly, said that China's policy towards Afghanistan was guided by the following points:

1. Efforts should be made to safeguard the sovereignty, independence and territorial integrity of Afghanistan. It is the basic principles of the UN Charter and international law that stipulate the respect for sovereignty, independence and territorial integrity of a country;
2. The Afghan people should be able to decide on the solution to their problem independently;
3. The future Afghan government should be broad-based, represent the interests of all ethnic groups in the country and develop good relations with Afghanistan's neighbouring countries;
4. Efforts should be made to maintain the peace and stability in the region;
5. The UN should play a more constructive role in solving the Afghan problem.[22]

In the backdrop of China's closer understanding with the Taliban prior to 9/11 attacks and its relative distance from the Northern Alliance groups, who appeared to have a stronger presence in the post-Taliban establishment in Kabul, the Chinese position was closer to Pakistan in this regard. Subsequently, when the agreement for an interim government was established in December of the same year and as the UNSC approved a multinational force to stabilize the situation in and around Kabul, China's Deputy Permanent Representative to the UN, Shen Guofang, suggested that other UN organs should also be involved in the reconstruction of Afghanistan.[23]

However, two significant events in Afghanistan indicated the limited Chinese influence in the region. First, from August 2003, the North Atlantic Treaty Organization or NATO-led 5,500-strong International Security Assistance Force was placed in Afghanistan. Second, in 2004, a new elected government under President Hamid Karzai came into being in Kabul. Although Karzai, over a period of time, evolved relations with all neighbours, the US influence was visible during his tenure. Nevertheless, Afghanistan was admitted as an observer in SCO and it also started participating in another Chinese-led multilateral grouping, Boao Forum for Asia.

At the diplomatic level, mutual visits promoted increasing understanding between the two countries. In May 2003, Vice President Nematullah Shahrani visited China and signed an agreement on economic and technical cooperation. President Karzai preceded this visit with a brief stopover at Beijing in February en route Tokyo.[24] In March 2004, Foreign Minister Abdullah Abdullah visited China, while President Hu Jintao met Karzai at the SCO Tashkent summit meeting.[25] The fiftieth anniversary of the establishment of diplomatic relations were marked in 2005. Chinese Foreign Minister Li Zhaoxing visited Kabul in April 2005 and attended the third meeting of Afghanistan Development Forum.[26] This visit was followed by Vice Foreign Minister Wu Dawei's visit in December to attend the Kabul conference on Regional Economic Cooperation.[27] In April of the same year, Afghan Vice President Khalili visited China to attend Boao Forum meeting.

President Karzai visited Beijing in June 2006, during which China and Afghanistan signed a treaty of friendship and cooperation.[28] President Hu Jintao, on this occasion, promised to 'actively participate' in Afghan reconstruction efforts, while Karzai pointed out that Afghanistan would be a 'bridge' between China and Central Asia. Ratified by the National People's Congress in November 2006, the treaty aims at enhancing 'more military and security cooperation' between the two countries.[29]

The highlights of the joint statement issued by both presidents included elevation of bilateral ties for 'comprehensive and cooperative partnership'; China was to provide about $10 million as gratis in 2006 and grant Afghanistan with zero-tariff treatment to 278 items of Afghan exports to China, along with 200 Afghan professionals to be trained by China, and so on.[30]

Institutional arrangements between the two indicate towards steady progress. From the June 2006 'comprehensive cooperative relationship', both graduated in June 2012 to 'strategic cooperative partnership'. In 2014, President Ashraf Ghani made China as his first visit abroad and in May 2016, a memorandum of understanding on China's BRI was signed. In November 2015, the Chinese and the Afghan government signed a cooperation agreement in the fields of security, reconstruction and education.

Safety of Chinese Citizens

During the fourth phase and subsequently, three major issues posed concerns for China vis-à-vis Central Asia and Afghanistan, security of its citizens living abroad, terrorism and drug trafficking. All of these, together with the general instability in the region, came to be known in the Chinese official discourse as a part of the 'arc of destabilization' in its periphery. Among these, one of the issues that came to the fore in the Chinese interactions with the outside world was the security of Chinese citizens living and working abroad.

As several Chinese started venturing abroad in the last 10 to 15 years, specifically in turbulent regions, their safety has become one of the main concerns for the Chinese government. With violent incidents being reported from several regions, such as Central Asia, West Asia and Pakistan, pressure started mounting on the Chinese government to tackle this issue through diplomatic means. The Chinese working in Afghanistan were also being targeted by Afghan-based groups. On 10 May 2004, for instance, 11 Chinese workers were killed and five were injured in terrorist strikes in Jalowgir area, which is 36 km from Kunduz in northern Afghanistan. A new terror group, reported to be closer to the Taliban, was suspected to have carried this mission.[31] These workers belonged to a Chinese railway company, Shisigu Group, and were involved in construction work. On this occasion, Afghan finance minister agreed to pay compensation of $5,000 per victim.[32] In May 2006, in another incident, a riot took place in Kabul, injuring some Chinese. The Chinese foreign ministry spokesman, on this occasion, requested the 'relevant' Afghan bodies to ensure safety of the Chinese.[33]

Since July 2014, Islamic State leader Abu Bakr al-Baghdadi's statement listing China for jihad has brought in a new element. The Islamic State Khorasan Province's (ISKP) activities were closely monitored by China. Although no major casualties of Chinese citizens took place in Afghanistan, China began demanding for repatriation of Uighurs from the Kabul government. In the October 2021 attack on a mosque at Kunduz, the ISKP militants led by Muhammad al-Uyghuri killed over 70 people.[34]

Counterterrorism

The above incidents are partly linked to the Chinese counterterrorism efforts. As Chinese forces unleashed 'strike hard' campaigns against Uighurs in Xinjiang, there were reprisals elsewhere. One of the major issues of Sino-Afghan relations recently has been around how to tackle Uighur unrest in Xinjiang. Afghanistan came into the picture after some of the Uighurs were reportedly trained and supported by the Al-Qaeda/Taliban and other groups.

In brief, while China's relations with the then Soviet Union suffered a setback from August 1960, differences between the two were reflected in covert actions of each against the other. Initially, such differences were reflected in 1960, when nearly 60,000 Uighurs migrated from Xinjiang to the Soviet Republics in Central Asia. The pan-Turkic movements spread during the anti-Soviet occupation of Afghanistan with the active support of the US, Pakistan and partly from China in 1979–89. It was reported that the Chinese leadership allowed NATO to put up listening posts in Xinjiang. Chinese transferred small arms to the Mujahideen against the Soviets in Afghanistan during this period, which appears to have boomeranged in the recent times, when the Al-Qaeda trained separatists started entering Xinjiang. Most of these are suspected to have been trained in Afghan and Pakistani camps. In camps near Mazar-i-Sharif, Uighurs were trained by Islamic Movement of Uzbekistan, headed by Tahir Yoldasev.[35] The then Chinese Deputy Chief of General Staff, Xiong Guangkai, estimated that nearly a thousand such armed separatists entered Xinjiang region. In Xiong's words: 'Over the years, the international terrorist forces, as represented by Osama bin Laden and the Taliban, have provided a great deal of support and assistance to the "East Turkistan" terrorists.'[36]

On the other hand, some argue that Beijing was piggybacking on the post-9/11 consensus to castigate Uighurs abroad as terrorists to cover up the repression and assimilationist policy it adopted in Xinjiang, and that intensified in recent years with allegations of over a million Uighurs being confined to detention centres. The estimated 2,000 Uighurs in Afghanistan, for instance, were apprehensive that they will be deported back to Xinjiang and incarcerated.

Nevertheless, to counter these, apart from joining international conventions on counterterrorism and military exercises, in the 1990s, China closed its Karakoram highway connecting with the Pakistan-occupied northern areas to stop the flow of separatists from Afghanistan into Xinjiang. Later, after the US launched its strikes on Taliban-held Afghanistan following the 9/11 incidents, China closed its borders with Afghanistan and Pakistan fearing that the fleeing Al-Qaeda/Taliban activists would sneak into Xinjiang.

During the US strikes on Afghanistan, Chinese troops blockaded its borders with Afghanistan. To cut any migration of militants through this region, specifically at Taxkorgan, China beefed up surveillance in this region and also restricted the movement of people.[37]

Another measure followed by China was to extend support to Afghan counterterrorism efforts. China provided nearly $5 million worth of arms and equipment to Afghanistan police since 2001, including small arms, motorcycles, computers, etc.[38] In 2005, during the visit of Lt Gen. Mohammed Fawzi, China announced ¥15 million as gratis.[39] In the penultimate days of the US presence in Afghanistan, China also made arrangements with the Kabul government to train security forces to control militants in Badakhshan province. In order to counter the spread of the ISIS (estimated at around 10,000) in Afghanistan, Defense Ministry's deputy spokesman, Muhammad Radmanish, stated that China had promised to provide $85 million for raising a mountain brigade in Badakhshan to protect the borders.[40]

Drug Trafficking

Dwindling narcotics supplies from traditional sources, such as Myanmar, provided an opportunity for Afghanistan to export drugs to China. According to Jacob Townsend, Afghanistan's drug exports to China increased and by 2004 constituted nearly 20 per cent of total Chinese heroin consumption. While such exports from the Wakhjir Pass between Afghanistan and China border are difficult due to terrain and climate factors, other possible routes, according to Townsend, include porous Tajik–China borders, with at least some passing through Pakistan–China border areas through the Karakoram Highway. With opium cultivation increasing in northern areas (specifically in bordering Badakhshan with more than 20 per cent increase) as compared to the traditional southern production provinces, the exports to China also increased from these areas via Central Asia.[41] Concerned about the drug trafficking and to curb channelizing funds to terrorist organizations, Chinese Assistant Foreign Minister Li Hui suggested at the sixth summit meeting of SCO in June 2006 that an anti-drug belt be built around Afghanistan.[42] This continues to be a concern for China.

CURRENT PHASE

The fifth phase of China's relations with Afghanistan witnessed multipronged measures that included intensifying contacts in Kabul at various levels. The current phase overlaps with the fourth phase and is predominantly influenced by the US decision to withdraw troops from Afghanistan and alternative arrangements at Kabul. As the drawdown began, China exhibited initiatives at four levels—unilateral, bilateral, trilateral and multilateral. These overlapped with the fourth phase as recounted above. The detaining of nearly 10 Chinese nationals by Afghanistan's National Directorate of Security in late 2020 for alleged espionage and infiltration into the Uighur groups was the highlight of one of the unilateral measures that China had undertaken in Kabul.[43] This, and other cases of China's involvement in Afghanistan, Nepal, Sri Lanka, Pakistan, Myanmar, Libya and other countries, suggest that despite its avowed policy of non-interference, China has been actively involved in interfering in the internal affairs of other countries.

A second indicator of China's growing influence can be seen in its links with the Taliban, specifically the Hekmatyar group and their confabulations at Kandahar, Kabul, Doha, Tianjin, Xian and other places. Even though China continued to deal with the Kabul government as mentioned above and despite its avowed policy of non-interference in internal affairs of other countries, China began structured dialogues with the Taliban representatives since 2014.[44] In 2014, officials of the Taliban in Doha visited Beijing. In May 2015, with the help of China, three senior Taliban representatives met in Urumqi with officials of the Afghan Ministry of Defense to discuss the terms of peace talks.

A third measure undertaken by China was the floating of

trilateral arrangement to include Pakistan and the Taliban of Afghanistan. This measure was significant in providing leverages to Inter-Services Intelligence agency of Pakistan to spearhead initiatives in Afghanistan and was visible in the indirect support that China exerted in terms of arms, drones, intelligence sharing to counter the Panjshir resistance movement in the last few months of 2021. In 2014, China promoted the first round of trilateral strategic talks between Afghanistan, Pakistan and China to be held in Kabul. In December 2017, the trilateral dialogue of foreign ministers of China, Afghanistan and Pakistan was held in Beijing to address the conflicts between Pakistan and Afghanistan and to discuss the issue of the extension of the China–Pakistan Economic Corridor (CPEC) to Afghanistan.

Finally, China also undertook to promote multilateral initiatives, such as the SCO–Afghanistan Contact Group, Istanbul Process, Himalayan Quad, and others. In 2014, China hosted the fourth meeting of foreign ministers of the Istanbul Process, involving parties for the reconstruction of Afghanistan. The fourth foreign ministerial conference of the Istanbul Process on Afghanistan (established in 2011 with 14 regional countries and 28 supporting partners was held in Turkey, Afghanistan and Kazakhstan) was held in Beijing in October 2014. On 10 July 2015, a preliminary meeting of concerned vice ministers was also held at Beijing. Other multilateral initiatives included China–Pakistan–Afghanistan–Tajikistan, China–Pakistan–Afghanistan–Uzbekistan and China–Afghanistan–Tajikistan–Russia. These were mainly intended to push through China's agenda in Afghanistan, minimize the costs for China in Xinjiang and also push Pakistan's influence further in the region, but under the Chinese guidance.

The current phase also witnessed intensifying role of the Special Envoys of Beijing towards Afghanistan for coordination with various capitals and the Taliban. China appointed a Special Envoy for Afghanistan—senior diplomats Sun Yuxi, Deng Xijun, Liu Jian and Yao Xiaoyong—to coordinate with Kabul but also with Pakistan, Russia, Turkey, Uzbekistan, Tajikistan and Iran as a part of its 'united front' drive.

At the 14 July 2021 SCO meet, foreign minister Wang Yi put forward five points as China's focal areas:

1. To prevent the US from shirking its responsibility
2. To prevent the resurgence of terrorist forces
3. To work together to boost the reconciliation process
4. To actively strengthen multilateral coordination
5. To continue to contribute to peace and reconstruction in Afghanistan[45]

On 28 July 2021, Chinese Foreign Minister Wang Yi met with Taliban leader Mullah Abdul Ghani Baradar in Tianjin. Wang stated: 'We hope the Afghan Taliban will make a clean break with all terrorist organizations including the ETIM and resolutely and effectively combat them to remove obstacles, play a positive role and create enabling conditions for security, stability, development and cooperation in the region.'[46] It was reported that while mentioning about economic development, Uighur leader Haji Furqan's extradition to China was raised. Given there was no progress on the last topic, there was Chinese reluctance to fund Afghan economic development. This is the context for foreign ministry spokesperson's comments on 16 August (as translated by the author): 'We hope that the Afghan Taliban will unite with all parties and ethnic groups in Afghanistan to establish a broad and inclusive political structure that suits Afghanistan's own national conditions and lay the foundation for the realization of lasting peace in Afghanistan. China expects these statements [of the Taliban on July 28] to be implemented.'[47]

On 2 September 2021, Assistant Foreign Minister, Wu Jianghao, had a phone conversation with Deputy Head of the Afghan Taliban's Political Office, Abdul Salam Hanafi, in Doha.[48] Wang Yi, again on 8 September, made three announcements, viz., $31 million in aid (grains, winter clothes and 3 million vaccines); management of refugees and migrants, as well as deepening anti-terrorism and anti-narcotics cooperation. Around the same time were President Xi Jinping's observations at the SCO and Collective Security Treaty Organization (CSTO) meeting in September 2021, the crux of which was to 'promote the smooth transition of the situation in Afghanistan as soon as possible; engage in contact and dialogue with Afghanistan; and to help the Afghan people tide over the difficulties. It is necessary to provide Afghanistan with humanitarian and anti-epidemic support'.[49] However, as we saw, China's assistance to Afghanistan has been meagre and calculated in nature.

ECONOMIC RELATIONS

This is also reflected in economy, trade and investment profile of China in Afghanistan. China's second-largest economic status, or its largest trading country status, or even its new image as global investor has no reflection in Afghanistan. For instance, in 2020, bilateral trade was $550 million which is a year-on-year decrease of 11.7 per cent. From 2019 to 2020, Afghanistan's total exports to China were $55.3 million and imports totalled $986.5 million. The previous year, in 2018, bilateral trade was worth $690 million—with $670 million in China's exports.[50] China's investments in Afghanistan were also negligible for a $16.9 trillion economy. China's total investment in Afghanistan stands at about $400 million. This is mainly in mining, telecommunications and road construction. Most of these investments are made by state-owned enterprises, those close to the party-state: China Railway 14th Bureau, China 19th Metallurgical, China Metallurgical Copper and Zinc, Huawei, ZTE and ZhengTong have participated in the construction of Afghanistan's telecommunications, power transmission and transformation lines, water conservancy and roads. In June 2018, China's Shuangdeng Group Co. Ltd and the Ministry of Energy and Water Resources of Afghanistan signed a 5.5 MW photovoltaic contract project in Daikondi Province.[51] According to Chinese assessments[52], the operating costs of Chinese companies is high as they have to deal with the central government, militants and local warlords, specifically in southern and western regions of eight dangerous provinces. Also, connectivity between resource exploitation centres and export sites are under-developed. There is also a lack of water for processing minerals before export. The infrastructure projects that were completed were mainly constructed by Chinese companies that have signed contracts with multilateral institutions like the International Monetary Fund or World Bank or Asian Development Bank. In 2020, Chinese companies signed a contract worth $110 million, with a year-on-year increase of 158.7 per cent, but later this saw a decline, given the transition in power. China demands that the Taliban provide security to Chinese companies. In December 2018, during the China–Afghanistan–Pakistan Trilateral Foreign Ministers' Dialogue held in Kabul, the three parties discussed the construction of cross-border railways from Peshawar to Kabul and Quetta to Kandahar, indicating that Afghanistan is actively seeking to integrate into the CPEC. However, it would be difficult for China to build the BRI, as Afghanistan has no political stability.[53]

COMPLEX RESPONSES TO THE US

Even though China and the US have worked together in the region with the common aim of countering the then Soviet Union and in fact supported the Mujahideen, China began taking a subtle critical position on the US role in Afghanistan. Earlier, at the SCO meetings, China nudged other states to pursue a 'withdrawal of US troops' position from the region. Later, as mentioned above, it began voicing concerns about the long-term presence of the US troops in the region and the implications to its security in Xinjiang and other western areas. However, the presence of the US in Afghanistan to a large extent deflected the Taliban/Al-Qaeda towards the US rather than China or other regional states.

Nevertheless, once the US decided to withdraw from Afghanistan after the Qatar deal in 2020 and later President

Joe Biden's formal announcement—initially partially and then completely—China began intensifying efforts to secure its interests as well as once again taking an explicit anti-US position in the hopes of combining with the countries of the region. For instance, on 8 July, Hua Chunying, the foreign ministry spokesperson reflecting on the US troops leaving the Bagram air base, said: 'It is like a thief leaving a house hastily before the owner returns home.'[54] In a press briefing on 17 August 2021, she added: 'Wherever the US sets foot, be it Iraq, Syria or Afghanistan, we see turbulence, division, broken families, deaths and other scars in the mess it has left. The US power and role is destructive rather than constructive... Solving problems with power and military means would only lead to even more problems.'[55]

Later, China's deputy representative to the UN responded to the UN resolution on Afghanistan on 30 August:

> The recent chaos in Afghanistan is directly related to the hasty and disorderly withdrawal of foreign troops. We hope that relevant countries will realize the fact that withdrawal is not the end of responsibility, but the beginning of reflection and correction... These countries should be responsible for what they have done in the past 20 years, and fulfill their commitments towards the peaceful rebuilding of Afghanistan.[56]

The academic and policy circles in China, too, have similar postures with ideological overtones. For instance, Tao Wenzhao, the US mission in Afghanistan should be seen not as a success but a failure.[57] According to another scholar, Zheng Yongnian, 'Afghanistan buried Western-style democracy.'[58] Zhang Yongle argued that the US departure from its previous informal 'imperial governance' model of extending control over the world through bases, dollar dominance and other policies and military occupation of Iraq and Afghanistan had led to several problems. Its departure from Afghanistan is the restoration of 'thrifty' tradition of imperial governance.[59]

Deal with the Taliban

China has been in constant touch with several groups in Afghanistan in pre-9/11 and post-9/11 period, including the time after the Taliban took over Kabul in August 2021. This provided China with a better understanding of the situation in Afghanistan and its policy responses.[60] Chinese analysts realize that even though the current Taliban has changed compared to what they were two decades ago, it is still not clear to the Chinese how popular are the Taliban, and whether they are 'progressive and civilized', in the words of Li Qingyan of China Institute of International Studies. According to Liu Zhongmin of the Shanghai International Studies University, the subjective promises of the Taliban to various countries and the objective condition of links with the Al-Qaeda and others need to be examined. Li suggested that the UN should provide legitimacy to the Taliban as a step towards diplomatic normalization with other countries. According to another Chinese scholar, Yun Sun, of the Stimson Institute, the US has no national interest in Afghanistan and that the withdrawal is aimed at countering China.[61] According to scholar Ye Hailin, the process of consolidation of the Taliban in Afghanistan is difficult. Even though the spiritual tradition of Afghans in opposing foreign interference united them, local kinship loyalties, differences between different factions, such as in Panjshir, and the slow process of centralization of power will take time to sort out. Hailin also warns of the Afghan characteristic of being an imperial graveyard.[62] Zhou Bo argued that China has the wherewithal to make its presence felt in Afghanistan through various measures.[63] These different assessments in China suggest the complex situation in Afghanistan and different pressures within China in addressing such challenges.

CONCLUSION

China's relations with Afghanistan have been tentative and tactical in nature, even though its intention has been to replace the then Soviet and currently the US influence in the region. This is due to the Chinese assessments of protecting Xinjiang from becoming unstable, lack of ethnic cohesion in Afghanistan, dangers of falling into the 'imperial graveyard' phenomenon that Afghanistan became known for historically, furthering regional dominance and others.

Clearly, China's policies in Afghanistan exhibited its nuanced policies with many others in the region, specifically with Russia and, more importantly, with the US. Working with the US since the 1970s against the Soviet Union provided China with leverages in Afghanistan through the Mujahideen. While the US relations with the Taliban became strained following the 9/11 attacks, China continued its equations with the various factions of the Taliban, including the Hekmatyar group. Even though China laid down the condition that the Taliban should curb Uighur activities, this has only divided the Taliban and the Al-Qaeda in terms of their equations with the ISKP.

While China floated several initiatives—unilateral, bilateral, trilateral and multilateral—these are intended to continue to negotiate, as is its practice, while preparing militarily and otherwise for regional dominance. Thus, China's aid for the reconstruction efforts in Afghanistan have been minimal, like its trade and investment profiles, even though its political decibels have been high. Compared to China, contribution by other coutnries, like India and Japan, to Afghanistan has been high and made difference at the ground level.

For the past few decades, China has been voicing ethnic reconciliation, non-interference, 'Afghan-owned, Afghan-led' process. However, uppermost in China's consideration is political stability in the contiguous Xinjiang. China's mobile military base in Tajikistan, the counterterror and counter-drug trafficking measures in the region are intended to block any infiltration and counter any challenge to the party-state rule in Xinjiang. As western sanctions on China's internment camps in Xinjiang have been intensified, it is expected that the party-state of China would make concerted efforts to counter these trends and the transition in Afghanistan will act as a crucial factor. It is likely that China could pressurize various groups in Afghanistan to create a buffer zone in Badakhshan, bordering Xinjiang, in the near future.

9

The Pashtun Movement in Pakistan and Its Afghanistan Strategy

Dr Shalini Chawla

'*Ye jo dehshat gardi hai, isske peechay wardi hai!* (The uniform is behind this terrorism!)'—this is one of the frequently heard slogans raised by supporters of the Pashtun Tahafuz Movement (PTM) in Pakistan.[1] Their lead anthem, *Da sanga azadi da*? (What kind of freedom is this?), is an emotion that aptly portrays the challenges faced by the Pakistani Pashtuns.[2] Slogans like these mark open defiance against the atrocities of the military targeting the Pashtuns in the Federally Administered Tribal Areas (FATA) and the Khyber Pakhtunkhwa (KPK) (the tribal areas were merged in the KPK province in May 2018).

The PTM, a civil rights non-violent movement demanding Pashtun rights, has attracted a large number of Pashtun youth and gathered strength through social media channels. The peaceful movement alleges serious human rights violations and alienation by the state authorities against the Pashtuns, who comprise the largest minority, making up approximately 15–20 per cent of Pakistan's population. The Pashtuns have been protesting against the targeted and encounter killings, forceful disappearances, arrests and harassment at multiple checkpoints in the region. The military rejects the claims of the PTM and tags the protesters as traitors.[3] The Pashtuns have faced discrimination in Pakistan for decades now and the leadership has always been conscious of the strong Pashtun sentiment that demanded a separate Pashtunistan at varied intervals, given the contentious status of the Durand Line. The Durand Line was a demarcation drawn by the British administrator Sir Henry Mortimer Durand in a pact with the Afghan Emir Abdur Rahman Khan in 1893. Pakistan inherited the border in 1947, but none of the Afghan regimes have accepted the border as the international boundary and the issue remains disputed.

Pakistan's strategy of seeking strategic depth in Afghanistan is rooted in two critical factors: first, its desire to control the Pashtun sentiment within Pakistan, which it views as an existential threat, and second, to have a pro-Pakistan regime in Afghanistan, which would eventually recognize the Durand Line as an international border. The Taliban takeover of Kabul in August 2021 was seen as a strategic victory by the Pakistani leadership and the religious fundamentalist groups in Pakistan. However, contrary to Pakistan's assumption, its strategy of having a Pakistan-friendly regime, the Taliban in Afghanistan does not seem to be fulfilling the former's strategic objectives.

The PTM is gaining momentum, Pashtun sentiment seems to be intensifying, the Taliban regime in Afghanistan has not shown any sign of recognizing the Durand Line and there have been disturbing news regarding skirmishes on the Durand Line between the Taliban and the Pakistani security forces. Videos of the Taliban seizing spools of barbed wire of the fence erected at the contentious Durand Line have gone viral on social media, adding to Pakistan's discomfort. In March 2017, Pakistan started fencing the 2,670-km-long border after there were repeated cross-border attacks on the civilians and military posts on Pakistan's side. The fencing was one of the major reasons contributing to the widening rift between the former Afghan President Ashraf Ghani and Islamabad. Pakistan in the beginning of 2022 claimed that it had completed the fencing of close to 94 per cent of the border.[4]

It would be useful to analyse the Pashtun movement in Pakistan and the state's response to the movement to be able to have a better understanding of Pakistan's Afghan policy.

THE PASHTUN SENTIMENT AND RISE OF THE PASHTUN MOVEMENT

The beginning of the non-violent Pashtun patriotic movement can be traced back to late 1920s in the North-West Frontier Province or NWFP, now FATA. Abubakar Siddique, a journalist with Radio Free Europe, in his book, *The Pashtun Question: The Unresolved Key to the Future of Pakistan and Afghanistan*, explained that the movement started after the British troops targeted and killed protesters of the movement called 'Organization for Promoting Reforms Among Afghans'. It was headed by Khan Abdul Ghaffar Khan (also known as Frontier Gandhi) and later came to be known as Khudai Khidmatgars or Servants of God.[5] The non-violent movement demanded an independent state for Pashtun, called the Pashtunistan. Khudai Khidmatgars inspired thousands of Pashtuns to adopt non-violent means to resist the British rule. Dinanath Gopal Tendulkar in his book, *Abdul Ghaffar Khan: Faith is a Battle*, quoted the oath taken by the Servants of God: 'Since God needs no service... I promise to serve humanity in the name of God. I promise to refrain from violence and from taking revenge. I promise to forgive those who oppress me or treat me with cruelty. I promise to devote at least two hours a day to social work.'[6]

The fact that the Pashtun movement was always inclined towards adopting non-violent means and demanding their political, social and economic rights, explains the character of the current Pashtun movement in Pakistan. The NWFP became part of the newly formed Pakistan in 1947. However, the tribal leaders in the region saw Pakistan as the continuation of the British rule and the Pashtun resistance as a part of Pakistan's evolution. Since 1947, the region has seen little development and faced consistent alienation from the federal government. For Pakistani leadership, the prospect of rise in Pashtun nationalism in Pakistan was perhaps the most significant threat to Pakistan's unity. Abubakar Siddique in his book very aptly described the

Pashtun identity: 'For at least the past six centuries, Pashtun history has been shaped by war, invasion and endemic local violence. These ordeals have shown that the Pashtun identity is resilient. While former nemeses such as that the Mughals exist today only in history books, the Pashtuns have survived to constitute a nation in the archetypal sense.'[7]

THE BIRTH OF THE PASHTUN TAHAFUZ MOVEMENT

In 2014, a small set of students of the Mehsud tribe formed a group called Mehsud Tahafuz Movement in Dera Ismail Khan. The objective of the movement was to campaign for the rights of their community, draw the attention of the state authorities towards the plight of the Pashtuns and demand clearance of the landmines in the Mehsud areas in Waziristan. While the practice of fake encounter killings was not new in Pakistan, what really caught social media by the storm was the killing of a 27-year-old owner of a clothes shop and an aspiring model, Naqeebullah Mehsud, by the Karachi police on 13 January 2018. The police team, commanded by Rao Anwar, claimed that Naqeebullah was associated with the Pakistani Taliban, Lashkar-e-Jhangvi and the Islamic State and his killing was a part of counterterror operation.[8] Naqeebullah had a significant fan following with no criminal background. PTM, under the leadership of its young and charismatic leader, Manzoor Pashteen, started holding a series of rally that attracted tens of thousands of Pashtuns whose relatives were missing or forcibly disappeared or arrested or killed during/after military's counterterrorism operations were conducted in FATA and KPK.

Secunder Kermani from BBC News in 2018 reported about the Pashtun struggles: 'A common thread is a feeling that Pashtuns have been caught between the militants and the military for years...on a single road there would be checkpoints by both the Taliban and the army. If you were clean-shaven the Taliban would accuse you of being pro-government, if you had a beard soldiers accused you of being an extremist."⁹

The PTM protest rallies were large but peaceful. Thousands of men, women and children held photos, birth certificates of their missing family members and demanded their release/ justice/ search. The Pashtuns found their voices through the PTM and admirable part of the movement was the amorphous leadership, which had no political linkage and no political agenda.

Ali Wazir, a PTM leader, wrote in *The Diplomat* on 27 April 2018 about the PTM's demands from the Pakistani leadership,

> We Pashtuns have been through hell... As the world's largest tribal society, the Pashtuns are known for their hospitality, commitment, and valor, yet we were falsely reduced to terrorist sympathizers despite the fact that we are their worst victims. Now that we [PTM] are protesting for change and demanding the state fulfill its most basic responsibilities, we are accused of treason and are being projected as enemies of the state.[10]

State Response to the PTM

The Pakistan state has tried to suppress the Pashtun voices and the region remains deprived of the national attention and the much-needed investment in the development. Rise of the PTM and its mass appeal was something unexpected for the Pakistan Army. History of Pakistan suggests that the military-run state has seldom opted to resolve the anti-state voices, concerns and complaints of the populace through a dialogue. The political and military culture in Pakistan has been inclined towards the use of brute force to curb the voices and any form of opposition for the State. Dismemberment of Pakistan and creation of Bangladesh in 1971 is a living example of the State's inability to address the grievances of the minorities. The State has always been troubled by strong ethnic loyalties and has seen them as a challenge to Islamic unity of the country. Hence, State's response for the PTM is no deviation from its past.

The military has publicly warned the PTM and said that its 'time is up'. The PTM members have been portrayed as traitors, agents of the enemy countries (India), anti-nationalists, etc.[11] It is ironic that Imran Khan's government (former), which had military support and consensus in critical decision-making, was in conversation to negotiate a peace deal with the deadly terrorist organization, Tehrik-i-Taliban Pakistan (TTP). Government's offer to TTP militants of granting amnesty in exchange of the TTP agreeing to giving up violence and arms triggered social outrage as the group was responsible for deadly terror attacks within Pakistan, including the assassination of Benazir Bhutto and killings at the Peshawar military school in 2014.

Use of Force

The military used force and tactics like enforced disappearances, arrests on the charges of sedition, hate speeches and encounters, etc., to deter the PTM supporters. While numerous cases came to the fore and several PTM leaders were arrested, one of the cases that caught international limelight was the arrest of Ali Wazir, (member of National Assembly and one of the leaders of the PTM). Wazir was arrested in December 2020 on the charges of making incendiary speeches against the state institutions at a PTM protest rally. The rally was organized to mark the anniversary of the TTP terror strike on December 2014 at the Army Public School in Peshawar, where more than 150 innocents were killed. Wazir had been behind bars for over a year, repeatedly denied bail and not allowed to attend parliamentary meetings. Although Wazir was granted bail in November 2021, he remains incarcerated as he stays implicated in another case.

Wazir's arrest caused strong reactions within the society, including lawmakers, journalists and analysts, apart from the PTM supporters within Pakistan. The State's hypocrisy was condemned specifically after Saad Rizvi, leader of a radical Islamist organization, Tehrik-e-Labbaik Pakistan (TLP), was released in November 2021.[12] The TLP has been staging violent anti-state protests, demanding the expulsion of the French ambassador from Pakistan on account of blasphemy.

Harassment tactics continue for Ali Wazir and his supporters. House of a senior lawyer, Qadir Khan, who is representing Ali Wazir, was raided by Sindh rangers in Karachi in January 2022. Mohsin Dawar, a Pashtun politician, termed this act as 'State terrorism' in his tweet: 'It seems Ali Wazir's incarceration was not enough; now his lawyer Qadir Khan and his family are terrorised and harassed through such despicable means. This is State terrorism. State agencies must desist from such tactics or they will face the wrath of the people.'[13]

Alamzeb Mehsud, one of the founding members of the PTM, was picked by the police in Karachi in 2019. His arrest led to massive social outcry and the Amnesty International issued a statement expressing concern of his disappearance. According to the PTM members, approximately 30,000 people have gone missing in the last 10 years from KPK and Balochistan.

Media Blackout

The Pashtuns have been very vocal about their grievances and demands from the government—seeking justice and basic civil rights. Their voices have unfortunately not been covered, and even when covered, they have often been misrepresented. The PTM coverage happens more on the social media rather than the Pakistani media houses. Allah Khan, a journalist in South Waziristan, who streams PTM events, on his Zhagh News (Voice News) and social media accounts, told VOA News, 'We journalists send stories on PTM to mainstream news outlets but they don't publish it… I was arrested and put in jail for 12 days for streaming the PTM protest before this last Ramadan [April 2021].'[14]

Pakistan has a history of military leadership coercing the media houses to fulfil their strategic objectives. Censorship of the PTM can be well understood in this background.

Blaming India

The PTM leaders and members are accused of working on behalf of India (and Afghanistan). This is the tactic the military is most confident about and feels would help it to rationalize and justify the State's unlawful and coercive actions against the PTM members. On 12 April 2018, Pakistan's Army Chief Qamar Javed Bajwan said that no anti-state agenda would be allowed under the garb of these protests.[15] On 14 April 2018, while speaking to the newly-graduated officers, Bajwa made a statement targeting India: 'Our enemies know they cannot beat us fair and square and have thus subjected us to a cruel, evil and protracted hybrid war. They are trying to weaken our resolve by weakening us from within.'[16]

The then Director General (DG) of Pakistan Army's media wing, Inter-Services Public Relations (ISPR), accused the PTM of receiving funds from the intelligence agencies of India and having an anti-state agenda. The PTM was now being portrayed as a part of India's Pakistan strategy, which, as perceived by Islamabad, aimed at the breakup of Pakistan. In April 2019, addressing a press conference at the General Headquarters, the DG ISPR (referring to the PTM) said, 'We want to do everything for the people [of tribal areas], but those who are playing in the hands of people, their time is up. Their time is up.' He further warned the PTM of strict action: '...the instructions of the army chief will be fully followed. People will not face any sort of problem and neither will any unlawful path be adopted.'[17]

PAKISTAN'S AFGHANISTAN STRATEGY

The Pashtun sentiments, calls for Pashtunistan and the growing popularity of the Pashtun movement in Pakistan have significantly guided Pakistan's desire to control Afghanistan. It will be interesting to look into Pakistan's objectives in Afghanistan, which have directed its actions and persistent patronizing of the terror groups/non-state actors.

After Pakistan's disintegration in 1971, the evolution of Pakistan's grand strategy was critical in shaping its strategic choices and alliances. The grand strategy after the 1971 India–Pakistan War incorporated two important objectives that decided the future course of action for the Pakistani leadership: first, to expand territory eastward (take Kashmir). This implied a rise in covert activities in Jammu and Kashmir, and added emphasis on radical Islam in the name of jihad. Thus, terrorism came to be adopted as a foreign policy tool. Nuclear weapons aimed at war prevention, providing a shield to the strategy of sub-conventional war; second, to expand their control westward (to gain leverage in Kabul). This implied creating 'strategic depth' in Afghanistan and also facilitating Pakistan-friendly governance.

Undoubtedly, Pakistan has been overly obsessed with the desire to 'gain strategic depth in Afghanistan'. The military and the intelligence agency, the Inter-Services Intelligence, authored and executed the policy of strategic depth since the late 1980s through the 1990s, when it strongly backed the Taliban. Till today, they deeply believe in having strong control over Afghanistan. At no stage was the policy of strategic depth logical or viable for Pakistan. Its adoption of the doctrine of strategic depth and, thus, control over Afghanistan is widely considered as a strategic blunder that actually facilitated Pakistan's drift into extremism and has not allowed it the option of altering its strategic calculus. In Pakistan's perception, the strategic depth policy has allowed it to maintain a conventional balance against India, but, on the other hand, this policy has led to a blowback in the form of intense militancy and extremism in Pakistan. There has been a change in the terminology regarding Pakistan's policy in Afghanistan and the term 'strategic depth' is not commonly used (now), but the underlying objectives pretty much remain unaltered.

Pakistan has been seeking rationalization of its control and influence in Afghanistan owing to the following reasons:

1. The lingering Afghanistan–Pakistan border issue based on the Durand Line, which separates the tribal areas of KPK of Pakistan from Afghanistan. No Afghan regime, including the Rabbani government and the Taliban regime in the '90s, has ever accepted the legitimacy of the border drawn by the British in 1893.
2. The issue of Pashtun nationalism, which demanded a separate Pashtunistan, has been critical. In Pakistan's view, control and influence over Afghanistan by a Pashtun-dominated (essentially Taliban) government would, therefore, reduce the demand for a separate Pashtunistan (within Pakistan) and yet have the Pashtuns under Pakistan's control.
3. Afghanistan provided Pakistan a safe haven to train the Islamist militants, such as the Harkat-ul-Mujahideen, Jaish-e-Muhammad and Lashkar-e-Taiba.
4. A pro-Pakistan government is a must to undermine the Indian influence in Afghanistan and that has always been a priority for Pakistan.

RECENT DEVELOPMENTS

Pakistan's support to the Afghan Taliban and the Haqqani network has been one of the critical factors contributing to the resurgence of the Taliban in 2003–04 (when the US was distracted in the Iraq War), strengthening of the Taliban, weakening of the democratic regime and failure of the US military operations in Afghanistan. Pakistan facilitated the negotiations between the Taliban and the US (excluding the Ghani government) and rejoiced post signing of the US–Taliban agreement on 29 February 2020. The sudden US exit, collapse of the democratic government and victory of the Taliban in August 2021 were seen as major strategic achievements by Islamabad.

Attempt to Equate the Pashtuns with the Taliban

Then Prime Minister (PM) Imran Khan tried to equate the Pakistani Pashtuns with the Afghan Taliban, and build a narrative that the Taliban is getting support from the tribal areas of Pakistan. In his speech in the United National General Assembly on 24 September 2021, he said:

> Then all along the tribal belt bordering Afghanistan— Pakistan's semi-autonomous tribal belt—where no Pakistan army had been there since our independence, people had strong sympathies with the Afghan Taliban, not because of their religious ideology but because of Pashtun nationalism, which is very strong. Then there are three million Afghan refugees still in Pakistan, all Pashtoons, living in the camps... They all had affinity and sympathy with the Afghan Taliban.[18]

On 11 October 2021, the PM, while speaking to the digital news agency, Middle East Eye, claimed that the Pakistani Pashtuns were sympathetic towards the Taliban owing to their ethnic affiliation: 'The Pashtuns on this side [Pakistan] were completely sympathetic with the [Taliban] Pashtuns [in Afghanistan]—not because of the religious ideology but because of Pashtun ethnicity and nationality, which is very strong.'[19]

The statement fetched immense criticism for Imran Khan from the Pakistani Pashtuns who suffered during military's counter-terror operations and have been frequently targeted by the Afghan Taliban and the TTP. Mohsin Dawar, who has been actively championing the cause of the Pashtun and was elected to the Pakistan National Assembly in 2018 as a member of the PTM, submitted a resolution against Imran Khan to the National Assembly, demanding an apology from the PM for equating the Pashtuns to the Taliban. In the resolution, Dawar's statement reflected anger of the Pashtuns against Imran's position: 'This is not the first time the PM has tried to portray the Taliban as representatives of Pashtuns. Baseless and racist generalizations like these have to be called out.'[20]

Fencing of the Durand Line

There have been repeated instances of clashes between the Pakistan military and the Taliban on the Afghanistan–Pakistan border. The fencing of the Durand Line was strongly opposed by the Ghani government and people from both sides whose families are divided between the two countries.

The contested Afghanistan–Pakistan border has always been a deep concern for the Pakistani leadership. The ruling elites have always been apprehensive about the Afghans claiming their right on the Pashtun areas of Pakistan. By putting up the fence, Pakistan wanted to physically demarcate the border and, in a way, put an end to the contentious nature of the border. Also, the leadership has been of the view that by fencing the borders, it could potentially reduce free flowing movement between the two sides, and restrict and monitor the support for the Pashtuns in Pakistan.

However, Pakistan miscalculated the Taliban's position on the border and contrary to its expectations, the Taliban have opposed the fence from the time they took over Kabul. Soon after the Taliban claimed victory, Taliban spokesman Zabiullah Mujahid said: 'The new Afghan government will announce its position on this issue [the fence along the Durand Line]. The fencing has separated people and divided families. We want to create a secure and peaceful environment on the border so there is no need to create barriers.'[21]

The Taliban have viewed the fence as a divider between the two nations, and Mujahid, while giving an interview to a local YouTube channel in Kabul, said, 'The issue of the Durand Line is still an unresolved one, while the construction of fencing itself creates rifts between a nation [sic] spread across both sides of the border. It amounts to dividing a nation.'[22]

The Pakistan government, on the other hand, has acknowledged the problem but has tried to downplay the issue. The then Foreign Minister Shah Mahmood Qureshi said, 'Certain miscreants are raising this issue unnecessarily, but we are looking into it and we are in contact with the Afghan government. Hopefully, we would be able to resolve the issue diplomatically.'[23]

CONCLUSION

In Pakistan, the Pashtuns are united and demand their rights from the ruling elites. The determination and appeal of the PTM is admirable. However, the response of the leadership remains indifferent and harsh, and there have been no signs of any change. The PTM has challenged the legitimacy of the military and the support base for the movement has expanded beyond the traditional boundaries. The PTM protests have attracted support from the Left wing Awami Workers Party. This is unacceptable in a military-run State, which consistently fears that the Pashtun issue has the potential to divide the country. The critical question is, 'Will the State coercion throttle the spirit of the PTM?' It does not look like it will, and the movement is fetching support from diverse sections. Gul Bukhari, a Pakistani journalist, said, 'Pakistan's powerful Pashtun Tahaffuz Movement is no longer just about the Pashtuns. In the past year, this extraordinarily brave and non-violent movement has brought into its fold the support of disaffected Sindhis, Mohajirs and the Baloch, who have also suffered enforced disappearances for decades.'[24]

The desire to contain the Pashtun nationalism and solve the disputed Durand Line issue in its favour contributed to Pakistan's Afghan strategy. The Taliban regime came into power in Kabul, but both the issues continue to pose serious challenges for Islamabad—neither has the Pashtun nationalism been contained nor is the new Taliban regime ready to accept the Durand Line as an international border.

Part III

AFGHANISTAN AND INDIA

10

Afghanistan and Its Effect on India's Strategic Security

Lt Gen. (retd) Syed Ata Hasnain

The eruption of crisis in Afghanistan, even as the world was emerging from the scourge of the coronavirus pandemic, threatened to once again bring turbulence to an already restive nation and region that affects the security of the world at large. The Afghan National Security Forces (ANSF) failed to live up to their promise. The doctrine 'Afghan led, Afghan owned and Afghan controlled' could not endure in its original intent, although in a pyrrhic way, the Taliban's arrival spelt the same.

The Taliban 2.0 unilaterally took control of Kabul and the rest of the country even before the mandated date of the US withdrawal. Pakistan's role and influence in the progression of events was fairly marked. Besides the local turbulence that the Taliban's return brought, it's the geopolitical and geostrategic impact on the South Asia and Central Asia regions, and to an extent on the world, that is of much concern. Many of the factors arising from the changed milieu impinge on India and its security considerations, too. That is also largely because the emerging situation in Afghanistan is considered to be mainly influenced by Pakistan, and China too has considerable interests there.

The US has been replaced by a plethora of influence seekers, with nations such as China, Pakistan, Russia, Turkey, Iran and some of the Central Asian Republics (CARs) in the lead. India has been characteristic by its absence. The US interest in the region continues despite its lack of physical presence, as it cannot ignore the developments there; the geostrategic significance of the region makes this obvious. However, its approach is still tentative and uncertain. International engagement with the Taliban continues primarily to seek options and prevent a humanitarian crisis in Afghanistan, which will have its own security implications. For India, which did not have a Plan B all these years, its over-reliance on the security it sought from the US presence could prove to be costly. However, nimbleness in policy and lack of any dogma regarding the past could help India recover the situation; its relationship with the people of Afghanistan remains its greatest asset.

HOW NON-TALIBAN GOVERNMENTS IN KABUL PROVED TO BE AN ASSET TO INDIA

Twenty years of friendly regimes in Afghanistan, along with the umbrella presence of the US security forces, has been helpful to India in no small way. The regimes could not be considered as friends of Pakistan, although they depended on it for many things. Pakistan invested heavily in cultivating elements in Afghanistan through the '80s and '90s. This ensured that its western borders were secure and an advantage of 'strategic depth' (Pakistan's terminology) was obtained with a pro-Pakistan regime in place, while the Taliban existed in power. It left Pakistan free to pursue various strategies in the East against India. Through the '80s, Pakistan worked on developing the tool of radical Islamic ideology to use the same to its advantage in extending its claim as a potential leader of the Islamic world. It was largely responsible for the clarion call for Islamic Jihad in 1980, which brought thousands of transnational, non-state actors to fight the Soviets at the behest of the US and Saudi Arabia.

It was the same line of strategy that was subsequently employed in Kashmir, while laying the groundwork in the '80s and exploiting the same when the proxy conflict was initiated in 1989. The virtual genocide of the Kashmiri Pandits was a manifestation of this strategy, which over the last 30 years also saw a sea change in the ideology of Kashmir, from the inclusive Sufi belief to the more obscurantist Islamic belief. This helped 'separatism' and 'alienation', two aspects on which Pakistan based its proxy war. The Taliban 1.0, which was created by Pakistan in the seminaries of the Afghan–Pak border to ultimately contest and then rule Afghanistan, came to power in 1996 and spelt major advantage for Pakistan[1]; it became an extension of the Pakistan's deep state, which controls the strings of power in Pakistan and directs its security and economic policies.

The moment the US-led Operation Enduring Freedom commenced and a defeated Taliban 1.0 was evicted from power in December 2001, the scenario changed substantially. Firstly, the presence of the US forces and those of the other constituents of the International Security Assistance Force (all democratic countries lined against obscurantist ideologies) ensured that it was no longer an advantage to Pakistan. A substantial part of the Pakistani security forces (Army and the Frontier Constabulary) had to be deployed and orientated towards the security of the West. At least two corps-sized forces remained committed to their primary task of holding and defending that border. The US-led Global War on Terrorism (GWOT) focussed considerably on Pakistan. It was not just the presence of Al-Qaeda leader Osama bin Laden or that of the top Taliban leadership within Pakistan, which brought it to glare, but also the networks that transcended the Durand Line. Networks related to finances, drugs, arms and ideology became the main drivers of irregular conflicts. The potential of these reduced considerably once Taliban 1.0 was overthrown in 2001, thus giving Indian security a reprieve.

India went on an overdrive through its soft power capability reviving the 'Kabuliwala' image of the Pashtun. It led to $3 billion worth of Indian investment in Afghanistan's infrastructure and people.[2] India built over 200 public and private schools, sponsored over 1,000 scholarships and hosted over 16,000 Afghan students with the hope that a post-US withdrawal Afghanistan would be a more inclusive, stable and middle-path nation, seeking good for its citizens through an enduring people-to-people relationship. Relations between Afghanistan and India received a major boost in 2011 with the signing of a Strategic Partnership Agreement, Afghanistan's first since the Soviet invasion of 1979. The Salma Dam, the Parliament House at Kabul and the Delaram–Zaranj Highway, besides 400 smaller but significant projects, could be completed or nearly completed because of the strategic agreement. The opening of the Indian consulates at Kandahar, Mazar-e-Sharif, Jalalabad and Herat meant extension of people-to-people contacts, greater visa outgo and flourishing medical tourism. The Indian Army trained over a 1,000 officer cadets and many more soldiers for the ANSF. This relationship has been flourishing over 20 years and all the above factors have added substantially to India's security considerations.

Pakistan at all times had to consider three areas for its security; Afghanistan in the west, India in the east (with specific reference to Jammu and Kashmir) and the internal security domain within itself, especially after it upset its own applecart by attempting to cultivate terrorists as trans-border strategic assets. In due course, these turned on Pakistan itself in the form of the Tehrik-e-Taliban Pakistan or TTP. Thus, Pakistan's three areas of security focus had to be carefully calibrated to accord the right priority for the concerned situation. The deep-set proxy hybrid war that it has been fighting against India may not have received the optimum attention because of inherent fears of crossing the Indian threshold and the US–India presence in Afghanistan. The altered situation could embolden Pakistan's deep state to think differently and recalibrate its objectives and strategy. This will have an impact on India's security, especially since the collusion between Pakistan and China appears to be of a higher order.

EFFECTS OF REGIME CHANGE IN KABUL

If any nation wrung its hands in glee on 15 August 2021, it was Pakistan. Its 20 years of two-timing Afghanistan came to an end. With its embassy intact, its protégés (the Taliban) in place, along with the strong proxies within the Taliban (the Haqqanis), Pakistan's days under the sun were beginning. The 20-year hiatus of not having control over the Afghanistan government in no way diluted Pakistan's larger strategy. In fact, it bided its time effectively and displayed sufficient stamina to await the opportune moment. What affects the region the most is Pakistan's ambition of being the centre of Islamic power. The deep state within Pakistan imagines this as the only way that Pakistan can realize its ambition of being counted—first in the Islamic world and then in the international community. Getting secession of J&K, keeping India on tenterhooks through its re-energized policy of a 'thousand cuts' and constantly seeking opportunities to embarrass India will remain on the cards.

Afghanistan's sudden turnaround affects India's security in different ways. First, it's all about the threat from terror, the very reason why the US decided to stay 20 years in that country. This needs detailed analysis. Second is the expansion of Chinese influence into a region where it was thus far a marginal player. Third is the rise in stakes for Pakistan, which impinges directly on India's interests. Fourth is the geopolitics of the New Great Game (NGG), which could now take a different turn. In fact, the NGG in the environment of the post-pandemic world order could have unpredictable factors influencing it and its outcome will surely have deep impact. Fifth, South Asian politics, reasonably predictable in the last 20 years, throws up possibilities for deeper effect on the neighbouring countries with the outcomes, which can be quite unpredictable.

The US presence in Afghanistan was always considered a positive factor for India's security. The US is also India's strategic partner for the Indo-Pacific in a far more enlarged way. This is not a zero sum game of security because the context of cooperation differs quite widely. India's concerns are many, both with China and Pakistan in the centre, with near equal focus on both. For the US, it is all about the rise of China. The US is taking a risk lowering its priority of the Middle East and the region of the NGG in order to focus on its priority domain, the Indo-Pacific. India, on the other hand, is concerned about China and its threats but is unwilling to reduce its focus from the threats emanating from the cardinal direction of the West. This phenomenon too needs a greater analysis.

TERRORISM, PROXIES AND HYBRID WAR

With Taliban reluctant to alter the basics of its foundation and only offer cosmetic changes to obtain some financial reprieve, the world is apprehensive. Islamic radicalism, which has been diluted to some extent in the last three years, is likely to get a shot in the arm even as it witnesses a downturn in the Middle East. Pakistan's original intent of creating the Taliban to control Afghanistan, spread its influence in the region of the NGG and use the strategic depth to its advantage against India in more ways than one has not changed. The Pakistan deep state always imagined this as the way it could hurt Indian interests too, disallowing access to CARs, while building a surge of Islamic radical ideology, which could unite the Islamic elements in the region including an outreach into J&K.

Even before Taliban 2.0 came back to power, Northern Afghanistan started witnessing a gravitation of terrorist elements. The sub-region has been lawless, with little government control, hence, giving scope for extension of illegal elements to establish their hold. Strategically, it's a sub-region close to Central Asia and not too far from the Chinese region of Xinjiang. The potential for spread of such an influence of terrorism is high in these areas that have disaffected populations, weak governance and security. There is also the scope for spread of networks of the Golden

Crescent (the narcotics networks), which generate enough money for active terror networks to thrive financially. Pakistan, as a state sponsor of terror with numerous outfits under its control, such as Lashkar-e-Taiba (LeT) and Jaish-e-Mohammad (JeM), is the net benefiter. Some anti-establishment outfits, such as TTP and Lashkar-e-Jhangvi, are also present in the country.

It is not as if Pakistan is dependent on all the above for resources to pursue proxy war in J&K or elsewhere in India. It is the inspiration from the long struggle and the eventual victory of the Pakistan-backed Taliban that could be used to muster resources and spread radical influence, not just in J&K but other parts of South Asia, too, including Sri Lanka, Maldives and Bangladesh as well. At the back is also the latent Pakistani desire to be the leader of the Islamic world.

The Pakistan deep state (Pakistan Army and Inter-Services Intelligence) does not appear to perceive too much worry from the potential spread of radicalism within Islam, where elements such as Tehreek-e Labayak carry on their activities with legitimacy. The fact that none of the terror related entities have scored at the electoral polls to establish a political stranglehold seems to be a solace for the deep state. The fact that for four years, one-third of the Pakistan Army was battling Islamic extremists within Pakistan as part of Operation Zarb-e-Azb is not considered as important by Pakistan.[3]

The potential to train terrorists for proxy war in neighbouring territories has now increased within the space of ungoverned Afghanistan. The cauldron has the potential to cause major problems for India, China and Russia (in the CARs in particular). The US presence had ensured a degree of clampdown on transnational criminal and narcotic networks; presence of intelligence agencies of a super power has an effect of caution on such networks. With that caution now removed, networks connected to illegal finance will be able to give a boost to terrorism. In fact, in many ways, the overall failure of the GWOT is likely to stoke such activities.

Lastly, it is important for India to realize that even as it focuses north towards China in terms of its security, the West will remain a potent threat as before. Pakistan itself is unstable with its polity bereft of any further options for democratic governance. The deep state is employing disruption within the country as a ploy to retain its unauthorized power. Pakistan's economy is in shambles as much as Afghanistan's. Together they offer a continuum of land mass and population base that is ripe for implosion, the kind not witnessed for long. India needs to war-game its options, should it confront such an eventuality.

EXPANSION OF CHINA'S INFLUENCE

The vacuum in Afghanistan caused by the US withdrawal has facilitated the move of China into a region it does not understand too well but nevertheless wishes to control and influence as part of its larger ambition. China is an important stakeholder in the NGG, which like the 'great game' of the early twentieth century has a lot to do with influence. Besides influence, it's the control over infrastructure (including pipelines, railway and roads), energy and, most importantly, ideology. Left without deliberate efforts to influence, there is likely to be gravitation of radical elements into the region, particularly the CARs.

China is most uncomfortable with the creeping threats towards the restive Xinjiang region. It would perceive that its adversaries would treat this as China's Achilles Heel. It is fully aware that India has good relations with the CARs and also the people of Afghanistan. It automatically follows that China would like to see the area devoid of Indian influence and linkages, even though India and China both form part of the Shanghai Cooperation Organization. The major concern lies in the fact that China is likely to be greatly influenced in Central Asia by Pakistan and the latter will no doubt attempt to cultivate an agenda totally against Indian interests.

China could also work towards excluding India from a

potential manoeuvre through Iran to link up with the CARs and the International North–South Transport Corridor. These are areas India has to work with on higher priority and also decisively. Our relationship with Iran is extremely important, for both access to the CARs and for balancing Sunni extremism in Afghanistan. Convergence of Indo-Iran interests may never have been so close. India's close relationship with Saudi Arabia and the UAE must not come in the way of its working in sync with Iran. What is important for India to project is the necessity of international relationships with multiple players, without harming the interests of any of them.

The possibility of China viewing Pakistan's activities in J&K as being in convergence with its own interests too is higher than ever before. This is because China has probably found disconcerting India's rise, its partnerships and its increasing strategic confidence as important factors in taking bolder security related decisions. J&K did not find much traction in Chinese diplomacy of the recent past. However, this new situation could bring Sino-Pak cooperation to tie India down in managing J&K's security. China has to remain mindful that a potential conventional conflict between India and Pakistan has all the chances of sucking it into the vortex, which might not turn out to be in its interest. Thus, while playing Pakistan as a foil against India, it has to ensure that things do not go overboard. The Russians who support and cooperate with the Chinese may not find it to their interests to see China intimidate India either in conjunction with Pakistan or by themselves.

We need not view China only from a negative point of view. It may not wish to see the NGG region unstable with potential threats to influence its Uighur population in Xinjiang. Its Belt and Road Initiative arteries are also vulnerable. The feasibility of China going overboard to assist Pakistan in its strategic intent is unlikely, and locking horns with India there may prove counter-productive. In the spirit of adjustment, India should consider engaging China on this. It need not be discouraged by China's knee jerk response at not attending the meeting of national security advisors in New Delhi in November 2021. It continues being an evolving situation.

IMPACT ON J&K

The region of India closest to the NGG is J&K (especially when we include Gilgit–Baltistan as per the Indian Parliamentary resolution of 1994). In fact, the NGG's side show is considered as being played out in J&K with the ideological intent of Pakistan— the spread of obscurantist Islam to dilute J&K's inclusive and secular existence, and convert it to radical ideology. Yet, given India's major concerns about the situation in Afghanistan and these directly impacting J&K, it is clear that the analogy of 1989 does not apply today. In those years, India was taken by complete surprise as none contemplated Pakistan's intent and the resources it could harness directly or indirectly from Afghanistan. The experience gained by India's security forces and intelligence agencies through 30 years stands it in good stead today.

It is neither the human resources (terror elements) nor the US arms and equipment left behind in Afghanistan that should worry India. The worry should be about the inspiration from the success of the Taliban against the sophisticated war machine of the West, the ability to retain stamina over 20 years and successfully resist any attempt at dilution of radical ideology. This inspiration can stir mass sentiment if instigated. While the Taliban government is not showing any overt animosity towards India and is in fact inviting Indian humanitarian aid, there can be no guarantee of what its security outlook will be. Either it will follow a very independent policy without enmeshing itself in the complex power games that Pakistan is playing, or simply be guided by Pakistan. At some point of time, there will be internal corrections, whereby Afghan interests will become the priority and will not clash with Indian stakes. However, in the short to medium term, while Pakistan probably guides Afghanistan's policy, an anti-India thrust is likely to continue.

Pakistan has attempted to refocus on J&K rather early after the turn of events in Afghanistan in the hope to regain traction. It has tried a twofold strategy. First, the use of proxies to target the minorities since this is the softest option to provide a short-term gain of proving Pakistan's relevance in the context of the changing situation in J&K. Second is an attempt to rebuild capability to strike in some of the areas in which terrorist activity has been limited for some years. The concentration on the Pir Panjal and the sudden flurry of operations in Bandipura prove this. The Indian response has been swift, although there have been fatalities. Pakistan's intent of establishing a stronghold in the Pir Panjal mountain range appears to have passed for the moment. Short of an all-out uprising in Kashmir, which will need leadership and resources, there is very little Pakistan may be able to do in the near future. This is the time for India to redouble its goodwill and outreach, improve administration and ready itself for the re-introduction of democracy in J&K, which is likely to happen in less than two years' time.

SOUTH ASIA AND THE INDO-PACIFIC

The sudden exit of the US and abandoning of Afghanistan has also been caused by the urgency it perceived in shifting its focus to the Indo-Pacific. It signed the AUKUS[4] and mounted a diplomatic initiative to take India along through the sphere of the 'Quad', which remains a non-military initiative for cooperation. For India, as the midway region between the NGG and the Indo-Pacific, it is essential to keep its strategic relationships right. First, it needs to ensure that its neighbourhood remains stable and any attempts to embroil it in local conflicts have to be curbed. It has to keep a tight control over external influence in the region if it wishes to retain its dominant strategic position in the Indian Ocean. Second, its attention has to remain balanced between the Indo-Pacific and the NGG region. For the former, the US is the main strategic partner and for the latter, it is Russia. Thus, the visit of the Russian president to New Delhi on 6 December 2021 and of the foreign ministers of the CARs on 20 December 2021 did not come a moment too soon. While India will be badgered for attention towards the Indo-Pacific, its security considerations for the NGG region must always remain balanced.

SUMMARY OF ACTIONS BY INDIA

The following issues spell some of the priorities for India's strategic security:

1. Maintain an outreach to the Taliban government with humanitarian aid and allow the people-to-people relationship to continue and develop. An online visa system should be considered.
2. Identify Indian stakes in the NGG and continue to maintain effective consultation with Russia and the CARs.
3. Iran remains one of the crucial countries. Relations with Iran have seen ups and downs in recent years. We will need to overcome reservations regarding the US objections and continue to pursue our interest-based relationship with Iran. Access to Afghanistan for humanitarian aid and maintenance of the facilities set up under soft power outreach should be done through the Iran route. This should be used for progressively improving relations with the Taliban.
4. We should expect some manifestation of Pakistan's attempts to regain traction in J&K. Our response should be strong, measured and surgical to ensure no loss of gains made in outreach in J&K.
5. We should ensure that the existing networks that support terror are systematically dismantled over the next few years. Reintroduction of democracy in J&K will help to counter Pakistan's moves in promoting alienation against India.
6. The tendency to consider only J&K as the territory where

Pakistan's strategies are likely to play out should be avoided. The whole of India is a likely playing field for Pakistan's deep state, especially relating to fourth and fifth generation warfare.

7. Pakistan's efforts will be based upon collusion with China to offset the chances of response from India, should the threshold be crossed. India should not be intimidated by this approach as China is unlikely to trigger any actions over which it may not have control.
8. India must maintain a strong relationship with the important Gulf countries to ensure an effective pushback against the potential rise of radical ideologies from the Middle East to Central and South Asia.
9. As an important player in the post-pandemic emerging global order, India has to balance its relationships in order to play an effective role in the Indo-Pacific as well as the NGG region. It should accordingly develop its relationships with the big powers.

The Taliban 2.0's arrival has changed the dynamics of international politics, but its current dispensation must not be considered permanent. Internal dynamics will determine the ultimate direction that Afghanistan will take. There is no permanence about the close coterie of powers that are perceived close to the Taliban 2.0. This is an evolving situation that will continue to have different manifestations. It needs flexibility of policy and a quick grasp of the complexities of phenomena, such as the NGG, to survive and emerge stronger.

11

India's Role in the Last Two Decades in Afghanistan

Amb. Jayant Prasad

On 4 January 1950, the landmark Treaty of Friendship was concluded between India and Afghanistan. It provided that the two countries respect the independence and rights of each other and that they would maintain everlasting peace and friendship.[1] During the Mujahideen rule in Afghanistan after the fall of the People's Democratic Party of Afghanistan regime (1992–96) and the rule of Taliban 1.0 in Afghanistan (1996–2001) when Afghanistan was conflict-ridden, there was a hiatus between India and the Afghan people. They felt that India had turned away from them. In the past two decades, India made amends and reconnected with the Afghan people through its development partnership, especially its small development projects, implemented through the length and breadth of the country, from Badakhshan to Kandahar and Herat to Nangarhar.

India has been, by far, the biggest contributor regionally in Afghanistan's development effort in the past two decades, despite the handicaps of not enjoying continuity with Afghanistan, the obstructive behaviour of Pakistan in prohibiting the export of Indian merchandise overland through its territory, preventing the use of the shortest route to Afghanistan, and India's resource constraints as a developing country. Afghans regarded India's contribution highly. They knew India sought a sovereign, united and peaceful Afghanistan, on the track of sustainable development, and that India's development partnership meant to assist the Afghan people. According to the annual confidential political surveys and opinion polls conducted by the Afghan Centre for Socio-economic and Opinion Research (ACSOR) as well as international polling agencies, a vast majority of Afghan respondents had a 'favourable' or 'very favourable' view of India's role in Afghanistan.

THE BEGINNING

Twenty years ago, there was no official Indian presence in Kabul. Within a week of the Taliban 1.0 abandoning the seat of government, an Indian contingent led by Ambassador Satinder Lambah, and comprising Joint Secretary of the Ministry of External Affairs, Arun Singh, the retired Vice Chief of the Indian Army, Lt Gen. R.K. Sawhney, and the Chief Liaison Officer (later ambassador), Gautam Mukhopadhyaya, arrived in Kabul on 21 November 2001. An army medical team of five professionals, including two doctors, carrying five tonnes of medicines, accompanied this team. The first disbursement of salary to the medical staff deployed at the Indira Gandhi Children's Hospital in Kabul was made out of Ambassador Lambah's briefcase. Word had quickly gotten around about the arrival of the Indian team, for when it reached the chancery building in Shahr-e-Nau, the entire local staff of the Indian embassy turned up to welcome the team.

Following the setting up of the Afghan Interim Administration and the election of President Hamid Karzai in October 2004, India pursued the following overall objectives in Afghanistan: the ending of the use of Afghan territory for the terrorist groups from Jammu and Kashmir (J&K), minimizing external interference in Afghanistan, encouraging the constitution of an inclusive and broad-based government, launching reconstruction and development activities with India's active participation, encouraging an active role for the United Nations (UN) and rapidly developing an effective Indian presence in Afghanistan.

In contrast to the considerable vicissitudes in India–Afghanistan bilateral relationship between 1979 and 2001, India enjoyed considerable success in pursuing a set of objectives. These included establishing an effective diplomatic presence, first through the appointment of a special envoy, followed quickly by setting up an appropriately staffed embassy and four consulates (in Herat, Mazar-e-Sharif, Jalalabad and Kandahar); linking Delhi and Kabul by air (first through Ariana Afghan Airlines, later supplemented by Indian Airlines, and Indian and Afghan private airlines); providing humanitarian assistance (first by holding a Jaipur foot camp, rehabilitating the Indira Gandhi Institute of Child Health, Kabul, setting up Indian Medical Missions in Kabul and the four major cities, and supplying wheat in the form of fortified biscuits for school-going children); contributing effectively to the reconstruction and development of Afghanistan through infrastructure projects and cooperation programmes; and sustaining a strong presence in Afghanistan through interaction and exchanges across almost all administrative, social and economic activities.

Quite quickly, as a significant donor to Afghanistan's reconstruction (ninth in aggregate commitments), India secured a place on the high table, with its views and contributions sought in discussions at United Nations Assistance Mission in Afghanistan and within the Joint Coordination and Monitoring Board, which oversees the implementation of the Afghan Compact, a strategy for rebuilding Afghanistan, agreed in London in January 2006.

This was in sharp contrast to India's exclusion from deliberations on Afghanistan's future held under the UN's aegis from 1997–2001 under the 'Six-plus Two' format, comprising the six contiguous States bordering Afghanistan (China, Iran, Pakistan, Tajikistan, Turkmenistan and Uzbekistan), plus the United States and Russia.[2]

FOCUS OF INDIA'S DEVELOPMENT EFFORTS

India's effort to rebuild Afghanistan over the past two decades went beyond financial support or constructing the Afghan Parliament, the Afghanistan–India Friendship Dam on the Harirud River, building roads, erecting transmission lines and a power station to bring electricity to Kabul, and executing the small development projects for education, health, micro-irrigation and solar electrification. India contributed to building institutions and developing human resources, training Afghan public officials and providing the country with a new generation of educated and skilled workers through the massive Indian scholarship programme there.

During this period of intense involvement, India's message to the Afghan political leadership had never been divisive. India consistently advised leaders of different ethnicities to work in cohesion with others for peace, stability, nation-building and what they considered the best for Afghanistan. India never sought a political or military role in Afghanistan in the past 20 years. In return for its development effort, India gained goodwill. It won back traction with Afghan men and women from all parts of the country. Yet, Pakistan is affronted by India's development role in Afghanistan, simply because the Afghan people appreciated it.

As a result of India's vigorous development programme since 2001, the Afghan people were convinced that India has a strong stake in the stabilization of their country and that it wants them to stand on their own feet and make their own decisions. They know India has worked for a sovereign and peaceful Afghanistan, on the track of sustainable growth. They believe there is a consonance between Indian and Afghan objectives, and that India regards Afghan successes equally as much as its own. India remained reluctant about the political accommodation of individuals, groups or Islamist entities associated with Al-Qaeda/Daesh and their associates since it believed this would subvert the Afghan nation and undermine the rights of the Afghan people, besides adversely affecting India's security interests.

An 'exit strategy' defined the US objective in Afghanistan since 2009. Since Afghanistan is in India's extended neighbourhood, India could not embrace any exit strategy and continued its constructive engagement until the Indian Embassy and its consulates were able to do so. India had welcomed Afghanistan's entry into the South Asian Association of Regional Cooperation in its New Delhi Summit in 2007. India, therefore, continued to stand by the people of Afghanistan and sustain its stabilization efforts with a long-term commitment.

THE SECURITY ASPECT

An Afghanistan that is subverted or destabilized or in the hands of terrorist networks will be a catastrophe for the region and the world. The 9/11 attacks amply illustrated this, as did, from our point of view, the free-run given to Lashkar-e-Taiba and Harkat-ul-Mujahideen (HuM) in eastern Afghanistan in the late 1990s. The hijacking of the IC-814 aircraft in December 1999 resulted in the release of the HuM leader, Maulana Masud Azhar, along with other terrorists, who were whisked off to Pakistan moments after they were released from the Indian custody.[3] A year earlier, after the bombing by Al-Qaeda at the US embassies in East Africa, the US bombed a training camp for terrorists in the Jawher Khel village near Khost after being alerted about the presence of Osama bin Laden in the camp. However, the principal target left before the American cruise missiles came down on the camp. Among those killed were Pakistan Army instructors and terrorists training to operate in J&K.

Given this background, sustainable peace and stability in Afghanistan are integral to India's security. India was, therefore, undeterred by the constant efforts to derail the India–Afghanistan development partnership by repeatedly attacking the Indian Embassy and its consulates, as also India's projects and development personnel. Notwithstanding India's critical security concerns, India never pressed Afghanistan for an increased role in the security domain and any assistance rendered was strictly in response to specific requests. There were lingering suspicions in certain quarters about India's strategic objectives in Afghanistan, particularly vis-à-vis Pakistan. Afghans, however, generally viewed India as pursuing development activities without any hidden agenda. The Indian Embassy sought to project India's profile as a non-partisan and constructive, behaving with responsibility and restraint in the rebuilding of Afghanistan.

HUMANITARIAN ASSISTANCE

Throughout the '90s, there had been little development in Afghanistan, especially in the health sector. Afghanistan needed, in the first instance, immediate support for buttressing its food distribution and health sectors. India promised a million tonnes of wheat, which Pakistan would not permit to be taken across by the shortest route between the Wagah and Torkham border crossing points. That is what compelled India to envisage a route to Afghanistan through the Iranian port of Chabahar. To reduce the quantity of wheat to be transported to Afghanistan by a factor of eight to one, in consultation with the World Food Programme (WFP), India embarked on the supply of fortified high-protein biscuits to be used in WFP's School Feeding Programme in Afghanistan, active in 32 of its 34 provinces. Pakistan grudgingly allowed transit of the biscuit packets through Pakistan on two conditions: that the consignment would be transported by the trucks of the National Logistics Cell (NLC) of the Pakistan Army and the cartons containing the packets would have no markings indicating their provenance from India. Both these conditions met Indian requirements because NLC's handling would ensure that there would be no pilferage and the biscuit packets contained within the cartons had the Indian and Afghan flags printed on them.

India also began medical missions in Kabul and in the four major cities where India's consulates were located—Jalalabad, Herat, Kandahar and Mazar-e-Sharif. This provided high-value, low-cost services in Afghanistan's critical health sector. Modern diagnostic equipment was provided to substantially upgrade the Indira Gandhi Children's Hospital in Kabul.

MAJOR INFRASTRUCTURE PROJECTS

In one of my not infrequent meetings with President Hamid Karzai, he referred to the positive impact of Indian assistance. He said that, given the quality of India's work, the package of $1.3 billion committed at that time was worth three to four times more, equivalent to $4 or $5 billion from any other source. Pointing to the chandelier in his room, he said that 'for this light, we have to thank India'.

He was referring to the construction of the 202-km transmission line from Pul-e-Khumri to Kabul by India. While the World Bank and Asian Development Bank were part of this transmission-line building effort, India built the most difficult part of the power grid, over the Salang Pass at 3,700 m, higher than the transmission lines built in any of the three Indian hill states, and a sub-station at Chimtala, just north of Kabul. With the capacity to handle 300 MW of electricity, this sub-station is the largest in Afghanistan. The idea was to bring electricity from Uzbek to Kabul, known until 2009 as 'the capital of darkness' and electrified only by generators. The Chimtala power station was for the distribution of imported electricity. The projects brought cheer and light to the residents of Kabul.

Soon afterwards, in January 2009, India completed the 218-km Zaranj–Delaram highway. It provides connectivity to the very end of southwestern Afghanistan by linking Zaranj, the capital of Nimroz province, to the Kandahar–Herat highway. It also furthers regional cooperation by encouraging new trade and transit, and provides Afghanistan with supplementary access to the Persian Gulf through the Iranian port of Chabahar, also being developed with funding from India. Two years ago, the viability of this route was proven when India shipped 75,000 tonnes of wheat through this port to Afghanistan.

Along with trade routes, the associated initiatives included unilateral tariff concessions, such as duty-free and quota-free access for Afghan goods, concessionary credit to boost commercial exchanges, investments and manufacturing, making a 5,000-tonne cold storage in Kandahar for perishable goods, encouragement of customs procedure harmonization, and initiation of motor vehicles and railways agreements among the states using this trade route.

SMALL DEVELOPMENT PROJECTS

People-oriented projects initiated by India in Afghanistan were the Small Development Projects (SDPs), which were community-oriented, quickly implementable projects, typically entailing an expenditure of between half a million to $2 million. From 2006, 400 SDPs have been implemented in all parts of Afghanistan. These include schools, clinics, micro-hydel, groundwater pumps and solar electrification projects. These quick-gestation projects in the social sector were conceived and executed by local and provincial authorities. After the initial success of the SDPs started in 2006, India accorded higher priority to more community-based SDPs because of their local ownership and quick delivery and results, in preference to large infrastructure projects with longer gestation.

India experimented with innovative schemes in response to Afghan requests. The Afghan Public Service Commission asked for Indian experts, advisors and coaches, in January 2007, for the different departments of the Afghan central government for capacity development of public institutions in Afghanistan, and promoting gender equality and empowerment of women. It was a joint United Nations Development Programme (UNDP), Canadian and Indian programme called 'Capacity for Afghan Public Service' (CAP), in which UNDP helped with the coordination, Canada provided with the funds and India sent their experts. The experts did not draw emoluments on the scale US or EU experts did, but far more modestly, so that they could be more acceptable to their Afghan colleagues. The embassy advised them to avoid line functions and demonstrate to their Afghan colleagues how they would perform or what they would do if asked to carry out a similar task in India. According to a UNDP survey, after the CAP project had been in operation for a year, the beneficiary satisfaction for the 40 coaches assessed ranged from 63 per cent (lowest) to 80 per cent (highest).[4]

Another innovation was successfully tried: forging public-private-NGO (Indian NGO) partnerships, considering the limitations in deploying Indian government personnel in Afghanistan. As a result, Sulabh International built 'pay and use' public toilets in several Afghan cities and trained Afghan sanitary staff in their maintenance. The Confederation of Indian Industry helped to establish training facilities for specific trades, such as tailoring, carpentry, plumbing, welding and masonry, in partnership with the nascent Afghan private sector industry, which assured employment for the trainees.

The Indian government's funding enabled one of the largest women's non-governmental organizations in the world: the Self-Employed Women's Association (SEWA) set up a vocational training centre in Kabul's Bagh-e-Zenana (a woman's only park) for training destitute women in employment-generating activities. Training the women to become entrepreneurs in association with each other was a significant part of the project.[5] The Hand in Hand International executed another supported project in some northern Afghanistan provinces, replicating a programme implemented successfully in Tamil Nadu.

What was most important was India's contribution to Afghanistan's soft infrastructure, nurturing institutions, developing human resources and training Afghan public officials in the same institutions in India where Indian public servants were trained. This was scaled up massively under the Indian Technical and Economic Cooperation Programme.

THE TALIBAN TAKEOVER

Two decades of progress in Afghanistan and the process of reconstructing India–Afghanistan relations came to an abrupt end with the fall of the Afghan government and the takeover of Kabul by the Taliban on 15 August 2021. The Afghan government collapsed because of America's ineptitude, Afghanistan's incapacity caused by faulty institutional support, a foisted leadership, and sanctuary, sustenance and support provided to the Taliban by Pakistan.

Afghanistan now faces an economic and humanitarian catastrophe. The *Afghanistan Times* recently quoted doctors from the Indira Gandhi Children's Hospital, Kabul, about the death rate among children going up by 50 per cent, the hospital's shortage of equipment and supplies, and its limited capacity, constraining them to treat only emergency cases. The challenge for India now will centre around how it resumes its historical engagement with the Afghan people.

To attenuate the present dire humanitarian challenge in Afghanistan, India is seeking ways to scale up humanitarian assistance and secure unconstrained access, so that assistance reaches the intended beneficiaries. The first consignment of half a million doses of Covid-19 vaccines and a tonne-and-a-half of medicines was delivered by air to the World Health Organization's representative office in Afghanistan (the latter for use in the Indira Gandhi Children's Hospital in Kabul in early December 2021). This is being followed up by the supply of a consignment of 50,000 tonnes of wheat, for which India had requested a passage from Pakistan.

Pakistan's prime minister and foreign minister maintain that Pakistan has been trying to get international aid flowing to

Afghanistan. After India's formal request to Pakistan to transport wheat materializes, more such shipments could follow as long as Pakistan gives access and the World Food Programme can handle unimpeded distribution within Afghanistan. India could also ship supplies through the ports of Kandla and Chabahar.

Indian policy will evolve as the situation unfolds in the present situation of flux. At the present, India cannot accord recognition to a regime that remains so unrepresentative of Afghan society. Meanwhile, in coordination with the regional countries and other interested countries, India will strive to provide the Afghan people with humanitarian assistance, ensure that Afghan territory is not used to spread radicalism or terrorism, preserve the social and economic gains made over the past two decades, establish inclusive governance, with the representation of women and minorities, allow the United Nations to play an important role, implement the United Nations Security Council resolution 2593, and forge a unified international response to the current situation. For now, the fourfold focus must be on the delivery of humanitarian assistance, getting the remaining foreigners and Afghan nationals wishing to leave their country out of Afghanistan, an inclusive and representative government in Kabul, and ensuring that Afghan territory is not used for terrorist acts.

Part IV

AFGHANISTAN AND THE WEST

12

United States's Dilemmas in Afghanistan

Amb. Arun K. Singh

Dilemmas of the United States (US) in Afghanistan did not end with its withdrawal on 31 August 2021. President Joe Biden pushed for ending US military presence, seeing the involvement as never ending. He seized on the Doha Agreement that was set by the Trump administration in February 2020, setting 1 May 2021, as the deadline for the US troop withdrawal, although he extended it till August, in view of the prevailing situation and logistics requirements. Seeing the clear US intent, the Taliban did not attack the US forces during this extended period. Biden did not repudiate the Doha Agreement, even though the Taliban did not fulfil its part of the commitments on working out political reconciliation with the government in Kabul, lessening of violence, or breaking links with designated and other terrorist groups. He stayed with this agreement, while undoing Trump's rejection of the Paris Climate Accord of 2015, and re-entering negotiations with Iran on revival of Joint Comprehensive Plan of Action, which Trump had abandoned in 2018.

Biden himself, as vice president in the Obama administration from 2009–16, had pushed for ending the US military involvement. He argued that the US needed to stop nation-building in Afghanistan. The military, according to him, was going beyond Obama's goals of defeating Al-Qaeda, preventing the Taliban from toppling the Afghan government and improving security.[1]

Biden said he and Obama agreed that 'we were not in Afghanistan for nation-building. We were not going to commit to provide and guarantee resources to build that country for the next ten years… the COIN [counterinsurgency] strategy was not appropriate for signing on indefinitely to a nation-building campaign'.[2] On the troops' withdrawal, on 19 December 2010, he said, 'We're starting it in July of 2011, and we're going to be totally out of there, come hell or high water, by 2014'.[3] He, however, had said in January 2011 that the US troops will stay in Afghanistan beyond 2014 if Afghans wanted them to.[4]

Obama was not able to go along fully with him in view of contrary advice from the Pentagon, and worried about his political legacy if there was to be a subsequent major terrorist attack on the US soil by groups based in the Afghanistan–Pakistan region. For this reason, Obama was also not able to declare 'mission accomplished' and order withdrawal of the US forces after the killing of Osama bin Laden in May 2011.

CRITICISM OF THE US ADMINISTRATION AFTER WITHDRAWAL

The eventual withdrawal in August 2021 and the chaos that took place in its wake ignited further political infighting within the US. Republicans criticized the administration for the disorganization, chaotic scenes at Kabul airport, terror attack on 26 August 2021, which took the lives of nearly 200 including 13 US service personnel, for leaving behind Afghans who had worked closely with the US and were now potential Taliban assassination targets, and abandoning the major effort of the past 20 years of developing a super structure of a modern democratic Afghan society.[5] They also claimed that the Doha Agreement was based on conditions, and that the US could have acted differently if the Taliban had not kept their part of the commitments.

Democrats and even some former members of the Trump administration criticized the Doha Agreement as 'capitulation', for effectively legitimizing and enabling a heightened international profile for the Taliban, and blamed Special Envoy Zalmay Khalilzad for not coordinating with and undermining the Afghan government and consequently destroying the morale of the Afghan security and defense forces, and forcing the release of 5,000 Taliban prisoners, many of whom joined the fighting against the government. There was also criticism regarding the deadline of 1 May 2021 for the withdrawal of the US troops, as it took away the pressure on Taliban to compromise for political settlement and over the Doha Agreement, which was not really conditions based, targeting the Trump administration for not calibrating its steps on Taliban's compliance.[6] They also sought to justify Biden's decision on the ground that the US military, on account of its own compulsions to show success and relevance, would have wanted to stay on indefinitely and so it had made false claims of progress for more than a decade, and that the Afghan government was mired in corruption, further undermining the US effort and bolstering support for the Taliban.

Strategic analysts have pointed to several challenges resulting from the withdrawal. Many have argued that the situation could have been sustained with a small US military presence, training and advising Afghan forces and enabling support by the US contractors, stating that 'you don't end wars by withdrawing, you only cede space to others', as had happened in Iraq, leading to rise of the Islamic State of Iraq and Syria (ISIS).[7] It was further stated that a major humanitarian crisis would arise because of the Taliban's lack of experience of governance, freezing of Afghan assets in the US and Europe, and erosion of international assistance, budgetary support and financial flows. Former US National Security Advisor (NSA), Lt Gen. H.R. McMaster, said that the Sirajuddin Haqqani group had links with ISIS and the Al-Qaeda, and as it was responsible for security in Kabul and at the airport on 26 August, one 'cannot rule out that the ISIS-K attack was coordinated with the Haqqani group to humiliate the US'.[8] Others are asking if the US, which had relied on the 'duplicitous' support from Pakistan earlier, was now wanting to rely on duplicitous Taliban support against various terrorist groups harbouring in Afghanistan. McMaster went on to describe the Taliban's advance in July-August as 'an ISI planned attack against the Afghan government'. Former US Ambassador Ryan Crocker said that US did not lose militarily. We just said we are tired of fighting and want to go home.[9]

In a US Senate hearing on 28 September 2021, the chairman of Joint Chiefs of Staff, Mark Milley, said, 'Taliban was and remains a terrorist organization and has continued its links to the Al Qaeda.' He went on to say that the Al-Qaeda and ISIS could reconstitute in Afghanistan in 12 to 36 months. He further described the US withdrawal as a 'strategic failure for the US…the enemy is in charge in Kabul'.[10] Chairman of the Senate Committee on Armed Services said that the Doha Agreement represented negotiations and agreement with terrorists.[11]

The US is now faced with new dilemmas about how it should engage with the Taliban to get some satisfaction over concerns of terrorism and to address the humanitarian situation, while not appearing as providing recognition or legitimacy to their regime. There are some markers it could adopt. The new governance structure should be required to show legitimacy through a vote by democratic or traditional Afghan processes, but not just by power grab through violence. There should be continued insistence on observance of human rights of ethnic groups, minorities, women and girls, and all within a truly inclusive governance structure.

US-TALIBAN RELATIONS: POSING NEW DILEMMAS

There are dilemmas related to Afghans who now find themselves in the diaspora after the Taliban takeover, those left behind but alienated from or targeted by the Taliban, or the refugee flows that could result from the Taliban violence or humanitarian and economic crisis. Another dilemma is around how should the US or democracies generally respond if there is a major terror attack threat emanating from the Af–Pak area. Further, as fundamentalists everywhere have been emboldened by the Taliban victory, while short-term interest may suggest some engagement with the Taliban for a superficial sense of stability, how should the long-term aim of not allowing fundamentalist elements to derive strength from the Taliban gain be pursued? The Taliban did not show willingness to compromise in the past. In 2001 or earlier, they had refused to hand over Osama bin Laden to the US. They did not honour their part of the obligations in the Doha Agreement. Then how can they now be expected to give in to pressure or inducement to take action against their hitherto partners in terrorism and violence, or to honour human rights, or form an inclusive governance structure?

The dilemma that the US is faced with is compounded by the fact that others, including its geopolitical rivals, are moving ahead with the Taliban. China, Russia, Iran, Turkey, UAE and Pakistan, are among the few countries that maintained their embassies in Kabul after the Taliban seized the country.[12] Several European countries are working on opening up a joint diplomatic mission.[13] Representatives of the Taliban, including some representatives of Afghan civil society, were in Norway from 23 January 2022, at the initiative of the Norwegian government for three days of talks. 'These meetings do not represent a legitimization or recognition of the Taliban. But we must talk to the de facto authorities in the country,' Norwegian Foreign Minister Anniken Huitfeldt said in a statement, adding that 'We cannot allow the political situation to lead to an even worse humanitarian disaster.'[14] Taliban representatives have, since August 2021, also visited Qatar, Iran, Pakistan, Uzbekistan, Russia and Turkey. Several countries have sent representatives to meet them in Kabul or in Qatar.

On 22 December, with US concurrence, the United Nations Security Council (UNSC) approved a UN sanctions carve-out for humanitarian assistance and other activities supporting basic needs in Afghanistan.[15] An earlier US version, seeking to authorize only case-by-case exemptions to the sanctions, was blocked by

China and Russia. In passing the text, the Council carved out an exemption for humanitarian assistance and other activities that support basic human needs from the sanctions imposed under resolutions 2255 (2015) and 1988 (2011) concerning individuals and entities associated with the Taliban. Key provisions now allow for processing and payment of funds, other financial assets or economic resources, and the provision of goods and services necessary to ensure timely delivery of humanitarian assistance. The UNSC resolutions, which was adopted unanimously, sought to reduce the legal and political risks of delivering aid to Afghanistan. It exempted humanitarian activities from the UN sanctions for a one-year period, and required updates to ensure that aid was not diverted to the Taliban.[16]

Donors to the Afghan Reconstruction Trust Fund (ARTF) agreed to release $280 million (€247 million) in aid to Afghanistan, the World Bank said on 10 December 2021.[17] The money was to be transferred from a frozen trust fund to two aid agencies—the World Food Programme (WFP) and children's agency United Nations International Children's Emergency Fund (UNICEF)—to support nutrition and health in Afghanistan. World Bank-administered ARTF will give $180 million to the WFP to scale up food security and nutrition operations and $100 million to the UNICEF. Using reconstruction trust fund money and channeling it through the WFP and UNICEF, both part of the UN family, appears to be a way to get funding into the country for basic needs in a manner that does not necessarily implicate the US sanctions against the Taliban.[18] Some 160 national and international organizations are providing critical food and health assistance, as well as education, water, sanitation and support to agriculture as of 2021.

On 11 January 2022, speaking in Geneva, UN Emergency Relief Coordinator Martin Griffiths said that $4.4 billion was needed for the Afghanistan Humanitarian Response Plan alone 'to pay direct' to health workers and others, not the de facto authorities. The scale of need is already enormous, as stressed by UN officials Griffiths and Filippo Grandi, who also warned that if insufficient action is taken to support Afghanistan and regional response plans, 'next year we'll be asking for $10 billion'.[19] Rejecting questions that the funding would be used to support the Taliban's grip on de facto government, Griffiths insisted that it would go directly into the pockets of 'nurses and health officials in the field', so that these services can continue, and are not to be seen as support for State structures.[20] However, such assistance, bypassing the Taliban, will also lessen the pressures on the Taliban to respond to the needs and demands of the people and the markers for governance advocated by the international community.

Earlier, in the September 2021 Geneva Conference, donors pledged more than $1.1 billion to help Afghanistan, where poverty and hunger had spiralled since the Taliban took over and foreign aid had dried up, raising the specter of a mass exodus.[21] In 2021, donors provided $1.5 billion for two humanitarian appeals, including $776 million of the $606 million required for the 'Flash Appeal' launched in September by the Secretary General, and $730 million of the $869 million sought in the Humanitarian Response Plan.[22] US Senator and former Democratic Presidential aspirant Bernie Sanders, on 19 January 2022, tweeted, 'Afghanistan is facing a humanitarian catastrophe. I urge the Biden administration to immediately release billions in frozen Afghan government funds to help avert this crisis and prevent the death of millions of people.'[23]

Another continuing US dilemma in Afghanistan has been about how to address the 'frenemy' role of Pakistan, which was acting simultaneously as both foe and friend of the US objectives and strategies. It allowed the transit of the US military personnel and supplies, but provided safe haven, funds, equipment and training to the Taliban. It enabled the terror-linked Haqqani network to seize control of Kabul in August, and thereafter dominate the key governance institutions of the Taliban, sidelining those who were the political face in the Doha negotiations. In a cable sent to Washington DC in 2009, US Ambassador to Afghanistan Karl W. Eikenberry said, 'Pakistan will remain the single greatest source of Afghan instability so long as the border sanctuaries remain.'[24] In a US Senate hearing in September 2011, Admiral Mike Mullen, Chairman of Joint Chiefs of Staff, said that the Haqqanis have 'long enjoyed the support and protection of the Pakistani government' and are 'in many ways a strategic arm' of Pakistan's ISI.[25] There is a need to also hold Pakistan accountable for the governance and humanitarian disaster facing Afghanistan because of the support it provided to the Taliban. But the US will also remain dependent on Pakistan for land and air transit, and for over-the-horizon counterterrorism action, even if that is much less effective now because of the absence of its ground presence.

The US strategy in Afghanistan had been, from the start, marked by confusion in objectives and messaging. Initially, immediately after the 9/11 attacks, it was described as a mission to bring Osama bin Laden and other perpetrators to justice and to decimate the Al-Qaeda. As the mission dragged out, it was described as an effort to bring democracy and development to Afghanistan. However, the overwhelming US presence itself prevented any organic consolidation of political process and structures. The US counterterror missions often ended up killing or brutalizing civilian populations, thus breeding fresh recruits for the Taliban and other terrorist groups. Former Afghan President Hamid Karzai had repeatedly called for the US to cease counter-terror operations, particularly at night and the resulting harassment of civilians and families, and to hand over responsibility for any such operations to Afghan security forces.[26] He suggested that the US forces should instead focus on interdicting movements of fighters from safe havens in Pakistan.

Even as the US effort in Afghanistan was stalling, it shifted focus to Iraq in 2003 through another military intervention there. The Afghanistan effort was, thereafter, short of resources and high-level attention. The Taliban violence started to ratchet up from

2005 onwards. Under pressure from the military, US President Obama, in 2009, agreed to expand significantly the number of US troops, but gave an 18-month deadline for drawdown, signalling a lack of political will to sustain the effort. President Trump took several steps further by repeatedly criticizing the US involvement, and eventually signing the Doha Agreement. But even he could not completely remove the US forces because of the continued security challenges, and left 3,000 troops by the end of his term.

As the situation in Afghanistan continues to be dire, the international community will continue to face dilemmas. Taliban has shown a consistent pattern of brutalization of its opponents and the people, in the past and now, and not paid heed to international demands. Pakistan has, in the past and now, been a key enabler of the Taliban, but has evaded any accounting. North Atlantic Treaty Organization (NATO) did not succeed in its first 'out of area' operations beyond its foundational European focus, and for the first-time invoking of the Article 5 of NATO Treaty on collective self-defense. But it is now seeking to define a role for itself in the Indo-Pacific region in its Agenda 2030, seeing US focus there. After the failure in Iraq, the setback in Afghanistan has put another firm nail in the coffin of policies to 're-order other societies'.

Many US analysts have said that the US does not see a threat to its national interest from enhanced Chinese presence and role in Afghanistan. However, with its long-term agreement with Iran and military supplies to Saudi Arabia, Afghanistan will provide contiguity for China through the China–Pakistan Economic Corridor and on to the Gulf region, potentially adding to the challenges for the US there. The Russia–China Joint Statement issued on 4 February 2022, after the visit of Russian President Vladimir Putin to coincide with the opening of the Winter Olympics, officially boycotted by the US, spoke of supporting each others' positions on security architectures in Europe and in the Asia–Pacific, and criticized the US' Indo-Pacific strategy.

Short of another terror strike on the US soil emanating

from the Af-Pak region, the US's attention will veer away from Afghanistan. Other challenges, from Russia in Europe and from China in the Indo-Pacific, will attract US's energies and attention. The administration will also need to compensate for the chaotic Afghan withdrawal by showing more robustness in other theatres. However, US actions in Afghanistan since 2001, or even the 1980s when it built up militant jihad to drive the Soviet Union out of Afghanistan, will have lasting consequences for Afghan society, people and for the US itself.

Part V
AFGHANISTAN IN THE GLOBAL CALCULUS

13

Afghanistan in the United Nations

Amb. D.P. Srivastava

Afghanistan was a member of the League of Nations. Membership of the League helped Afghanistan establish the international status of the country after it emerged as a completely independent nation in 1919. It joined the United Nations (UN) on 19 November 1946 as the Kingdom of Afghanistan. Afghanistan opposed Pakistan's admission to the UN; its entry into the world body preceded Pakistan's creation. The Soviet invasion in 1979 thrust it on the world stage. During the Cold War, the decision-making in the United Nations Security Council (UNSC) remained paralysed. However, Afghanistan received considerable attention in the UNSC. The General Assembly adopted a key resolution in January 1980 after the debate was transferred to it following the stalemate in the Security Council. The General Assembly resolutions gave the Office of the Secretary-General a mandate to seek a political settlement. This created a mechanism to pursue political reconciliation. Though this did not change the situation on the ground, it kept the issue in focus.

Apart from the UNSC and the General Assembly, the secretary generals have also played a role in shaping the debate on Afghanistan. Following the UN General Assembly resolution, Secretary General Kurt Waldheim appointed Javier Perez de Cuellar as his personal representative on Afghanistan. After the latter was elected as the secretary general, he, in turn, appointed Diego Cordovez as his personal representative on Afghanistan.

Cordovez was followed by Benon Sevan. Since then, there has been a succession of UN mediators. Currently, Roza Otunbayeva is the special representative of the secretary general on Afghanistan.

There is an inherent irony underlying the UN dynamics. Without the support of the permanent members (P5), the UNSC cannot take major decisions. The council gets some space to act when there is no clashing interest among the P5. However, the absence of interest is not necessarily a good basis for effective action. The spasmodic action by the UNSC gave Pakistan a relatively free hand to continue to interfere in Afghanistan in the 1990s. This was the period when the collapse of the Soviet Union had resulted in the waning of the United States' (US) interest in Afghanistan. It is worth recalling that the UN is an inter-governmental body. Its successes or failures reflect those of the member States. This is as true in the case of Afghanistan as in many other countries.

The UN may have had a light footprint on the ground in Afghanistan. But it played a key role in political reconciliation. The UN brokered the Geneva Accords of the 1980s, which led to the withdrawal of Soviet forces from Afghanistan. It also played a significant role in setting the normative agenda. Both the UN General Assembly and the UNSC adopted resolutions, which invited attention to gender discrimination and the threat of terrorism. The destruction of Bamiyan Buddhas brought out the medieval mindset of the Taliban. Most importantly, the UNSC Resolutions 1267 and 1333 adopted and deepened sanctions against the Taliban. The author was involved in negotiations with the major powers, which eventually led to the adoption of these resolutions. These ensured that despite their victory on the ground, the Taliban regime could not get international recognition. The Taliban was also denied the Afghan seat in the UN.

EARLY YEARS

The UNSC adopted a resolution on 29 August 1946 recommending admission of Afghanistan along with Iceland and Sweden in UN membership.[1] There, the UNSC passed another resolution on Afghanistan on 9 January 1980, after 36 years. This was approved after the Soviet invasion of Afghanistan, only to transfer the issue to the General Assembly after the Soviet Union had exercised a veto on a draft resolution, calling for its forces to withdraw from Afghanistan. The resolution invoked Uniting for Peace procedure to call for an emergency session of the General Assembly.[2]

The General Assembly adopted the resolution captioned 'The Situation in Afghanistan and its Implications for International Peace and Security' on 14 January 1980. It reaffirmed 'the respect for sovereignty, territorial integrity and political independence of every State', and stated in operative Paragraph 2 that it 'Strongly deplores recent armed intervention in Afghanistan'. The operative Paragraph 4 'Calls for the immediate, unconditional and total withdrawal of the foreign troops in Afghanistan in order to enable its people to determine their own form of government and chose their economic, political and social systems, free from outside intervention, subversion, coercion or constraint of any kind'. Resolution ES-6/2 was adopted on 14 January 1980 by a vote of 104 in favour, 18 against and 18 abstained. India abstained on vote on the resolution.[3]

Fear of the Soviet veto kept Afghanistan off the agenda of the UNSC during the Afghan War of the 1980s. Cordovez brokered Geneva Accords, which were signed on 14 April 1988. The council adopted Resolution 622 on 31 October 1988 endorsing them. The resolution confirmed the agreement to temporarily dispatch to Afghanistan and Pakistan, military officers from existing UN operations to assist in the mission of good offices. The operation—the United Nations Good Offices Mission in Afghanistan and Pakistan (UNGOMAP)—had been established earlier in May 1988 to assist in the implementation of the Geneva

Accords 'and report possible violations of any of the provisions of the Agreements'.[4] It was a short-lived operation and was wound up on 15 March 1990. Pakistan was opposed to the extension of its mandate, as it constrained its continued interference in Afghanistan even after the withdrawal of the Soviet troops. Contrast this with Pakistan's enthusiasm for United Nations Military Observer's Group for India and Pakistan to highlight the Jammu and Kashmir issue.

GENEVA ACCORDS

The UN played a key role in the negotiations with the personal envoy, Cordovez, undertaking trips to Afghanistan and Pakistan. The Geneva Accords ensured the withdrawal of the Soviet forces. But this did not bring an end to the fighting. The reason was that neither was there any agreement on the transitional government nor any agreement to cease arms supplies to the two sides by the principals. These were not simple omissions. Pakistan and supporters of the Afghan War in the US suggested 'negative symmetry' 'to refrain from providing military aid to any party'. This placed the Najib government on the same level to that of the Mujahideen. That was a departure from the original understanding where the Soviet Union had agreed to withdraw their troops from Afghanistan in return for the US's agreement to end any aid in the resistance. The Soviet Union resisted but eventually agreed on a variant of the formula. This was 'positive symmetry', where both sides would continue arms supply to their respective clients.

The absence of an agreement on a transitional government and continued supply of arms to both sides set the stage for strife. The implementation of the Geneva Accords was to be monitored by the UNGOMAP. This included a military section under a Finnish general and a political section under Benon Sevan. The mission was empowered to receive complaints from either side. However, the UNGOMAP was wound up within 20 months itself. The withdrawal of the super powers and the absence of an effective monitoring mechanism allowed Pakistan to continue meddling in Afghanistan. Indeed, it stepped up interference in its neighbouring country, now that there was no longer any threat of Soviet retaliation.

The Geneva Accords were silent on the formation of a transitional government. Sensing military victory, Pakistan and Mujahideen avoided any commitment to a transitional government in which elements of People's Democratic Party of Afghanistan (PDPA) could be accommodated. The Jalalabad offensive by the Mujahideen supported by the Inter-Services Intelligence (ISI) and Pakistan Army failed. Mohammad Najibullah successfully held on till the collapse of the Soviet Union ended petrol supplies for his troops. The UN negotiator Sevan also unwittingly played a part in the drama. He persuaded Najibullah to announce that he would step down without winning Pakistan's approval for a transitional government in place. Najibullah's fall led to the start of a civil war.

Comparing Geneva Accords of the 1980s with the Doha Agreement four decades later, the contrast cannot be greater. In the negotiations in the 1980s, the Mujahideen were not given a seat on the table. The Geneva Accords for withdrawal of Soviet troops was brokered by the UN and signed by Afghanistan and Pakistan governments with guarantees by the two super powers. At Doha, the US negotiated with the Taliban; the elected government of Afghanistan was not a party. It was no surprise that the outcome of the Doha Process collapsed so soon after the US withdrawal.

After Soviet withdrawal, the Najibullah government went on fighting till at least three years. The Afghan government unravelled only after the collapse of the Soviet Union in December 1991.

THE 1990s

The end of the Cold War led to an unprecedented increase in the activities of the UNSC. While the first 45 years of the UN saw the adoption of 687 resolutions by the UNSC, this number doubled in the 1990s. However, this activism was not reflected in the Afghanistan issue. The UNSC adopted a merely six resolutions on Afghanistan between January 1990 and December 2000. This showed an absence of interest in Afghanistan on the part of great powers. Afghanistan had reverted to being a regional issue.

While the UNSC had distanced itself from the Afghanistan issue following the Soviet withdrawal and collapse of the Soviet Union, the General Assembly took up the issue. The General Assembly adopted a two-part resolution every year in the 1990s. The first part dealt with humanitarian assistance to Afghanistan. The second part captioned 'The situation in Afghanistan and its implications for international peace and security' dealt with the political issues. It called for ensuring transfer of power through the urgent establishment of a fully representative and broad-based authoritative council with authority. Its significance lies in the contemporary context. This resolution was adopted in February 1996, when the Taliban came knocking at the gate of Kabul.

The General Assembly repeated its call next year in February 1997, when the Taliban had captured Kabul. The General Assembly resolution dated 13 February 1997 called for 'a lasting political settlement of the conflict and establishing a fully representative and broad-based transitional government of national unity'.[5] It highlighted the fact that the Taliban control of much of the country was based on denial of due representation to other ethnic groups.

Resolutions adopted by the UNSC during this period were: UNSC Resolutions 647 (1990), 1076 (1990), 1077 (1996), 1193 (1998), 1214 (1998), 1267 (1999) and 1333 (2000). The first four essentially dealt with periodic extension of the mandate of United Nations Assistance Mission in Afghanistan (UNAMA). The last two were significant; these related to the renewed interest of the great powers in Afghanistan. This time impetus did not come from great power rivalry, but the concern with the use of Afghan territory for sponsoring terrorist activities. The US interest was aroused by the bombings of the US missions in Tanzania and Nairobi by the Al-Qaeda, whose leader, Osama bin Laden, was ensconced in Afghanistan. The resolutions called on the Taliban to hand over Osama. There was not much concern about fallout within the region. Pakistan was using Afghanistan as a sanctuary and a training ground for undertaking terrorist activities against India. The nexus became very clear with the hijacking of IC-814 in 1999.

UNSC RESOLUTION 1267

The UNSC resolution 1267 was adopted in October 1999. It signalled the return of great power interest in the region. The resolution focussed on the terrorism issue. The Operative Paragraph 1 stated that it

> Insists that the Afghan faction known as the Taliban, which also calls itself the Islamic Emirate of Afghanistan, comply promptly with its previous resolutions and in particular cease the provision of sanctuary and training for international terrorists and their organizations, take appropriate effective measures to ensure that the territory under its control is not used for terrorist installations and camps, or for the preparation or organization of terrorist acts against other States or their citizens, and cooperate with efforts to bring indicted terrorists to justice.[6]

As the wordings make it clear, the UNSC treated the Taliban only as one of the Afghan factions. This was indeed the main motive of the resolution. India had played a role; the author was involved in the earliest bilateral negotiations with the US State Department as well as the Russian side. This put a brake on the moves towards recognition of the Taliban regime, despite the considerable momentum it had gathered on the ground.

A key demand in the resolution was the Taliban handing over Osama bin Laden. The Operative Paragraph 2 stated that it

> Demands that the Taliban turn over Usama bin Laden without further delay to appropriate authorities in a country where he has been indicted, or to appropriate authorities in a country where he will be returned to such a country...

The Operative Paragraph 3 stated that it 'Decides that on 14 November 1999 all States shall impose the measures set out in paragraph 4 below...'[7]

In the UN parlance, 'measures' related to sanctions against the Taliban unless it complied with the demands made by the UNSC. These were listed in Operative Paragraph 4 and included: (i) flight ban and (ii) freezing of funds. All States were to 'deny permission for any aircraft to take off from or land in their territory if it is owned, leased, or operated by or on behalf of the Taliban...' Similarly, all states were to 'freeze funds and other financial resources, including funds derived or generated from property owned or controlled directly or indirectly by the Taliban, or by any undertaking owned or controlled by the Taliban, as designated by the Committee...' To administer the sanctions, a committee was to be established. The UNSC resolution 1267 was adopted by consensus. However, the Taliban refused to comply with it.[8]

Over a period of time, the work of this committee, also known as the 1267 Committee, expanded. The Afghan delegation while supporting the resolution stated,

> We are of the view that the set of measures contained in the draft resolution is an adequate signal to the Taliban and to their Pakistani mentors: it indicates that the international community is extremely concerned about the adventurist policy of Pakistan and the Taliban, which is a major threat to international peace and security.[9]

The Afghan representative added, 'Despite the mild and limited nature of the draft resolution to be adopted today, the political message which it contains is strong.' There were statements made by other delegates also. The US delegate said,

> The United States has consistently expressed its concern with the policies of the Taliban. As this draft resolution makes clear, the Council shares our deep concern over the continuing violations of international humanitarian law and of human rights, particularly discrimination against women and girls. We are also disturbed by the significant rise in illicit opium production under areas of Taliban control and the deplorable treatment of Iranian diplomatic personnel and journalists. The Taliban's actions pose threats to their neighbors and to the international community at large.[10]

Malaysia expressed reservation on 'the use of sanctions to affect the desired changes on a targeted regime'. It added, 'Therefore, sanctions directed at the Taliban will have a direct and indirect effect on the general population...' Similarly, China in a statement, after the vote, expressed a sense of discomfort with the resolution, which it had voted to support. This dual policy reflected multiple agendas of China. It wanted to satisfy its Pakistani client without breaking ranks with other members of the UNSC. It stated: 'In principle, China does not approve of the frequent use of sanctions. We entirely endorse the views expressed by the representative of Malaysia.'[11]

UNSC RESOLUTION 1333

Failure of the Taliban to comply with the UNSC Resolution 1267 led to an increase in pressure by the UNSC, which adopted Resolution 1333 on 19 December 2000. Operative Paragraph 1 read:

> Demands that the Taliban comply with resolution 1267 (1999) and, in particular, cease the provision of sanctuary and training for international terrorists and their organizations, take appropriate effective measures to ensure that the 3 S/RES/1333 (2000) territory under its control is not used for terrorist installations and camps, or for the preparation or organization of terrorist acts against other States or their citizens, and cooperate with international efforts to bring indicted terrorists to justice.[12]

The paragraph had particular relevance to India's interests. Nearly a year prior to the resolution, the Indian Airlines flight IC-814 was hijacked and taken to Kandahar, where Masood Azhar received a hero's welcome. He, thereafter, surfaced in Pakistan. The episode betrayed the Taliban's links with the ISI and complicity in terrorist activities in India. The resolution reiterated the demand that the Taliban 'turn over' Osama bin Laden.

The UNSC resolution added arms sanctions to the list of sanctions against the Taliban. Its Operative Paragraph 1 stated:

> Prevent the direct or indirect supply, sale and transfer to the territory of Afghanistan under Taliban control as designated by the Committee established pursuant to Resolution 1267 (1999), hereinafter known as the Committee, by their nationals or from their territories, or using their flag vessels or aircraft, of arms and related materiel of all types including weapons and ammunition, military vehicles and equipment, paramilitary equipment, and spare parts for the aforementioned.[13]

The resolution also had other important provisions, which hinted at Pakistan's support to the Taliban, though that country was not specifically mentioned. It prohibited their nationals from providing 'technical advice, assistance, or training related to the military activities of the armed personnel under the control of the Taliban.'

The resolution also stated that all States shall 'withdraw any of their officials, agents, advisers, and military personnel employed by contract or other arrangement present in Afghanistan to advise the Taliban on military or related security matters, and urge other nationals in this context to leave the country.'[14]

While the UNSC Resolution 1267 was adopted unanimously, the UNSC Resolution 1333 was adopted by a vote of 13 for, none against and two abstentions. China and Malaysia abstained from voting on the resolution. The Afghan representative, who spoke on the resolution stated: 'The Pakistan/Taliban/bin Laden alliance has categorically refused to cooperate with the international community or to put an end to the training and haven it provides to international terrorists.' Afghan representative, however, noted that the draft resolution 'does not deal with a peaceful settlement of the present conflict in Afghanistan, and it is silent on Pakistan's well-known aggression in Afghanistan. The draft resolution addresses one specific issue: the terrorism originating from that part of Afghan territory that is under military occupation by the diabolical Pakistan-Taliban-bin-Laden alliance.'[15]

Malaysia reiterated its reservations voiced earlier when the previous Resolution 1267 was adopted. China claimed that 'a new round of sanctions would undoubtedly make that situation even worse.'[16] Both countries abstained on the vote on the resolution. The Russian representative, who had presided over the session, made a national statement on behalf of his country after the vote. He supported the resolution, and, in particular, the arms embargo by stating: 'there had been reference today to the fact that the arms embargo in the text was one-sided in nature. That one-sided nature, he said, was fully justified. The Taliban banked specifically on military solutions. They had also provided their territory for use by terrorists, including Chechnyans, Uzbeks, Tajiks and other extremists.'[17]

THE 9/11 ATTACKS

The events of the 9/11 brought back renewed interest to Afghanistan. The UNSC adopted the Resolution 1368 on 12 September 2001, which is mentioned in its Operative Paragraph 1 as: 'Unequivocally condemns in the strongest terms the horrifying terrorist attacks which took place on 11 September 2001 in New York, Washington, D.C., and Pennsylvania and regards such acts, like any act of international terrorism, as a threat to international peace and security'. Operative Paragraph 5 'expresses its readiness to take all necessary steps to respond to the terrorist attacks of 11 September 2001, and to combat all forms of terrorism, in accordance with its responsibilities under the Charter of the United Nations.'[18] The US Congressional Research Service report mentioned, 'This was widely interpreted as a U.N. authorization for military action in response to the attacks, but it did not explicitly authorize Operation Enduring Freedom to oust the Taliban. Nor did the Resolution specifically reference Chapter VII of the U.N. Charter, which allows for responses to threats to international peace and security.'[19]

Normally, authorization of the use of force requires a Chapter VII resolution. Resolution 1368 is mentioned in the preamble as 'Recognizing the inherent right of individual or collective self-defense in accordance with the Charter.'[20] This, together with the domestic legislation adopted by the US House and Senate, was considered adequate by the US to launch Operation Enduring Freedom, which overturned the Taliban regime. The US, of course, had full justification for taking such a step. This also has relevance to the situation India faces in the sub-continent. India has suffered repeated terror attacks that were planned and sponsored by Pakistan.

After the fall of the Taliban regime, UN mediator Lakhdar Brahimi was brought back; he earlier resigned in 1999. The UNSC Resolution 1378 was adopted on 14 November 2001, calling for a central role for the UN in establishing a transitional administration and inviting member states to send peacekeeping forces to promote stability and aid delivery.[21]

The Bonn Conference established a post-Taliban interim administration headed by President Hamid Karzai on 5 December 2001. The outcome of the Bonn Conference was endorsed by the UNSC Resolution 1385 (6 December 2001). This was followed by the UNSC Resolution 1386 (20 December 2001), which gave formal UNSC authorization for the international peacekeeping force (International Security Assistance Force or ISAF).[22] To support the implementation of the Bonn Agreement, the UNSC adopted Resolution 1401 (March 2002), establishing the UNAMA. This has been the backbone of the UN's mediatory efforts in Afghanistan. Its tasks include the provision of good offices, the organization of elections, protection of human rights, gender equality, humanitarian assistance and development priorities. The UNSC resolution 2596 (2021) has recently extended its mandate to 17 March 2022.

Use of force was kept outside the UN command and control. This was true as much of the beginning of Operation Enduring Freedom as subsequent operations of the ISAF, which worked under the North Atlantic Treaty Organization command. The limitation of the system put in place by the US was that it left untouched sanctuaries provided by Pakistan to the Taliban. President Pervez Musharraf allowed religious parties, which had openly opposed the US military operation against Taliban in Afghanistan in 2001, to come to power in two key border provinces—North-Western Frontier Province and Balochistan.

The adverse situation on the ground facing the US-led coalition was reinforced by the policy of 'engagement' with the Taliban. The Doha Process legitimized the Taliban without extracting any concession from them. Russia sponsored talks with the Taliban in Moscow. These competitive processes, often with clashing agendas, were conducted outside the UN framework. They left the elected government of Afghanistan outside the ambit of negotiations, undermining it in the process.

RETURN OF THE TALIBAN

After the return of the Taliban to Kabul in August 2021, the UNSC adopted two resolutions: S/Res/2593 on 30 August and 2596 on 17 September. The first one was adopted after the 26 August attack at Hamid Karzai International Airport. The resolution condemned the attack, which was claimed by the Islamic State in Khorasan Province, an affiliate of Daesh. It noted the Taliban's condemnation of the attack. Given the immediate context perhaps, it did not provide any pathway to the future beyond stating that it 'encourages all parties to seek an inclusive, negotiated political settlement'. There was no hint of the UN's recognition of Taliban.'[23]

Resolution 2596 on 17 September extended the mandate of UNAMA till 17 March 2022, signifying the UN's commitment to maintain its role in Afghanistan. The resolution refrained from conferring any status of government on the Taliban. It was otherwise a very mild resolution. It relegated even the issue of terrorism to preambular paragraphs. It gave no direction about the future of the country. It was adopted after the Taliban had proclaimed a new cabinet on 7 September 2021, dominated by hard-liners with no representation of minorities or women. The UNSC's silence could suggest that the world body upholds the values of inclusion and diversity, but was not prepared to press the point. The Special Representative of the Secretary General (SRSG), Deborah Lyons, gave a briefing to the UNSC on the same day the resolution 2596 was adopted. She described the Taliban as 'de facto authorities'. She added, 'The de facto authorities have assured us that they want a UN presence, and they value our assistance.'[24] She recalled the assistance provided to Afghanistan by the international community in the past and stated: 'But with the Taliban takeover, the Afghan people now feel abandoned, forgotten, and indeed punished by circumstances that are not their fault. To abandon the Afghan people now would be a historic mistake—a mistake that has been made before with tragic consequences.'[25]

While the Taliban obviously want international assistance to bail out collapsing economy, they have not shown any inclination to moderate their behaviour. The UNSC Resolution 2596, as well as SRSG's briefing, took place on 17 September, 10 days after the Taliban had announced their new cabinet. As SRSG acknowledged: 'We continue to call for a more inclusive administration, in which government institutions reflect Afghanistan's broad diversity. We have seen limited progress on this issue, however. The composition of the caretaker cabinet, so-called by the Taliban themselves, the composition of this cabinet remains entirely male, essentially Pashtun, and almost all Taliban.'[26]

The SRSG gave a sympathetic treatment of the Taliban's aspirations to be recognized as a government:

> My general impression is that the Taliban however is making genuine efforts to present itself as a government. These efforts are partly constrained by the lack of resources and capacity, as well as a political ideology that in many ways clashes with contemporary international norms of governance so present in this chamber. The Taliban have not yet established full trust with much of the Afghan population or convinced them of their capacity to govern.[27]

Her characterization of the Taliban's political ideology as clashing with the values promoted by the UN is worth noting. Even more sobering is the acknowledgment that the group has not yet established 'full trust with much of the Afghan population'. The images of Afghans thronging Kabul airport to catch the flight before the 31 August deadline will continue to haunt the public imagination. In the meantime, the food situation is worsening. As SRSG mentioned: 'As we move into winter and households consume their very limited food stocks we fear and predict that up to 23 million Afghans will be in crisis or emergency levels of food insecurity.'[28] Afghanistan under the Taliban regime is set to have long winters.

The Afghan seat at the UN is occupied by the permanent representative appointed by the previous government. The Taliban have been denied recognition of the world body. Apart from upholding universal values, the UN has played a key role in providing assistance to Afghan refugees in Pakistan and Iran. Its developmental role has been highlighted again in channeling food aid to Afghanistan from a host of bilateral donors. The UN Office on Drugs and Crime has kept the opium production and drug trafficking in Afghanistan under scanner.

Afghanistan's history has seen many violent turns. Outside powers have not always been successful in shaping the events. The UN is most useful, precisely when the great powers have withdrawn. Afghanistan cannot be left alone at Pakistan's mercy—to turn into its protectorate. The UN has a unique legitimacy, which can be used as a tool for conflict resolution. However, engagement with Afghanistan cannot come at the expense of universal values which the UN Charter proclaims.

Part VI

AFGHANISTAN: INTERNAL SITUATION

14

Understanding the Taliban: Origin, Composition and Philosophy

Rana Banerji

After the Soviet withdrawal and fall of President Mohammad Najibullah (April 1992), the Mujahideen came to power briefly in Kabul (1992–96). Burhanuddin Rabbani, leader of the Jamiat-e-Islami, Afghanistan, became the president. In 1992, Ahmed Shah Massoud was a signatory to the Peshawar Accord, a peace and power-sharing agreement in the post-communist Islamic State of Afghanistan. He was appointed minister of defense as well as the government's main military commander. His militia initially fought to defend Kabul against those led by Gulbuddin Hekmatyar and other warlords, who were bombing the city. Various factions of the Mujahideen quickly began to fight among themselves. In a sense, it can be said that this continuing bloodshed amidst the Mujahideen gave rise to the radical Taliban movement.

ORIGINS

The founding meeting of the Taliban was held in the late autumn of 1994 at the historic white mosque in Sangesar, Kandahar. Mullah Omar was the designated commander and he took an oath of allegiance (*bayat*) from everyone present (about 40–50).[1] They also swore to fight against corruption and the extortionist criminal gangs of the Mujahideen warlords.

On 20 September 1994, following an incident involving the rape and murder of some Herati boys and girls travelling through the area, after they had been accosted by a bandit Mujahideen group at a post 90 km north of Kandahar, Mullah Omar took over the tax collection posts outside Kandahar.[2] The common people welcomed this freedom from the rapacious yoke of these tax collectors. This added to Omar's growing charisma. He joined the Herati family for the funeral of the deceased girl, where he may have met Col. (retd) Sultan Emir Tarar, a retired Pakistani Army officer with experience in the Army's Special Services Group and the Inter-Services Intelligence (ISI), who was then Consul General of Pakistan in Herat. Tarar later took on the military training of the Taliban, acquiring in the process, the mystical name of 'Imam'.[3]

At this stage, the Taliban benefitted from the help provided by the government of Pakistan, the second Pakistan People Party's regime under the leadership of Prime Minister Benazir Bhutto. Pakistan was trying to open a land route to Central Asia. A convoy of trucks from Quetta, destined for Turkmenistan, had been accosted by local warlords en route, and the trucks were being held hostage. Maj. Gen. (retd) Nasrullah Babar, interior minister, asked the ISI to take the Taliban's help to get the trucks released, which was achieved through Mullah Omar's intervention. A grateful Pakistan government then provided them access to the Pasha Dump, a cache of arms and equipment stored in 17 underground tunnels near Kandahar, used to fight against the Soviet invaders, which were 'enough to equip a corps'.[4]

Even as the Taliban started making inroads against the coalition government of the Afghan Mujahideen, President Burhanuddin Rabbani provided monetary assistance to the tune of $3 million through Mullah Naqibullah, then governor of Kandahar. Till now, the Taliban had only sought assistance of petrol and food from the ISI for their fight against local warlords supporting both Gulbadin Hekmatyar and Ahmed Shah Masoud. Saudi intelligence also started helping the Taliban at this stage, routing funds to them through the ISI.[5] After gaining control in the southwest, the Taliban began to function independently in Kandahar. They laid siege to the capital, Kabul, in January 1995 after the city had underwent fierce fighting.

Mullah Mohammad Rabbani Akhund, a Kakar tribal leader belonging to the Hizb-e-Islami Khalis and Mullah Abdul Razzak, a Noorzai tribal leader from Spin Boldak, Kandahar, were invited to join thereafter, uniting what broadly came to be regarded as three main factions of the Taliban at that stage. A 10-member Shura or Leadership Council was formed as its apex ruling body. Some of them became ministers in the Taliban government in Kabul (1996). Three Shuras were placed under different commanders— the Peshawar Shura (then under Mullah Mansour), the Quetta Shura (first under Mullah Omar, and later, under Mullah Abdul Ghani Baradar) and the Miramshah Shura (under Jalaluddin/later Serajuddin Haqqani).[6]

The formal leadership structure also had provision for deputy leaders, other executive officers, 12 specialist commissions, including the military commission, the political commission, the economic commission, the commissions for education, prisoners' affairs, martyrs and the differently-abled, and the Council of Ulema. The most important of these commissions, the military, had a subsidiary in Peshawar to manage affairs of the eastern province.

Over the years, the Taliban went on to use Pakistan, with active support from the latter's military and Intelligence establishment[7] as a rear base and logistic supply hub, both for training and recruitment of fighters, as also for rest, recuperation and medical relief.

IDEOLOGY

The Taliban's ideology has been described as combining an 'innovative' form of Sharia Islamic law based on Deobandi fundamentalism and militant Islamism, along with Pashtun social and cultural norms known as Pashtunwali, as most Taliban are Pashtun tribesmen. Deobandi Islam is identified with an Islamic revivalist movement within Sunni (primarily Hanafi) Islam that formed during the late nineteenth century around the Darul Uloom Islamic seminary in the town of Deoband, India, from which the name derives.[8]

Strong historical and etymological links between madrasa students (Taliban literally meaning 'the seekers of knowledge') and the Taliban movement that emerged from a network of Pakistani and Afghan madrasas in the 1990s are well established. In the mid and late '80s, about 10 per cent of deeni madarsa students in the North-West Frontier Province or NWFP, now Khyber Pakhtunkhwa, came from Afghanistan. During and after the Soviet invasion, the clergy from these religious schools guided, to a considerable degree, the guerilla war in Afghanistan.[9] The Darul Uloom Haqqania, Nowshera, run by Maulana Sami-ul-Haq, had a large proportion of these students. The Binori Town mosque, Karachi, also acquired cult status in training the Taliban. Some madrasas in Pakistan, notably those located in or near the Afghan refugee settlements in Peshawar and Quetta, were used by radical religious-political leaders to create popular support for their distinct versions of Islam, to advance particular political agendas, and to recruit to militant groups. These madrasas also functioned as an organizational base for militants. They were also used as transit points for militants and for providing military training facilities.[10]

RHETORIC OF IDEOLOGY AND VIOLENCE

Taliban rhetoric, their ideology and political ideas became instrumental in enabling the movement to maintain high levels of violence over the years. Rhetoric had an impact at individual, institutional and societal levels. The Taliban case for violence provided motivation and reassurance to individual Afghans recruited in the movement, giving them a moral cover for the violent actions they committed. This justification of violence became the core of the Taliban's collective raison d'etre.[11]

In the first phase of their ideological consolidation (1994–96), this rhetoric asserted that the Taliban were engaged in a righteous jihad aimed at establishing a divinely ordered Islamic system in Afghanistan. In its second phase, from 1996–2001, the ascendant Taliban established its Islamic emirate. In the first two phases, the Taliban fought exclusively against Afghan forces. The third phase, from 2002–06, saw insurgency in reaction to the establishment of the post-2001 Afghan government, supported increasingly by international forces. After the rapid collapse of their government in late 2001, small armed groups of the Taliban fought international forces and the new Kabul government, mostly in the south and east of the country. The fourth phase, from 2007–14, saw an intensification of the insurgency, during which the Taliban sought to expand their influence beyond its traditional power bases in the south and east. Though still militarily weak, they spread military operations to all regions of the country and operated a parallel administration in rural areas. During the second half of 2014, the Taliban military started launching attacks with larger groups of fighters, attempting to seize territory in each region of the country.

Taliban rhetoric focussed on four major themes: national sovereignty, military strength, the sacredness of its jihad and the authority of the Islamic Emirate.[12]

DOCTRINAL ISSUES[13]

Under the theme of sacred jihad, the Taliban asserted that their use of violence constituted a legitimate fight, as they were the true Mujahideen, maintaining the legacy of martyrs in previous Afghan conflicts. Active participation in, or support of, this jihad was obligatory for Afghan Muslims. Failure to comply would be seen as a rejection of Islam. Under the theme of the Islamic Emirate, the Taliban rhetoric asserted that decrees and orders issued by the movement and its officials had the authority of Islam and that all Afghans should accept the Islamic shariat, and the only way to do so was to submit to the authority of the emirate.

The Taliban evolved an organizational culture that enabled the movement to survive for 20 years, seemingly immune to the hazards of patronage politics, which weakened and divided other Islamist organizations. The main element of this culture was reverence for the leader as Amir-ul Momineen. It also envisaged centralization of moral and temporal authority, denial of personal responsibility, conformism or suppression of dissent, and religiosity. The Taliban were instructed to accept insecurity of tenure, resistance to permanent hierarchy, blurring of civil-military distinctions and follow a spartan ethos, rejecting cliques of tribalism.

Drawing from the Koran, the Taliban prescribed some guidelines—*Islami Adalat* (Islamic Justice), for administrators and judges, *De Mujahid Toorah, De Jihad Shari Misalay*, to guide decision-making on how to make or break truces and how to distribute booty. Other rules of conduct were issued from time to time, through successive edicts of guidance to the Mujahideen, generally known as the Lahya.

Focussing on internal affairs, the Taliban stressed, in particular, on maintaining cohesiveness. They were ruthless in enforcing their doctrine of obedience to the emir. A Pakistani Islamist scholar and mentor of the Taliban leadership, Mufti Rasheed, published a document titled 'Obedience to the Amir' in Urdu in 2000, after touring Afghanistan with the Taliban. He headed the Rasheed Trust during the Taliban's period in power, between 1996 and 2001. Operating from a campus in Karachi, his organization was involved in religious education and welfare activities. Officials serving under Mufti Rasheed had access to the Taliban leadership, including Mullah Omar, and sought to advise him on the challenges of building the Islamic state.

Rasheed essentially argued that the Taliban's success depends on all members of the movement maintaining unity and their obedience to the emir through the command chain leading up to the supreme leader (Emir-ul-Momineen), Mullah Omar. He said that God and the emir knew better why the Taliban had to do things that individual members of the movement might not fathom. God works through the emir, and so obedience to the emir was to be equated with obedience to the Prophet and to God.

Sound leadership decision-making depended on availability of good advice. Shuras (representative assembly) as a council of the grandees of the movement could give such advice, though their size or appointment was not specified. The shura's role would be strictly advisory. The emir would make his decisions after considering the advice, which would alert him regarding all possible perspectives on the matter at hand. Decision-making authority would rest unambiguously with the emir, and in the case of a disagreement between the shura and emir, the shura would obey, falling in line the same way as ordinary members did.

Another organizational principle prescribed was that of rotation of civilian personnel to the military fronts, to avoid the emergence of a gap between combatants and non-combatants, and to imbue managers with the spirit and morale of the armed ranks. This served to remind the rank and file that violence was essential to jihad. Rasheed suggested that the tenure in civilian or military commands should be relatively short. A rationale for the spartan element of the Taliban's organizational culture was laid down, calling on the leadership to avoid allowing privilege to attach to office, to ensure that no post became so comfortable that others should covet it, and to discourage personal ambition and lust for office within the movement.

SUICIDE OPERATIONS[14]

One striking feature of the Taliban's cult of violence has been their reliance on one of the most extreme combat tactics—that of suicide bombing. The first suicide bombing in recent times occurred on 9 September 2001, when two Al-Qaeda activists blew themselves up to assassinate Northern Alliance leader, Ahmad Shah Massoud. In the early stages of the Taliban insurgency, suicide attacks were rare—an average of one per year, between 2001 and 2004. However, after this period, they became an integral part of the Taliban campaign, with 25 attacks occurring in 2005 and more than a 100 per year, thereafter.

The Taliban rapidly developed an infrastructure to train suicide bombers, plan and execute the attacks. Until 2014, much of that infrastructure was located in Pakistan's North Waziristan Agency. In military terms, these suicide operations became the Taliban's preferred strategic weapon, controlled and deployed by the military leadership against its targets of choice. In cultural terms, suicide operations became part of a cult of militarism. The explosives-filled waistcoat, known as a suicide jacket, came to symbolize an elite cadre of Muslim warriors, those who had been trained to conduct suicide operations. The Koranic verse most commonly invoked was *ayat* 111 of sura Al Tawba, which refers to the believer's covenant with Allah, according to which they have a place in heaven but first must be prepared to fight and die for Allah. Fidayeen talk of the merit of jihad in general and martyrdom in particular. The rhetoric frequently uses the term *isteshadi*, or one seeking martyrdom, rather than the more common *shaheed*, a martyr. This was a nuance designed to emphasize the desire for martyrdom, which would be meritorious, as opposed to an intention to commit suicide (which would be reprehensible). Talking about martyrdom, they say that it is a divine blessing and a passport to eternity, citing a *hadith* that on the Day of Judgment, God will laugh with the martyr who fought on the front line. Another expresses the obligation to jihad: 'All those born in the Muslim religion, have the *kalma*, and so must bleed for their religion until the unbelievers leave.'[15] Justification of suicides suggested a convergence of the Taliban and Al-Qaeda narratives. Further, significantly, the lack of effort to rationalize the Taliban's violence against fellow Afghans illustrated how the Taliban failed to build a case for ending 'the continuation of war' beyond the international troop withdrawal. This doctrinal reservation also portends dominance of the Haqqani network's narrative, in the context of impending power struggles between the Taliban factions now in power.

The above narrative explains how far the Taliban have moved from traditional Sufi, especially Naqshbandi Islamic moorings prevalent in Afghanistan. Fear, not popularity, impels an almost reluctant acceptance of their advent and now, consolidation of power over the whole of Afghanistan. Though strict followers of the Hanafi Fiqh, their thoughts were not in line with the thinking of Egyptian scholars of the Muslim brotherhood, such as Hassan al Banna, or those followed by the puritanical Al Azhar school, as also other 'classical' Mujtahids (those who interpret the religion based on their scholarly credentials). As a discerning academic describes this phenomenon, 'At an intellectual level, the Taliban had no business enforcing Sharia law because their knowledge of it was rudimentary and flawed.'[16] This view was supported by the Al-Azhar trained Egyptian clerics, who met with the Taliban leaders in a failed attempt to forestall the destruction of the Bamiyan Buddhas in 2001. They were appalled to find that 'because of [the Taliban's] circumstances and their incomplete knowledge of jurisprudence, they were not able to formulate rulings backed by theological evidence...their knowledge of religion and jurisprudence is lacking because they have no knowledge of the Arabic language, linguistics, and literature and hence they did not learn the true Islam.'[17]

From this discourse, it also follows that the Taliban 2.0 will not be much different from the Taliban 1.0 in respect to their basic ideology and policies, though efforts may be made to project a more media savvy information front, only to further prospects of international legitimacy, acceptance and diplomatic recognition.

EMERGING TRIBAL SCHISMS AND FACTIONAL INFIGHTING

Though doctrinally, the Taliban are not supposed to be influenced by tribal loyalties, in practice, Afghan tribal society has been riven by hostility between the ruling Durrani elites, the Barakzai and Popalzai sub-clans and the commoner Ghilzais. Of the approximately 40 per cent Pashtuns in Afghanistan, Durranis comprise about 12 per cent, while Ghilzais account for about 15 per cent. The Zadran, progenitor of the Haqqani clan, are more in number, spreading in the eastern provinces of Nangarhar, Paktia and Khost. They are considered lower in the tribal pecking order, compared to the 'blue blooded' Barakzais and Popalzai, or the Ghilzais. Even among Ghilzais, there have been intra-tribal grudges between Ahmadzais and Ishaqzais, both sizably numerous sub-clans of Ghilzais, or between Ishaqzais and Noorzais.

Mullah Omar was a Hotak Ghilzai from Kandahar. He had fought against the Soviet in Afghanistan on behalf of the Hizbe-Islami Khalis, sustaining injuries and losing one eye. He died of tuberculosis in a Karachi hospital in April 2013, but this was not publicly revealed by the Taliban. It was made public by the Afghan National Defense and Security Forces (ANDSF) only in July 2015. Succession battles within the top Taliban leadership perhaps accounted for this effort at secrecy.

Mullah Akhtar Mansour's accession to the top post of Emir al-Mu'minin was not smooth. He was an Ishaqzai (Afghan tribe of the Durrani clan of the Pashtun people). A rival commander, Mullah Rasool, who had influence in Nimroze and Farah, disputed his leadership. He also had support from Mansoor Dadullah, half-brother of Dadullah Akhund, a Kakar from Uruzgan, who was killed in fighting with the British forces in Helmand (2007). After reports of alleged contacts with the ANDSF, he was arrested by the Inter-Services Intelligence (ISI) in 2016.[18]

Since the elevation of Akhtar Mohammad Mansoor

as acting leader, Ishaqzais from his home area of Band-e-Timur, in Maiwand district, Kandahar, received several senior appointments. Both the Taliban director of finance, Gul Agha, and his senior adviser, Samad Sanai, were Ishaqzais. Though both Mansour and Rasool were Ishaqzais, they fell out over control of respective drug empires and links in Iran, as also on other issues of finance dispersal for the local commanders against the Afghan security forces.

Other aspirants like the young Mullah Yaqoob, son of Mullah Omar, and Mullahs Zakir (an Alizai), Ibrahim Sadr (Alikozai) and Mullah Rauf (late), prominent field commanders fighting in Helmand and Uruzgan were unhappy with Mansour's leadership, as was the main ISI protégé, Serajuddin Haqqani.[19]

Mansour was observed travelling frequently to Iran. His family and property assets were reportedly present there. His possible distancing from Pakistani control and progressive reliance on Iran was not liked by Taliban handlers in ISI. He was killed in a US drone attack in May 2016, inside Balochistan, while on his way back from Iran. Though the taxi carrying him was completely incinerated, his Pakistani passport in the name of Muhammad Wali was found outside, leading to suspicion about an ISI tip-off to the Americans.[20]

Haibatullah Akhundzada, a Noorzai from Panjwai in Kandahar, was chosen the third emir of the Taliban. He hailed from a respected religious family and had served as the head of Sharia courts in the Taliban's previous dispensation. From the outset, his approach as leader was consensual and great pains were taken to brush factional differences under the carpet. Serajuddin Haqqani and Mullah Yaqub were brought in as deputy leaders.[21] These changes occurred under close ISI supervision.

To complicate matters further, Mullah Baradar, a Popalzai and co-founder of the Taliban, was brought in as a third deputy emir in 2018. He had been under Pakistani custody from 2010 for having initiated talks with President Karzai and the Americans without a go-ahead from the Pakistani Army. He was released in October 2018 under prodding from the US Special Envoy, Zalmay Khalilzad, to lend impetus to the Doha talks. Baradar was entrusted with the responsibility of interacting with the Americans at Doha, along with the hardline 'Guantanamo Five', and the Taliban leaders still under house arrest there.[22]

The Haqqani network was founded by Jalaluddin Haqqani, a Zadran tribal leader having influence in Paktia and Khost provinces. When the Soviet invasion took place, he became a militant commander. He was cultivated as an asset of the Central Intelligence Agency and received tens of millions of dollars in cash for his work in fighting the Soviet-led Afghan forces in Afghanistan.[23] While fighting the Russians, he was able to take US senators, notably Charlie Wilson, a Democrat, to the war theatre to observe firing of the US made stinger missiles made available to the Mujahideen.[24] He also received funds from Arab sources. He was not an original member of the Taliban, but in 1995, just prior to the Taliban's occupation of Kabul, he switched his allegiance to them. In 1996–97, he served as a Taliban military commander north of Kabul, and later, as minister of borders and tribal affairs, and governor of Paktia. He had seven sons, prominent among them being Burhanuddin, Nasiruddin (both deceased) and Sirajuddin, current interior minister of the Taliban government. Another son, Anas Haqqani, is much younger. He was in custody of the ANDSF but was released in terms of the Doha Accord, 2020.

Despite dependence on the ISI for years of sustenance in safe havens, and for rest and recuperation facilities inside Pakistan, some Taliban leaders, especially those hailing from the Kandahar Loya, harbour resentment over the ISI's excessive control or dominance. In his book, *My Life with the Taliban*, Abdul Salam Zaeef, Taliban's Ambassador to Pakistan (2000–2001), referred to the Pakistani military establishment derisively as 'men with forked tongues'. He told the US ambassador in Pakistan not to trust ISI missives about alleged Taliban reluctance to open dialogue channels.[25]

This issue rankled with the Pakistanis even earlier, when Sayyed Tayyab Agha, Mullah Omar's close associate, along with another influential leader, Agha Jan Motasim, reached out to Barnett Rubin, a US academic close to the CIA, in 2010, and with interlocutors in the Royal United Services Institute, UK, in 2017, in an apparent quest to start a peace dialogue with the Americans through the Taliban's Doha office. Another idea of insurgent peace-making, through some field commanders, was also floated.[26] Tayyab Agha was arrested by the ISI for a while in Islamabad. Both he and Motasim now remain in exile, possibly in the UAE.

Exactly two years back, in August 2019, an IED blast at the Khairul Madaris Mosque in Qasim Killay, Kuchlak, frequented by the Taliban's Quetta Shura, killed Haibatullah Akhundzada's brother, Hafiz Ahmadullah, who was the main preacher there. The chowkidar at the mosque, an Afghan national, was arrested by the Pakistani authorities. Claims of responsibility for the blast, made on behalf of Mullah Rasool's dissident faction of the Taliban could not be established, though Mullah Rasool continued to remain under detention of the Pakistani authorities.[27]

Interestingly, in what may be a subtle message to the Taliban leadership by the ISI, two days after the Taliban entered Kabul, Mullah Rasool was released from custody on 17 August 2021. This news was blacked out in the Pakistani media.[28]

Pulls and pressures from rival Taliban factions may have delayed formation of their 33-member interim cabinet, which could be announced only on 8 September 2021, almost three weeks after they took charge in Kabul. These included 15 from the Loya Kandahar, 10 from Loya Paktia and five other Pashtuns.

Mullah Yaqub is the present acting defense minister, with Mullah Zakir as one of his deputies. Mullah Ibrahim Sadr is accommodated as deputy interior minister, under Serajuddin Haqqani. Only one Uzbek, two Tajeks were inducted, including the army chief (Fasihuddin), one Hazara came in a later expansion, but no woman representative was present.[29] The Ministry of

Women Affairs was replaced and renamed as the Ministry for Prevention of Vice and Promotion of Virtue. Rumours of persisting differences within the Cabinet abounded when reports surfaced of a major fracas between Mullah Baradar and the Haqqanis in the Presidential Palace in early September 2021.[30] Mullah Baradar went back to Kandahar, sulking.

On 28 September 2021, Abdul Hakim Sharaey, Taliban's acting justice minister, announced during a meeting with the Chinese ambassador in Kabul, Wang Yu, that the Islamic Emirate will follow the 1964 Constitution of Afghanistan for a temporary period, without paying heed to any content that would contradict Sharia law.[31] It remains to be seen what adjustments are made in its observance. Though it provided for an elected Parliament, these provisions may well be deemed as not conforming to the Sharia.

TALIBAN AND TEHREEK-E-TALIBAN PAKISTAN

On 17 August 2021, shortly after the Taliban entered Kabul, they released several prisoners from Pul-e-Charkhi jail. Among them was a prominent Tehreek-e-Taliban Pakistan (TTP) leader, Maulvi Faqir Muhammed.[32]

Though reiterating their resolve not to allow use of Afghan territory for disruptive terrorist activities elsewhere, Zabiullah Mujahid, Taliban spokesperson and now deputy minister, information and culture, indicated that the issue of the TTP is one that the Pakistan government must resolve, not Afghanistan.[33] They clearly indicated that they were reluctant to take any conclusive action against the TTP, especially when elements within the Taliban favoured TTP's idea of bringing Pakistan under Islamic rule. Such action could alienate groups within the Taliban, affecting internal unity so essential to the Taliban's hold in Kabul, at a time when there are reports of various factions fighting internally for power.[34]

This reluctance stemmed from the same refusal the Taliban doggedly displayed when pressed by former Pakistani Director

General, ISI, Lt Gen. Mehmood Ahmed, to give up Osama bin Laden to the Americans in 2001. The ideological affinities and bonds that developed between the Al-Qaeda, Afghan Taliban and subsequently emerged radical Islamic outfits, like TTP, were deep and lasting. Atiyah Abd al-Rahman and Abu Yahya al-Libi, close religious advisers of Osama, sent detailed instructions to the TTP leaders at the time of its formation in 2007, urging them to 'trust the rule of the Amir of the Believers-Mullah Muhammad Umar Mujahid and consider him as their emir'.[35]

These developments also raised the possibility of the Afghan Taliban using the TTP as a bargain or leverage in its dealings with Pakistan, perhaps even to facilitate talks between the TTP and Pakistani state institutions to settle, but they would ignore Pakistani demands to expel TTP from Afghanistan or to act against TTP over their differences.[36]

However, Pakistani Prime Minister Imran Khan claimed that the Taliban leadership had been approached to mediate and had agreed to intercede on behalf of the Pakistani establishment for talks with the TTP as well.[37] Reports of one of the TTP factions from North Waziristan announcing a three-month ceasefire in its operations emerged subsequently.[38] More recently, Pakistan's Minister of Information and Broadcasting, Fawad Chaudhry, claimed that agreement had been reached with the TTP for a full ceasefire.[39]

TTP's new leader, Mufti Noor Wali Mehsud, appointed after the death of Mullah Fazlullah, is a Pashtun from the Mehsud tribe, hailing from South Waziristan. The TTP's various splinter factions reunited recently and Mehsud declared his intention to ideologically justify, operationally sustain and morally legalize the group's violent struggle in the Afghanistan–Pakistan border region in the post-US withdrawal scenario. He said that the TTP would work for separating the ex-Federally Administered Tribal Areas (FATA) region, now merged with Khyber Pakhtunkhwa province, from Pakistan through a jihadist struggle and transform it into a Sharia-ruled state.[40] The TTP's statements of the last two years reveal constant references to two main themes: 'Islamic principles and tribal customs' and the 'Pashtun tribal nation'. These themes can also be found in the first chapter of Noor Wali Mehsud's book *Inqilab-i-Mehsud*.

The TTP seems to be making these rhetorical and operational changes to circumvent being lumped with global jihadist groups, such as the Islamic State Khorasan Province (ISKP) or the Al-Qaeda in Afghanistan. This rhetoric is consistent with the Afghan Taliban's position of not recognizing the Durand Line as a legal border and opposing its fencing by Pakistan. They also seek to avoid the US-led over-the-horizon counterterrorism strikes. As they no longer control territory in FATA, these changes in strategy and rhetoric were also necessary for the TTP to continue to benefit from sanctuaries in Afghanistan, under the Afghan Taliban's umbrella, without creating international legal challenges for the former.

Latest reports indicate that Taliban's Interior Minister, Sirajuddin Haqqani, has taken the initiative to oversee peace negotiations between the TTP and the Pakistani military establishment. Efforts were underway, apparently, to thresh out modalities of a ceasefire agreement. The TTP was resisting pressure to unconditionally disarm and was demanding release of prisoners. Details in this regard are understandably couched in secrecy at present.[41]

TALIBAN AND THE ISLAMIC STATE KHORASAN PROVINCE

Ties with the Islamic State Khorasan Province (ISKP) or Daesh splinter cells existing in parts of Afghanistan's eastern provinces and in some towns like Jalalabad, Asadabad (Kunar), even Kabul, may prove to be more difficult to handle.

When the Taliban released prisoners from Pul-e-Charkhi jail on 17 August 2021, they killed Ziya-ul-Haq aka Abu Omar Khorasani, a Pashtun tribal from Khyber Agency, then ISKP's known leader since April 2017.[42] The Taliban have also been accused of killing Farooq Bengalzai, an Islamic State of Iraq and the Levant leader from Pakistan, while he was travelling in southwestern Afghanistan. On 28 August 2021, the Taliban was accused of arresting Abu Obaidullah Mutawakil, a well-known Salafi scholar, in Kabul. A week later, Mutawakil was found dead. The Taliban denied any part in Mutawakil's death, however suspicions of their complicity were not allayed. Deputy Minister of Information and Culture, Zabihullah Mujahid, recently told Al Jazeera that the Taliban would actively 'hunt down those who are sowing chaos' in the country.[43] The Taliban spokesperson in Kabul recently claimed that a major ISKP hideout in Kabul had been raided.

On the evening of 26 August, just 11 days after the Taliban takeover, the ISKP claimed responsibility for a bombing at Kabul's Hamid Karzai International Airport that killed more than 180 people and injured hundreds of others.[44] On 22 September 2021, ISKP militants carried out two bombings and a gun attack on Taliban supporters, killing at least two Taliban fighters and three civilians.[45]

The ISKP emerged in 2014 from various splinter groups operating across the Afghan-Pak border. Described as a *wilayah* (province) of the Islamic State, and Khorasan, it espoused the Daesh's ideology, seeking to establish a global, transnational caliphate that is governed by Islamic jurisprudence. Hafiz Khan Saeed, a former TTP commander from Orakzai, was its first emir. Thereafter, Aslam Farooqi, a 43-year-old Pakistani Afridi became its leader. He was arrested by the Afghan NDS. Later, a new faction emerged under Muawiya Khorasani aka Sayvaly Shafiev, formerly an Islamic Movement of Uzbekistan commander. Some reports suggest Shahab al-Muhajir is the ISKP's new emir in Afghanistan. In June 2021, the United Nations estimated that ISKP consists of a core group of fighters numbering between 1,500 and 2,200 and are based in provinces such as Kunar and Nangarhar.

The Islamic State's motto, '*baqiyawatatamaddad*' (remaining and expanding), calls on other Muslims to migrate to the group's fledgling caliphate. Though these ideological moorings were similar to those of groups like Al-Qaeda, the ISKP refused to acknowledge the Taliban as a legitimate Islamic leader. Their newsletter, *al-Naba*, has pursued a long-standing propaganda effort to brand the Taliban as nationalists with narrow parochial interests in Afghanistan—contrasted with the ISKP's global aims. This hostility intensified, especially after the Taliban started peace negotiations with the US in March 2020. From January 2020 to July 2021, the ISKP conducted 83 attacks, resulting in 309 fatalities. They targeted Hazaras in Bamiyan, as also security forces, including North Atlantic Treaty Organization (NATO) troops and Afghan military. Thirteen of the incidents since January 2020 were attacks or violent clashes against the Taliban forces.[46] On 2 November 2021, the Kabul Military Hospital was attacked by gunmen, killing at least 19 people, including Hamdullah Mokhlis, a key commander of the Haqqani network. The attack was later claimed by the ISKP.

The ISKP has had links in the past with the Haqqani network. Elements of the Haqqani Network allegedly coordinated with ISKP on some occasions. The Afghan Ministry of Defense claimed that at least one 2018 attack claimed by ISKP was in fact carried out by Haqqani network fighters. Al-Muhajir, who was behind organizing frequent attacks in Kabul, was previously an ISKP planner/mid-level commander of the Haqqani network.[47]

The reduction in the international counterterrorism and intelligence footprint in Afghanistan after the withdrawal of the US and NATO forces gave the ISKP strategic breathing room to regroup and increase its attacks. They were afforded a 'replenishable and diverse recruitment pipeline' of experienced militants from existing groups on both sides of the Af-Pak border, which could enable it to expand its local base.[48]

A lot would depend on how seriously Taliban's Interior Minister, Sirajuddin Haqqani, deals with this complicated problem of disciplining or neutralizing the ISKP, which is now believed to be also getting help from former disgruntled elements who deserted the Afghan National Army. This could also condition the international response to the Taliban's quest for diplomatic recognition.

15

Afghan National Defence and Security Forces: From Collapse to Regrouping?

Brig. Rahul Bhonsle

Afghanistan as a nation-state has faced multiple fracturing criticalities in the last four decades and has entered another period of transition from an Islamic Republic to an emirate. What is significant is that this change, like others before, has occurred through the use of asymmetric force by a non-state actor, the Taliban, a group that has been internationally sanctioned. Combating North Atlantic Treaty Organization (NATO) led by the United States Armed Forces, a military alliance of the most advanced armed forces of modern times, the Taliban's success has raised many questions due to the sudden collapse of the Afghan National Defence and Security Forces (ANDSF).

While the US intelligence, as is now being revealed through hearings in the US congressional committees, expected a 'risk of fracture and government collapse after the departure of US forces', the consensus was that this may occur by the end of December in 2021.[1] The discomfiting collapse of the ANDSF has led to much recrimination of the power elite in Republican Kabul. A detailed review of the reasons behind the failure of the ANDSF will be discussed herein. This will be followed by a descriptive survey and projection of how the Taliban or the so-called Islamic Emirate is going about rebuilding a national army and what are the prospects of viable security stability in Afghanistan.

ANDSF COLLAPSE OF AN ARMY OR STATE FAILURE

Belying expectations

In Afghanistan's turbulent history of recent decades, 15 August 2021 was another significant day. A dominant insurgent movement moved into Kabul, which by now has witnessed a change of regime by use of force for the fifth time in the past four decades. The sudden departure of the elected president of the republic, Mohammad Ashraf Ghani, secretively by helicopter, marked the end of an era that saw many tangible gains for the Afghan people—yet it seems high politics in the country had seen little transformation. It was easy to blame the fall of the Republican Kabul on collapse of the army, yet the reality may be far more complex. While the ANDSF failed to offer resistance that was expected of them, there is a need for a deeper analysis of underlying factors that led to the catastrophic capitulation.

The US Secretary of Defense, Lloyd J. Austin III, appearing before the United States Senate Committee on Armed Services on 28 September 2021 outlined the cause for failure of the ANDSF: lack of will of the force to sustain the fight despite having been provided the best of weapons and equipment. Lloyd, a former head of the United States Central Command, which was directly responsible for US operations in Afghanistan, said in his prepared remarks to the United States Senate Committee on Armed Services on 28 September 2021: 'We provided the Afghan military with equipment and aircraft and the skills to use them. Over the years, they often fought bravely. Tens of thousands of Afghan soldiers and police officers died. But in the end, we couldn't provide them with the will to win. At least not all of them.'[2]

Yet years before in 2017, another American general, John W. Nicholson, commander of the US forces in Afghanistan deposing before the United States Senate Committee on Armed Services, lauded the offensive ability of the Afghan forces in decimating the Taliban. He said: 'Since the start of the Taliban's campaign in April that year, the ANDSF prevented them [Taliban] from accomplishing their stated strategic objective of overtaking provincial capitals... The ANDSF consistently retook district centers and population areas within days of a loss, whereas in 2015 it sometimes took them weeks to recover.'[3]

The then Afghanistan Minister of Defence, Asadullah Khalid, stated that 'he had worked to shift regular forces out of their defensive posture...their mind-set has changed from defensive to offensive.'[4]

An important point to note is that during this period, the ANDSF was operating as the lead offensive force, with the NATO coalition having assumed the role of training and guidance in the form of the Resolute Support Mission (RSM).

Other American agencies, however, were less optimistic of the capabilities of the ANDSF. Special Inspector General for Afghanistan Reconstruction (SIGAR), tasked to report to the US Congress on effective employment of resources allocated for rebuilding of the State in Afghanistan, in a quarterly report to the United States Congress in 2017 highlighted the numerous challenges faced by the Afghan forces. The SIGAR report read:

> The ANDSF faces many problems: unsustainable casualties, temporary losses of provincial and district centers, weakness in logistics and other functions, illiteracy in the ranks, often corrupt or ineffective leadership, and over-reliance on highly trained special forces for routine missions. In addition, about 35% of the force does not reenlist each year, so even full recruitment to cover attrition might dilute its quality.[5]

In a frank confession before the United States Senate Committee on Armed Services on 28 September 2021, Austin questioned whether the coalition had the right strategy and the ability to build effective institutions. Austin said, 'Did we have the right strategy? Did we have too many strategies? Did we put too much faith in our ability to build effective Afghan institutions—an army, an air force, a police force, and government ministries? We helped build a state, but we could not forge a nation."[6]

Quite evidently, two narratives emerge from the ANDSF's capability, indicating a variation between organizational and operational effectiveness. Yet in 2021, it appeared that the operational resistance too had crumbled between 6 August, when the first provincial capital in Afghanistan, Zaranj in Nimroz province, fell to the Taliban, and 15 August, when formal military resistance collapsed. The reasons for this travesty will be debated by military historians and scholars for years ahead.

Raising the ANDSF

The legacy of fielding a national army in Afghanistan has been weak. The State has over the years relied on military controls through a patchwork of militia led by local satraps, while a central force has been the glue that has ensured writ of the seat of power Kabul ran across the country. Antonio Giustozzi, noted analyst on military and security organization, in Afghanistan wrote:

> It is interesting to note that even in 1938, as the Afghan Army for the first time had just adopted a modern divisional structure, there remained a heavy reliance on tribal levies to pump up the size of the armed forces. It was then expected that in the event of war, 300–400,000 tribal warriors would join the 90,000 men of the regular army.[7]

The International Security Assistance Force (ISAF), led by the NATO, hoped to break this jinx and create a viable national security force. The ISAF had to begin from scratch. At the beginning of 2002, Afghanistan's security institutions, including its national army, police and judiciary had collapsed or were severely damaged after Operation Enduring Freedom. During the Taliban rule from 1996–2001, the army had disintegrated and was replaced by ethnic and regional militias. The Afghan national police force had also withered away.

Thus, for the first time, an attempt to form a military on the lines of a modern state was made in Afghanistan, starting from 2002. While initially assessed to fight criminal and sundry terrorist groups, this force, which went on to become the ANDSF, faced a highly complex threatening environment over the next two decades. By the end of 2020, the challenge was that of high intensity militancy waged by multiple regional and global groups with the Taliban as the central 'enemy' of the State. These groups were aided from across the Durand Line in terms of political support, sanctuaries, funding, arms munitions and a safe passage, along with a typical doublespeak from Pakistan. The strength of the militant groups has been variously estimated at 70,000 plus mostly hard-boiled fighters. They operated on slim logistics and were adept at living off the land.

In such an environment, the Afghan military had to control security of at least 30 of the 34 provinces, spread across 652,000 sq. km, covering a population of 30 million. While initially, the number of personnel sanctioned for the ANDSF in 2002 was 43,000, the final figures were 352,000 Afghan National Army (ANA) and Afghan National Police personnel, including the Afghan Air Force and Afghan Special Security Forces, along with 30,000 Afghan local police officers. On the ground, there were roughly 275,000–300,000 forces, a deficit of around 20 per cent.[8]

In terms of force to space ratio for fighting an active insurgency, the numbers were inadequate. How the figure of 352,000 was arrived at is not clear. It may have been determined by the ability for providing long-term funding to such a force. The deficit in the ANDSF numbers were partially made up by well-trained and equipped support from the NATO forces for much of the time from 2003 onwards. But as the latter dwindled and western troops' numbers went down, expecting the Afghan military to deliver on its own appears to be too optimistic now in hindsight.

In tandem with the army and the police, Afghan Air Force (AAF) was raised as a combat support with an inventory of 174 helicopters and 50 light combat aircraft, all of which were very effective in operational and logistics support to the ANDSF.[9] The bases, however, were operated by American coalition forces and the private defence contractors that supported them and were almost 15,000 in number in 2021. This support wilted away once the US forces started withdrawing and the AAF was faced with challenges in operating at full potential.

Apart from the numbers, raising the ANDSF had been a complex process, involving multiple nations and agencies. The US had led the army reforms, and Germany, the police reforms. Multiple national contingents of NATO had been involved on the training front—each contingent and trainer had a tenure of six months. In addition, a number of private contractors from DynCorp Aerospace Technology had also been employed to train and equip the police as well as advising the Ministry of Interior. Private contractors had also been involved in construction and maintenance support.

In the initial stagem, the NATO-embedded teams had been deployed in Afghan Kandaks or battalions for imparting 14 weeks of training for officers and non-commissioned officers. This period included six weeks of basic training, six weeks of advanced individual training and two weeks of collective training.[10] There were bound to be deficits owing to the short period and quality of training that was imparted to the ANDSF recruits. The period of voluntary service for a soldier in the Afghan Army was five years—this implied the need to train a far larger number of recruits as the re-enlistment rate remained low.

The training of the ANDSF was progressively improved and ethnic balance was maintained. The Pashtuns formed the largest community in Afghanistan at around 40 per cent. The Tajiks, Hazaras and Uzbeks made up amongst other ethnicities. Despite the ANDSF progressively increasing in numbers, sustained support by the ISAF was necessary, and it was provided from 31 December 2003 onwards. This mission continued till the end of December in 2014, and on 1 January 2015, the RSM was put into place, which 'focused primarily on training, advice and assistance activities at the security-related ministries, in the country's institutions and among the senior ranks of the army and police.'[11]

Apparently, a realistic assessment of ANDSF's ability to survive a full-blown Taliban onslaught without the support of the US and NATO partners was never done. In addition, there were some structural deficits in the ANDSF, which could not be overcome.

ANDSF: What Could Not Be Overcome?

A military reflects the characteristics of the society from which it is raised. While noble efforts were made to build a national army with professional values, the challenge was to create a proficient force from a multi-ethnic pantheon of historical ethnic divisions with schisms embedded over the years. Another challenge at hand was corruption. SIGAR Report of 2017 mentioned earlier stated: 'One recent indicator of the severity of difficulties confronting U.S. efforts to stand up and sustain an effective ANDSF were apparent in a March 28, 2017, announcement by the Afghan Ministry of Defence that the ministry had sacked 1,394 of its officials for corruption in the past year.'[12]

Leadership was another challenge. While there were many leaders who were no doubt competent in the field, their record was marred in terms of human rights and corruption. Status and grade were significant factors in the Afghan military hierarchy. Thus, ANDSF emerged as a top-heavy organization, and throughout history, Afghan national forces have had more generals than what can be decently scaled. In fact, then President Ashraf Ghani was unpopular as he sought to dismiss or downgrade some of the bloated higher ranks who parked themselves in the comfort zone in the Ministry of Defence and the Interior as well as the subordinate formations.

The US Secretary of Defense, Lloyd J. Austin III, appearing before the United States Senate Committee on Armed Services on 28 September 2021 summarized these challenges by saying: 'We need to consider some uncomfortable truths: that we did not fully comprehend the depth of corruption and poor leadership in their senior ranks, that we did not grasp the damaging effect of frequent and unexplained rotations by President Ghani of his commanders...'[13]

The last-named factor of unexplained change in command made by the President undoubtedly had a role to play in the collapse of the ANDSF. 'Over the years, we met Afghan generals praised by the U.S. military, only to find out later the generals were replaced for incompetence or corruption,' remarked one commander.[14] Asadullah Khalid, defence minister of Afghanistan in 2018, was curiously removed in 2020 and later brought in days after the provincial capitals started collapsing only to be replaced by Bismillah Mohammadi, a veteran Tajik commander. President Mohammad Ashraf Ghani appointed General Abdul Satar Mirzakwal as the acting minister for interior affairs in the month of June 2021. Meanwhile, in the heat of the battles so to say, commander of 215 Maiwand Afghan Army Corps, Gen. Sami Sadat, was appointed to lead the Special Operations Corps, replacing Gen. Hibatullah Alizai who was appointed the chief of army staff, replacing Gen. Wali Ahmadzai who had been appointed in June. Playing musical chairs at a time of acute military crisis was hardly a strategy to defeat the Taliban.

Lack of professional oversight by the US and NATO military and civil leadership to the Afghan president was more than evident at this critical juncture. Finding himself out of depth in crisis, Ashraf Ghani, former director at the World Bank, fumbled to the detriment of his State and people.

As the ANDSF saw the main bulwark of support of NATO dwindling over the years, the impact on morale and fighting potential may also have been heavy, though there are no surveys of the same so far. But the steady draw-down of troops would have certainly developed a sense of abandonment.

General Mark E. Milley, the US chairman of the joint chiefs of staff, in the hearing of the United States Senate Committee on Armed Services on 28 September 2021, said:

Beginning in 2011, we steadily drew down our troop numbers, consolidated and closed bases, and retrograded equipment from Afghanistan. At the peak in 2011, we had 97,000 US and 41,000 NATO troops in Afghanistan. 10 years later when Ambassador Khalilzad signed the Doha Agreement with Mullah Berader on 29 February 2020, the US had 12,600 US troops, 8,000 NATO and 10,500 contractors in Afghanistan.[15]

In April 2021, when US President Joe Biden announced the final drawdown date of the US and consequentially that of NATO troops, there were 2,500 American troops in Afghanistan at the time.[16]

Austin said that the Doha Agreement also had a demoralizing impact on the Afghan Soldiers. Austin remarked in September that the US military did not anticipate 'the Doha agreement itself had a demoralizing effect on Afghan soldiers...'.[17] The perception of desertion by a key ally even as the battle was being joined may have led to deep diffidence in the ANDSF, a sentiment that the Taliban deftly exploited as will be highlighted in the next part.

Taliban's Winning Operational Strategy

The Taliban, having failed to seize even a single provincial capital in numerous battles in 2017 and 2018, seemed to have sensed victory with the signing of the Doha Agreement on 29 February 2020 or even prior to that as there was a declaration of intent of the US and NATO forces leaving Afghanistan as early as in 2010 at the London Conference. Thereafter, the markers were 2014, the year of transition of NATO mission from combat to support—RSM.

While it is not clear when the Taliban actually began their planning with the obvious assistance of Pakistan's intelligence and military planners, the Doha Agreement in February 2020 perhaps heralded the multifaceted campaign of information, psychological warfare and military operations to gain control of districts and provinces. Austin said that the Doha Agreement was also a start of deal-making by the Taliban with local leaders. The US military did not anticipate the 'snowball effect caused by the deals that Taliban commanders struck with local leaders in the wake of the Doha agreement', he added.[18]

Acknowledging debility of the US and NATO military position in January 2021, Secretary of State, Antony John Blinken, in his opening statement in the hearing before the United States Senate Committee on Foreign Relations on 14 September 2021 said, 'By January 2021, the Taliban was in its strongest military position since 9/11—and we had the smallest number of troops on the ground since 2001.'[19] The hard-boiled Taliban fighters having years of experience in combating foreign militaries may have derived similar conclusions as the campaign for control of the Afghan provincial space was launched with full vigour.

In 2020, the US armed forces saw the Taliban gaining control of areas in numerous provinces. US Chairman of the Joint Chiefs of Staff, Mark Milley, during his hearing to the United States Senate Committee on Armed Services on 28 September stated, 'The Taliban strengthened its positions around several provincial capitals in anticipation of the departure of foreign forces and, over this time period, enemy-initiated attacks increased by over 50% and were above previous seasonal norms.' Simultaneously, Milley stated that targeted attacks were launched in 2020 to undermine and coerce the people at large and, '...Taliban violence against women, human rights defenders, journalists, and government officials continued, with almost 1,000 targeted killings attributed to the Taliban, up from 780 in 2019.'[20]

As per Milley's testimony of the 419 districts in Afghanistan, Taliban controlled approximately 78 districts in February 2021, which rose to over 100 in mid-June and 200 by mid-July, with at least 15 provincial capitals under threat.[21]

The Taliban also worked on the ANDSF psychology. Well-worn themes such as success in forcing the US to agree to a pullout and Islamic messaging were used to effect to degrade the capability of Afghan soldiers and police to resist. Money is also said to have played a major role, and corruption has been a major issue with the Afghan forces in the past. Supplies were pilfered, with arms, ammunition and other equipment sold in the black market.

The systematic campaign to achieve local dominance that was undertaken by the Taliban no doubt weakened the determination of the ANDSF, but the extent of the same cannot be assessed as of now. One option was to delay NATO pullout. Department of Defense leadership seems to have sought to convey to American presidents—first Donald Trump and later Joe Biden—about the perils that may befall continuing with the pullout. But perhaps, these fell on deaf ears, given the domestic political compulsions as well as the firm personal belief held by both Trump and Biden for leaving Afghanistan.

A high operational tempo was maintained by mobile fighters, moving from one district to another, concentrating a superior force against isolated posts and picquets of the Afghan Army and the police. The strategy of the ANDSF of holding a large number of small outposts with limited strength in the belief that this was essential to ensure support to the Republic regime was operationally disastrous. Gen. John Nicholson, commander of the US forces, in Afghanistan, while deposing before the United States Senate Committee on Armed Services, warned of this weakness in 2017 and said: 'Besides poor leadership, the widespread ANDSF use of static checkpoints is still the greatest contributing factor to increased casualties. There is significant social and political pressure to maintain these checkpoints around villages and along highways. However, the ANDSF are not trained in how to defend these small outposts, conduct local security patrols or ambush would-be attackers.'[22]

The Taliban obviously exploited this weakness.

As the Taliban cut off the lines of communications supporting these isolated posts, arms and munitions could not be provided to the latter, and supply by the AAF did not prove economical.

Thus, the morale and motivation, lacking basic wherewithal, is expected to have withered away.

The backstop to military action was negotiations with the US initially and then with the Afghan Republic government, both of which were employed to good effect to obtain release of a large number of prisoners, divide the leadership in Kabul and finally lead to an agreement for transfer of power, as per the statements now made by the then US Special Envoy for Afghan Reconciliation, Zalmay Khalilzad. He claimed in multiple forums, after having officially resigned, that President Ghani rescinded the agreement for transition in Kabul before his last-minute departure by helicopter, leaving behind a power vacuum.

Bitter Lessons of Collapse of ANDSF

The famous saying that 'success has many fathers, but failure is an orphan' rings true in the collapse of the ANDSF. Many Afghan soldiers and NATO personnel fought bravely in the past two decades, even though they did not live up to the expectations in the last phase of resistance against an internationally recognized terrorist group—the Taliban supported by the intelligence and military establishment of Pakistan. Apart from deficit in military organization, such as paucity of numbers, distribution in penny packets, logistics and resupply failures, poor national and military leadership, and corruption, preparation of the battlefield by the Taliban, added to the rapid collapse of the ANDSF. These are, of course, preliminary lessons based on the available inputs and are subject to review as more details emerge in the days and months ahead.

TALIBAN AND NATIONAL ARMY

Taliban 1.0's Experience

Noted scholar on Afghan military history and organization of forces, Antonio Giustozzi, recounted the fighting force raised by the Taliban after they came to power in Kabul in 1996. With ambitions of creating a national army, the Taliban had reportedly failed to raise a viable force despite assistance from Pakistan. The Taliban, he said, had established a central army corps and an armoured brigade in Kabul, and three regional army corps in Kandahar, Paktia and Herat. Professionalism was lacking as personal relations and charisma was substituted for competence to promote leaders. Giustozzi recounted that the hardcore army included 45,000 personnel, which also constituted many foreign volunteers, mostly Pakistanis.[23] A number of local militias, which were loyal to the Taliban, were organized in tandem.

The Taliban had gained experience of handling armoured vehicles and artillery, but the force wilted under the combined pressure of the US special forces and the local militia in the Operation Enduring Freedom sweep that followed the 9/11 attacks. At the same time, the Taliban gained control of most of Afghanistan through patchwork force, even pushing the legendary Ahmad Shah Masood into Panjshir. How the circumstances, which were effective for Taliban 1.0, will set the stage for the Taliban 2.0 remains to be seen. There is very limited information of the Taliban plans and processes of creating a national army, though a desire for the same has been expressed by many senior officials.

From Fighters to Soldiers

The first transition for the Taliban in building a national army would be converting fighters to soldiers—moulding raw aggression and courage into a disciplined operator. Aware of the possibility of fighters continuing on a triumphant rampage, acting Minister of Defense, Islamic Emirate of Afghanistan (IEA), Mullah Mohammad Yaqoob, warned the Taliban fighters that a general amnesty had been granted and thus arbitrary actions should not be taken. 'Behave well with people, do not defame IEA with your arbitrary actions, stop taking unnecessary photos and videos, and do not enter to government administrations unless you need to,' said the statement, as complaints of fighters evicting citizens from their homes, extortion and harassment of women were found to be growing.[24]

How much impact this had on the Taliban fighters is unclear, as targeting former Afghan police and intelligence forces in acts of revenge has continued. Cadres on the loose—renegade Taliban fighters—have been conducting door-to-door visits of those who worked with the US and NATO forces, threatening them with dire consequences. Bringing order to their own rank and file is the biggest immediate challenge that is faced by the group.

Mindful of the accusations, the Taliban launched a joint commission to weed out those who were indulging in acts of intimidation. The so-called supreme leader of the Islamic Emirate, Hibatullah Akhundzada, ordered the formation of a military court. TOLOnews reported that Mawllavi Obaidullah Nizami was appointed as the head of the court and Mawllavi Sayed Agha and Mawllavi Zahid Akhundzada were appointed as judges.[25] The court is to investigate complaints against the staff of the defense and interior ministries as well as intelligence department. How effective this will be remains to be seen.

Initial Force: Focus on Counterterrorism

The Islamic State of Khorasan Province (ISKP) poses a primary security challenge to the Taliban in Afghanistan. The ISKP is now active in all the provinces as per a recent report submitted to the United Nations Security Council. The ISKP has been responsible for a suicide bombing at Kabul airport in August 2021 and recent multiple bombings on Shia mosques. There are also reports of former military commanders joining the ISKP. To counter the ISKP, a series of operations have been launched and counterterrorism forces, such as Lashkar-e-Mansoori and Badri 313 Battalion, have been raised.

Badri 313 Battalion has secured the presidential palace and other important sites in the city. It was reportedly providing 'security' at the Kabul Airport and is named after the Battle of Badr, which took place in AD 624, when Prophet Muhammad led a victorious battle with 313 men. The Badri Battalion is ideologically aligned closely with the Al-Qaeda, while 313 Battalion is known to be close to the Haqqani network.

Lashkar Mansouri (Mansouri Battalion) forces have been formed in Badakhshan, Takhar and Balkh. Taliban has been showing off 'special forces' on social media, soldiers in uniforms equipped with looted American equipment to demonstrate their strength. The effectiveness of these forces will be determined based on their ability to curb the threat of the ISKP, which for now is a work in progress. In other words, how successful are the Taliban in converting an insurgent movement into a counter-insurgent one thus remains to be seen.

Ambitions for a Regular Army

Simultaneously, attempts to raise a regular army have been ongoing. Mullah Mohammad Yaqoub, the acting defence minister, and Mohammad Afzal Mazlom, first deputy defense minister, have announced the intent to form a regular army. Afzal reported that the army will defend the country's borders, while the Taliban will strive to have an 'independent' army. 'We should try to have a free and independent army and we must work to preserve the freedom we have gained,'[26] Mazlom said, while introducing Mawllawi Attaullah Omari as the commander of the Balkh army corps. Omari meanwhile said he will try to train the soldiers at the military corps. 'We will provide military training,' he added.[27]

Earlier, Taliban's acting Army Chief of Staff, Qari Fasihuddin, announced two weeks after the seizure of power in Kabul that the so-called IAE is working to form a 'regular' and 'strong' army. 'Our dear country should have a regular and strong army to easily defend and protect our country,' he said. 'Those who have received training and are professional should be used in our new army. We hope this army should be formed in the near future,' he added.[28]

In a contrary statement, Afghan Minister of Foreign Affairs, Emir Khan Muttaqi, said in Islamabad in November 2021 that Afghanistan does not need a large military on the lines of the former ANDSF, while speaking at Institute of Strategic Studies, Islamabad. It is not clear if this statement was made after serious consideration or to appease his Pakistani guests.

Separately, Wahidullah Hashemi, a senior Taliban official, said that the Taliban planned to set up a new national force that would include its members as well as government soldiers willing to join. 'Of course we will have some changes, to have some reforms in the army, but still we need them and will call them to join us.' Hashemi called for pilots to return and join the group. 'And we have asked them to come and join, join their brothers, their government. We called many of them and are in search of (others') numbers to call them and invite them to their jobs.'[29]

Taliban statements welcomed former government army personnel, however these reports of the soldiers of the ANDSF joining still needs confirmation. A news report on 10 October 2021 quoted cultural commission officials of the IAE saying that they will hire experienced soldiers in forming an Afghan Army.

The Taliban has announced reorientation of various corps' headquarters at the same location as that of the ANDSF, but have renamed those. The Kabul Military Corps became the Central Corps. The 201 Selab Military Corps in Laghman is now Khalid bin Walid Military Corps, 203 Thunder Military Corps is now Paktia Mansoori Military Corps, 215 Atal Military Corps in Kandahar is Al-Badr Military Corps, 207 Zafar Military Corps in Herat is Al-Farooq Military Corps, 209 Shaheen Military Corps has become Al-Fath Military Corps in Mazar-e-Sharief, 215 Maiwand Military Corps is Azm Military Corps in Helmand and 217 Pamir Military Corps has been changed to Omari Military Corps in Kunduz. Commanders have also been nominated to the corps. These appear to be the initial steps for formation of a regular force and an attempt to consolidate on NATO equipment may be an objective.[30]

Training

In an attempt to recreate a regular army, the Taliban is carrying out training and orientation at the corps locations. Pajhwok

Afghan News reported that 400 security personnel have completed one-month military training in the Mazar Military Corps Training Centre recently. A 75-member unit has been trained and graduated at the 203rd Thunder Corps headquarters in southeastern Paktia province. In Kabul, a parade was held for the graduation ceremony of 250 freshly trained soldiers. Details of the training carried out and the outcomes is yet to be assessed.

IEA National Army: An Illusion

While detailed information of the plans of formation of a regular army based on outcomes achieved is not available, this review is based essentially on statements made by the acting defence minister and army chief of the Taliban, legacy of raising a force and assessment of its capability to form a regular army. As of now, formation of a regular army may prove to be a very difficult challenge for the Taliban unless there is active support extended by an external state. Nations are unlikely to risk the wrath of the US by aiding the Taliban in creating a regular force, while assistance to building counterterrorism capability may be in the offing. Pakistan, which is involved in guiding the Taliban, is unlikely to welcome a professional military in the neighbourhood. Pakistan may insist on the use of counterterrorism rather than a conventional force.

Given wider security challenges, particularly by the ISKP, became evident within just a few months of the Taliban takeover of Kabul, the ability of the Taliban to form an effective counterterrorism force will be the first test. Thereafter, organization of a regular force will depend on the stability of the Taliban government, intragroup rivalries and funding. While large quantum of captured equipment is available, acquiring of munitions and fuel may pose a challenge, which the Taliban obviously lacks the money for. Clearly, at this point of time, the ambition of building a national army or even an effective counterterrorism force may be an illusion, yet the moves need to be watched carefully.

Part VII

ROAD AHEAD

16

The Return of the Taliban: Options for India

Amb. Gautam Mukhopadhaya

A little more than a year after the military takeover of Afghanistan amidst political confusion and very little resistance from the forces of the Islamic Republic of Afghanistan, hopes and wishful thinking that the Taliban would bring even a semblance of peace, security, stability and perhaps even a measure of inclusive government under the flag of an Islamic Emirate of Afghanistan (IEA), have not borne fruit. If anything, the political, economic, social, humanitarian and security situation in Afghanistan have become murkier than ever.

Politically, the country is deeply divided along multiple lines. The economy is in shambles. One set of security threats have been replaced by another. There is an atmosphere of fear and loathing against the Taliban that is taking a dangerously ethnic character. The Taliban still governs by the threat and use of force and appeal to religious virtue and tribal affiliation but lack legitimacy or the support of the Afghan people as a whole. Not a single political figure from the Islamic Republic has been accommodated in the Taliban power structure.

The Taliban violence and terrorism of the past against the Islamic Republic and its citizens have been replaced by harsh repression and reprisal killings, and by terrorism at the hand of the Islamic State Khorasan Province (ISKP) with Shia Hazaras as the principal target. However, other ethnicities too are not immune. Women have been virtually disenfranchised and subjected to apartheid—voiceless, faceless and nearly invisible.

The Taliban priorities are contrary to the existing humanitarian situation. Although better placed than between 1996–2001, when only three countries recognized the Taliban, the latter remains in a diplomatic limbo with some 15 resident foreign missions in Kabul, but no official international recognition as yet. Relations with its closest neighbour, Pakistan, are subject to strains over the fencing of the Durand Line, the Tehrik-e-Taliban Pakistan (TTP) presence in Afghanistan, and overbearing Pakistani tutelage over them.

Any roadmap of how countries should respond to the situation in Afghanistan must begin with an appreciation of the political and security situation, the internal, regional and geopolitical forces at work, the balance of such forces, and an insight into the foreseeable future and the longevity of the authority in power. But with a severely reduced and curtailed domestic media, and virtually no objective international presence in Afghanistan, reliable information on a complex reality is scarce to come by. Much of what is gathered through the limited media and chatter on social media is filtered through echo chambers and predilections of a deeply divided Afghanistan and Afghanistan watchers. Navigating these waters with Indian interests and values in mind would be challenging even in the best of times.

Although there are many in India today who look at Afghanistan purely in terms of the military plunder and depredations of the medieval past and the instability, with recent additions of conflict and terrorism, the rich trade and cultural legacy of Afghanistan–India relations, Afghanistan's timeless strategic location between West, Central and South Asia, its untapped economic and human resources, the close political ties since Independence, and the overwhelming affection that Afghans hold for India cannot be gainsaid. Politically, they constitute a huge political capital that we can ignore or squander only at our peril. Even if circumstances have distanced us from Afghanistan post August 2021, as it did during the period of Taliban rule from 1996–2001, India must find ways to maintain its relationship with the Afghan people and assist them in times of distress.

POLITICAL SITUATION

Despite known divisions and factions within the Taliban, most notably between the now Kandahari 'shura' and the Haqqani network, visible even during the Taliban takeover of Kabul, combined with 'acting' or interim nature of the Taliban government, and discernible internal differences over principles and policies (such as over girl's education), the Taliban have maintained an impressive show of unity under the authority of Mullah Haibatullah Akhundzada. Although recent decrees indicate a shift in decision-making to Kandahar and the invocation of Mullah Haibatullah by name[1] amongst the prophet's companions in Friday prayers and sermons in Ghazni and perhaps other provinces, may be signs of an attempt to consolidate power. Harsh crackdowns against any kind of dissent and preemptive actions, intended to foreclose any armed uprising or resistance by recalcitrant quarters, chiefly among the Tajiks, Uzbeks and Hazaras, appear to have consolidated the military control of the Taliban over Afghanistan.

However, false hopes and wishful thinking of an inclusive government, let alone a representative one, or any relaxation of their harsh interpretation of the Islamic shariat or social codes on women, have been dashed amidst initiatives that have only reinforced their radical conservatism and exclusionary vision. However, some still believe that the Taliban can be reformed. As if to underline their steadfastness to their puritanism and hard line, after abolishing the Ministry of Women's Affairs during their occupation and replacing it with a Ministry for the Propagation of Virtue and the Prevention of Vice, they are continuing to dismantle the structures of democracy and human rights that were established during the time the country was an Islamic

Republic. The offices of the Afghanistan constitutional council, the Afghanistan High Peace Council, the secretariats of the upper and lower houses of the Afghan Parliament, the Meshrano and Wolesi Jirga, and the Afghanistan Independent Human Rights Commission, among other Republican era institutions, were closed down in May 2022. Meanwhile, there are reports of the Taliban purging non-Pashtuns from military commands and administrative posts over differences in policies like education for women.[2]

Calls for a traditional Loya Jirgah by leaders, like former President Hamid Karzai, to facilitate unity and reconciliation too have been ignored. Instead, they have announced a 'Return and Communications' commission, which is to hold a national-level meeting to try to persuade those outside to drop their opposition to the Taliban rule and return to an uncertain future, even as they hold top leaders, who stayed behind like ex-President Hamid Karzai, Dr Abdullah, and Lower House Speaker Abdul Hadi Muslimyar, under house arrest. (However, latter two were allowed to leave Afghanistan briefly).[3]

OPPOSITION

With the advent of the Taliban, the political and social class that presided over the Islamic Republic is now dispersed internationally, with concentrations in Turkey, Tajikistan, the Gulf, the US and Europe. They have been meeting mainly in Turkey to form a common front, vis-a-vis the Taliban, with some recent signs of progress.

In Afghanistan, while street protests and demonstrations around the Afghan flag and rights of women, after the Taliban took over, have more or less fizzled out under the menacing presence of the Taliban gunmen, symbolic acts of protest continue; pockets of armed resistance have begun appearing mainly in Tajik areas of the northeast and elsewhere, too. The National Resistance Front (NRF), an armed resistance led by

Ahmed Massoud, son of the legendary Ahmed Shah Massoud, together with former Vice President Amrullah Saleh, based in Tajikistan, has been marshalling its forces and resolve to fight in tandem with a variety of other resistance forces. The latter claim to have conducted armed attacks in many parts of Afghanistan, notably Panjshir, Baghlan, Takhar, Badakshan, Parwan, Kapisa, Balkh, Samangan, Jawzjan, Ghor, Sar-e-Pul, Nangarhar and Kandahar, among other places.[4] Unlike in the late 1990s, when the Northern Alliance were known to be backed by Iran, Russia and India, it is not clear what external support and funding the resistance forces may be getting other than shelter in Tajikistan and other neighbouring countries.

On the political front, Uzbek leader Marshal Abdul Rashid Dostum hosted a meeting of jihadi leaders, including Ustad Atta Noor, Ustad Mohammad Mohaqeq, Ustad Karim Khalili, Ustad Abdur Rassoul Sayyaf, Mir Rahmani Rahmani, Mohammad Alam Ezedyar, and representatives of Salahuddin Rabbani and Ismail Khan, among others, on 17 May 2021 in Ankara, Turkey. In the meeting, he announced the formation of a Supreme Council of National Resistance for the Salvation of Afghanistan with a collective, rotational leadership, and also that of Ahmed Massoud's NRF as part of it.[5] Building on an earlier meeting held in October 2021, the Supreme Council of National Resistance has drawn up an agenda for Afghanistan that includes a more decentralized and parliamentary political system, an offer of dialogue with the Taliban, an endorsement of the ongoing nascent-armed resistance against the Taliban, and preparations to escalate the struggle. Together, the first serious stirrings of a coherent political organization and armed resistance seem to be beginning, although these are accompanied by deep internal divisions, rivalries, egos and personality clashes.

While this is a positive news, internally, Taliban-ruled Afghanistan is strained politically along multiple lines—Taliban–non-Taliban, north-south, Pashtun–non-Pashtun, inter-ethnic, intra-Taliban, intra-Pashtun and Taliban–ISKP. Of particular concern is a visible sharpening of ethnic fault-lines and revival of bad historical memories going back to the harshest periods of Afghan history, casting a shadow on Tajik-Pashtun, Hazara-Pashtun and even Tajik-Hazara relations.

Although, the anti-Taliban Pashtun leadership and most Pashtuns do not share this sentiment, more and more articulate non-Pashtuns are venting out feelings that the Taliban agenda is essentially Pashtun chauvinist in nature, that they have little in common with their version of Islam, that most Pashtuns are willing to countenance Taliban rule and regulations because they are not so opposed to their values or believe that the Taliban can be reformed, and are more likely not to support an armed resistance as they do. Many conservative Pashtuns, on the other hand, feel that the gains of peace and restoration of Pashtun authority in Kabul after 20 years of terrorism, misrule and skewed political power balance, are not worth another round of bloodshedding.

These concerns are complicated by the presence of multiple radical armed outfits who have fought shoulder to shoulder with the Taliban in Afghanistan and Pakistan over the last 20 years or more. These include the TTP and Pakistan-based anti-India outfits, who are now awaiting their turn to pursue their struggles against Pakistani establishment. This has worrying implications for its neighbours, not just Pakistan, which is already feeling the foretaste of the Taliban radicalism radiating from Afghanistan through the TTP.

Overall, the political and security situation in Afghanistan has remained highly dynamic. While the Taliban have consolidated themselves militarily and are unlikely to be easily dislodged by resistance in the near future, opposition and resistance groups are only just getting their act together, and are likely to grow and attract greater local and international support in future. Many of the latter are old jihadi commanders who have large followings among their ethnic groups and areas, and are experienced in fighting but have lost standing in the eyes of the people at large over the last 20 years of the Islamic Republic during which they were seen as amassing personal wealth and not doing much for the public. A newer generation of resistance, drawn largely from the old, has made an appearance but is untested politically or in the battlefield.

The emergence of more radical outfits like the ISKP, the shot in the arm provided by the Taliban to like-minded old and new regional groupings around Afghanistan from Central Asia to Chinese Turkestan, Pakistan and Iran, and ethnic frictions in Afghanistan and Pakistan spilling over into neighbouring states, carry the danger that unlike in the late 1990s, when there was a straightforward contest between the Taliban and the Northern Alliance, this time there could be a multi-cornered contest with several ethnic and radical extremist outfits in competition with each other.

Together, they have raised the spectre for the first time in a century of a de facto division of Afghanistan along ethnic, north–south lines around Farsiban Khorasan and Pashtunistan, with cross-boundary spillovers that could change the political geography of the region. While the emergence of the NRF and the Supreme Council of National Resistance for the Salvation of Afghanistan should avert such a scenario, the possibility of a Syria-like conflict in and around Afghanistan cannot be ruled out and must be kept in mind of contingency planners.

INTERNATIONAL RELATIONS

On a diplomatic plane, too, despite the Taliban efforts at securing recognition and international legitimacy and the good offices of well-wishers in the West and Islamic world for the sake of peace in Afghanistan, the Taliban have not had much success. Fifteen embassies have either maintained their missions in Afghanistan through the takeover, including Pakistan, China, Russia, Iran and some CARs, or returned to Afghanistan since then, including the European Union—the number has been considerably more than the number of maintained missions between 1996–2001. However, none have formally recognized the Taliban. Some, like the EU, have reopened their missions without acknowledging diplomatic recognition. The US conducts its relations through Qatar.

Though the Taliban have been active diplomatically through an acting foreign minister and ministry mainly through their office in Doha, the Afghan Permanent Mission to the United Nations (UN) as well as most of its embassies, including in India, continue to be manned by officials appointed and loyal to the Islamic Republic, albeit in a political and financial limbo. Russia is reported to have upgraded the Taliban presence in Moscow. Recent media reports[6] suggest that India might be contemplating a modest presence in Kabul to coordinate necessary activities, including humanitarian aid and consular services that have been paralysed since the temporary closure of the embassy after 15 August 2021, at the request of the Taliban. These reports have been followed up by a visit of a senior delegation from the Ministry of External Affairs to Kabul on 2 June 2022.[7] A resumption of consular services would be a welcome move for Afghans who are facing a virtual freeze on their e-visa applications.

The litmus test for greater recognition (even more than the demands for an inclusive government or even guaranteed of counterterrorism activities, which no one really believes) has been the treatment of women. However, far from fulfilling their vague promises on women's education or denying territory to the Al-Qaeda and other international terrorists, recently reiterated by Sirajuddin Haqqani to CNN's Christiane Amanpour (likely for western consumption) to gain greater acceptability[8], the Taliban have shown little interest or capacity of delivering on either, or to provide basic governance, security or stability. If anything, their idea of governance remains limited to the imposition of their radical version of the shariat. Women are being subjected to increasing restrictions and gender apartheid, confined to homes, forced to don hijabs and full burqas, unable to move without familial escorts, and denied prospects of education or employment. The Taliban promises to resume secondary education for girls after Nowruz in 2022 were reneged on after being announced.

Regionally, relations with Pakistan have been showing signs of strain over the Durand Line and its fencing by Pakistan, and the presence of the TTP inside Afghan territory, where local populations suspected of harbouring them have been subjected to artillery and aerial attacks by the Pakistani military ostensibly to neutralize the TTP attacks inside Pakistan. Pakistani tutelage over the Taliban remains strong but is coming under increasing questioning from within the Taliban. Many Taliban commanders spoke out against the fencing, which their leaders and spokespersons did not contradict but deflected diplomatically. The Haqqanis brokered one ceasefire between the TTP and the Pakistan Army towards the end of last year, but it did not last. A second round of talks in Kabul, headed by former ISI chief and present Peshawar Corps commander, Faiz Hamid, was followed by a third round in Pakistan, mediated by Sirajuddin Haqqani. The latter resulted in an 'indefinite ceasefire'.[9] But given the differences over Federally Administered Tribal Areas' merger that the TTP wants reversed, the disbandment of the TTP as an armed group, which it opposes, tribal solidarity between the Taliban on both sides of the Durand Line, and the contradiction between Pakistan blessing the Taliban ideology in Afghanistan and opposing it in Pakistan, a lasting resolution seems improbable.

Iran continues to deal with the Taliban elements that it has cultivated. The treatment of Afghan refugees and migrants, however, has become an increasingly emotive issue. Central Asian Republics and Russia are wary of the currents of Islamic radicalism emanating from regional extremist and terrorist groups that have been fighting together with the Taliban in Afghanistan and Pakistan over the last 20 years. The Gulf countries, particularly Qatar, continue to believe that the Taliban can be moderated. Turkey, too, is trying to make them acceptable to the international community, but at the same time has given refuge to anti-Taliban leaders.

Internationally, Europe and the West, in general, have downgraded their involvement in Afghanistan to humanitarian assistance. The US has stepped back to a primarily counterterrorist monitoring role, but suspicions that the US military withdrawal was at least partially intended to destabilize the region to check the its own strategic and regional rivals, notably China, Russia, Iran and perhaps even Pakistan, may be heightened with the Russia–Ukraine War and the temptation to use Central Asia as another point of pressure or distraction. With Imran Khan's departure, the US would try to wean Pakistan away from its budding relationship with Russia and rebuild long-standing ties with the Pakistani military with an eye on Afghanistan, Central Asia and Iran. China is keeping a watchful eye on Afghanistan to extract political, diplomatic, economic and strategic advantage westward towards Iran and the Gulf. Chinese Foreign Minister Wang Yi is one of few international figures to have visited Kabul post August 2021.

INDIA

As far as India is concerned, its actions since 15 August 2021 suggest a cautious and security-centric approach towards Afghanistan. Although India has been criticized for not reaching out to the Taliban earlier so as not to betray its constituency in the Islamic Republic, it is now apparent that feelers were put out before the Taliban launched its May 2021 offensive to take over Afghanistan that stood in good stead during the evacuation of the Indian Embassy, Indian nationals and Afghan Sikhs from Afghanistan, immediately after 15 August. The earlier decision to evacuate its remaining open consulates in Kandahar and Mazar-e-Sharif, and eventually the Embassy in Kabul, was taken on security grounds. It did not foreclose the option of returning when security conditions are better or when the Taliban fulfill certain basic conditions for legitimacy that meet minimal conditions for Afghans, India and the international community as a whole, such as a more inclusive government, guarantees that Afghan territory will not be used by extremist groups against Indian targets and interests amongst others, and that commonly understood minority and women's rights that are practised in the Islamic world are respected.

It is clear that India has built upon previous informal diplomatic contacts through the US- and Russia-led 'peace' processes, and moved to more through the Indian Embassy in Qatar. The Taliban statements on India have tried to reassure India that it has no interest in fanning the situation in Kashmir and that it would conduct its relations with India (and others) independently and not let third countries determine it. Likewise, Indian statements on the Taliban rule and takeover through sessions of the United Nations Security Council, where it came up during India's presidency of the council and after, have been moderate and circumspect. While India has opposed and condemned the Taliban military takeover of Afghanistan and spoken up for an inclusive government and for the human rights of women and others, it has not gone out of its way to alienate the Taliban completely. It has followed this up with concrete actions of support for the Afghan people by providing 20,000 tonnes of wheat overland via Pakistan (out of a promised 50,000), and four planeloads (13 tonnes) of medicines, and 500,000 doses of Covid-19 vaccine (plus another 1 million doses to Iran for Afghan refugees there)[10] as part of a humanitarian effort to ease the suffering of the Afghan people in the face of a humanitarian crisis. Such steps have been publicly appreciated by the Taliban.

Where India has seriously faltered, is on the issue of visas for Afghans wishing to leave Afghanistan in the aftermath of the Taliban takeover; speedy solutions for Afghan students studying in India, those stranded in Afghanistan mid-course and those wishing to study in India; and a more sympathetic arrangement for those wishing to study or stay temporarily in India while the situation in Afghanistan is hostile. Existing valid visas were annulled and a new e-visa facility was announced for those wishing to leave for or via India, for third countries with some fanfare, ostensibly for security reasons. But actual approvals have been so restrictive that it has cast doubts among Afghans about its sincerity and purpose.[11] While welcome steps have already been taken to extend the tenure of Afghans students in India, many who returned to Afghanistan during Covid-19, remain stranded there without visas.

All these amount to a mindless harassment of hapless Afghans seeking to flee repression in their country, and is also contrary to India's tradition of hospitality towards persecuted neighbouring people. While there have been instances of criminal activities, such as drug trafficking from time to time and a few cases of Afghan jihadis in Kashmir in the 1990s, there is not much evidence of Afghan participation in causing disturbance or terrorism in Kashmir to warrant such suspicion. Hopefully, this sore will be at least partially relieved with reports of possible resumption of consular services for visitors, students and medical visits.

HUMANITARIAN AND ECONOMIC SITUATION

The humanitarian and economic situation remains dire and needs to be addressed pragmatically and on priority, even at the cost of some principles. The advent of the IEA in August 2021 was accompanied by a desperate flood of Afghans seeking to escape Taliban rule, massive internal displacement, a prior drought, and dire warnings of a humanitarian, financial and economic crisis, as international aid and budgetary support dried out overnight with the international pullout, freezes and sanctions that followed.

The banking and financial systems were crippled, depriving ordinary Afghans any access to their own savings. While that situation may have improved, given the major reductions in funds, revenues and budget, security, stability, diplomatic ties, connectivity, trade, investment, development projects and economic opportunities have plummeted. Millions have been forced into poverty. According to the estimates by the International

Labour Organization and the US Special Inspector General for Afghan Reconstruction, almost between 500,000 and 900,000 jobs have been lost since August 2021, spurring another wave of migration, estimated at nearly 1 million via migration routes to Iran.[12] Other recent reports speak of 95 per cent of Afghanistan facing food insecurity and 45 per cent, malnutrition or worse, starvation. The United Nations has appealed for international humanitarian assistance for Afghanistan, but the response has been insufficient and complicated by issues of aid delivery, including lack of experienced personnel and Taliban demands that they be channelized to their priorities. India has been among the most generous with supply of wheat and medicines.

SECURITY SITUATION

With the transition of the Taliban from being the biggest source of insecurity as a terrorist insurgency to the ruling power, it was expected that security, at least, would improve. On the contrary, while security on the streets and highways may have improved, major terrorist attacks attributed to the ISKP, have accompanied the takeover by the Taliban, starting with attack on those trying to flee the Taliban at Kabul airport in August 2021, and subsequently against Shia Hazara targets, especially in mosques and schools. These have been taking place with sickening regularity at places as far apart as Kunduz, Kandahar, Kabul and Mazar-e-Sharif, inviting charges of a genocide.[13] While veteran Afghan watchers and journalists have also observed and reported a significant increase in ISKP attacks against the Taliban[14]—apart from one high profile attack against a senior Taliban military commander at the Daud Khan hospital in Kabul shortly after the takeover—most of these appear to have been a settling of scores between the Taliban and ISKP commanders at a local level, suggesting a large area of sectarian commonality and perhaps even a common guiding hand.

This insecurity has not been limited to the Hazaras. Despite a promise of amnesty after the takeover, house-to-house searches, interrogations, confiscations of property, vehicles and weapons of those associated or suspected to harbour loyalties to the Islamic Republic, especially Tajiks, and brutal reprisals and killings of former Afghan National Defense and Security Forces personnel and their families, have been constant. Military operations against Tajiks in Panjshir, Kabul, Andarab, Badakshan and other places, and ethnic cleansing and displacement of Hazaras and Tajiks, and resettlement of Pashtuns, reported from places like Uruzgan and Panjshir, have spawned twitter hashtags of Tajik genocide as well. There have also been reports of conflicts over land rights between Taliban-backed nomadic Kuchis and local residents in Jawzjan.

There is no serious evidence that the Taliban are cracking down on the Al-Qaeda and other terrorist groups against the US and its allies, let alone kindred regional and sectarian terrorist outfits affiliated with them in Afghanistan and Pakistan for nearly two decades, including Pak-based, anti-Indian terrorist organizations, like the Lashkar-e-Taiba (LeT) and Jaish-e-Mohammad (JeM). The latest 13th Report of the Analytical Support and Sanctions Monitoring Team of the United Nations Security Council noted that the Taliban 'cabinet' and senior levels of the 'government' includes 41 individuals on the UN sanctions list for terrorism and warned that the Al-Qaeda now has 'increased freedom of action' in Afghanistan. This was inclusive of 180–400 cadres of a weakened Al-Qaeda in the Indian sub-continent that has now renamed itself to shift focus from Afghanistan to Kashmir. The JeM is reported to maintain eight training camps in Nangarhar, three of them directly under the control of the Taliban, and three in Kunar, under the LeT.[15] Meanwhile it is ironical to note that Interior Minister Sirajuddin Haqqani, on whom there is a $10 million reward by the FBI for any information leading to his arrest, has been given a much-publicized interview by Christiane Amanpour on CNN.

OPTIONS FOR INDIA

Given this background and assessment of the situation in Afghanistan, what kind of policy should India pursue, and are there lessons that we can learn from the past? This may not be the place to go into a detailed analysis of India's relations with Afghanistan in the historic or recent past, but a few conclusions can be briefly drawn to guide policy making.

First, notwithstanding the negative historical experiences dating to the late medieval past that some elements in India are trying to play up for domestic reasons, the overall image of India–Afghanistan political, cultural and economic relations, restored over the last 20 years of various governments after the Soviet intervention and the Mujahideen–Taliban phases, has been overwhelmingly positive, and should be built upon.

Second, although the current situation does pose some security challenges to India, it would be a mistake to look at Afghanistan and the region from a prism of security alone. It should not be forgotten that cross-border terrorism emanates from Pakistan, not Afghanistan. Actual instances of Afghan jihadi involvement in Jammu and Kashmir are few and dated. India can still use its political capital in Afghanistan to mitigate and manage its security challenges.

Third, the strategic environment, too, has changed significantly against India, with the western military pullout and diminution of political interest in Afghanistan, the fall of the Islamic Republic in which we had invested, the military takeover of Afghanistan by the Taliban with ties to Islamic extremist outfits in the region and beyond, Pakistani influence over the Taliban, and a looming Chinese strategic interest in the region. India needs to counter it with a strategy of its own.

Fourth, India, too, has strategic interests in the region stemming from its historical and cultural influence in the region, its location vis-à-vis Pakistan, it's still untapped mineral, agriculture-horticulture and human potential, the terrestrial route it offers towards Central Asia, Iran and Eurasia. India, now also has to ensure that the region is not used by China and Pakistan against it in terms of 'strategic depth' or 'geo-economics'.

Fifth, far from the security challenges from the region being a reason for India to turn its back on Afghanistan, every effort must be made to remain engaged in Afghanistan to forestall its fall. It may mean dealing with both the Taliban and the opposition, and, if and when necessary, making hard choices in line with India's values and interests.

Sixth, at present, the Taliban are dominant, but the resistance is only just raising its head after the trauma of the US pullout. The last time the Taliban ruled, it lasted for five to six years, and a single incident, the 9/11 attacks, and the Taliban association with the Al-Qaeda, triggered their downfall and brought about 20 years of Republican rule, albeit flawed. Beneath Taliban control, Afghanistan is seething with discontent. This could turn again. Any moves that we make towards the Taliban should bear in mind this probability.

Seventh, the Taliban do not enjoy popular support. They represent an alien ideology without an organic base in Afghanistan. Their hold over the Afghan people is fragile and based on use or threat of use of force, and manipulation of religious sentiments and tribal loyalties, not political consent. Despite grievances with the past regime, even the more conservative rural Pashtun areas of Afghanistan have changed over the last 20 years, especially in regard to girls' education and sentiments towards Pakistan. While some are ready to settle for a repressive peace, most are looking for a way out. Many are ready to fight but do not have the wherewithal. The resistance has little international support as yet, but that too could change.

Eighth, in weighing options for the future, India should be able to deal with the short term but not lose sight of the long term, its moderate and democratic values and its friends. A strong, united Afghanistan that is friendly to India is in India's best interest. A progressive Afghanistan is more likely to be loyal to India than an extremist one. India should continue to explore political options to reconcile hostile and opposing groups as the best option for Afghanistan and India, but be prepared to take sides in support of progressive values in its national interest, if necessary. It should be proactive, not passive. It should explore coalitions of the willing for solutions, but be prepared to chart an independent policy and shape the political environment rather than 'go along with the crowd', following countries with their own agendas that have brought Afghanistan to its present state. As Pakistan–Taliban strains widen over various issues and hated Pakistani tutelage, there will be opportunities for India to play a constructive role in Afghanistan.

Ninth, India should adopt a pragmatic political approach to keep its doors open to the Afghan people, and continue to provide humanitarian and consular assistance and facilitate bilateral trade, which has been a lifeblood of India–Afghanistan relations historically, including land-based trade through Pakistan. It should not sacrifice its traditional people-to-people ties with the Afghans to punish the Taliban.

In particular, India must adopt an enabling visa policy, keep an open door for Afghans seeking to escape the repressive rule of the Taliban for the sake of their life, liberty, security, education, medical treatment, trade and travel; these could include media personalities, think tanks, scholars, intellectuals, artists, musicians, poets, writers and civil society activists. News that India may reopen its consular section in Kabul has been welcomed. The e-visa policy, too, needs to be liberalized and supported by a complimentary temporary residence and work policy. It should be understood that they are short-term permits, not long-term refugees.

Afghans seeking temporary stay in India to escape persecution share precisely the values of moderation, freedom, and civil and political liberties that we share against the religious extremism of the Taliban. It would be the ultimate irony and tragedy if we were to close our doors to such a constituency when they face life and death issues in Afghanistan, and go along with a misled world in legitimizing an extremist Pakistani creation that we would oppose in India, in the name of 'reality'.

Tenth, India should engage the Taliban politically and be prepared to maintain a minimal necessary presence in Afghanistan to keep in touch with its constituency (Afghans living under the Indian influence) in Afghanistan, short of diplomatic recognition until the Taliban moderates its positions on an inclusive government, bearing in mind that its real loyalties lie elsewhere. More than almost any other country, recognition by India matters the most to the Taliban, not least because of the historic, cultural and religious ties with India. It should not be bartered cheaply.

Timing is important. It should also take into account the increasingly regressive steps being taken by the Taliban at present with regard to persecution of minorities, treatment of women, use of violence, and inclusivity and the status of the resistance. If conditions are right, modalities for doing this range from opening an 'interests section' in a friendly country embassy, to appointing a liaison office to look after India's interests (as India did initially in 2001 before the Karzai was sworn in as interim president after the Bonn Accord in December 2001), or opening a mission at the level of a Charge d'Affaires below full diplomatic relations.

Eleventh, India should modulate its development assistance in Afghanistan that could strengthen the Taliban vis-à-vis democratic forces, but expand assistance to Afghans in India and third countries in the form of education facilities, health treatment, support for Afghan media and think tanks in India.

Twelfth, India should keep a close eye on presence and activities of the extremist outfits of various persuasions and their links with the Taliban, Pakistan and international jihadi outfits, as also ethnic tensions or conflicts that might irrupt with cross-border implications. In this regard, the Tajikistan Security Dialogue of National Security Advisors or their equivalents held in May 2022 attended by the National Security Advisor of India, Ajit Doval, provided a good platform for consultations with the region, including China and Pakistan.

Although the Taliban disavow interest in 'exporting' its ideology outside Afghanistan, the presence of so many foreign fighters from Pakistan, Central Asia and Pakistan, including dedicated anti-India outfits, like the LeT and JeM, and that of the Al-Qaeda and its affiliates, which it continues to host, indicate that while the Taliban per se may not internationalize its jihad, it will provide an umbrella for others to do so and not crack down on its 'guests' in Afghanistan. In addition, the idea of the IEA is itself transnational in concept. India has good reason to be wary of its appeal.

Next, India should also be carefully tracking geopolitical developments that could leave a positive or negative impact on the situation in Afghanistan. In this respect, India should watch the already fragile situation in Pakistan, which is facing challenges in the political heartland from Imran Khan and the Pakistan Tehreek-i-Insaf, and resurgent ethnic insurgencies in Pashtun and Baluch areas, and closely follow the regional moves of China, Pakistan, the US, Russia, Iran, Turkey, Central Asian Republics, the interested Gulf states (Qatar, Saudi Arabia and the UAE), and cooperate with them or check their moves as necessary. Pak–Chinese moves, in the name of 'geo-economics', are essentially intended to reorient Afghanistan's economy from its largest historical market that is India to Pakistan, Central Asia and China. This requires to be particularly watched.

Finally, if the Taliban do not evolve in a positive direction, India should not shy away from taking bolder steps in favour of the political and military opposition in Afghanistan, including providing space or platforms for the Afghan political diaspora and the new generation of Afghans that embody the gains of the last 20 years and are currently dispersed worldwide to conduct political activity and shape the future of Afghanistan. India could also play a helpful role in bringing opposing factions together. When the rest of the world has virtually abandoned and betrayed freedom-loving Afghanistan and Afghans, India must sustain and uphold the idea of freedom from fear and extremist Islamist rule and Pakistani tutelage, in India, if not in Afghanistan itself. Such an approach would multiply the pro-India constituency in Afghanistan. In a worst-case scenario, military or financial support to resistance groups should not be foreclosed.

Such an approach would also chart a new approach to realist diplomacy, one not overly dependent on the government in power through the use of force or alignment with big powers, but a government based on the power of forward thinking Afghans in line with India's External Affairs Minister, Dr S. Jaishankar's insight that 'future of Afghanistan cannot be its past.'[16] India should also not forget that it has been a beacon for freedom in Asia since its independence struggle, and that it has the power and the political capital in Afghanistan that it often underestimates, to influence the situation in favour of basic freedoms in its immediate neighbourhood. It should exercise that option that it, too, often forecloses out of timidity.

Notes

Chapter 1
1 This essay is based on the following book: Chakrabarti, Dilip K., *The Borderlands and Boundaries of the Indian Subcontinent: Baluchistan to the Patkai Range and Arakan Yoma*, Aryan Books, Delhi, 2018.
2 For the major literary references to 'Gandhara', see Raychaudhuri, H.C., *Political History of Ancient India,* University of Calcutta, 1938, pp. 59–62.
3 Hayat, Ambrin, 'The Rise and Fall of Gandhara', *The Friday Times*, 17 February 2017, https://bit.ly/3BIfRwj. Accessed on 16 September 2022.
4 The first three passes link Kabul area and northern Afghanistan. It is claimed that this is the route Alexander took while travelling across the Hindu Kush via the Khawak Pass and the Kushan Pass in 327 BC. It is also possible that the Kushan Pass is named after the Kushan dynasty, which has a number of sites, like Surkh Kotal and Rabatak, in the area to the north of the three passes.

Chapter 2
1 A.K., Warder, *Indian Buddhism*, Motilal Banarsidass Publishers, Delhi, 1991, p. 239.
2 Majumdar, Gayatri Sen, *Buddhism in Ancient Bengal*, Mahabodhi, Kolkata, 2013, p. 36.
3 Majumdar, R.C, *The History of Bengal, Vol. I,* B.R. Publishing Corp, 2003, New Delhi, p. 122.
4 Margit, Koves, *Buddhism among the Turks of Central Asia*, International Academy of Indian Culture and Aditya Prakashan, New Delhi, 2009, p. 33.
5 Hazra, Kanai, Lal, *The Rise and Decline of Buddhism in India*, Munshiram Manoharlal Publishers Pvt. Ltd, 2009, p. 16.
6 A.K., Warder, *Indian Buddhism*, Motilal Banarsidass Publishers, New Delhi, 1991, p. 9, pp. 32–3.
7 Kapilvastu was the kingdom of the Sakyans in eastern India where Buddha spent 29 years of his life.
8 Beal, Samuel, *Si-Yu-Ki: Buddhist Records of the Western World,* Low Price Publications, Delhi, 1884, Bk vi, p. 21; Watters, Thomas, T.W. Rhys Davids and S.W. Bushell, *On Yuan Chwang's Travels in India., Vol. 2,* Munshiram Manoharlal Publishers Pvt. Ltd, Delhi, 2012, p. 9.
9 Ibid. Bk I, p. 52–53, Bk III, p. 133, p. 128, n. 29–131.
10 Jayaswal, K.P, *Hindu Polity: A Constitutional History of India in Hindu Times,* The Bangalore Printing and Publishers, 1943, p. 128, 143.
11 A.K., Warder, *Indian Buddhism*, Motilal Banarsidass Publishers, New Delhi, 1991, p. 235.

12. Hiebert, Fredrik, and Pierre Cambon (eds), *Afghanistan: Crossroads of the Ancient World*, British Museum Press, 2011, p. 131.
13. Beal, Samuel, *Si-Yu-Ki: Buddhist Records of the Western World*, Low Price Publications, Delhi, 1884, Bk I, p. 55.
14. Barthold, W., *Turkestan Down to the Mongol Invasion*, The EJW Gibb Memorial Trust, 1968, p. 77.
15. Ibid.
16. Information given by the National Museum, Kabul. The bowl was seen by the author during her visit to the museum.
17. Dupree, Nancy Hatch, *A Historical Guide to Afghanistan*, Afghan Air Authority, Afghan Tourist Organization, Kabul, 1977, p. 219.
18. *The Life of Hiuen Tsiang*, Samuel Beal (trans.), D.K. Publishers Distributors, Delhi, 2001, p. 50–1.
19. Ibid. 48.
20. Beal, Samuel, *The Life of Hiuen-Tsiang by the Shaman Hwui Li*, Low Price Publications, 1911.
21. Ibid. 56.
22. Bagchi, P.C., *India and China: A Thousand Years of Cultural Relations*, 1981, pp. 255–9.
23. Ibid. 258.
24. Puri, B.N, *Buddhism in Central Asia*, Motilal Banarsidass Publishers Pvt. Ltd, 2000, pp. 103–4.
25. Ibid. 103.
26. Ibid.
27. Beal, Samuel, *Si-Yu-Ki: Buddhist Records of the Western World*, Low Price Publications, New Delhi, 1884, p. 51.
28. Ibid. 143.
29. Sharma, R.C., *The Splendour of Mathura Art and Museum*, D.K. Printworld Pvt. Ltd, Delhi, 1994, pp. 8–9.
30. Hiebert, Fredrik, and Pierre Cambon (eds), *Afghanistan: Crossroads of the Ancient World*, British Museum Press, 2011, p. 162.
31. Sharma, R.C., *The Splendour of Mathura Art and Museum*, D.K. Printworld Pvt. Ltd, Delhi, 1994, p. 84.
32. Litvinsky, B.A, Zhang Guang-da and R. Shabani Samghabadi, *History of Civilizations of Central Asia Vol III*, Motilal Banarsidass Publishers Pvt. Ltd, New Delhi, 1999, p. 427.
33. Ibid. 425
34. Beal, Samuel, *Si-Yu-Ki: Buddhist Records of the Western World*, Low Price Publications, New Delhi, 1884, Bk XII, pp. 283–4.
35. Dupree, Nancy Hatch, *An Historical Guide to Afghanistan*, Afghan Tourist Organization, 1977, p. 191.
36. Banerji, P., *New Light on Central Asian Art and Iconography*, Abha Prakashan, Delhi, 1992, pp. 84–90.
37. Ibid. 91.
38. Director General, *Archaeological Survey of India, A Challenge to World Heritage*, Visual Publication, 2002, p. 3.

Chapter 3

1. 'Afghanistan Population 2022 (Live)', World Population Review, https://bit.ly/3FuMLBd. Accessed on 15 November 2022.
2. Verma, Lalmani, 'Adityanath Offers Kabul River Water at Ram Janmabhoomi', *The Indian Express*, 1 November 2021, https://bit.ly/3DZ8GS5. Accessed on 26 September 2022.
3. Mookerji, Radhakumud, *Chandragupta Maurya and His Times*, Motilal Banarsidass Publishers, New Delhi, 1999.
4. KUWAYAMA, Shosh, 'Historical Notes on Kāpiśī and Kābul in the Sixth-Eighth Centuries', March 2000, Institute for Research in Humanities, Kyoto University, https://bit.ly/3X2jVQw. Accessed on 14 November 2022.
5. Mishra, Yogendra, *The Hindu Sahis of Afghanistan and the Punjab, A.D. 865-1026: A Phase of Islamic Advance into India*, Vaishali Press, Bihar, 1972.
6. Ibid.
7. Ibid.
8. 'Dōst Mohammad (1826–39; 1843–63)', Britannica, https://bit.ly/3fgN3SO. Accessed on 26 September 2022.
9. 'The First Anglo-Afghan War, 1839-1842', Military History Matters, 1 October 2010, https://bit.ly/3C7xJ3U. Accessed on 26 September 2022.
10. Constitute, 'Afghanistan's Constitution of 1964', constituteproject.org, 27 April 2022, https://bit.ly/3W51vOR. Accessed on 27 October 2022.
11. Suba Chandran, D., 'Chronicling the Afghanistan Tragedy—VI The Saur Revolution gone Sour', Indian Institute of Peace and Conflict Studies, 23 October 2001, https://bit.ly/3VbqaAO. Accessed on 4 October 2022.
12. Solomon, Christopher, '40 Years After His Death, Hafizullah Amin Casts a Long Shadow in Afghanistan', *The Diplomat*, 31 December 2019, https://bit.ly/3Cx6vDO. Accessed on 4 October 2022.
13. 'Gorbachev, Leader Who Pulled Soviets from Afghanistan, Says U.S. Campaign Was Doomed from Start', NBC News, 17 August 2021, https://nbcnews.to/3Cx2srt. Accesed on 4 October 2022.
14. United Nations Security Council, 5 December 2001, https://bit.ly/3C6kXBp.

Chapter 4

1. Khan, Riaz Mohammad, *Untying the Afghan Knot: Negotiating Soviet Withdrawal*, Progressive Publishers, Lahore, 1993.
2. Khan, Riaz Mohammad, *Afghanistan and Pakistan: Conflict, Extremism and Resistance to Modernity*, Oxford University Press, Karachi, 2011.
3. Ibid. 166.
4. Ibid. 315.
5. Ibid. 170.

Chapter 5

1. M Latifi, Ali, and Qais Azimy, 'Remembering the 'Lion of Panjshir', Aljazeera, 9 September 2012, https://bit.ly/3BPNnPV. Accessed on 23 November 2022.

2   Lushenko, Paul, 'ISKP: Afghanistan's New Salafi Jihadism', Middle East Institute, 19 October 2018, https://bit.ly/3E1U6sR. Accessed on 23 November 2022.
3   Xia, Lena, 'The China Alternative–Tajikistan', China Briefing, 12 August 2011, https://bit.ly/3UhVv3X. Accessed on 8 November 2022.
4   Mirovalev, Mansur, 'Uzbekistan: 10 Years after the Andijan Massacre', *Al Jazeera*, 12 May 2015, https://bit.ly/3ChN8OZ. Accessed on 29 September 2022.
5   Beehner, Lionel, 'ASIA: U.S. Military Bases in Central Asia', Council on Foreign Relations, 26 July 2005, https://on.cfr.org/3Tjuls7. Accessed on 23 November 2022.
6   Matusiak, Marek, 'Uzbekistan Withdraws from the CSTO Once Again', Centre for Eastern Studies, 11 July 2012, https://bit.ly/3SzDmgQ. Accessed on 29 September 2022.
7   'Session of CSTO Collective Security Council', 23 August 2021, bit.ly/3AEflhU. Accessed on 29 September 2022.
8   Weitz, Richard, 'Central Asia's Taliban Surprise', Middle East Institute, 16 September 2021, https://bit.ly/3O4VxtA. Accessed on 23 November 2022
9   'Tajikistan Calls Up Reservists to Bolster Border as Afghan Troops Flee Taliban', Reuters, 6 July, 2021, https://reut.rs/3DMgFAc. Accessed on 8 November 2022.
10 'Tajikistan Asks Russia-led Bloc for Help on Afghan Border', Reuters, 7 July 2021, https://bit.ly/3YpopkY. Accessed on 15 November 2022.
11 Funaiole, Matthew P., and Joseph S. Bermudez Jr., 'Afghan Military Aircraft Land in Uzbekistan, Move to Tajikistan (Updated)', Center for Strategic & International Studies, 26 August 2021, https://bit.ly/3SRFEYD. Accessed on 23 November 2022.
12 'President Mirziyoyev Proposes Unfreezing Afghan Assets in Foreign Banks', KUN.UZ, 17 September 2021, https://bit.ly/3UAeHts. Accessed on 23 November 2022.
13 'SCO Is Not Discussing Recognition of Taliban — Russian Foreign Ministry', Russian News Agency TASS, 23 September 2021, https://bit.ly/3M2dM1Q. Accessed on 4 October 2022.
14 'Tajikistan: President Demands Tajik Role in Running Afghanistan', eurasianet, 25 August 2021, https://bit.ly/3C8n3AU. Accessed on 4 October 2022.
15 'Speech by the President of the Republic of Tajikistan at the General Debates within the 76th Session of the UN General Assembly', Ministry of Foreign Affairs of the Republic of Tajikistan, 24 September 2021, https://bit.ly/3zVaqbW. Accessed on 4 November 2022.
16 'In Afghanistan, Panjshir resistance folds up for now', *The Tribune*, 24 September 2021, https://bit.ly/3Mbwqo4. Accessed on 4 October 2022.
17 'Uzbekistan Is Committed to Non-Interference to the Internal Affairs of Afghanistan - Abdulaziz Kamilov', *The Tashkent Times*, 9 September 2021, https://bit.ly/3UjRb4a. Accessed on 23 November 2022.
18 'Uzbekistan Launches Construction of Trans-Afghan Railway Line

Connecting Termez-Mazar-i-Sharif-Kabul–Peshawar', KUN.UZ, 29 March 2022, https://bit.ly/3CdAEqK. Accessed on 23 November 2022.
19   'Sector Assessment (Summary): Energy', North–South Power Transmission Enhancement Project, https://bit.ly/3YiCqAS. Accessed on 15 November 2022.
20   Jalilov, Orkhan, 'Turkmen, Uzbek Leaders Discuss Expansion of Trade Ties', Caspian News, 7 October 2021, https://bit.ly/3Cffokk. Accessed on 6 October 2022.
21   'UN Temporarily Moving Some International Staff from Afghanistan to Kazakhstan', Radio Free Europe, 19 August 2021, https://bit.ly/3CCCqmv. Accessed on 6 October 2022.

Chapter 6

1   Hasnain (Retd), Lt Gen. Syed Ata, 'The Iran Factor in Post Afghanistan Geopolitics', Chanakya Forum, 22 September 2021, https://bit.ly/3V92lJA. Accessed on 24 November 2022.
2   'Film on 1998 Iranian Diplomats' Murder in Mazar-i-Sharif Premieres in Tehran', *Tehran Times*, 25 August 2015, https://bit.ly/3fGCXe5. Accessed on 24 November 2022.
3   A term invented by the former US President George W. Bush, and originally included Iran, Iraq and North Korea, a few months after the 9/11 attacks.
4   'The Joint Comprehensive Plan of Action (JCPOA) at a Glance', Arms Control Association, https://bit.ly/3rByf46. Accessed on 24 November 2022.
5   Kaura, Vinay, 'Iran's Influence in Afghanistan', Middle East Institute, 23 June 2020, https://bit.ly/3ykv70h. Accessed on 24 November 2022.
6   'Ayatollah Raisi in a Phone Call with His Chinese Counterpart: Promoting Cooperation with China at Top Foreign Policy Priority for New Iranian Govt', Islamic Republic of Iran, Ministry of Foreign Affairs, 18 August 2021, https://bit.ly/3CfQ9yd. Accessed on 24 November 2022.
7   'President in a Meeting with Pakistani FM', Islamic Republic of Iran, Ministry of Foreign Affairs, 26 August 2021, https://bit.ly/3SLaaUl. Accessed on 24 November 2022.
8   'Ayatollah Raisi in a Phone Call with the President of Russia: Cementing Ties with Russia a Key Priority in Iran's Foreign Policy', Islamic Republic of Iran, Ministry of Foreign Affairs, 18 August 2022, https://bit.ly/3RD1sGx. Accessed on 24 November 2022.
9   Ibid.
10 Dorsey, James M., 'To Include or Not Include? China-led SCO Weighs Iranian Membership', Substack.com, 12 September 2021, https://bit.ly/3CjCnuF. Accessed on 24 November 2022.
11 'President: US Military Defeat, Withdrawal from Afghanistan Should be an Opportunity to Restore Life, Security, Lasting Peace in Afghanistan', Islamic Republic of Iran, Ministry of Foreign Affairs, 16 August 2021, https://bit.ly/3V7JjDv. Accessed on 24 November 2022.
12 Ibid.

13 'The Latest: Iran President Calls for Election in Afghanistan', AP News, 5 September 2021, https://bit.ly/3Tl74GL. Accessed on 24 November 2022.
14 'As Taliban Claim Victory in Panjshir, Iran Slams Pakistan Military's Role', 6 September 2021, https://bit.ly/3VdJn4D. Accessed on 24 November 2022.
15 'Iran Urges Inclusive Afghan Govt., Warns Against Foreign Intervention', Press TV, 8 September 2021, https://bit.ly/3Mgcksw. Accessed on 24 November 2022.
16 Sharifi, Arian, 'The Fatemiyoun Army: Iran's Afghan Crusaders in Syria', *The Diplomat*, 23 April 2021, https://bit.ly/3SW18DW. Accessed on 24 November 2022.
17 Majeed, Zaini, 'Anti-Taliban Resistance Front Leader Ahmad Massoud Arrives in Iran to Meet Ismail Khan', 7 November 2021, Republic World, https://bit.ly/3Elpvqo. Accessed on 24 November 2022.
18 'Taliban Reveal Details of New Agreements with Iran', Tasnim News Agency, 6 October 2021, https://bit.ly/3ehjwIE. Accessed on 24 November 2022.
19 Hameed, Mansoor, 'Raisi Urges Formation of Inclusive Govt in Afghanistan', *The Siasat Daily*, 17 September 2021, https://bit.ly/3RH8nOP. Accessed on 24 November 2022.
20 'Ayatollah Raisi in a Meeting with Indian FM: With a New Look, We Will Take New Steps in the Development of Tehran-New Delhi Ties', Islamic Republic of Iran, Ministry of Foreign Affairs, 6 August 2021, https://bit.ly/3CGEl9u. Accessed on 24 November 2022.
21 'The Text of the Speech by the Respected Minister of Foreign Affairs at The 2nd Meeting of Foreign Ministers of Afghanistan's Neighboring Countries', Islamic Republic of Iran, Ministry of Foreign Affairs, 28 October 2021, https://bit.ly/3yn7tAe. Accessed on 24 November 2022.

Chapter 7

1 Baker, Peter, 'Why Did Soviets Invade Afghanistan? Documents Offer History Lesson for Trump', *The New York Times*, 29 January 2019, https://nyti.ms/2WnIhF4. Accessed on 24 November 2022.
2 'U.S. Army to Buy 30 Russian Mi-17 Helicopters for Use in High, Hot Areas of Afghanistan', Military+Aerospace Electronics, 18 June 2013, https://bit.ly/3AGjdz2. Accessed on 24 November 2022.
3 Figures are correct as of November 2022.
4 Herb, Jeremy, 'Five Key Pieces of Trump's Afghanistan Plan', CNN, 22 August 2017, https://cnn.it/3Cn9CwY. Accessed on 24 November 2022.
5 Bolton, John, *The Room where it Happened: A White House Memoir*, Simon & Schuster, New York, 2020.
6 Chernova, Anna, Zahra Ullah and Rob Picheta, 'Russia Reacts Angrily after Biden Calls Putin a "Killer"', CNN, 18 March 2021, https://cnn.it/3ejG5fN. Accessed on 24 November 2022.
7 'U.S Believes Russia Has Stakes in Secure, Stable Afghanistan', *The Frontier Post*, https://bit.ly/3ViXR3u. Accessed on 11 October 2022.
8 'Joint Statement on Trilateral Meeting on Afghan Peace Process', U.S.

Embassy in Afghanistan, 27 April 2019, https://bit.ly/3VhJo7P. Accessed on 24 November 2022.
9   'Putin Says US Presence in Afghanistan Good for Security', Russian News Agency TASS, 25 October 2020, https://bit.ly/3epr7F1. Accessed on 11 October 2022.

Chapter 8

1   Shu, Yang, *Zhuanxing de Zhongya he Zhongguo* [Central Asia in Transformation and China], Beijing University Press, Beijing, 2005, pp. 80–6.
2   Ibid. 81
3   Segal, Gerald, 'China and Afghanistan', *Asian Survey*, vol. 21, no. 11, 1981, pp. 1158–74.
4   Jiaxuan, Tang, *Zhongguo Waijiao Cidian* [Dictionary of China's Diplomacy], World Knowledge Publications, Beijing, 2000, p. 2.
5   *China's Foreign Relations: A Chronology of Events (1949–1988)*, Foreign Languages Press, Beijing, 1989, pp. 137–9.
6   Dong, Wang, *Zhongguo Afuhan bianjie tiaoyue*, [China–Afghan Border Treaty], 2000, p. 462.
7   Cooley, John, *Unholy Wars: Afghanistan, America and International Terrorism*, Pluto Press, London, 1999, pp. 65–79.
8   Shu, Yang, *Zhuanxing de Zhongya he Zhongguo* [Central Asia in Transformation and China], Beijing University Press, Beijing, 2005, p. 86. According to Yang Shu, Afghanistan situation is riddled with several contradictions, mainly including those between Russia and the US (who are vying for influence); between Islamic religious feelings and the US policies; contradictions within Islam and amid the policies of the western countries and Central Asia and those of Russian interests in the region.
9   'Ghafoorzai's Statement to AFP, After His Visit to China, Is at "China to Pressurise Pakistan into Talks with Kabul"', News, 1 March 1996.
10 Yujun, Ren, and Wang Nan, 'Afghanistan: Ethnic Factions Cross Swords', *People's Daily*, 28 January 1997.
11 'Sino-Pak Consensus on Peace in Afghanistan', *Pakistan Times*, 26 October 1996.
12 'Pakistan Seeks Support of USA, Others for Afghan Peace Moves', *Dawn*, 2 January 1997.
13 'Taliban and China Reportedly Sign a Defence Pact', *Frontier Post*, 12 December 1996.
14 'Sino-Afghan Trade Ties May Affect Pakistan Products', *Nation*, 25 February 1999.
15 Gangadharan, Surya, 'The China-Taliban Equation', *Aakrosh: Asian Journal on Terrorism and Internal Conflicts*, vol. 3, no. 6., 2000, pp. 55–77; Shankar Sahay, Tara, 'Taliban-China Deal Puzzles Diplomats', Rediff, 12 February 1999, https://bit.ly/3j472WV. Accessed on 14 December 2022.
16 'Chinese Team in Kabul for Talks with Taliban', *Nation*, 1 February 1999.
17 Khan, Ilyas, 'Islamic Extremism - Afghan Connection', *Herald*, January 2000.

18. 'Afghanistan Centre of Terrorism: Chinese Scholar', *News*, 11 November 2000.
19. 'Chinese Envoy to Pakistan Meets Taliban Supreme Omer', *News*, 14 December 2000. The Chinese foreign ministry spokesperson, on this occasion, said that China supports UN sanctions on the Taliban.
20. 'Protest to UN Security Council Members', Afghan Islamic Press, 23 December 2000.
21. 'China Urges Broad-Based Government in Afghanistan', *China Daily*, 21 November 2001, https://bit.ly/3yN7Sfs. Accessed on 25 November 2022.
22. 'Tang Jiaxuan Urges "Political Solution" to Afghan Issue Through Dialogue', Xinhua, 12 November 2001.
23. 'China Hopes UN Move Can Promote Stability in Afghanistan', *China Daily*, 21 December 2001, https://bit.ly/3DXI8jB. Accessed on 25 November 2022.
24. *China's Foreign Affairs 2004*, World Knowledge Publications, Beijing, 2003, p. 76.
25. Ibid. 73.
26. 'Afghan President Meets with Li Zhaoxing and Welcomes Chinese Entrepreneurs to Invest in Afghanistan', The Office of the Chargé d'Affaires of the People's Republic of China in the Republic of Lithuania, 4 April 2005, https://bit.ly/3ggHiVN. Accessed on 25 November 2022.
27. *China's Foreign Affairs 2006*, World Knowledge Publications, Beijing, 2005, p. 74.
28. 'China, Afghanistan to Step Up Security Co-op: Presidents Say', Xinhua, 19 June 2006.
29. 'China Ratifies Four Treaties', China.org.cn, 1 November 2006, https://on.china.cn/3Vkyr4u. Accessed on 25 November 2022.
30. 'Joint Statement Between China, Afghanistan', Embassy of the People's Republic of China in Jamaica, 20 June 2006, https://bit.ly/3iHCCcO. Accessed on 7 November 2022.
31. Nei, Guo, 'New Terror Network Attacked Chinese Workers', *China Daily*, 14 June 2004, https://bit.ly/3Thpf0o. Accessed on 25 November 2022.
32. 'Afghan Government to Compensate Chinese Terror Victims', *China Daily*, 20 June 2004, https://bit.ly/3s6DzwF. Accessed on 25 November 2022.
33. 'China Urges Afghanistan to Ensure Safety for Chinese Citizens', Xinhua, 30 May 2006.
34. Soliev, Nodirbek, 'Why Is the Islamic State in Afghanistan's Propaganda Targeting China?', *The Diplomat*, 26 October 2021, https://bit.ly/3s1gfQQ. Accessed on 25 November 2022
35. Gangadharan, Surya, 'The China-Taliban Equation', *Aakrosh: Asian Journal on Terrorism and Internal Conflicts*, vol. 3, no. 6, 2000, pp. 55–77.
36. Guangkai, Xiong, *International Strategy and Revolution in Military Affairs*, Qinghua University Press, 2003, pp. 145–6. In a subsequent edition, Xiong, however, raised this figure of those trained by the Al-Qaeda from 1,000 to 10,000. See Guangkai, Xiong, *International Situation and Security Strategy*, Qinghua University Press, 2006, p. 346. Incidentally, Xiong was the training

official for the Mujahideen during the anti-Soviet operations.
37. 'Journalists Banned from China–Afghanistan border', *Taipei Times*, 8 October 2001, https://bit.ly/3s3lpMd. Accessed on 25 November 2022.
38. 'China Donates Police Equipment to Afghanistan', Xinhua, 12 June 2006.
39. *China's Foreign Affairs 2006*, World Knowledge Publications, Beijing, 2005, p. 75.
40. 'China to Create Mountain Brigade for Afghan Army in Badakhshan', Ariana News, 29 December 2017, https://bit.ly/3V9LxAY. Accessed on 25 November 2022.
41. Townsend, Jacob, 'China and Afghan Opiates: Assessing the Risk | Silk Road Paper', Central Asia-Caucasus Institute Silk Road Studies Program, Uppsala University, Sweden, June 2005, https://bit.ly/3Tc4ymq. Accessed on 25 November 2022.
42. 'SCO to Build Anti-drug Belt around Afghanistan', *China Daily*, 12 June 2006, https://bit.ly/3D4Lgtj. Accessed on 25 November 2022.
43. 'China "Unaware" of Any Afghan Deportation of Chinese on Spying Charges', Reuters, 7 January 2021, https://reut.rs/3D7Retr. Accessed on 25 November 2022; Gupta, Shishsir, 'Afghanistan Busted Chinese Spy Ring, Kept it a Secret. NDS Chief Explains Why', *The Hindustan Times*, 6 January 2021, https://bit.ly/3eDLSwX. Accessed on 19 October 2022
44. Wang, Paul, 'China's Approach to the Taliban: A Reflection of Realpolitik', Modern Diplomacy, 5 September 2021, https://bit.ly/3CIBM5K. Accessed on 19 October 2022.
45. 'Shanghai Cooperation Organization Holds Meeting of Foreign Ministers on Afghan Issue', The State Council, The People's Republic of China, 16 July 2021, https://bit.ly/3MJIBbH. Accessed on 24 November 2022.
46. Fatima, Sakina, 'China Hopes Taliban Will Make Clean Break with Terrorist Outfits Including ETIM', *The Siasat Daily*, 29 July 2021, https://bit.ly/3VwgTmS. Accessed on 19 October 2022.
47. 'What does Afghanistan's "Changing Sky" Mean to China?', Manohar Parrikar Institute for Defence Studies and Analyses, 19 August 2021.
48. 'China Will Maintain Their Embassy in Kabul, Says Taliban', ANI, 3 September 2021, https://bit.ly/3FGBakl. Accessed on 25 November 2022.
49. 'Xi Jinping Puts Forward 3 Opinions and Suggestions on Afghanistan', Manohar Parrikar Institute for Defence Studies and Analyses, 17 September 2021.
50. The information is based on China's foreign ministry annual yearbooks, *China's Foreign Affairs*.
51. Lanyu, Liu, 'Research on Afghanistan Security Risks under the Background of "One Belt One Road"', *Xinjiang University Journal*, Philosophy, Humanities and Social Sciences Edition, 2019.
52. Mei Xinyu, a researcher, argued that due to the domestic uncertainty in Afghanistan, China should not make any commitments for large-scale fixed asset investment projects, but can supply consumer goods for civilian use, provided the Afghan government pays for this and give security. Mei argued that due to the domestic uncertainty, Afghanistan is unlikely

to undertake any BRI projects; Xinyu, Mei, 'Do Not Blindly Revel in the Economy of Afghanistan in the Post-American Era, 18 August 2021, https://bit.ly/3WqAfKb. Accessed on 26 November 2022. Mei suggested that China provided ¥30 million in emergency supplies in December 2001 when the Kabul government was formed, and later ¥2 billion for aid in 2015–17.

53. Rizwan, Saman, 'Can China Fill the Major Power Vacuum in Afghanistan?', Centre for Strategic and Contemporary Research, 18 September 2021, https://bit.ly/3glyWw8. Accessed on 19 October 2022.
54. @SpokespersonCHN, Twitter, 8 July 2021, 9.30 p.m., https://bit.ly/3I1W7aD. Accessed on 26 December 2022.
55. 'Foreign Ministry Spokesperson Hua Chunying's Regular Press Conference on August 17, 2021', Embassy of the People's Republic of China in the Lao People's Democratic Republic, 17 August 2021, https://bit.ly/3VCZFEs. Accessed on 19 October 2022.
56. 'Explanation of Vote by Ambassador Geng Shuang on the Security Council Draft Resolution on Afghanistan', Permanent Mission of the People's Republic of China to the UN, 30 August 2021, https://bit.ly/3VI6g0j. Accessed on 25 November 2022.
57. Wenzhao, Tao, 'Insufficient Success, More than Failure-Comment on the US War in Afghanistan', aisixiang.com, 17 July 2021, https://bit.ly/3Eto9cD. Accessed on 25 November 2022.
58. Yongnian, Zheng, 'Afghanistan Is a Great Failure of Western Democratic Utopianism', Manohar Parrikar Institute for Defence Studies and Analyses, 16 August 2021.
59. Yongle, Zhang, 'Sub-healthy Empire and Headquarters with Heavy Loads', aisixiang.com, 27 August 2021.
60. Lun Tian, Yew, 'As Taliban Advances, China Lays Groundwork to Accept an Awkward Reality', Reuters, 16 August 2021, https://reut.rs/3NRBcaX. Accessed on 8 November 2022.
61. 'What Does Afghanistan's "Changing Sky" Mean to China?', Manohar Parrikar Institute for Defence Studies and Analyses, 19 August 2021.
62. Hailin, Ye, 'Afghanistan | The Flag at the Head of the city Has Changed. Where Is the Person Who Planted the Flag?', The Paper, 17 August 2021, https://bit.ly/3UyBF3Y. Accessed on 8 November 2022.
63. Bo, Zhou, 'In Afghanistan, China Is Ready to Step into the Void', The New York Times, 20 August 2021, https://nyti.ms/3UCItxx. Accessed on 8 November 2022.

Chapter 9

1. Khan, Omer Farooq, 'Pak Punjab government Projects Pashtuns as Terrorists', The Times of India, 17 September 2018, https://bit.ly/2xsBz4Z. Accessed on 25 November 2022.
2. Khan, Ghulam Qadir, 'Pakhtun Renaissance', Dawn, 3 April 2018, https://bit.ly/3rOAu3X. Accessed on 25 November 2022.

3   Afzal, Madiha, 'Why Is Pakistan's Military Repressing a Huge, Nonviolent Pashtun Protest Movement?' Brookings, 7 February 2020, https://brook.gs/3fYxkYI. Accessed on 25 November 2022.
4   'Pakistan Completes 94% of Border Fence, Despite "Isolated" Incidents', Ariana News, 6 January 2022, https://bit.ly/3CMXFlS. Accessed on 26 November 2022.
5   Siddique, Abubakar, *The Pashtun Question: The Unresolved Key to the Future of Pakistan and Afghanistan*, C. Hurst and Co., London, 2014, p. 36.
6   Tendulkar, D.G., *Abdul Ghaffar Khan: Faith is a Battle*, Gandhi Peace Foundation, 1967, p. 59.
7   Siddique, Abubakar, *The Pashtun Question: The Unresolved Key to the Future of Pakistan and Afghanistan*, C. Hurst and Co., London, 2014, p. 12.
8   Ali, Imtiaz, 'Anger on Social Media after Waziristan Man Killed in Karachi "Encounter"', *Dawn*, 18 January 2018, https://bit.ly/3fVzwAd. Accessed on 26 November 2022.
9   Ilyas Khan, M., 'Manzoor Pashteen: The Young Tribesman Rattling Pakistan's Army', BBC, 23 April 2018, https://bbc.in/3ekjYFO. Accessed on 26 November 2022.
10 Wazir, Ali, 'What Does the Pashtun Tahafuz Movement Want?', *The Diplomat*, 27 April 2018, https://bit.ly/2wzo0kf. Accessed on 26 November 2022.
11 Masood, Salman, Mujib Mashal and Zia ur-Rehman, '"Their Time Is Up": Pakistani Army Targets Pashtun Protest Movement', *The Irish Times*, 29 May 2019, https://bit.ly/3fXbnJT. Accessed on 26 November 2022.
12 'Saad Rizvi Is Released but Waziristan's Elected Rep Ali Wazir Remains Behind Bars', *The Friday Times*, 18 November 2021, https://bit.ly/3SPGDZP. Accessed on 26 November 2022
13 @mjdawar, Twitter, 7 January 2022, 7.16 a.m., https://bit.ly/3iR9L5T. Accessed on 9 December 2022.
14 Takar, Nafees, 'Anti-Taliban Pakistani Political Movement Struggles to be Heard', VOA News, 5 August 2021, https://bit.ly/3fQTlZE. Accessed on 26 November 2022.
15 'Won't Allow "Anti-state Agenda in Garb of Engineered Protests" to Succeed: COAS', Geo News, 12 April 2018, https://bit.ly/3G8p8jR. Accessed on 26 November 2022.
16 Sajjad Syed, Baqir, '"Hybrid War" Imposed on Country to Internally Weaken It, Says Bajwa', *Dawn*, 15 April 2018, https://bit.ly/3ElX8Ii. Accessed on 26 November 2022.
17 '"Time Is Up": DG ISPR Warns PTM Leadership in Press Conference', *Dawn*, 29 April 2019, https://bit.ly/3NVmC2m. Accessed on 26 November 2022.
18 'Statement by the Prime Minister of Pakistan H.E. Imran Khan to the Seventy-sixth Session of the UN General Assembly 24 September 2021', https://bit.ly/3hrWVKp. Accessed on 26 November 2022.
19 Siddique, Abubakar, and Israr Alam Mohmand, 'Pakistan's Imran Khan under Fire for Claiming Pashtuns are Taliban Sympathizers', Radio Free

Europe | Radio Liberty, 15 October 2021, https://bit.ly/3SPI6iN. Accessed on 26 November 2022.
20. Ibid.
21. Khan, Omer Farooq, 'Taliban Consider Governance Models, Oppose Pakistan Fence on Durand Line', *The Times of India*, 31 August 2021, https://bit.ly/3fT8l9V. Accessed on 26 November 2022.
22. Khan, Tahir, 'Pak-Afghan Border Fencing Issue Will Be Addressed through "Diplomatic Channels": Taliban', *Dawn*, 4 January 2022, https://bit.ly/3EwOGqc. Accessed on 26 November 2022.
23. 'Afghanistan's Taliban Regime Not to Allow Any Fencing along Durand Line by Pakistan', *The New Indian Express*, 6 January 2022, https://bit.ly/3CJPmXF. Accessed on 26 November 2022.
24. Bukhari, Gul, 'Year after Pashtun Protests, Pakistan Military Is on Spree as Civilians Fight Back', *The Print*, 11 February, 2019, https://bit.ly/3TrjLiz. Accessed on 26 November 2022.

Chapter 10

1. 'This is Taliban 1.0 with Pakistan's ISI Fingerprints All over It: India's Former Diplomats on New Afghan Govt', Zee News, 8 September 2021, https://bit.ly/3Mu4s71. Accessed on 26 November 2022.
2. 'India Invested More than $3 Billion in Afghanistan: MoS Muraleedharan', *Business Standard*, 5 February 2022, https://bit.ly/3V7w19G. Accessed on 26 November 2022
3. Pakistan Army launched Operation Zarb-e-Azb, an offensive targeting various militant groups in North Waziristan, an area in the Khyber Pakhtunkhwa province of Pakistan, in 2014 on the border between Pakistan and Afghanistan.
4. Announced on 15 September 2021, AUKUS is a trilateral security pact between Australia, the UK, and the US. Under the terms of the pact, the three nations will share advance technologies in the areas of nuclear-powered submarines, artificial intelligence, underwater systems, among others; Ward, Alexander and Paul Mcleary, 'Biden Announces Joint Deal with U.K. and Australia to Counter China', *Politico*, 15 September 2021, https://politi.co/3yA2YlV. Accessed on 26 November 2022.

Chapter 11

1. 'Treaty of Friendship between the Government of India and the Royal Government of Afghanistan', Ministry of External Affairs, Government of India, 4 January 1950, https://bit.ly/3RThhsB. Accessed on 26 November 2022.
2. 'Meeting for First Time in Afghanistan, "Six plus Two" Group Backs Peace Process', United Nations, 11 March 2002, https://bit.ly/3Vogtih. Accessed on 26 November 2022.
3. 'IC-814 Hijackers Received Strong Pakistan Intelligence Support: Doval',

The Express Tribune, 15 January 2017, https://bit.ly/3CVnkc6. Accessed on 26 November 2022.
4. 'Assessment Of Development Results: Evaluation of UNDP Contribution', United Nations Development Programme, May 2009, https://bit.ly/3SZW3e6. Accessed on 26 November 2022.
5. 'Vocational Training Centre at Bagh-e-Zanana', *Afghan News*, 6 January 2007, https://bit.ly/3BQHeEa. Accessed on 26 November 2022.

Chapter 12

1. Landler, Mark, 'Obama's Growing Trust in Biden Is Reflected in His Call on Troops', *The New York Times*, 24 June 2011, https://nyti.ms/3u1QrVI. Accessed on 27 November 2022.
2. Ambinder, Marc, 'Biden, on the Afghanistan Debate, in His Own Words', *The Atlantic*, 3 August 2010, https://bit.ly/3XzhHZl. Accessed on 27 November 2022.
3. 'Biden: US out of Afghanistan in "14 "Come Hell or High Water"', *New York Post*, 19 December 2010, https://bit.ly/3u5TpZg. Accessed on 27 November 2022.
4. "Biden: U.S. Willing to Stay in Afghanistan beyond 2014." CNN Politics, 11 January 2011, https://cnn.it/3G3e0Ew. Accessed on 20 December 2022.
5. Kane, Paul, 'Biden Receives Heated Criticism from Republicans, Questions from Some Democrats after Kabul Airport Attack', *The Washington Post*, 26 August 2021, https://wapo.st/3XD3hre. Accessed on 27 November 2022.
6. Crowley, Michael, 'A Veteran Diplomat, a "Tragic Figure," Battles Critics in the U.S. and Afghanistan', *The New York Times*, 16 November 2021, https://nyti.ms/3UcLGn5. Accessed on 27 November 2022.
7. Crocker, Ryan, 'Afghanistan 2001-2021: U.S. Policy Lessons Learned', Carnegie Endowment for International Peace, https://bit.ly/3V4osAF. Accessed on 27 November 2022.
8. Rasmussen, Sune Engel, and Nancy A. Youssef, 'In Taliban-Ruled Afghanistan, Al Qaeda-Linked Haqqani Network Rises to Power', *The Wall Street Journal*, 26 August 2021, https://on.wsj.com/3VvYfLb. Accessed on 27 November 2022.
9. 'Afghanistan in Hindsight: Lessons From Two Decades of War', Council on Foreign Relations, 22 October 2021, https://on.cfr.org/3Vp0PC4. Accessed on 26 December 2022.
10. '"Strategic failure": Top US General's Testimony on 20-Year War in Afghanistan', *India Today*, 29 September 2021, https://bit.ly/3YM27tT. Accessed on 26 December 2022.
11. 'Taliban Failed to Honour Doha Accord, Says Top U.S. General Mark Milley', *The Hindu*, 29 September 2021, https://bit.ly/3AP4Nwl. Accessed on 27 November 2022.
12. Stancati, Margherita, 'Taliban Intensify Efforts to Take Control of Afghanistan's Overseas Embassies', *The Wall Street Journal*, 18 January 2022, https://on.wsj.com/3ijMZmV. Accessed on 27 November 2022.

13 Irish, John, 'France, Europeans Working to Open Joint Mission in Afghanistan—Macron', Reuters, 4 December 2021, https://reut.rs/3V4sh8Z. Accessed on 27 November 2022.
14 'Taliban Delegation Due in Norway for Humanitarian Talks', Reuters, 21 January 2022, https://reut.rs/3T1XR6p. Accessed on 27 November 2022.
15 'Security Council Unanimously Adopts Resolution 2615 (2021), Enabling Provision of Humanitarian Aid to Afghanistan as Country Faces Economic Crisis', United Nations, 22 December 2021, https://bit.ly/3g5kmbR. Accessed on 27 November 2022.
16 Crowley, Michael, and Alan Rappeport, 'As Humanitarian Disaster Looms, U.S. Opens Door for More Afghanistan Aid', *The New York Times*, 22 December 2021, https://nyti.ms/3Vcc2H3. Accessed on 27 November 2022.
17 Welle, Deutsche, 'Afghanistan: Donors Back Release of $280 Million in Aid', *Frontline*, 11 December 2021, https://bit.ly/3sedFat. Accessed on 27 November 2022.
18 'Donors Back $280m Transfer for Afghan Food, Health Schemes', *Dawn*, 12 December 2021, https://bit.ly/3gyZGd6. Accessed on 27 November 2022.
19 'Afghanistan: UN Launches Largest Single Country Aid Appeal Ever', United Nations, 11 January 2022, https://bit.ly/3S2FHQC. Accessed on 27 November 2022.
20 Ibid.
21 Farge, Emma, and Michelle Nichols, 'Donors Pledge $1.1 Billion for "Collapsing" Afghanistan"', Reuters, 13 September 2021, https://reut.rs/3XwMmqh. Accessed on 27 November 2022.
22 'Harsh Winter Fuels Ongoing Humanitarian Crisis in Afghanistan | UN News', United Nations, 4 January 2022, https://bit.ly/3gAbR9v. Accessed on 27 November 2022.
23 @SenSanders, Twitter, 19 January 2022, 1.52 a.m., https://bit.ly/3Vuz1wz. Accessed on 27 November 2022.
24 Schmitt, Eric, 'U.S. Envoy's Cables Show Worries on Afghan Plans', *The New York Times*, 26 January 2010, https://nyti.ms/3ECUwWZ. Accessed on 27 November 2022.
25 Joscelyn, Thomas, 'Admiral Mullen: Pakistani ISI Sponsoring Haqqani Attacks', *FDD's Long War Journal*, 22 September 2011, https://bit.ly/3EG8MNa. Accessed on 27 November 2022.
26 Motevalli, Golnar, 'Afghanistan Government Accuses US Special Forces of Civilian Death and Torture', *The Guardian*, 24 February 2013, https://bit.ly/3Ua0bHZ. Accessed on 27 November 2022.

Chapter 13
1 'Admission of New Members to the United Nation', https://bit.ly/3Tr9vYc. Accessed on 27 November 2022
2 'Overview of Security Council Resolutions', Security Council Report, 9 January 1980, https://bit.ly/3CHqVJj. Accessed on 27 November 2022.

3   'The Situation in Afghanistan and its Implications for International Peace and Security: Resolution / Adopted by the General Assembly', United Nations Digital Library, 1980, https://bit.ly/3NLE7ls. Accessed on 27 November 2022.
4   'Afghanistan / Pakistan - UNGOMAP—Mandate', United Nations Good Offices Mission in Afghanistan and Pakistan, https://bit.ly/3EmKKrD. Accessed on 27 November 2022.
5   'United Nations General Assembly Fifty-First Session', 13 February 1997, https://bit.ly/3GjbvOA. Accessed on 26 December 2022.
6   'Resolution 1267 (1999)', United Nations Security Council, 15 October 1999, https://bit.ly/3eAbevD. Accessed on 27 November 2022
7   Ibid.
8   Ibid.
9   'United Nations Security Council Fifty-Fourth Year', 15 October 1999, https://bit.ly/3FyOln1. Accessed on 7 December 2022.
10 'United Nations Security Council Fifty-Fourth Year', 15 October 1999, New York, https://bit.ly/3UUFiB4. Accessed on 12 December 2022.
11 Ibid.
12 'Resolution 1333 (2000)', United Nations Security Council, 19 December 2000, https://bit.ly/3VMyFma. Accessed on 27 November 2022.
13 Ibid.
14 Ibid.
15 'United Nations Security Council Fifty-Fifth Year', 19 December 2000, New York, https://bit.ly/3BrKYvI. Accessed on 12 December 2022.
16 'Security Council Imposes Wide New Measures Against Taliban Authorities in Afghanistan, Demands Action on Terrorism | Resolution 1333 (2000) Calls for Closure of Training Camps, End to Provision of Sanctuary; Ban Imposed on Military Assistance', United Nations, 19 December 2000, https://bit.ly/3F6q73b. Accessed on 27 November 2022.
17 Ibid.
18 'Resolution 1368 (2001)', United Nations Security Council, 12 September 2001, https://bit.ly/3ThgdR0. Accessed on 27 November 2022.
19 'Afghanistan: Post-Taliban Governance, Security, and U.S. Policy', Congressional Research Service, 13 December 2017, https://bit.ly/3Fw3c08. Accessed on 19 December 2022.
20 Ibid.
21 Ibid.
22 'Security Council Authorizes International Security Force for Afghanistan; Welcomes United Kingdom's Offer to be Initial Lead Nation', United Nation Human Right Office of the High Commissioner, 20 December 2001, https://bit.ly/3Eih0vU. Accessed on 27 November 2022.
23 'Resolution 2593 (2021)', United Nations Security Council, 30 August 2021, https://bit.ly/3CL7fnM. Accessed on 27 November 2022.
24 'SRSG Lyons Briefing to the UNSC on the Situation in Afghanistan', United Nations Assistance Mission in Afghanistan, 17 November 2021, https://bit.ly/3gfapbY. Accessed on 27 November.

25 Ibid.
26 Ibid.
27 Ibid.
28 Ibid.

Chapter 14

1   Linschoten, Alex Strick van, and Felix Kuehn (eds), *Abdul Salam Zaeef: My Life with the Taliban*, C. Hurst & Co., London, 2010, p. 65.
2   Nawaz, Shuja, *Crossed Swords: Pakistan, its Army and the Wars Within*, Oxford University Press, 2008, p. 478.
3   Ibid. 479–80.
4   Ibid. 479.
5   Coll, Steve, *Ghost Wars: The Secret History of the CIA, Afghanistan, and Bin Laden*, Penguin Books, 2004, p. 296.
6   Giustozzi, Antonio, *The Taliban at War: 2001–2018*, Oxford University Press, 2019, pp. 77–108.
7   Gall, Carlotta, *The Wrong Enemy: America in Afghanistan: 2001–2014*, Houghton Mifflin Harcourt, USA, 2014.
8   Malik, Jamal, *Colonization of Islam: Dissolution of Traditional Institutions in Pakistan*, Vanguard Books, 1996, p. 4.
9   Roy, Olivier, *Islam and Resistance in Afghanistan*, Cambridge University Press, 1986.
10 Borchgrevink, Kaja, 'Beyond Borders: Diversity and Transnational Links in Afghan Religious Education', *Peace Research Institute Oslo* paper, September 2010, https://bit.ly/3CP8Rgh. Accessed on 27 November 2022.
11 Semple, Michael, 'Rhetoric, Ideology and Organisational Structure of the Taliban Movement': Peaceworks, 2014, https://bit.ly/3VF822l. Accessed on 27 November 2022.
12 Ibid.
13 For a more detailed study of the material discussed under this subhead, please refer to endnote number 11.
14 Ibid.
15 Semple, Michael, 'Rhetoric, Ideology, and Organizational Structure of the Taliban Movement', Peaceworks, https://bit.ly/3F87g6z. Accessed on 7 November 2022.
16 Barfield, Thomas J., *Afghanistan: A Political and Cultural History*, Princeton University Press, 2010, p. 262.
17 Ibid.
18 Khan, Tahir, 'Breakaway Taliban Faction Mired in Uncertainty', *The Express Tribune*, 29 August 2019, https://bit.ly/3Wz5GTg. Accessed on 27 November 2022.
19 Banerji, Rana, 'Can the ISI Keep the Taliban United?', Rediff.com, 26 August 2021, https://bit.ly/3WpHq5E. Accessed on 27 November 2022.
20 Boone, Jon, and Sune Engel Rasmussen, 'US Drone Strike in Pakistan Kills Taliban Leader Mullah Mansoor', *The Guardian*, 22 May 2016,

https://bit.ly/3eMHsnq. Accessed on 27 November 2022.
21. Watkins, Andrew, 'Taliban Fragmentation: Fact, Fiction and Future', United States Institute of Peace Report, 23 March 2020, https://bit.ly/3sd0g24. Accessed on 27 November 2022
22. Arif, Sibte, 'Mulla Baradar Released from Pak Jail', *The News International*, 22 October 2018, https://bit.ly/2ELvKqu. Accessed on 27 November 2022.
23. Coll, Steve, *The Bin Ladens: An Arabian Family in the American Century*, Penguin Books, 2008.
24. Jones, Seth G., *In the Graveyard of Empires: America's War in Afghanistan*, W.W. Norton & Company, Manhattan, 2010, p. 105.
25. Zaeef, Abdul Salam, *My Life with the Taliban*, C. Hurst & Co., London, 2010.
26. Semple, Michael, Theo Farrell and Anatol Lieven, 'Taliban Perspectives on Reconciliation', The Royal United Services Institute for Defence and Security Studies, 10 September 2012, https://bit.ly/3UD6aWY. Accessed on 27 November 2022.
27. Yousufzai, Rahimullah, 'Taliban Claim Arrest of Mosque Chowkidar after Friday's Blast in Kuchlak', *The News International*, 18 August 2019, https://bit.ly/3yUOygC. Accessed on 27 November 2022.
28. Mohan, Geeta, 'Leader of Taliban Splinter Group Freed after Five Years in Pakistani Prison', *India Today*, 18 August 2021, https://bit.ly/3zX15k9. Accessed on 27 November 2022.
29. Taieb, Rajab, 'New Cabinet Members Announced, Inauguration Cancelled', TOLO News, 21 September 2021, https://bit.ly/3EtTjAE. Accessed on 27 November 2022.
30. 'Taliban's Baradar Says Reports He Was Hurt in Internal Clash are False', Reuters, 16 September 2021, https://reut.rs/3EuGHJO. Accessed on 27 November 2022.
31. 'Taliban to Implement Monarch-era Constitution in Afghanistan', Sada Elbalad English, 28 September 2022, https://bit.ly/3EdjmMh. Accessed on 27 November 2022.
32. 'Taliban Releases TTP's Maulvi Faqir Mohammad, Other Terrorists from Afghan prisons', ANI, 18 August 2021, https://bit.ly/3EpUQIe. Accessed on 27 November 2022.
33. 'TTP a Matter Pakistan Must Take Up, Not Afghanistan: Taliban Spokesman', Geo TV, 28 August 2021, https://bit.ly/3PHOE1Z. Accessed on 20 December 2022.
34. Behuria, Ashok K., 'Tehrik-e-Taliban Pakistan and its Relations with Afghan Taliban', Manohar Parrikar Institute for Defence Studies and Analyses, 16 September 2021, https://bit.ly/3fd0OSS. Accessed on 27 November 2022.
35. Scott-Clark, Cathy, and Adrian Levy, *The Exile: The Stunning Inside Story of Osama bin Laden and Al Qaeda in Flight*, Bloomsbury, USA, 2017.
36. Basit, Abdul, 'Tehreek-e-Taliban Pakistan's Discursive Shift from Global Jihadist Rhetoric to Pashtun-Centric Narratives', The Jamestown Foundation, 24 September 2021, https://bit.ly/3D7DLRk. Accessed on 27 November 2022.

37. 'Govt in Talks with TTP Groups for Reconciliation Process: PM Imran', *Dawn*, 1 October 2021, https://bit.ly/3TIkAV9. Accessed on 27 November 2022
38. Nasaruminallah, 'As Talks Advance, TTP Announces Ceasefire', *The Express Tribune*, 2 October 2021, https://bit.ly/3SAqHJW. Accessed on 27 November 2022.
39. 'Cabinet Seeks World Support to Avert Afghan Crisis', *The Express Tribune*, 9 November 2021, https://bit.ly/3SAyZBH. Accessed on 27 November 2021.
40. 'Pakistani Taliban Leader Reacts to Afghan Gains after US Withdrawal', CNN World, July 2021, https://cnn.it/3W4K9kB. Accessed on 20 December 2022.
41. 'Pakistan Taliban Demand Prisoner Release as Condition for Talks—Sources', Reuters, 6 November 2021, https://reut.rs/3TmvEGy. Accessed on 27 November 2022
42. Allen, Felix, 'SLAUGHTERED ISIS Leader Abu Omar Khorasani "Executed by Taliban" at Afghan Prison as Jihadis Wage War after Afghanistan's Collapse', The Sun, 27 September 2021, https://bit.ly/3s8cZmK. Accessed on 27 November 2022.
43. Haris, Mujtaba, and Ali M. Latif, 'Taliban Takes on ISKP, Its Most Serious Foe in Afghanistan', Aljazeera, 27 September 2021, https://bit.ly/3eGUW49. Accessed on 27 November 2022.
44. Ibid.
45. Shah, Saeed, and Yaroslav Trofimov, 'Islamic State Attacks in Eastern Afghanistan Challenge Taliban Rule', *The Wall Street Journal*, 22 September 2021, https://on.wsj.com/3jjpN8y. Accessed on 27 November 2022.
46. Doxsee, Catrina, Jared Thompson and Grace Hwang, 'Examining Extremism: Islamic State Khorasan Province (ISKP)', Centre for Strategic & Islamic Studies (CSIS), 8 September 2021, https://bit.ly/3TWDAzH. Accessed on 27 November 2022.
47. Ibid.
48. Ibid.

Chapter 15

1. 'Statement of General Mark A. Milley, USA 20th Chairman of the Joint Chiefs of Staff Department of Defense Afghanistan Hearing', Senate Armed Services Committee, 28 September 2021, https://bit.ly/3zPwO6t. Accessed on 30 November 2022.
2. 'Secretary Of Defense Lloyd J. Austin III Prepared Remarks before the Senate Armed Services Committee', U.S. Department of Defense, 28 September 2021, https://bit.ly/3gJKIAV. Accessed on 30 November 2022.
3. 'Statement for the Record by General John W. Nicholson Commander U.S. Forces – Afghanistan Before the Senate Armed Services Committee on the Situation in Afghanistan', 9 February 2017, https://bit.ly/3THDoUu. Accessed on 30 November 2022.
4. Nordland, Rod, and David Zucchino, 'As U.S. Nears a Pullout Deal, Afghan Army Is on the Defensive', *The New York Times*, 12 August 2019, https://nyti.ms/2YQQo25. Accessed on 30 November 2022.

5 'Quarterly Report to the United States Congress', Special Inspector General for Afghanistan Reconstruction, 30 April 2017, p. 5, https://bit.ly/3Fd0hdF. Accessed on 30 November 2022.
6 'Secretary Of Defense Lloyd J. Austin III Prepared Remarks Before the Senate Armed Services Committee', U.S. Department of Defense, 28 September 2021, https://bit.ly/3gJKIAV. Accessed on 30 November 2022.
7 Giustozzi, Antonio, 'Re-building the Afghan Army', The London School of Economics and Political Science and University of Bonn, June 2010, https://bit.ly/3VljhMK. Accessed on 30 November 2022.
8 'Enhancing Security and Stability in Afghanistan', U.S. Department of Defense, 12 June 2020, https://bit.ly/3E4E0ym. Accessed on 30 November 2022.
9 Ibid.
10 'Afghan Security Efforts to Establish Army and Police Have Made Progress But Future Plans Need to be Better Defined', United States Government Accountability Office, 30 June 2005, https://bit.ly/3uabs0v. Accessed on 30 November 2022.
11 'Resolute Support Mission in Afghanistan (2015-2021)', North Atlantic Treaty Organization, 30 May 2022, https://bit.ly/3f5o2ud. Accessed on 30 November 2022
12 'Quarterly Report to the United States Congress', Special Inspector General for Afghanistan Reconstruction, 30 April 2017, p. 5, https://bit.ly/3Fd0hdF. Accessed on 30 November 2022.
13 'Secretary Of Defense Lloyd J. Austin III Prepared Remarks before the Senate Armed Services Committee', U.S. Department of Defense, 28 September 2021, https://bit.ly/3gJKIAV. Accessed on 30 November 2022.
14 Bowman, Tom, and Monika Evstatieva, 'The Afghan Army Collapsed In Days. Here Are the Reasons Why', CapRadio, 20 August 2021, https://bit.ly/3t33hT1. Accessed on 30 November 2022.
15 'Statement of General Mark A. Milley, USA 20th Chairman of the Joint Chiefs of Staff Department of Defense Afghanistan Hearing', Senate Armed Services Committee, 28 September 2021, https://bit.ly/3zPwO6t. Accessed on 30 November 2022.
16 Ryan, Missy, and Karen DeYoung, 'Biden Will Withdraw all U.S. Forces from Afghanistan by Sept. 11, 2021', *The Washington Post*, 13 April 2021, https://wapo.st/3t34slp. Accessed on 30 November 2022.
17 'Secretary Of Defense Lloyd J. Austin III Prepared Remarks before the Senate Armed Services Committee', U.S. Department of Defense, 28 September 2021, https://bit.ly/3gJKIAV. Accessed on 30 November 2022.
18 Ibid.
19 'Blinken's Prepared Remarks for Today's Hearing on Afghan Pullout', *First State Update*, 13 September 2021, https://bit.ly/3t32a5M. Accessed on 30 November 2022.
20 'Statement of General Mark A. Milley, USA 20th Chairman of the Joint Chiefs of Staff Department of Defense Afghanistan Hearing', Senate Armed Services Committee, 28 September 2021, https://bit.ly/3zPwO6t. Accessed on 30 November 2022.

21. Ibid.
22. 'Statement for the Record by General John W. Nicholson Commander U.S. Forces—Afghanistan before the Senate Armed Services Committee on the Situation in Afghanistan', 9 February 2017, https://bit.ly/3THDoUu. Accessed on 30 November 2022.
23. Giustozzi, Antonio, 'Re-building the Afghan Army', The London School of Economics and Political Science and University of Bonn, June 2010, https://bit.ly/3VljhMK. Accessed on 30 November 2022.
24. 'Taliban Urges its Fighters to Respect Amnesty Given to all Afghan Government Officials', ANI, 24 September 2021, https://bit.ly/3gOi7dv. Accessed on 30 November 2022.
25. Achakzai, Abdullah, 'Islamic Emirate to Form Military Court', TOLOnews, 11 November 2021, https://bit.ly/3DeDUm8. Accessed on 30 November 2022.
26. Musavi, Sayed Mohammad Aref, 'Balkh, MoD Official Urges Troops to Guard the Nation', TOLOnews, 17 October 2021, https://bit.ly/3zPyv3P. Accessed on 30 November 2022
27. Ibid.
28. Omeri, Abdulhaq, 'Taliban Says it Will Build Regular Army, Include Former Members', Tolonews, 15 September 2021, https://bit.ly/3TKcjjG. Accessed on 30 November 2022.
29. 'Exclusive-Council May Rule Afghanistan, Taliban to Reach Out to Soldiers, Pilots-Senior Member', Reuters, 18 August 2021, https://reut.rs/3t6o7kI. Accessed on 30 November 2022.
30. Ibid.

Chapter 16

1. @sayedsalahuddin, Twitter, 2 June 2022, 7.13 p.m., https://bit.ly/3gkJds9. Accessed on 30 November 2022.
2. Khalid, Sakhi, 'Taliban to Clear its Ranks of Non-Pashtun Commanders', *Hasht-e-Shubh Daily*, 31 May 2022, https://bit.ly/3ByjnsL. Accessed on 14 December 2022.
3. Earlier this year, Abdul Hadi Muslimyar and Abdullah were allowed to leave for Dubai and Delhi, respectively, but Hamid Karzai was prevented from attending the funeral ceremonies of the Abu Dhabi Emir, Sheikh Khalid al Nayhan.
4. These include forces led by former Interior Minister, Massoud Andrabi, in Andarab; the Tehreek-e-Azadi Afghanistan (Afghanistan Freedom Front) led by Gen. Yasin Zia, and possibly, former Defense Minister Bismillah Khan; the Afghan Islamic National and Liberation Movement of Afghanistan led by Abdul Matin Sulaimankhail, a former special forces commander; the Noor Guerrillas affiliated with Ustad Ata Noor; the 'Wolf Unit' of Yar Mohd. Dostum, elder son of Dostum; Hazara militias associated with Abdul Ghani Alipur and the soldiers of Hazaristan; lesser-known outfits, like the Freedom Front, Freedom and Democracy Front, National Front for Free Afghanistan, the Turkestan Freedom Tigers, etc; Security

Risk Research, 'Mapping Afghan Resistance Movement', Security Risks, https://bit.ly/3FPwfgs. Accessed on 14 December 2022.

5. There have also been contacts between Ahmed Massoud/NRF and the Taliban leaders in Iran and Tajikistan to explore the possibility of an inclusive government.

6. Subramaniam, Nirupama, 'India Looks at Reopening Mission in Kabul Minus Senior Diplomats', *The Indian Express*, 17 May 2022, https://bit.ly/3SdnsI8. Accessed on 30 November 2022; Sahay, Anand K., 'India's Return to a Key Role in Kabul: Ticklish Issue Emerges', *The Asian Age*, 31 May 2022, https://bit.ly/3Db52mY. Accessed on 30 November 2022.

7. Kumaraswami, Sridhar, 'Indian Team to Visit Kabul for First Time in Taliban Region', *Deccan Chronicle*, 3 June 2022, https://bit.ly/3GerTPd. Accessed on 26 December 2022.

8. Amanpour, Christiane, 'Exclusive: Amanpour Speaks with Taliban Deputy Leader', CNN, https://cnn.it/3TzUYcU. Accessed on 30 November 2022.

9. Khan, Ismail, 'Islamabad, TTP Agree to an Indefinite Ceasefire', *Dawn*, 31 May 2022, https://bit.ly/3VDs2Bx. Accessed on 30 November 2022.

10. 'India's Humanitarian Assistance to Afghanistan', Ministry of External Affairs, 2 June 2022, https://bit.ly/3Te9zuN. Accessed on 1 December 2022.

11. There have been instances of holders of diplomatic passports being turned back and of Afghans not being allowed to board despite having valid tickets and e-visas, all under instructions that were reportedly issued by the Ministry of Civil Aviation.

12. Karlekar, Hiranmay, 'Will the Taliban Cookie Crumble'? *The Pioneer*, 21 May 2022, https://bit.ly/3CKZ9Mb. Accessed on 30 November 2022; there are also numerous reports of parents selling their underage daughters in marriage and those of others selling their organs, to survive. Visuals of women in blue burqas outside naan bakeries, waiting for handouts of food for their families from those more fortunate are commonplace.

13. In many such cases, Taliban guards have prevented bystanders from shooting footage or photos from the scene and even donating blood.

14. Jones, Seth G., 'Countering a Resurgent Terrorist Threat in Afghanistan', Council of Foreign Relations, 14 April 2022, https://on.cfr.org/3eEDfSP. Accessed on 30 November 2022; Goldbaum, Christina, and Yaqoob Akbary, 'Over a Million Flee as Afghanistan's Economy Collapses', *The New York Times*, 3 February 2022, https://nyti.ms/3CPY85i. Accessed on 30 November 2022.

15. G., Sampath, 'Looking at the UN Report on the Taliban Regime', *The Hindu*, 1 June 2022, https://bit.ly/3SlwfYC. Accessed on 30 November 2022.

16. Haider, Suhasini, 'Future of Afghanistan Cannot be its Past: Jaishankar', *The Hindu*, 14 July 2021, https://bit.ly/3N0rfI5. Accessed on 30 November 2022.

List of Contributors

Dr Dilip Kumar Chakrabarti is professor Emeritus, Department of Archaeology, Cambridge University and Editor, Vivekananda International Foundation (VIF) History Volumes.

Sunita Dwivedi is a Silk Road traveller and author. She has authored a tetralogy on the Buddhist heritage of Asia.

Dr Arvind Gupta is the director of VIF, New Delhi. He was the deputy national security advisor and secretary, National Security Council, Government of India during 2014–17.

Amb. T.C.A. Raghavan is a former Indian high commissioner to Pakistan.

Amb. Skand R. Tayal is a former ambassador of India to Uzbekistan and the Republic of Korea.

Amb. Sanjay Singh is a former secretary (east), Ministry of External Affairs, New Delhi, and a former Ambassador to Iran.

Amb. P.S. Raghavan is a former Indian diplomat and former chairman of India's National Security Advisory Board. He is a Distinguished Fellow of VIF, New Delhi.

Dr Srikanth Kondapalli is the dean of School of International Studies and a professor of Chinese studies at Jawaharlal Nehru University, New Delhi.

Dr Shalini Chawla is a distinguished Fellow at the Centre for Air Power Studies, New Delhi.

Lt Gen. (Retd) Syed Ata Hasnain PVSM, UYSM, AVSM, SM, VSM & Bar is a retired General of the Indian Army.

LIST OF CONTRIBUTORS ♦ 279

Amb. Jayant Prasad is former director general, Institute for Defence Studies and Analyses, New Delhi. He is a former ambassador to Afghanistan, Algeria, Nepal, and Permanent Representative of India to the Conference on Disarmament, Geneva.

Amb. Gautam Mukhopadhaya is a former ambassador to Myanmar, Syria and Afghanistan.

Amb. Arun K. Singh is a former ambassador to the United States, France and Israel.

Amb. D.P. Srivastava is a former ambassador to Iran, and Distinguished Fellow, VIF.

Rana Banerji is former special secretary, Cabinet Secretariat.

Brigadier (Retd) Rahul K. Bhonsle is managing a strategic risk and knowledge management consultancy (security-risks.com), focussing on strategic culture and security trends in South Asia, future warfare and human security.

Index

9/11, xvi, 30, 47, 78, 79, 108, 109, 111, 112, 116, 124, 125, 160, 176, 192, 227, 230, 252

Afghan National Defense and Security Forces, ANDSF, 208, 210, 218, 219, 220, 221, 222, 223, 224, 225, 226, 227, 228, 229, 233
Al-Qaeda, xvi, 47, 48, 64, 65, 96, 115, 116, 122, 124, 125, 145, 159, 160, 169, 171, 172, 176, 187, 206, 213, 214, 216, 232, 244, 250, 252, 255
Ashoka, 4, 14, 17, 35

Bactria, 5, 9, 18, 35
Balkh, 16, 17, 18, 19, 20, 23, 34, 35, 36, 38, 39, 63, 107, 232, 241
Balochistan, 133, 193, 209
Baluchistan, 10, 15, 42, 77
Bamiyan, 8, 9, 15, 17, 19, 20, 22, 23, 24, 25, 28, 29, 32, 38, 182, 207, 216
Biden, Joe, xvii, 47, 96, 123, 169, 170, 171, 175, 226, 228
Buddha, 14, 15, 16, 18, 19, 20, 22, 23, 24, 25, 26, 27, 28, 29
Buddhist, xviii, 6, 13, 14, 16, 18, 19, 20, 21, 22, 23, 24, 25, 26, 27, 28, 29, 35, 36, 48, 107, 278

Central Asia, xiii, xvi, xviii, 4, 5, 6, 7, 16, 18, 20, 22, 27, 28, 30, 31, 35, 36, 41, 48, 62, 63, 64, 65, 75, 76, 78, 85, 88, 91, 92, 94, 99, 100, 101, 104, 105, 107, 111, 113, 114, 115, 117, 143, 148, 150, 200, 243, 246, 252, 255
Central Asian Republics, CARs, 64, 65, 67, 69, 74, 75, 143, 148, 149, 150, 151, 154, 243, 245, 255
Chabahar, viii, 84, 161, 163, 166
China, viii, ix, x, xii, xv, xviii, 8, 11, 16, 17, 21, 22, 29, 35, 36, 48, 58, 65, 79, 80, 81, 86, 87, 93, 94, 95, 96, 97, 99, 100, 101, 102, 103, 104, 105, 106, 107, 108, 109, 110, 111, 112, 113, 114, 115, 116, 117, 118, 119, 120, 121, 122, 123, 124, 125, 126, 143, 146, 148, 149, 150, 151, 155, 158, 173, 174, 177, 178, 189, 191, 243, 246, 252, 254, 255
China–Pakistan Economic Corridor, CPEC, ix, 79, 119, 177, 122
Cold War, xvi, xviii, 45, 58, 89, 90, 103, 181, 185
constitution, xvii, 33, 44, 45, 93, 157

Daesh, 159, 194, 214, 215
Doha Agreement, 47, 48, 169, 170, 172, 173, 177, 185, 226
Durand Line, xvi, xix, 3, 8, 33, 43, 55, 59, 88, 89, 128, 136, 138, 139, 145, 214, 222, 238, 245

INDEX • 281

Gandhara, 3, 4, 6, 14, 15, 23, 25, 26, 28, 34
Geneva, 54, 174, 175, 182, 183, 184, 185, 279
Ghani, Ashraf, xv, 48, 69, 97, 114, 128, 219, 224, 225
Ghazni, 10, 11, 19, 22, 24, 25, 27, 32, 34, 38, 39, 41, 42, 49, 239
Greek, 4, 5, 14, 17, 32, 34, 35, 48

Haqqani, ix, xii, 65, 136, 171, 175, 201, 207, 208, 209, 210, 211, 214, 216, 232, 239, 244, 245, 250
Hekmatyar, 109, 118, 125, 199, 200
Herat, 5, 6, 7, 13, 17, 19, 32, 33, 34, 36, 38, 40, 41, 63, 83, 146, 156, 158, 162, 200, 230, 233
Hindu Kush, 3, 5, 8, 9, 11, 15, 16, 17, 28, 31, 36, 38, 77
Hindu Shahi, 6, 7, 13, 27, 28, 32, 37, 38

Iran, vii, viii, x, xi, xii, 4, 5, 7, 11, 35, 66, 70, 72, 76, 77, 78, 79, 80, 81, 82, 83, 84, 85, 86, 89, 90, 93, 102, 107, 119, 143, 151, 154, 158, 169, 173, 177, 196, 209, 241, 243, 245, 246, 247, 249, 252, 255, 278, 279
Iraq, 65, 77, 78, 91, 98, 99, 123, 136, 171, 176, 177, 215
Islamic Emirate of Afghanistan, IEA, 72, 75, 230, 234, 237, 248, 255
Islamic State of Iraq and Syria, ISIS, 70, 91, 92, 94, 96, 99, 101, 117, 171, 172
Islamic State of Khorasan Province, ISKP, 65, 83, 115, 125, 214, 215, 216, 217, 231, 232, 234, 237, 241, 243, 249
Israel, 80, 279

Jaish-e-Mohammad, JeM, 136, 149, 250, 255
jihadi, viii, ix, 90, 99, 241, 242, 251, 254

Kabul, x, xii, xvii, xix, 3, 5, 6, 7, 8, 9, 10, 11, 13, 14, 17, 21, 23, 24, 25, 27, 28, 29, 32, 33, 34, 36, 37, 38, 39, 40, 41, 42, 43, 46, 48, 49, 55, 57, 62, 63, 69, 70, 72, 73, 74, 75, 77, 80, 82, 83, 90, 93, 94, 98, 101, 102, 108, 109, 110, 111, 112, 113, 115, 117, 118, 119, 122, 124, 128, 135, 138, 139, 143, 144, 146, 147, 157, 158, 159, 162, 164, 165, 166, 169, 170, 171, 172, 173, 175, 186, 194, 195, 199, 201, 203, 210, 211, 212, 214, 215, 216, 218, 219, 221, 229, 230, 231, 232, 233, 234, 238, 239, 242, 244, 245, 246, 249, 250, 253
Kandahar, xvi, 4, 5, 7, 10, 13, 17, 19, 23, 31, 32, 34, 35, 36, 37, 39, 40, 83, 109, 110, 111, 118, 122, 146, 156, 158, 162, 163, 190, 199, 200, 201, 208, 209, 210, 211, 212, 230, 233, 239, 241, 246, 249
Kanishka, 19, 22, 26, 27, 35
Karzai, Hamid, 93, 113, 157, 162, 176, 193, 194, 215, 240
Kazakhstan, x, xi, 64, 67, 68, 73, 74, 99, 119
Khalilzad, Zalmay, 47, 95, 171, 210, 229
Khan, Daud, xvi, 45, 249

Khan, Imran, 70, 84, 132, 137, 213, 246, 255
Khyber Pakhtunkhwa, KPK, 127, 130, 133, 136, 202, 213
Khyber Pass, 7, 11, 17, 42
Kunduz, 9, 13, 20, 21, 24, 83, 115, 233, 249
Kyrgyzstan, xi, 64, 66, 67, 68, 74, 75, 99

Laden, Osama bin, 47, 57, 64, 116, 145, 160, 170, 173, 176, 187, 188, 190, 213
Lashkar-e-Taiba, LeT, 149, 250, 255

Massoud, Ahmad Shah, xvi, 64, 65, 66, 68, 69, 71, 206
Mohammad, Dost, 33, 42, 43, 63
Mughals, 7, 10, 32, 40, 62, 130
Mujahideen, 46, 56, 77, 89, 108, 116, 122, 125, 136, 156, 160, 184, 185, 199, 200, 203, 204, 210, 251

Nagarhara, 14, 19, 20, 21, 22, 23, 25, 27
Najibullah, Mohammad, 46, 56, 185, 199
Nangarhar, 156, 208, 215, 241, 250
National Museum, 18, 19, 20, 24, 26, 28, 29
National Museum of Afghanistan, 18, 19, 20, 24
North Atlantic Treaty Organization, NATO, 48, 49, 64, 66, 87, 100, 101, 113, 116, 177, 193, 216, 218, 220, 221, 222, 223, 224, 225, 226, 227, 228, 229, 231, 233
Northern Alliance, viii, xvi, 64, 65, 78, 91, 97, 106, 112, 206, 241, 243
North-West Frontier Province, NWFP, 59, 129, 202

Obama, Barack, 47, 169, 170, 177
Omar, Mullah, 64, 109, 111, 199, 200, 201, 204, 205, 208, 209, 211
Oxus, 4, 16, 17, 18, 23, 27, 36, 63

Pakistan, vii, viii, ix, x, xii, xv, xvi, xvii, xviii, xix, 7, 8, 9, 11, 35, 45, 46, 47, 53, 54, 55, 56, 57, 58, 59, 60, 61, 63, 65, 70, 72, 73, 77, 79, 80, 81, 82, 86, 87, 89, 90, 91, 92, 93, 94, 95, 96, 97, 101, 102, 103, 104, 105, 108, 109, 110, 111, 112, 114, 116, 117, 118, 119, 122, 127, 128, 129, 130, 131, 132, 133, 134, 135, 136, 137, 138, 139, 143, 144, 145, 146, 147, 148, 149, 150, 151, 152, 153, 154, 155, 156, 158, 159, 160, 161, 165, 166, 170, 172, 173, 175, 176, 177, 181, 182, 183, 184, 185, 187, 188, 190, 191, 192, 193, 196, 200, 201, 202, 206, 210, 212, 213, 214, 215, 222, 226, 229, 230, 234, 238, 242, 243, 245, 246, 247, 250, 251, 252, 253, 254, 255, 278
Panjshir, 37, 63, 64, 68, 69, 70, 71, 82, 83, 119, 124, 230, 241, 250
Pashtun, xvi, xviii, xix, 31, 45, 49, 55, 70, 89, 91, 127, 128, 129, 130, 131, 133, 134, 136, 137, 138, 139, 145, 195, 201, 202, 208, 213, 214, 241, 242, 252, 255
People's Democratic Party of Afghanistan, PDPA, 46, 77, 156, 185

Persia, 17, 30, 31, 32, 34, 35, 36, 38, 40, 41, 48, 62, 88
Peshawar, 3, 11, 19, 25, 26, 33, 34, 37, 38, 41, 42, 57, 64, 72, 109, 110, 111, 122, 132, 199, 201, 202, 245
Putin, Vladimir, 67, 81, 88, 96, 98, 99, 100, 102, 177

Qatar, 86, 95, 101, 106, 123, 173, 244, 245, 247, 255

Russia, vii, viii, x, xi, xii, xviii, 17, 42, 66, 67, 68, 70, 78, 79, 80, 81, 86, 87, 88, 89, 90, 91, 92, 93, 94, 95, 96, 97, 98, 99, 100, 101, 102, 103, 119, 125, 143, 149, 154, 158, 173, 174, 177, 178, 193, 241, 243, 244, 245, 246, 247, 255

Safavids, 7, 32, 40, 62, 76
Shah, Nadir, 7, 33, 41, 44
Sharia, 30, 47, 201, 209, 212, 213
Shia, 7, 31, 62, 76, 77, 79, 83, 231, 237, 249
Shuja, Shah, 33, 41, 42
Silk Road, 16, 62, 77, 107, 278
Singh, Ranjit, 7, 33, 41, 42
Soviet Union, xvi, xviii, 44, 45, 46, 56, 64, 89, 90, 115, 122, 125, 178, 182, 183, 184, 185, 186
Sunni, 7, 31, 62, 77, 80, 151, 202

Tajikistan, x, xi, 16, 35, 64, 65, 66, 67, 68, 69, 70, 71, 72, 74, 75, 78, 81, 82, 83, 99, 100, 101, 119, 125, 158, 240, 241, 254

Tashkent, 63, 71, 72, 113
Tehreek-e-Labbaik Pakistan, TLP, 132
Tehreek-e-Taliban Pakistan, TTP, 53, 56, 132, 137, 146, 149, 212, 213, 214, 215, 238, 242, 245
Timurid, 6, 32, 39, 40, 76
Trump, Donald, 47, 94, 95, 169, 170, 171, 177, 228

Uighur, 45, 111, 115, 118, 120, 125, 151
United Arab Emirates, UAE, 57, 69, 80, 151, 173, 211, 255
United Nations Security Council, UNSC, 109, 111, 112, 173, 174, 181, 182, 183, 185, 186, 187, 188, 189, 190, 191, 192, 193, 194, 195
United Nations, (UN), vii, xi, xii, 46, 70, 83, 93, 111, 112, 123, 124, 157, 158, 173, 174, 175, 181, 182, 183, 184, 185, 188, 192, 193, 194, 195, 196, 244, 250
Uttarapath, 14, 16, 17, 23, 25, 31
Uzbekistan, x, xi, xii, 35, 64, 65, 66, 67, 68, 69, 71, 72, 73, 75, 81, 99, 100, 116, 119, 158, 173, 215, 278

Western Turks, 14, 36, 37

Xinjiang, 8, 11, 104, 106, 107, 109, 111, 115, 116, 119, 122, 125, 126, 148, 150, 151
Xuanzang, 9, 15, 19, 21, 23, 27